FIXER-UPPER MYSTERIES

A High-End Finish
This Old Homicide

BIBLIOPHILE MYSTERIES

Homicide in Hardcover
If Books Could Kill
The Lies That Bind
Murder Under Cover
Pages of Sin (novella; e-book only)
One Book in the Grave
Peril in Paperback
The Cookbook Conspiracy
The Book Stops Here
Ripped from the Pages

CROWNED AND MOLDERING

A Fixer-Upper Mystery

Kate Carlisle

AN OBSIDIAN MYSTERY

OBSIDIAN
Published by New American Library,
an imprint of Penguin Random House LLC
375 Hudson Street, New York, New York 10014

This book is an original publication of New American Library.

First Printing, November 2015

For more information about Penguin Random House, visit penguin.com.

ISBN 978-0-451-46921-2

Printed in the United States of America
10 9 8 7 6 5 4 3

Penguin
Random
House

Chapter One

I gazed up at the neglected beauty and tingled with excitement. I was so ready to turn this old eyesore into the grand masterpiece it had once been.

The venerable lighthouse mansion was situated on a large tract of land surrounded by a once-lovely green lawn that had become overgrown and scruffy with crabgrass and brown weeds. A fine layer of sand covered the entire expanse, having been carried by the wind from the dunes that bordered the beach nearby.

The lighthouse tower stood a few yards away to the north of the house. To the west, the rough, rocky breakwater speared into the sea. Waves crashed and a fine mist of salt water was spewed in every direction.

"I love my job," I murmured as I grabbed the thick roll of blueprints from the narrow backseat of my truck. I slammed the door shut and marched across the sprawling lawn.

The rough March wind gusting off the ocean lifted my mop of wavy red hair and blew it around until I couldn't see straight. I finally had to stop at the bottom of the stairs leading up to the front porch or risk tripping on the steps. I set down the tool chest I was carrying and shoved the hair back off my face. And that's when I beheld the wondrous sight before me at the top of the stairway.

MacKintyre Sullivan, world-famous, bestselling thriller writer and former Navy SEAL, stood with his arms crossed as he leaned against one of the smooth Doric columns that braced the roof covering the wide porch. The man looked for all the world like some handsome, dashingly entitled lord of the manor—*if* the lord of the manor happened to be an unrepentant pirate with a wicked smile and a gleam in his dark blue eyes.

Mac had moved to Lighthouse Cove, California, a few months ago and almost immediately looked into buying the famous mansion by the lighthouse. The purchase had to be approved by both the town Planning Commission and the Historical Society. Not only was the mansion a local landmark with a lot of history attached to it, but the new owner of the home would have to be responsible for upkeep of the lighthouse—for which our town was named. Mac was willing to do the work.

"Those are the new blueprints?" Mac asked, pointing at the thick roll of papers in my hands. "So this is it? No more delays?"

"No more delays—I promise you." I picked up my tool chest and made my way up the eight steps and onto the sturdy wooden porch. Flashing him a determined smile, I added, "And no more red tape from the Planning Commission. No more whining from the Historical Society. And, especially, no more tiny white rats to send me screaming from this house again."

He laughed, and I couldn't blame him. It was still a source of deep embarrassment to me that a few weeks ago, I had spotted the little-bitty rodent skittering across the kitchen floor. With a shriek, I had dashed out of Mac's kitchen and hadn't stopped until I'd made it all the way across the wide lawn to my truck.

What can I say? Rats creep me out.

"Then we're finally ready to get started." He pushed away from the column and strolled toward me. "I've cleared my schedule for the next two weeks."

"Perfect." Because, to be honest, Mac's busy schedule had also produced a number of holdups lately. Flying off to New York, meeting with editors, dining with agents, going on book tours. Deadlines. The world-famous writer was a busy man.

I recalled one more unhappy distraction that had occurred recently and prayed there would be no more funerals, please. We didn't need anyone else dying in Lighthouse Cove. Besides being unbearably sad, the recent suspicious death of a dear friend had indeed thrown a shocking wrench into the schedule, causing yet more delays to Mac's plans to start the renovation of his new home.

Another gust of wind rushed up from the ocean, but before it could whip my hair into a greater tangle of curls, I turned toward the wind and lifted my face to catch the mist.

"Man, I love it out here," Mac said, sliding his hands into the pockets of his Windbreaker.

"It's a good day." Cold, windy, with dark clouds forming out on the horizon; there would be rain within a few hours. Still, it was wonderful to be here, ready to begin the job of rehabbing the most iconic house in Lighthouse Cove for the hunky Mac Sullivan.

I checked my watch, eager to begin. Once my guys and I finished going through the house with Mac, I would work out a schedule and make up a list of supplies and equipment we would need. And within a few days, my crew and I would start restoring this wonderful old Victorian to its former glory.

That was why Mac had hired me, after all. My name is Shannon Hammer, and I'm a building contractor specializing in Victorian-home renovation and rehab. I had taken over my father's construction business five years ago when Dad suffered a mild heart attack and decided to retire. Since then, I liked to think I'd proven to my clients that the best man for the job is often a woman. Namely, me.

"Wade and the guys should be here any minute," I said, referring to my foreman, Wade Chambers, and two of my most reliable crew members, Sean Brogan and Johnny Schmidt.

"In that case," Mac said, "I'll get this out of the way." And with that, he pulled me into his arms and kissed me.

I didn't protest. I should've, but instead I sighed and wrapped my arms around his neck, reveling in the warmth of his touch. This really was not a good idea. And I would put a stop to it any minute now.

A truck horn sounded out on the highway and I jolted and took a quick step backward. It took me a moment to catch my breath. "Uh, that must be the guys."

Mac was smiling broadly as he let go of me. "Must be."

I coughed softly, knowing the guys' truck wouldn't actually show up in front of Mac's house for another minute or two. I just needed to give myself a few more seconds to recover from the unexpected kiss. "Hmm."

He laughed and stroked my hair. "I'm crazy about you, Irish."

I was kind of crazy about him, too. But since I was

afraid of setting myself up for a fall, I gave him a weak smile and said nothing.

Mac and I had grown close over the past few months, since he'd moved to Lighthouse Cove. It helped that he'd rented the guest apartment over my garage and lived only a few yards away from me. We'd had a few late-night adventures while chasing down a killer and, yes, there had been a few kisses. I had hoped that maybe we'd grow closer and, well . . . Anyway, things got complicated the morning I saw him escorting a gorgeous blond supermodel out of his apartment. Ever since then I'd been rethinking the idea of getting involved with one of the most sought-after bachelor millionaires in the world.

I probably should've demanded to know what he'd been thinking by flirting with me while seeing some supermodel on the side. But it wasn't like me to be pushy that way, an obvious flaw in my character. Don't get me wrong—I could be plenty assertive in other areas, but when it came to men and dating and such, I tended to hold back. Considering my checkered dating history, it made sense. In the past nine years, I'd dated exactly three men. One turned out to be gay, another was a car thief, and the third ended up dead—or, to put it more bluntly, murdered. Was it any wonder that I didn't want to probe too much? Better to just walk away with my sanity and ego intact.

That was one more reason why I should've ended the kiss as soon as it began. Another was that kissing a client on the job probably wasn't the most professional thing I could've been doing right then, especially with my crew guys about to drive up at any second. But did that stop me? Obviously not.

In my defense, Mac was a world-class kisser.

I shook off those thoughts and took the opportunity to study the elegant old porch. It was wide and stretched across most of the front and halfway along the north side of the house, following the curve of the corner tower. Double Doric columns gave the graceful, circular porch a worldly style that belied the mansion's utilitarian roots. With its incomparable ocean view, the porch could be turned into a wonderful outdoor living/dining space.

Currently, though, it was pretty shabby. The floor planks were dull and a few of the boards around the outer edges were spongy and crumbling after sustaining years of damage from the sun and ocean air. Once those boards were replaced, we could re-sand the surface and add several coats of clear varnish, and all of it would be shiny and new again.

Things wouldn't go so easy for the beams above our heads. The porch roof had actually begun to sag from water damage, and those rotten headers and crossbeams would need replacing immediately. The sooner we started work on this portion of the house, the better. I figured if I could see the wood decomposing with my own eyes, it had to be even worse beneath the surfaces.

I jotted down more notes on my tablet and then used the device to take some photographs of the decaying beams in order to remind myself how bad the damage was.

Wade's truck finally came into view and Mac jogged down the steps and over to meet the guys. I took the moment to regroup, breathing in more ocean air and staring at the spectacle of waves tumbling and crashing against the rocky coastline.

Once I'd cleared my head and regained my senses—that kiss really was more potent than I'd realized—I was able to relax and watch Wade's truck jerk and buck to a stop. There was nothing wrong with his truck; the lurching was due to the timeworn cracks and potholes that pitted Old Lighthouse Road, right up to the edge of Mac's property. I had a feeling he would want to repave the path eventually, unless he liked replacing tires on his SUV more often than usual.

I waved to my guys, who were unloading their tool chests and ladders, with Mac lending a hand. Since they had things under control, I continued making notes on the exterior repairs needed to make to bring the house back to its former splendor.

For some unknown reason, people in Lighthouse Cove had always called this place the lighthouse mansion. Yes, the house stood within a few yards of the lighthouse, but it was the *mansion* part of the phrase that had always seemed misleading. That was because our town was famous for its abundance of breathtakingly massive Victorian homes, while Mac's new place wasn't all that large. But the home had a quiet, stately presence, unencumbered by the ostentatious gingerbread detailing that Victorians were known for. The term *mansion* just seemed to suit it.

Despite the lack of decorative clutter, the mansion still had many of the classic Queen Anne features, including the convoluted roof lines, the seemingly random placement and sizes of the windows, the multiple chimneys, and the many different surface textures that changed from floor to floor and gable to gable.

On the second floor, a shingled overhang sheltered a set of arched Palladian windows braced by more Doric columns. I made a note to check those charming old fish-scale shingles for termite damage. A small balcony off the master bedroom on the second floor cried out for a new railing. The copper gutters circling the third-floor tower would have to be replaced. I could see the gaping holes from where I was standing.

I hadn't seen the basement yet, but according to the blueprints, it ran the entire length and width of the house. You didn't see that feature in many Victorian homes, and if Mac wanted to, he could probably create the biggest man cave in town. But chances were good that some load-bearing posts and a beam or two would have to be replaced before any other work could occur. Wind and water damage was the price a homeowner paid to have a house this close to the shoreline.

I took a quick walk down the steps and around to the south side of the house, where a jewel-box-sized solarium had been built to connect with the first-floor parlor, or living room. It was a true rarity, made of strong white galvanized wrought iron and tempered-glass panels. I stared through one of the windows and saw the worn brick floor in a room just large enough to contain a few dozen plants and some potted trees, along with a small conversation area made up of a settee and a chair or two. It would be the perfect sunny place to read a book or take a nap.

The presence of a solarium might've seemed frivolous at first glance, but I'd read that the navy had built it specifically to grow citrus trees in pots, in order to provide juice for the sailors who were once stationed here. No scurvy for those boys.

Past the solarium was the root cellar with its thick wooden door, detached, deteriorating, and leaning against the side of the house. As I'd noted on my last visit, there were shutters hanging off their frames and several bricks missing from the chimney at the back of the house. The paint on most of the exterior walls was peeling badly, but there was plenty of other work to be done before we could start scraping, sanding, and painting.

Call me perverse, but seeing all the damage just made me more excited to explore the entire house. I took a quick moment to stare up at the spectacular sight of the lighthouse tower standing sentinel over the town and this stretch of the coast. It never failed to impress me with its clean white surface shooting one hundred feet into the sky. I'd climbed its spiral wrought-iron staircase many times over the years and knew the view at the top was sensational. Gazing up at the glass-walled lantern room at the very top, I wondered if Mac had ever been up there. I would have to remember to ask.

I circled back to the front where Sean, Johnny, Wade, and Mac were trudging up to the porch with tool chests, a ladder, and other equipment for the walk-through.

"Hey, boss," Sean said, laying his eight-foot ladder down at the far end of the porch and out of the way.

"Hi, guys," I said. "Are we ready to get started?"

"You bet," Wade said.

Johnny nodded. "Let's do it."

Even though I had a key to the front door, I gestured to Mac. "You go ahead. It's your new home."

He unlocked the door, walked in, and looked around. I knew he was familiar with the first- and second-floor rooms, but he'd never seen the whole place from attic to basement. Mac had bought the house after barely half an hour of walking through a few rooms and strolling around the property. That was all the time it had taken for him to fall in love and make an offer.

"I had the power and water reconnected a few weeks ago," Mac said, "so the lights should work."

"If there are still any bulbs in the fixtures," Wade said.

Mac grinned. "Right."

Wade flicked the nearest light switch and the foyer lit up nicely, thanks to the old-fashioned chandelier hanging from the twelve-foot-high ceiling. "Oh, man. This place is awesome. Look at all that mahogany paneling."

"It's beautiful, isn't it?" I ran my hand over the rich wood surface of the stairwell. Unlike some Victorian entryways that were dark and narrow and barely had room to hold an umbrella stand, this one was a large square, well-lit room. On one side of the foyer was a double doorway leading into a paneled living room, and on the other was an arched doorway that led to a formal dining room.

The broad staircase hugged the wall from the second landing down, until it curved and widened to meet the parquet flooring of the foyer. Roomy staircases always made me think of my father, who specialized in them because the old-fashioned, steep, skinny Victorian stairways made him claustrophobic.

The ceilings of all the first-floor rooms were twelve feet tall with ten-inch-wide crown molding, a picture rail below that, and carved plaster medallions in the centers of the ceilings that created a base for hanging chandeliers. In addition, the dining room had twelve-inch-high baseboards and a chair rail. Even though some of the crown molding, the leaf-patterned cornices, and the stone corbels were crumbling with age, the rooms had maintained their elegance. And we could easily replicate and replace the damaged embellishments.

Sean walked over to the living-room fireplace and studied the mantel. "Holy moly," he muttered, running his hand along the smooth, highly varnished, six-inch-thick piece of wood. "This is fantastic."

Mac joined him. "From what I was told, it was taken off the ship that went down in Lighthouse Cove Bay."

Sean's eyes bugged out. "Seriously? This is from the *Glorious Maiden*?"

"That's what the guy from the Historical Society told me. It was part of the ship's bow. Apparently the Coast Guard members stationed here would occasionally find pieces of the ship washed up on the rocks and were able to put some of them to good use."

"Cool," Sean whispered. "The fireplace is great, too."

I agreed. Beneath the wood mantel, the chimneypiece was made of black marble and the fender was cast iron. Whimsically painted tiles lined the jambs. The inner brick walls were blackened from decades of fire and smoke. I thought the fireplace suited Mac perfectly, giving the room a strong, masculine vibe.

"Let's see what condition it's in," Wade said. He got down on one knee and bent over to get a look at the flue. "Looks clear." He reached in and fiddled with the damper. "Seems to move well. I'll make sure everything's working once we've started the job."

"Thanks," Mac said. "I appreciate it."

"Part of the service," Wade said, standing and slapping his hands together to get rid of the soot he'd gotten on him.

I wandered over to the floor-to-ceiling bay window at the opposite end of the room from the foyer. It was one of my favorite features of the house and it faced north, giving Mac a fantastic view of the coastline. The windows looked to be in good condition, but, given their age, I suspected we'd have to replace the sashes and hardware and, in some cases, the glass itself.

Wade went out to the porch and carried a card table

into the house. He set it up in the living room and I spread the blueprints out, rolling them backward a few times to get them to lie flat. Now I'd be able to refer to the new prints anytime I needed to.

I pulled out my tablet again. "If you're ready, I thought we could start at the top with the third-floor attic and work our way down. The only room I've really seen is this one, plus the kitchen, although I didn't stick around in there long enough to make many notes. We'll take another look before we leave."

"Yeah, we've all heard about your adventures in the kitchen." Sean snickered.

I groaned out loud. "Okay, fine. So I was freaked-out by a rat."

Johnny blinked dramatically. "Rat? I heard it was the tiniest mouse ever seen in these parts."

"It was a rat," I said through clenched teeth. It had indeed been tiny, but I wasn't going to mention that.

Johnny and Sean laughed at my expense and I finally had no choice but to join in. What could I say? I suppose I was glad my guys were comfortable enough around me to give me grief on a daily basis. I would've hated to have a crew that treated me like the boss.

As we climbed the stairs, Mac talked about turning the attic space into another bedroom. I thought that was a smart idea, even though the house already had six bedrooms. I assumed the attic was a finished room since it had probably been used as a dormitory bedroom during World War II, when the mansion was famously occupied by a group of coastguardsmen charged with safeguarding the Northern California coastline from Japanese submarines.

The stairs leading from the second floor to the attic

were a bit steeper and narrower than the main staircase. Back in the day, the attic might have been where the lowliest servicemen bunked, or it may have been used as servants' quarters. As a rule, no one was very concerned over the help having to carefully maneuver down a scary staircase.

At the top of the stairs was a short hallway that ended abruptly. There was only one door and it was locked. Mac used his key to unlock the door and jiggled the handle a few times when he couldn't get it open.

"I got it unlocked, but it's stuck."

"Let me try," Sean said with a grin. "I'm younger and in better shape than you."

Everyone laughed. Mac was in fabulous shape and only a few years older than Sean, but Sean was the biggest, strongest guy on my crew. That was saying a lot, because the men who worked for me were plenty sturdy. But Sean was my expert when it came to demolishing a room with a single sledgehammer.

Mac stepped aside and Sean grabbed the doorknob with both hands, pulling as hard as he could. He gave it a few more tugs before admitting defeat. "That door is stuck."

Mac patted him on the back. "You gave it a good try."

Sean stared at the door, scratching his head, unwilling to give up the fight.

I looked at Mac. "Do you mind if we break it down and replace it later? It's probably swollen shut from years of water damage so you'll probably want to get a new one, anyway."

"Yeah," he said with a shrug. "Might as well."

"You'll need a sledgehammer," I said.

"I'll get one from the truck," Johnny said, and hustled

downstairs and outside. He returned in less than two minutes, carrying a sledgehammer and a powerful-looking ax. He held them out and Sean, who had pulled his work gloves on in the meantime, reached for the ax. Mac, Wade, and I moved quickly down the stairs and out of Sean's swinging range.

"Everyone safe?" Sean asked.

"Yeah," Johnny said, stepping out of Sean's way. "Take your best shot."

Sean lifted the ax and brought it down, splintering through the center of the door. After three more strikes, the door was hanging off its hinges with wood shards everywhere. He used the haft or handle of the tool to break up and push the remaining splinters and shards of wood out of the way. Then he gripped what was left of the door and ripped it away from the jamb, hinges and all.

"Okay, guess you're a pretty strong guy," Mac acknowledged.

Sean grinned and stepped into the dank, dark room. Johnny was right behind him.

Mac, Wade, and I scrambled up the stairs to join them, but before we could make it to the attic door, Sean said, "You guys should check this out. Looks like someone was living in here."

"What the heck?" Mac was there in an instant, and Wade and I were right behind him. "Oh, man. That's funky."

"Ick," I said. We all stared at the dirty old mattress spread out on the floor by the window. The thing sagged in the middle and there were unspeakable stains scattered across the top. I didn't want to think about all the bugs and bacteria crawling around inside it.

I stepped farther into the room and looked around. Despite the lack of lighting, I could see that the walls were nicely finished with lath and plaster, supporting my theory that this room had been used as a bedroom or dormitory sometime in the past. After I glanced around the dim space, my gaze returned to Mac. "I don't see any sheets or clothing or anything else besides the mattress. Do you?"

Mac had been walking the perimeter, checking the walls and windows. He stopped when he reached the mattress. "No. I'm pretty sure whoever once crashed here is long gone."

"There aren't any closets up here," Wade observed, and aimed his powerful Maglite around the room. "Just the dumbwaiter."

We all stared at the small cupboard door on the far wall. "Did you look inside?"

"I tried," Wade said. "It must be locked. But, look, if you really care about some ratty old sheets, we can check the basement. Maybe they tossed them down the chute."

Mac nodded. "Yeah, maybe."

I stared at him for a long moment. "Are you okay? This is kind of weird."

He shrugged. "As long as whoever was crashing here is gone now, I'm fine. But we've got to get that mattress out of here. I don't even want to think about what it might've been used for."

I grimaced at the possibilities.

"Johnny and I'll drag it downstairs before we leave today." Sean looked at the mattress again and frowned. "As soon as I find a hazmat suit."

"Thanks," Mac said. "I'll be glad to help."

I made a note on my tablet about the mattress. And since we were up there anyway, I got my guys to open the windows and check the condition of the shingles on the third-floor exterior. I couldn't see the gables clearly enough from the ground, so I would normally wait until the scaffolding was in place. But this was a quick and easy way to get a general idea of what, if any, damage would need repair. Also this window faced the front of the house and featured a decorative cutout wooden panel on a narrow overhang. Wade wanted to get a closer look at it.

Maneuvering to a sitting position on the window's ledge, he leaned back to take a look. "It'll have to be taken down," he shouted over the crashing of waves. "The wood has a bunch of holes that'll need to be filled, and the paint will have to be stripped off and then re-applied."

It was a small detail that would make a difference once the entire exterior was finished and looking new.

"Okay," I said, making notes. "Now come in off that ledge before you give me a heart attack."

After Sean removed the demolished attic door from its hinges and leaned it against the wall, we moved downstairs to the second floor to explore the bedrooms and bathrooms in depth. Wade ran down to grab the blueprint sheet for this floor, and we checked it and made notes as we walked. The bay windows in the rooms facing west showed off the spectacular ocean and breakwater views and allowed the afternoon sunshine in to light up the rooms. The windows filled the walls and were beautiful—or they would be once we'd fully refurbished them.

Every bedroom contained old, dark, shabby wallpaper that would have to be stripped off, and the walls painted. I noted the places where the oak floor planks would have to be replaced. The upstairs bannister would need a complete overhaul. As in the downstairs rooms, many of the ceiling moldings and cornices upstairs were beginning to disintegrate.

Mac and I had discussed opening up the master bedroom, but a load-bearing wall presented a complication. My thought was to join the master bedroom with a smaller bedroom next door, opening the wall wide enough to allow a sizable passageway while maintaining the integrity of the wall. The smaller room would be a sitting room—or, as he called it, a high-tech playroom. Another small bedroom on the other side would become a walk-in closet.

"It's not like I have a ton of clothes," Mac explained, "but I'd like the space to walk around and see what I've got."

Also, since each of the bedrooms had a maximum of two electrical outlets, I planned to add at least a dozen more on this floor alone.

And it went without saying that every bathroom in the house would be redone from top to bottom.

In the hallway, Mac stopped and studied what looked like another cupboard built into the wall around waist level. "What's this?"

"Open it."

He pulled on the small handle and the cupboard opened. "Is that a laundry chute?"

"Yes. Isn't it great? I love those kinds of features."

He stuck his head up close to the opening. "I can't see farther than a few feet."

"I assume it goes to the basement," I said, "but since it's underground, it'll be too dark to see anything." I took a peek through the opening and ran my hand along the interior. "This one's made of wood, so you'll want to replace it with a galvanized-steel chute. We'll add a self-closing door at the bottom to comply with the fire code."

He grimaced. "The last thing I want to do is ignore any fire codes."

An hour later, we had finished the second-floor walk-through and returned to the ground floor. The good news was that we didn't find any clothing or sheets that might've been used by the person who had brought the mattress into the attic. But that just led to more unanswered questions that would have to be investigated at some point.

"Let's take another look at the kitchen and the exterior," I said. "And then I think we'll be finished."

"I've decided I'd like to redo the kitchen," Mac admitted. "It's too old and funky to deal with."

"Sounds like a plan," I said. "And not that it matters to you, but the Historical Society won't care about the kitchen."

He chuckled. "You know I live to keep the Historical Society happy."

Wade grinned. "Even though they've fought you every step of the way."

"Not me," Mac said, aiming his thumb in my direction. "Shannon. She's the one who's been dealing with all of their demands and requirements."

I waved off the comment. "That's what I'm here for."

We walked into the kitchen and looked around at the dark-stained wood cabinets that had been there as long as the house had been standing. It would take an army of housecleaners to scrub off more than a hundred years' worth of food spills and grime.

Mac might not want them, but those cabinets were real wood and too darn good to throw away. I was already making a mental list of where I might use them once they were stripped down to the bare wood and varnished to a high shine.

I mentioned this to Mac, then said, "So unless there's something in the old kitchen you want to keep, we'll do a complete demo of the room. I'll give you some catalogs and magazines to look at that'll give you some ideas of what materials and colors you might want to use. Meanwhile, you can think about all the fun stuff, like whether you'd like a bigger window over the sink, or if you want French doors instead of the single door that leads to the back area."

"French doors might be nice," Mac muttered, wandering around the room. "Hey, maybe a deck off the French doors." He peered through the window screen to the outside and made a face. "Would a deck drive the Historical Society folks crazy?"

"If it can't be seen from the road or the beach, I don't see why they'd care. They've signed off on the project, so I'd say it's ultimately your decision." I stared at the cabinet built into the far wall. "Hey, I forgot about the dumbwaiter. Do you want to keep it?"

Dumbwaiters were another fascinating feature of many Victorian homes, and I couldn't wait to see how this one operated. The last time Mac and I had been here, I'd had every intention of checking out the dumbwaiter, but that darn white rat had distracted me.

"Let's check it out," Mac said, and joined me in front of the cabinet. "Do you think I'll ever use it?"

"They're very practical in a two- or three-story house," I said. "You'll want to keep it if you decide to entertain abovestairs."

"Abovestairs, huh?" He grinned at me. "I just might. Do they make them more modern-looking than this?"

"The outer frame can be anything you want it to be. You could get a sleek stainless-steel front or a nice blond

Douglas fir to match the rest of the cabinetry. Whatever you decide, it'll look fabulous."

I unbolted the dumbwaiter's vertical sliding door and lifted it. The old wood was stiff and heavy, but I managed to get it opened all the way. I stuck my head inside and looked up, but it was too dark to see anything, so I grabbed Wade's flashlight and took another look. "I'm not sure the old pulley mechanism is still working. It looks like the platform is stuck upstairs somewhere." I pulled my head out and glanced at Mac. "If you want to keep using it, I can install a new electric motor with an automatic control. The shaft runs from the attic all the way down to the basement, and it's a good-sized space. At least two and a half feet square."

He calculated the size with his hands. "That's not bad."

"I wonder if I can get it unjammed," I said, and reached inside to tug at the pulley.

"Boss, wait," Sean said. "Why don't you let me take a look at that?"

I frowned at him. Did he think I was afraid of getting dirty? I gave the ropes another yank and felt them go slack just as a loud cracking, splintering sound erupted from above and echoed through the shaft. I yanked my hand out of there just in time; the entire dumbwaiter platform shattered and fell three stories and crashed onto the basement floor.

The strong whoosh of air and dust coming from the shaft knocked me back a foot. Mac pulled me farther away from the opening. "Are you all right? What the hell was that?"

"The platform must've rotted out." I let out an unsteady breath. "The whole thing broke apart and dropped straight down to the basement."

"You could've been killed," he muttered, and rubbed my shoulders while I tried to calm my rapidly beating heart. I didn't want to admit how close to the truth his words were.

Once the dust had settled, I ventured over to the shaft and leaned inside to see what damage had been done. Shining the flashlight's powerful beam downward, I caught a glimpse of the pile of splintered wood—and something else.

"What the—" I jerked my head out of that dark, empty space as fast as I could move. The flashlight fell from my hand, hitting the floor with a bang. I stared at my empty hands and watched them tremble uncontrollably. I shook my head back and forth. "Oh my God."

Mac grabbed my arms. "Shannon, what is it?"

"What's wrong, boss?" Johnny demanded. "Did you see another rat?"

I couldn't believe I was still shaking, unable to tell what I'd just seen. Could I have been mistaken?

Sean grabbed the flashlight off the floor and leaned inside the dumbwaiter to see for himself what I was freaking out about.

"Holy moly," Sean said, backing away from the space.

"What is it?" Mac said. "What's wrong with you guys?"

Sean's cheeks puffed out and he exhaled heavily. "In the basement. There's, like, bones down there."

"Jeez, you guys, relax," Wade said cynically. "It's probably a dead raccoon."

"No," I said, my voice sounding scratchy and far away. "It's more like a dead human."

Chapter Two

"Why am I not surprised to see you here?" Police Chief Eric Jensen said at the sight of me standing on the porch with the others.

I wasn't sure how to respond. Just because I'd been on the scene of two previous murders didn't mean I had something to do with any of them. But didn't it just figure I'd be the one to spot the bones in the basement first? Which probably made me the number-one person the Chief would want to interrogate.

"Hello, Chief Jensen," I said, deciding to keep the conversation as cordial as possible—and trying not to feel insulted or hurt that I was automatically seen as a suspect.

And it was too bad, because we'd been getting along so well lately. I liked Chief Jensen—Eric—a lot. He was gorgeous, for one thing. Like, Nordic-superhero gorgeous. Tall, blond, muscular, beautiful clear blue eyes. In my mind, I'd called him Thor since the first time I'd ever seen him. Which was, admittedly, at the scene of a grisly murder awhile back. One that he'd suspected me of committing. Not the best start to a friendship, but I thought we'd come a long way since then.

He'd gotten over his suspicions—or so I thought. On a good day, he was nice and friendly to me. He had a dry sense of humor that I found appealing. He cared about people. I sort of thought he liked me—not that we'd ever been out on a date or anything. And we never would if I kept showing up at crime scenes like this.

But, then, who was to say this was a crime scene? A skeleton didn't necessarily mean someone had been murdered, right? Maybe whoever those bones belonged to had died of natural causes. Heck, maybe it was a suicide.

And maybe I'd win the lottery tomorrow. On both fronts I was living in a fantasy world. Because, seriously? There was a human skeleton in Mac's basement! And until it could be determined that someone had lived a good, long life and had passed away peacefully in his sleep—while stuffed inside the dumbwaiter of Mac's remote, empty mansion—this was very much a crime scene.

That hideous thought brought a whole new round of chills, and my shoulders commenced shaking again.

Eric glanced at Mac. The two men had become friends, so Eric knew that Mac was about to start the rehab on the house. "You know we'll have to halt any renovations you were planning until we clear this up."

"No problem," Mac said, sounding strangely buoyant. Of course Mac would be happy. Could life get any better for a thriller writer than to find an actual skeleton in his new home? It had to be the coolest thing on earth. For him, anyway.

"Where are these bones?" Eric asked.

"In the basement," Mac said. "You want me to show you how to get down there?"

"Yeah." Eric glanced at the four of us. "Who found them?"

Mac gave me a contrite smile. "Shannon spotted them first."

Eric let loose a sigh of sheer aggravation. I knew that sound. I'd heard him make it more than once.

"I found them when I looked through the dumb-waiter," I explained. "None of us has actually been down to the basement."

"Well, that's something," Eric muttered.

Another dark SUV bounded around the curve and came to a bouncing stop at the edge of the lawn. It was Tommy Gallagher, assistant chief of police and my old high school boyfriend. Tommy had been happily married for many years to my worst enemy, but I didn't hold that against him most of the time. We were still good friends, although I couldn't say the same for me and his wife, Whitney.

"Hey, guys," Tommy shouted from the car before he slammed the door shut and jogged over to the house. With a broad grin, he said, "Hey, Shannon."

"Hi, Tommy." No one had ever looked more jovial at a crime scene than Tommy Gallagher. He'd always been that way, cheerful and even-tempered, even after the times he was clobbered on the football field in high school. He was like an adorable golden retriever—always happy and friendly. The guy had a wonderful attitude, especially for a cop.

"Hey, Chief, I heard from the sheriff on my way over." Tommy jogged up the stairs. "It'll be at least two hours before one of his guys can get out here."

In our area, the Mendocino County sheriff served as coroner and could declare somebody officially dead. But if the death was suspicious and necessitated a more elaborate CSI facility, our police chief would call on the

Sonoma County Sheriff's Office, about a hundred miles away in Santa Rosa. And if he required even more detailed forensic or pathology services or other autopsy-related services, he would call the forensic medical group located in Fairfield over in Solano County, more than 150 miles southeast of Lighthouse Cove.

Unfortunately, I was pretty sure the chief would be needing all of those services, along with the forensic odontology expert attached to the group, who would, with luck, be able to match the dental records.

And how weird was it that I knew all this stuff? After being involved with a few homicide cases up close, I'd become sort of an expert myself. And by *expert* I mean I just knew who to call to take care of things.

Eric frowned and rubbed his neck. "I don't suppose we're in a huge hurry, since those bones have probably been there for a while. But keep in touch with him, Tom."

"You got it, Chief."

"We'd better go take a look."

Mac led the way back into the house, and Eric and Tommy followed. I looked at my guys and, without saying a word, the three of us walked quietly behind them. When Mac reached the hallway, he stopped. Shaking his head, he admitted, "You know, I'm not quite sure how to get to the basement. I've never been down there." He looked back at me. "Shannon?"

Since I'd spent a lot of time staring at the blueprints, I pointed the way. "Through the kitchen and out to the service porch."

He jerked his head in that direction. "You lead the way."

I got to the service porch and found the basement door. It was unlocked, so I opened it and stared down into blackness. I knew Mac had arranged weeks ago to have water and electricity restored to the place, so I searched the closest walls, found a light switch, and flipped it on. I looked back at Eric. "Here we go."

"Wait." He glanced at the others. "I'll go first. Tom, Mac, you're with me. The rest of you wait up here."

Relief rushed through me. I didn't mind staying upstairs at all. I'd had too many weird things happen in basements, the worst of which was stumbling over a dead body in one a few months ago. So I would've just as soon avoided getting any closer to that skeleton than I had to.

Sean, Wade, Johnny, and I returned to the front porch. Knowing that the work on Mac's house would have to be postponed for a few days at least, Wade and I got on the phone with my second foreman, Carla Harrison. The three of us held an impromptu meeting to rearrange schedules, crew members, and equipment. Sean and Johnny offered a few suggestions but mostly kibitzed in the background.

Once the call with Carla ended, the four of us chatted for a few minutes about work in general and then settled down with our own thoughts. I sat on the steps and scanned my notes on the lighthouse mansion, then started prioritizing the jobs that would have to be done once the house was available to my crew and me. Inevitably, as it did so often these days, my mind circled back around to the subject of the new men in my life, Mac and Eric.

Eric was a newcomer to Lighthouse Cove, having moved to town four months ago to take over the job of police chief when Chief Ray retired after thirty years. I had a feeling there was something in Eric's past that made him reticent to get involved with anyone too quickly. But that didn't stop my girlfriend Lizzie from asking him on a regular basis if he'd like to go out on a date with one of her friends. So far he'd refused her attempts.

In Lizzie's defense, she simply wanted all of her friends to be as happily married and settled down as she was. And we continually assured her that we wanted that, too. But not if it involved a blind date. I'd learned that lesson the hard way.

Mac had moved to town only about two months ago and he was already enveloped in the social life. It helped that he was handsome as sin, charming, and very wealthy. But he was also the sweetest guy in the world and so much fun and easy to talk to, and he loved animals.

I hadn't needed Lizzie to set me up with Mac because we'd met by accident when I wrecked my bike out on Old Cove Highway between the lighthouse and town. He'd been driving by and saw me go flying over the handlebars. He stopped to help and ended up driving me home and carrying me up the stairs to my door. Shortly after that, he decided to rent one of my two garage apartments until his house was ready, and we'd been growing friendlier every day. Well, until that blond supermodel showed up. Mac had tried to explain about her, but I'd cut him off before he could say more than a word or two. I really didn't want to hear about her.

I mean, come on. A supermodel? What was there to explain? She's gorgeous. He's a guy. End of story.

Looking around, I was struck by sudden guilt. Here I was, thinking about handsome men and my own feelings and petty jealousies in connection with them, while all this time someone was lying dead in the basement of the lighthouse mansion. How long had the body been there? Whose was it? Did I know him or her? Maybe it was a stranger, a drifter. An old sailor, perhaps, who'd climbed off his boat and found shelter in the house, hiding in the attic and somehow, some way, eventually dying in the dumbwaiter. The image made me feel queasy. What in the world had happened out here?

I checked my watch. Eric and the others had been downstairs for about a half hour. I couldn't sit around a minute longer, so I pushed myself up from the steps and said, "I'm going to go find out if the chief needs us all to wait. If not, you guys can go off to another job site and get a good day's work in."

"Great idea, boss," Sean said. I just noticed he'd been using a chisel to peel old paint from the window sills. Sean was someone who liked to keep busy, and I couldn't ask for a better quality in an employee.

At that moment, I heard heavy footsteps approaching from inside the house. The front door swung open and Chief Jensen stepped outside, followed by Mac and Tommy. They looked somber, as anyone would who'd been staring at death for the past thirty minutes.

"Do you know who it is?" I asked.

"We might've found a clue," Tommy said, earning a narrow look from Eric. Tommy was my best source of information and Eric probably knew it.

The chief seemed to argue with himself for a moment, then shook his head. "Might as well show you three since you all grew up around here, but I'd prefer you not spread the news all over town."

"We won't," I assured him, and all three of my guys nodded in agreement.

Eric held something up in his gloved hand. "Did you ever know anyone who wore something like this?"

The three of us had to get close up to see the faded

red letters stamped onto a thin silver band affixed to a cheap silver chain.

Sean gasped beside me.

Eric focused on him. "Do you recognize it?" His voice was steady, not accusatory, although I knew Sean would hate having the chief's attention directed at him.

"I—I don't know."

"It's one of those MedicAlert bracelets," I said. "Did it belong to . . ." I hesitated before asking the next question, wondering what I was supposed to call those bones. A skeleton, yes, but was that what the police would call it? Or would they refer to it as a body? A human? A victim? Was it a man? A woman? "Did it belong to the . . . person in the basement?"

"That is yet to be determined," Eric said, his tone turning official. He continued moving the metallic object this way and that so we could get a better look. "Look familiar?"

Wade squinted at the bracelet. "What's it say on the back?"

Eric must have memorized the information and didn't have to look to answer. "Bee allergy. Anaphylaxis."

Sean gasped again, so abruptly I thought he might pass out.

"Are you okay?" I asked.

He shook his head. "No."

"Do you recognize it?" Eric repeated.

I scowled at the chief and grabbed Sean's arm. "Come over here. Sit down." Dragging him to the front steps, I practically pushed him to a sitting position, his elbows resting on his knees. "If you think you're going to pass out, put your head between your knees and try to breathe."

"Does he recognize the bracelet?" Mac asked quietly.

"I don't know." I sat down next to Sean and put my arm across his broad shoulders. "Tell me what's wrong."

He took in a whopping gulp of air and let it out, but didn't speak. Looking at the expression of shock and fear in his eyes, I wasn't sure he could.

"Sean," I whispered nervously. "You need to talk to Eric. If you recognize that bracelet . . ."

He groaned and fell backward slowly until he was sprawled on the porch. He laid his arm over his eyes.

Concerned, I glanced over and met Mac's gaze, then Eric's. "Just give him a minute."

Looking down at Sean, I could see tears starting to leak and stream down the side of his face. I scrambled over to his side and knelt down. I'd known him most of my life but had no idea how to comfort him. He'd always been so big and strong, so easygoing. I'd never seen him this overwhelmed and upset before.

Except once.

Oh no. I was starting to feel sick myself.

I reached out and squeezed his arm. "Sean, honey, you can tell me what's wrong."

He sniffled, then whispered, "It was Lily's."

Oh God.

"What'd he say?" Eric asked.

"I didn't know she was allergic," I said, and mentally smacked myself. That had to be the dumbest thing I could've said. But having just received one of the biggest shocks of my life, a stupid comment like that was about all I was capable of uttering.

"Who's Lily?" Eric demanded.

My heart was pounding wildly in my chest. I tried to swallow, but my throat was too dry. Lily Brogan had been a friend of mine back in high school. She was also Sean's older sister. And fifteen years ago, Lily Brogan disappeared off the face of the earth, never to be seen or heard from again.

"I just want to talk to him."

"Please give him a few more minutes," I begged the chief as I watched Sean prowl the edges of the mansion property. "He's not going anywhere."

A few feet away, Mac leaned against the porch rail, silently observing us. Wade and Johnny had gone off to another job site to work for the rest of the day.

"If Sean's innocent," Eric argued in low tones, "he shouldn't mind talking to me."

"Innocent?" I argued. "Of course he's innocent. Look, I know you're the police chief, but people are not all divided up into suspects and victims. There are other slots to put us in. Like maybe hurting family member. How about a little compassion?"

"He should want answers, just like I do," Eric countered, a stern, unyielding look on his face. "Look, I'm not going to arrest him, Shannon. Why wouldn't he want to talk to me?"

"I wonder." I laughed softly. "I mean, because you're always so open-minded."

He folded his arms across his chest and leaned back against one of the porch pillars. "That's right."

"Oh please." I couldn't help but smile at his defensive posture. "You thought I was guilty of murder the first time you ever laid eyes on me."

His frown was expected. "You have to admit the evidence was compelling. And, besides, I didn't even know you yet."

I wanted to argue, but he was right. The murder weapon had been one of my favorite work tools. "Okay, I'll give you that. But look. You need to cut Sean some slack. He's just had a terrible shock."

"I understand that."

"I'm not sure you do." I wanted to make him understand. Would it be so hard to bend a little? The people of Lighthouse Cove already liked him, especially after so many years of dealing with the incompetent Chief Ray. So how could I make it clear to Eric that he didn't have to play the hard-nosed cop all the time?

"Here's the thing," I continued. "Sean has devoted the past fifteen years of his life to finding his sister. I mean, he's never stopped searching. When Lily disappeared, we were all upset, but Sean was flattened. His way of dealing with the loss was to dedicate every spare minute he had to finding her, tracking her down. It consumed him. And now to find out she never left town after all? That she was here all along? Dead, shoved inside a dumbwaiter shaft in the lighthouse mansion?" I rubbed my arms from the sudden chill. "He's got to be devastated. I mean, what was she doing out here? Who was she with? And how did she get inside that dumbwaiter?"

"That's for the police to figure out," Eric said.

My mind flashed on the image of those bones I'd seen through the dumbwaiter shaft. There was something wrong with that picture, but I couldn't figure out what it was.

"Do you think she was already dead when someone put her in the dumbwaiter? Or did she die once she got inside? Maybe she was hiding from someone. Could she have suffocated? Oh God." I had to rub away more chills from my arms. The thought of poor Lily being treated that way ...

"Stop it, Shannon," Eric warned. "Don't start painting scenarios. I don't want you thinking you can investigate this crime. If that's what it was. After all, you could be right about her hiding in there. Maybe she got stuck and couldn't get out."

"Oh, that's horrible."

He seemed to regret planting that image in my head. "Look, anything could've happened. The last thing I need is for you to be dreaming up theories and motives on your own."

"All right, all right." This wasn't the first time I'd heard him lecture me on this point, obviously.

"Tell me more about Sean's relationship with Lily," Eric said.

"Okay."

"Mind if I take notes?"

"Not at all."

He pulled out a spiral notepad and pen and turned to a blank page.

"Okay, there are three Brogan kids. Lily and Sean and their younger sister, Amy. They were always really close. I think it's because their father was such a bad guy. The three kids protected each other."

"Where was their mother?"

I hesitated, then admitted, "She was a big drinker."

Mac had been listening silently, but now he jumped into the conversation. "How old were you when all this was going on?"

"I was a sophomore in high school. Sean and I were in the same grade. I've known him since kindergarten. So, when we were sophomores, Lily was a senior and their little sister Amy was a freshman. Same grade as my sister, Chloe."

Eric looked up from his notepad. "You said Sean's been trying to find his sister all this time. Do you know how he's gone about doing that?"

"He's tried everything. He's got a private eye that he contacts whenever he has any extra cash. And whenever any new technology comes out, Sean learns how to use it to do more in-depth searches." My heart hurt for my friend and I threw a quick glance over my shoulder to check on him before turning back to Eric. "To this day, he's constantly online, checking new sources, thinking she's got to be out there somewhere. He's lived in hope of finding her one day, so now it's like he has nothing. I'm worried he'll slip into a depression, or worse."

Eric frowned. "Does he have a girlfriend?"

"No. And, believe me, Lizzie has tried to set him up a dozen times."

Eric smiled briefly. "Does he socialize at all?"

"He'll go out after work for a drink or dinner at the pub with the guys and me. And he plays on a softball team. But that's about it."

Mac nodded in understanding. "An obsession like that would put a damper on any personal relationships he tried to have."

I sighed. "Most people in town thought Lily ran away because her father used to beat her."

"Did he?" Eric asked. "Did he beat his children?"

I winced. I knew that giving information to a cop wasn't the same as gossiping, but I really didn't like talking about my friends. "Yeah. I mean, I think so. Everybody thought so. It was pretty obvious."

"If he did," Mac said, "then it's reasonable to suspect she ran away."

Eric wrote it all down, then looked at me. "Do you know the father's name?"

"Hugh Brogan. He was awful. A mean, violent man." I frowned, recalling some of the stories Chloe used to tell me. "One day Amy came to school with a black eye and a swollen jaw and told everyone she'd fallen down the stairs. Their homeroom teacher reported her injuries to the police, who must've gone to the house to question her parents. After that, Amy was out of school for almost a week, and when she came back she had a broken arm and was limping badly."

"Sounds like Hugh needed to be kicked in the teeth," Mac muttered.

I scowled. "Unfortunately, he's dead, or I'd be happy to see you go over there and bash his face in."

"Didn't the police ever arrest him?" Eric wondered.

"Oh yeah. He'd spend some nights in jail, and then Sean's mother would show up crying and whining that she needed him at home. And I heard that she called Amy a liar."

Mac's eyes narrowed in anger. "Did the cops ever question Amy?"

"Yes, but she wouldn't say a word. It would just mean a worse beating. So, what could the police do?"

Seething, Mac pounded his fist into his palm. "They could believe what they saw with their own eyes and lock the creep up for good."

Eric nodded and said, "You have no idea how many times we would like to do just that. But we have to follow the law, whether we agree with it or not."

I told them how Sean eventually grew to be taller and stronger than his old man and was able to give him a taste of his own medicine once or twice. After that, Sean became the buffer between his father and his sisters.

"But then Sean's mother would yell at him whenever he threatened his dad. She'd call him insolent and vicious and stuff like that. He told me she used to slap him for daring to disobey his father's orders."

"A classic enabler," Mac said, shaking. "Sometimes I wonder which is worse."

"The father was worse," I said flatly. "For a while, Sean was in and out of trouble himself. He spent some time in juvenile hall in his teens, but then he straightened himself out. And, believe me, there's nobody more easygoing and helpful in the whole world. He talked me into giving him a job when I took over the company, and I couldn't be happier with my decision. He's the perfect employee, a great worker, and a real sweet guy. And a dear friend."

I looked out at the silhouette of my friend sitting on the rocks. The sun had all but disappeared and a phalanx of dark clouds formed the background. "He doesn't deserve this."

Mac nodded and followed my gaze. "Poor guy."

"There's something else you probably should know," I said uncertainly.

Eric glanced up from his notes. "Let's hear it."

"It's just that, at the time, the local police didn't give Lily's disappearance much attention."

"Because they thought she ran away."

"Right. But still, they could've searched harder. I remember my father talking about it. He told me the cops sent a few inquiries to other police departments in the area and they questioned a few people around town. But that was about it."

"Do you remember who was questioned?"

"Her mom and dad, of course, and Sean and Amy. And her boyfriend at the time. I remember the cops showing up at school to question Lily's guidance counselor and a few of her girlfriends. I can't think of anyone else, but my dad would probably know. And I'll bet Sean would know, too."

Eric was jotting down the names. "I'll talk to all of them."

"Apparently nobody knew much and the police chief quickly gave up the search. He made a point of brushing off Lily's disappearance as just another teenage runaway."

Eric looked at the big man in the distance, sitting alone and broken. "Sean couldn't stop looking, though."

"No. I think it was partly because he felt so guilty. He always wondered if he could've done more to protect her from their father's brutal temper."

"Is his mother still around?"

"No, she died years ago."

"What about the sister, Amy?"

I smiled. "She's happily married to a doctor and lives up in Eureka. They have a couple of kids."

Mac gave a brief nod. "Good for her."

"She probably still has a few emotional scars," Eric mused.

"I know she does." I sighed. "I just wish the police had devoted a little more time to Lily's case. Someone had to have known that the mansion was being used as a crash pad. Stuff like that didn't just fall through the cracks. People drive out here all the time to go to the lighthouse, and the gift shop is nearby, too. Somebody must've seen something. But as far as I know, nobody came forward."

"I'm sorry," Eric said.

"Me, too," I said, knowing he was apologizing for the police in general. "I hate to say it, but Chief Ray wasn't very good at protecting and serving. He probably would've been fired years earlier, but he had his cronies on the town council and they kept him in the job a lot longer than they should have."

"I've heard about that guy," Mac said. "Nobody seems to have had much respect for him."

"Sadly, there are plenty of lazy cops who are more than willing to let things slide than do the legwork." Eric's jaw tightened, though he managed to bank his anger. "But there's a new chief in town, and I'm determined to get to the bottom of this case."

"Good," I said, smiling at his tough words. "You don't know how happy that makes me."

He pointed toward Sean, still sitting on the rocks. "But to do it, I'm going to need to talk to your guy."

I gazed in that direction and shivered. What had been a blustery-cold but beautiful day had turned grim and menacing. Those dark clouds were closing in, threatening to open up and dump icy rain on us at any minute.

I knew I would have to be the one to convince Sean to talk to the police and I'd have to do it soon. I'd already persuaded Eric to wait for the better part of an hour. If Sean continued to resist, Eric might go ahead and arrest him just to get him down to police headquarters and question him. I didn't want that to happen. Sean was already traumatized enough.

I glanced from Mac to Eric, then nodded. "I'll go get him."

Chapter Three

"For God's sake, Shannon," Sean shouted. "If you think I had anything to do with the death of my sister, you're not the person I thought you were."

I winced from the anger in his tone. "Of course I don't think that. I know you would never hurt Lily. Or Amy either. You three were always close."

"Then what are you doing out here?"

"I want you to go talk to Chief Jensen."

"Why? The police won't do anything. They don't give a hoot."

I couldn't blame him for having that attitude ingrained into his DNA, but in this case he was wrong.

"Come on, Sean," I said, grabbing his arms and forcing him to look at me. Believe in me. "Eric is nothing like Chief Ray and you know it."

He huffed out a breath and narrowed his eyes into a squint. "What if he arrests me?"

"He's not going to arrest you—I swear it." I prayed I was right. And if Eric did arrest Sean, he was going to get an earful from me. "He just wants to find answers. That's what you want, too, isn't it?"

He pressed his lips together like a stubborn six-year-old but finally relented. "Yeah."

"He needs your help." I wove my arm through his and nudged him away from the breakwater. "Let's go inside. It's freezing out here and it's going to start pouring rain any minute."

"I don't care."

"Well, I do," I countered. "If you get a cold and miss a day of work, I'll hunt you down and kick your butt."

He couldn't help but smile, but then shook his head soberly. "For Pete's sake, Shannon. It feels like I've been looking for Lily my whole life. And now to find out she was here all along? It hurts." He rubbed his chest absently.

"I know, honey." I grabbed his hand and held it tightly for a long moment. Finally, we linked arms again and he allowed me to lead the way, stepping off the rocks and onto the sandy path at the edge of Mac's property. "It hurts me, too, Sean. Lily and I were friends, remember? You'll laugh, but when she left, I thought it was because she didn't like me anymore. I was such a baby back then."

"Aw, come here," he said gruffly, and wrapped his muscular arms around me.

I couldn't help the tears as the memory of losing my friend took over. But as Sean's warm hands rubbed up and down my back and he murmured words of sympathy, I realized that even in his misery, he was more interested in soothing my pain than in wallowing in his own.

Finally I broke away and stared up at him. "Let's go talk to Eric. He'll help—I promise. And we'll both feel better if we talk it through and take some action."

"Yeah, okay," he said. Biting back a smile, he added, "You're the boss."

I slugged his arm and heard a deep chuckle echo inside that burly chest of his. It was the best sound in the world. . .

I watched Sean carefully as he glanced around at the pale green walls of the police department's interrogation room. He took in the thin brown carpet and the utilitarian conference table and chairs before turning to glare at Chief Jensen. "I want Shannon to sit in with us."

I already knew what Eric would say, but I waited patiently for him to tell me to get lost. I felt bad, though, because poor Sean sounded like a little kid begging for his mom to stay with him. I knew he would be fine without me, but it hurt to realize that he'd never had anyone be there for him. Except Lily. And with that realization, I prepared myself to fight Eric's decision.

"Sure, she can stay," Eric said.

My eyes widened in shock. "Really?"

"Yeah." He pointed to the seat at the far end of the small conference table. "Just sit over there and don't say anything."

"Okay, okay," I said, holding up both hands. "Don't worry. I'll be as quiet as a mouse."

Seriously, you could've knocked me down with a feather. I'd been involved in several murder cases since Eric had moved to Lighthouse Cove, and whenever I'd tried to fill him in on some background info or share my opinion or suspicions of something or someone around town, he'd given me a hard time. I couldn't blame him, since he was adamant that civilians shouldn't be involved in police activities. But still, if you had information to give to the police, shouldn't they welcome it? I had a sneaking feeling he was trying to protect me, so I suppose I could appreciate that. Sort of.

Meanwhile, this was a real switcheroo. A good one. Especially for Sean. He seemed even happier than I was that I was being allowed to stay in the room with him.

It made me think that Eric really meant it when he said he only wanted to have a conversation with Sean, not an interrogation. So that was a relief. I mean, I understood why Sean would be the first person Eric wanted to question, but I had to admit I was also concerned. Was Eric suspicious that Lily's sweet-natured brother might've been the one who hurt her?

I was pretty sure that this would simply be a fact-finding mission and that Sean would be able to go home in a little while, where he would have to deal with his own personal new world order: namely, his sister Lily was dead and he could no longer go through life hoping that she would return someday.

And wasn't that depressing?

I made a mental note to get in touch with Wade and see if he and the guys would take Sean out to dinner or a beer tonight and for the next few nights. If they weren't available, then I would take him out myself. And was it too soon to call Lizzie to see about lining up a few dates for him? Probably. Besides, how could I endorse anyone going out on a blind date when I was so adamantly opposed to it myself?

Eric sat down at the table and placed a manila file folder in front of him. "I called ahead and asked a clerk to pull all the records on your sister's disappearance. I haven't had time to read through them, but I will."

"That's good," Sean said, staring uneasily at the thin folder. "Doesn't look like you'll learn much from the cops who investigated Lily. They didn't go beyond the basics, but maybe they wrote up some background info that'll help."

Eric's lips pursed in thought for a moment. "I want to apologize to you for my predecessor's sloppy work."

Sean blinked a few times, clearly as surprised as I was. "Oh. Well, uh, that's okay. Not your fault."

"No, it's not. But it pisses me off when I hear about cops doing shoddy work. It makes us all look bad."

"Well, thanks for that." Sean nodded, discomfited by the chief's clear admission. "I appreciate it."

"I do, too," I said, even though I'd promised to keep my mouth shut. I couldn't help it, though. I was so pleased by Eric's words.

"So, let's talk about Lily," Eric said, and flipped open the folder.

Within minutes of skimming the pages, Eric found the date Lily was reported missing. "It says that your sister Amy called the police to report her missing. Where were you?"

Sean had that stubborn look on his face again. "I wasn't home."

"Away at camp? Visiting relatives? Where were you?"

I gave Eric a dark look. He was starting to sound like an interrogator. He ignored me.

"Do you remember where you were, Sean?" Eric continued. "This was a pretty memorable moment in your life. Can you remember what you were doing when you heard the news that your sister had disappeared?"

"I remember." But Sean clenched his teeth together and I was afraid he would refuse to answer. Within a few seconds, though, his shoulders sagged minutely and he relented. "I was in the county juvenile detention facility over in Ukiah. I was there for ten days. I didn't know Lily was gone until I got home and Amy told me."

Eric might have had the most professional poker face

ever, but I caught a fleeting look of relief in his eyes. Nanoseconds later it was gone, replaced by the stoic gaze I was used to seeing whenever he was holding his cards close to his vest.

I had no such poker face. I almost jumped up and cheered at the news that Sean had an alibi. Not that I ever doubted his innocence, but it helped to know that official county records would corroborate his story.

While Eric and I might've been happy at the news, Sean looked completely mortified. Was it because he'd been forced to confess the news of his incarceration to the chief of police? Or was it the fact that his boss— me—was sitting in the room with him? I hated that he might be worried about what I was thinking.

"I remember you used to get into trouble," I said, trying to sound casual. "But after Lily left, it seemed you straightened up pretty quickly."

"I had to," he said. "I realized that if I hadn't been such a screwup and had been around more, Lily might not have left. So I needed to clean up my act in case she came back someday. And I also needed to protect Amy."

I reached over and squeezed his hand. "I know you've blamed yourself all these years, but I hope you know that it wasn't your fault. You're a good brother, Sean, and a good friend. I'm really proud of you."

He brushed away tears. "You should probably stop talking, boss. Otherwise I'm going to start blubbering like a baby and we'll never get through this."

My own tears were threatening, but I was smiling. "Okay, okay." I made a zipping motion across my lips. "Quiet as a mouse."

As the two men talked, I wondered whether the coroner had arrived at the lighthouse mansion yet. Tommy and a uniformed officer had volunteered to wait while Eric drove back to the station to interview Sean. Would the coroner immediately recognize that the skeleton was that of a seventeen-year-old female? I'd heard that the size and shape of the pelvic bone was the clearest way to detect gender. Were there other ways?

Would he be able to determine that the MedicAlert bracelet had been worn by the victim? What if Lily's bracelet had fallen off somehow and the victim was clutching it when he or she died? Maybe Lily was alive and the bracelet had slipped down the dumbwaiter shaft to land in the pile of bones. Anything was possible, right?

But despite all my internal questions, I wouldn't voice any of them to Sean. I couldn't give him any more false hope when I truly believed it was Lily Brogan who'd died in the dumbwaiter of Mac's new home. The thought was realistic but depressing enough that I forced myself to brush it away and tuned back in to Eric and Sean's conversation.

"Until we hear from the medical examiner," Eric was saying, "we won't know for sure how the victim died."

"Or if it's even my sister?" Sean asked.

"Frankly, we won't know that for certain until we check dental records and run DNA tests."

"I'll be happy to submit my own DNA if you need a comparison."

"I'd appreciate it."

"Not a problem," Sean said. "I want answers even more than you do, Chief."

"I know that." Eric paused in his official tone and manner long enough to give Sean a small sympathetic smile. "And I promise we'll do everything we can to get them for you. And for your sister."

"Thanks."

Eric stood. "Let me get a swab of your DNA and then you're free to go. I'll be in touch as soon as we know anything."

The two men shook hands and the interview was over. But I couldn't have been more pleased that they had formed an alliance to find justice for Lily.

It was pouring rain by the time we left the police station. I dropped Sean off at his small Craftsman-style house on the east side of town, after extracting a promise that he'd meet me and some of the guys at the pub later for dinner. I was relieved that he seemed grateful for the invitation and I didn't have to strong-arm him into accepting our company. Not that I could actually strong-arm him myself. Sean could swat me away like a fly. But I was willing to send Wade or one of the other guys over to do the job for me.

Before he jumped out of the truck, Sean turned to me, wearing a sheepish look. "I guess you were right."

"How so?"

He shrugged. "Eric seems like a good guy, so I'll call him if I think of anything that might help with the case."

I grabbed him and gave him a hug. It warmed my heart to hear him say it. I hoped it meant that he wouldn't turn into a gloomy hermit anytime soon.

As I drove home, my thoughts were consumed by Sean and Lily. The closer I got to my house, the more the weight of the discovery of Lily's bones hit me. I began to tear up again and knew I needed to pull myself together or I wouldn't be able to continue driving. It was bad enough that there were bucketfuls of rain hampering my visibility. Tears would not help matters at all.

Lily Brogan had been a beautiful girl with dark red hair and perfect skin. She was two grades ahead of me, so it was a shock the first time she ever spoke to me back in grade school. She'd said, *"Sorry to hear about your mom, Shannon."*

My mother had died a slow death from complications brought on by diabetes. It wasn't easy watching her fade away. A week after her funeral, I finally went back to school.

"Thanks, Lily," I'd said, feeling tears form in my eyes. *How was it possible to cry this much? "I really miss her."*

Lily must have heard the catch in my voice, because she'd put her arm around my shoulders and squeezed a little. *"It's a blessing to have good memories of your mother. You should cherish those, because not everyone is that lucky."*

At the time, I was too wrapped up in my own grief to realize what she was really saying or to recognize how mature her words were for someone so young. But years later, in high school, I found myself alone with her again while we waited for the library to open.

"Hey, Shannon," she'd said.

"Hi, Lily. You look so pretty. I love that blouse you're wearing."

"You sure? You don't think pink clashes with red hair?"

"Not at all," I'd said, wondering if she was fishing for a compliment. *"I'd wear it anytime. It looks perfect with your complexion. Who told you it clashed?"*

She had made a face. *"My mother. She said I looked like a whore."*

I was stunned to know that any mother could talk that way to her own daughter. *"Well, don't tell her I said so, but she's totally wrong."*

Lily had brightened. *"I won't say a word—promise. We redheads have got to stick together."*

I'd loved the thought that we could be in some exclusive club together. *"You know it."*

"Does your mother ever say stupid stuff like that? Oh, wait." She'd given herself a sharp smack in the head. *"I'm so sorry, Shannon. Boy, am I an idiot."*

"That's okay. I'm just sorry your mom hurt your feelings."

I had been surprised to see her eyes get watery, but she'd quickly sniffed away the tears and gritted her teeth. *"I don't care. I won't have to live at home much longer."*

"Are you going away to college?"

"One way or another. I've applied for a bunch of scholarships, so I'm hoping to get one of them."

"You will," I had said with enthusiasm. *"You're really smart and talented. Everyone's going to send you offers."*

"You're sweet, Shannon."

Memories faded as I stopped at another red light at the edge of the town square and watched the rain pour down on the windshield. Everyone in town had been shaken when Lily disappeared only a few days before the opening of the annual high school spring play. Especially since Lily had been chosen to play Sandy, the lead in the musical *Grease*. I thought she was even prettier than Olivia Newton-John, and she had a beautiful singing voice. I used to hear her sing every night at rehearsal, because I was head of the carpentry crew, even though I was only a sophomore. And that happened because our drama coach and everyone in town knew that I'd been working in construction most of my life, ever since my mom died and my dad had starting taking my sister and me along to his job sites. Who better to teach a crew of tough senior boys how to hammer nails and saw wood than someone who'd been doing it since she was a little kid?

I braked at a stop sign. Thinking about those conversations with Lily was stirring up memories of my mother's death. Somehow our brief chats had always revolved around our mothers. Because of that we had shared an oddly special bond, despite our two-year age difference. Now I wondered if Lily had wished her own mother were dead. Or if, after seeing my pain, she might have tried to bridge that gap and make an effort to be closer to her mom.

Sadly, that would've been a lost cause. Mrs. Brogan, in her own way, had been as awful a parent as their father had been. And now I could see maybe Mac had been right earlier when he said that it was sometimes hard to tell which was worse, the abuser or the enabler.

Lily's mother's words had been terribly hurtful. And those were just the words Lily had told me. There had to have been so many more instances that were even worse. So yes, Lily had been physically beaten by her father, but I wondered if the kind of emotional thrashings she'd had to endure from her mother might've been just as devastating and probably longer lasting.

Wow. It really made me appreciate my parents and the relatively easy childhood they'd given me.

A few blocks from home, I remembered that I needed to pick up a pound of coffee and a quart of half-and-half for the morning. I pulled into the supermarket parking lot, found a place, and turned off the engine. I had to sit there for a minute, as all the confusion and heartache of those days came rushing back. It was painful to find out that Lily had never really disappeared; she'd been in town all this time. But nobody had ever thought to search for her inside the deserted lighthouse mansion. Could she have been saved? We would never know.

A dreadful thought occurred to me. Even if someone had thought to search for her in the mansion, would they have found her curled up inside the dumbwaiter? As soon as I pictured it, I had to shake off the image of Lily inside that cramped space. I jumped out of the car and ran through the rain into the market.

As I reached the dairy section, I heard a man say my name. "Well, well. Shannon Hammer."

It wasn't a friendly greeting. My stomach clenched as I turned to see Cliff Hogarth standing near the orange-juice display. He was impeccably dressed in a well-tailored black suit with a white shirt and a gold silk tie. He looked wealthy and dangerous and not at all at home in the dairy section of the local supermarket.

Cliff had grown up in Lighthouse Cove, but moved away after high school. Rumor had it that he'd made a killing in the real estate business in Chicago. Then a few months ago he'd returned to town to open a construction company. Ever since then, he'd been making life miserable for me and the other contractors around town. He had tried to poach our crews and thought nothing of drastically underbidding our jobs. It was infuriating and a little scary. The man had no integrity at all when it came to his professional dealings, not to mention his personal interactions. But why would I expect him to? He'd hounded me and a lot of other girls all through high school.

And staring at him now, I remembered that Cliff had dated Lily Brogan during her senior year in high school.

How was that for a coincidence? Seeing him on the same day that Lily's remains were discovered made me question his real motive for moving back to Lighthouse Cove.

Ordinarily I might not be so suspicious of someone, but Cliff was a jerk of the highest order. I wouldn't be surprised to find out he'd been involved in Lily's death. Maybe that was unfair of me, but I couldn't help it. The man was purposely aggressive and intimidating.

Paying no attention to him, I opened up the dairy case and took a quart container of half-and-half off the shelf. As I started to walk away, Cliff took hold of my arm.

"Hands off, pal," I said in my toughest voice.

"You're still a snob, aren't you?"

I wrenched my arm back. "And you're still a clueless oaf."

He moved closer. I backed up a step. He was big and loathsome, a real bully, yet his breath was minty fresh. It was unexpected and creepy. Without warning, he grabbed my arm again and squeezed.

I struggled to pull away. "I told you to get your hands off me."

"When are you going to learn that it pays to be nice to me?" he said through clenched teeth.

"You're wrong. Now let me go."

"Maybe once I've put you out of business you'll realize you should've paid better attention to me."

"Fat chance of that." I tried to push him, but he was as solid as stone. "I'm going to scream if you don't leave me alone."

"Of course you'll scream, because you're nothing but a weak little girl." He laughed, but his eyes were hard. "By the time I'm through destroying your little company, you'll be begging me for a job."

"You're crazy." I finally managed to break loose. "Stay away from me, or you'll be sorry."

His upper lip curled as he snorted. "Now I'm scared."

I walked away as fast as I could, but I could hear his evil laugh all the way up to the cash-register line.

Minutes later, I was home and dashing to the kitchen door. I let myself inside and quickly locked the door, concerned that Cliff might've followed me home. I tried to shake him from my mind as I stomped on the rug to dry my shoes.

I took a careful peek out the window and didn't see anyone loitering outside. The lights were on in the garage apartment, and I wondered if Mac might want to join me and my crew for dinner. I always enjoyed Mac's company, but tonight I had to admit I'd feel a lot safer going with him to the pub rather than going alone.

I hung up my coat on the hat rack by the back door and rubbed my arms to brush away the chill. The encounter in the dairy section wasn't the first time Cliff had tried to frighten me, but he was growing more aggressive. A few weeks ago I'd gone to the pub to pick up dinner and was sipping a beer while I waited. Cliff had walked over and sat down next to me. I'd tried to ignore him, but he moved in close—he always liked to get too close for comfort— and told me I should be careful about drinking too much because I was asking to be taken advantage of.

It was such a stupid, sexist thing to say, I'd almost laughed. But he'd had the weirdest, coldest look on his face, so I just turned my back on him. He then yanked me around and said, "Don't think you can treat me the same way you did in high school. I've got power now and I can make life miserable for you."

The bartender had brought my food just then, and I

left without saying a word to Cliff. But he had followed me outside and told me it could be dangerous to walk home alone at night. I'd dashed back inside and called my girlfriend Jane to come pick me up. I hadn't seen Cliff since, until a few minutes ago at the market.

The phone began to ring and I rushed to pick up the kitchen extension, careful to stand on the rag rug to avoid tracking water onto the tile floor. I was surprised to hear Eric's voice on the other line.

"Mind if I stop by for a few minutes?"

"Not at all," I said, relief flooding through me. Not that I'd thought Cliff Hogarth would call me, but hearing Eric's deep voice helped me breathe easier. "What's up?"

"I hope I won't regret asking, but I need some background info on this situation."

"Situation? You mean Lily?"

"Yeah, sorry. Lily."

"Okay." I decided to ignore his line about regret for now. "I'm going out later, but I'll be around for the next few hours."

"Thanks. See you in ten minutes." He hung up, and I stared at the phone for a long moment. I wasn't sure how I felt about this. Oh, I was definitely thrilled that Eric trusted me enough to want to talk. But I was annoyed that he felt he might regret it. I was also worried that Sean would think I was talking behind his back. Thrilled? Annoyed? Worried? There were plenty of each buzzing through me, but I decided to feel *cautiously thrilled* for the time being. At least it meant that Eric was no longer looking at me as a prime suspect in anything that went wrong in town.

I raced upstairs to change out of my rain-soaked blue jeans and into a pair of comfy yoga pants and a warm tunic sweater. In the bathroom, I grabbed my hair dryer and blasted it to get rid of my wet-puppy-dog look.

Speaking of puppy dogs, I glanced over at the bathroom doorway and saw Robbie—short for Rob Roy, since my little white-haired darling was a West Highland terrier—waiting patiently for my attention.

Tiger, my fluffy marmalade cat, had no such compunctions. She pranced into the room and straight over to me, where she, meowing loudly, wove her soft, furry body in and out and around my legs. And there was the difference between cats and dogs. Dogs will wait while cats demand.

"Hello, my darlings," I crooned over the blast of the hair dryer. "We're expecting company, so please be on your best behavior."

Robbie's bark was loud and enthusiastic, so I knew he understood completely. Tiger ignored the dog and head-bumped my ankles repeatedly. "I'll feed you—don't worry. I just need another minute to tame this mop so I don't scare off the chief."

A minute later the doorbell rang and Robbie barked again, then ran off down the stairs. Tiger tried to remain haughty and pay no attention to whatever was going on downstairs, but seconds later she strutted away to join Robbie, probably hoping our guest had brought food.

"I'll be there in a minute," I said, as though I expected Tiger to convey my message to the chief. I chuckled at myself, gave my hair one more gust of hot air, and turned off the hair dryer. Checking the mirror, I saw that my hair was still a tangle of red curls, but at least they were dry and bouncy, as opposed to stringy and wet. I quickly applied a coat of clear gloss to my lips, and hurried downstairs to greet the chief.

"Sorry to keep you waiting," I said as I swung open the front door. "Come in."

"Thanks for seeing me." He stepped inside and removed his wet leather jacket. I took the jacket, and he glanced down at the small puddle on the hardwood floor. "Sorry about the mess."

"Don't worry about that. Let me hang this up." He followed me into the kitchen, and while I hung his jacket on the service-porch rack to dry, he grabbed several paper towels and walked back to the front door to sop up the rainwater.

"It's pouring out there," he said a minute later as he returned to the kitchen.

"I know. My hair was sopping wet by the time I made it home."

"It looks great now."

"Oh," I said, foolishly pleased by the compliment. "Thanks."

Robbie had been patient long enough. He let out a quick bark and toddled up to Eric's feet, where he sat expectantly.

"Hey, buddy," Eric said, and bent down to scratch Robbie's back.

Tiger joined them, and Eric gave the cat's neck and ears a soft rubbing.

I almost sighed out loud. My pets recognized an animal lover when they saw one. And I did, too. Eric had recently adopted Rudy, a German shepherd he was training to become the first member of the Lighthouse Cove K-9 patrol. There had been a run on pet adoptions last month when the local no-kill animal shelter had rented a booth at the town's Valentine's Day Festival.

Mac was another one who'd taken advantage of the pet-adoption service and found himself a beautiful black cat. He'd named him Luke, short for Lucifer, and it was sweet to see how instantly they'd adapted to each other. At the time, I wasn't sure how my Tiger would feel about sharing her backyard territory with Luke. But the two felines had scrutinized and sniffed and circled each other for a little while before they slowly decided to become new best friends.

Mac had since assured me that he'd be paying another visit to the pet-adoption booth to find himself a big, clumsy, lovable dog, as soon as he moved out of the small garage apartment and settled into his new life in the lighthouse mansion.

"Let's sit in here," I said to Eric, gesturing at the kitchen table. "I didn't have lunch, so I was going to throw together something to eat. Do you have time to join me?"

"I'd love to. I missed lunch, too."

"I need to feed these two ragamuffins first, if you don't mind. Otherwise, they'll be begging for scraps."

"I don't mind at all."

Eric took a seat and watched me fill the pet bowls with food and give them fresh water to drink. Then, rather than prepare a real meal for Eric and me, I pulled out my favorite snacks and put them all on a platter. There were pickle spears, potato chips, cheese, crackers, pistachios, some rolled-up ham slices, and olives. I placed the goodies on the table, along with napkins and utensils and small plates for each of us.

"Would you like something to drink? I've got bubbly water, soda, beer?"

"Just water. I appreciate it, Shannon."

Once I'd poured two glasses of sparkling water, I sat and we began to munch. He seemed perfectly happy to enjoy a quiet moment, but I was dying of curiosity. So after a few minutes of small talk, I prompted him. "You said you need some background information on Lily."

He nodded and finished chewing a slice of ham. "Yes. I've debated back and forth about saying anything. I realize you're very loyal to Sean."

"I am, and I hope you don't believe for one minute that he could have anything to do with Lily's death."

"Not so far."

"I guess I'll have to be satisfied with that for now." I reached for a slice of cheese. "But I was also a friend of Lily's and I would love to know what happened to her. So I'll help you in any way I can, and I promise that anything you tell me will be kept in complete confidence."

"I'll count on that," he said, "because I don't want one word of this getting out. I know how things operate in this town."

"You mean Gossip Central?"

"Exactly," he said, shaking his head. "It's amazing how fast news travels around here."

"Well, if anyone hears anything, it didn't come from me. I know you're worried about that, but don't be. I won't tell a single soul."

He grabbed a potato chip and popped it in his mouth. He chewed slowly and appeared to be internally debating the question of my discretion. I sat back and waited. It was no hardship. The man was too attractive for my own good. In fact, thanks to the recent arrivals of both Eric Jensen and Mac Sullivan, the women of Lighthouse Cove—especially me—were a very happy group.

But time was marching on, so I gave Eric another nudge. "So, what do you want to know about Lily?"

"Well, that's the thing: we still don't even know if the deceased is Lily Brogan." He sounded exasperated.

"You'll know soon enough."

"It's never soon enough," he grumbled.

I hid a smile. "It's only been a few hours."

"Yeah, but you know me—I'm a results-oriented kind of guy." He gave me a half smile, easing my fears that this conversation might devolve into another interrogation.

"Did you talk to the medical examiner yet?"

"Yeah. He hasn't had a chance to study the skeleton yet, but the coroner said that he thought it was a young woman."

"I guess he would know," I said. As the sheriff-coroner, the man had probably seen his share of skeletons. Still, the ME would make the final determination.

"The coroner also said that her skull was crushed in."

I winced. "Ouch. Does he mean crushed by a bat or some other kind of weapon? Or was it crushed from falling through the dumbwaiter's shaft?"

"My guess is that it happened a long time ago, so the fall through the shaft wouldn't be a factor. But, again, the ME will know more once he gets everything back to the lab."

"Did you give him the MedicAlert bracelet?"

"Yeah. If there's a trace of DNA on the surface, he'll find it."

I thought about the bracelet and tried to remember if I'd ever seen it on Lily's wrist. And that was when I realized what it was that had struck me as so odd about the image of those bones in the basement. "Did you find anything else down there besides the bracelet?"

His eyes narrowed. "Like what, exactly?"

"Like remnants of clothing or personal effects?"

"Good question. But no."

"Nothing?"

"Nothing. No clothing was found in the basement or anywhere else in the house."

"I knew it. I knew something was wrong when I first saw the bones. There was no sign of any clothing."

"That struck me, too."

My next thought made me a little sick to my stomach, but I had to ask. "Was there any hair left on her skull?"

"Not that I could see, but the medical examiner will be able to check more closely. Chances are, if the remains are, in fact, Lily Brogan's, it means that she'd been in that shaft for fifteen years. The close quarters might've protected her body from rodents and such, but not from insects like moths and beetles. Because of the ocean air and the closed-in conditions, the space would be humid, which would attract bacteria. Her hair would have been consumed within two or three years."

Consumed. I clutched my stomach and had to take a few slow breaths to ease that queasy feeling. "I just thought, since she was a redhead, you'd be able to tell right away that it was Lily. If there was any hair left on her head."

"It's a good point."

A sickening point, but a good one. After a few sips of bubbly water, my stomach calmed down a touch. "Did you see the mattress in the attic?"

"Yeah. Tommy's got the crime-scene gals working on it. They searched the entire house all over again after we left and they didn't find anything, either. No clothes, no bed sheets, no towels." He shook his head in frustration. "Nothing that would indicate that someone might've actually lived there or even crashed there occasionally. Nothing except that mattress and the bones."

I rubbed my arms, suddenly chilled. "That's creepy, don't you think? I mean, she couldn't have been running around the house naked all the time. Someone must've taken the clothes and sheets to hide the evidence."

"Evidence?" he said. "Like what?" It was obvious that he already knew the answer. So this was a quiz, maybe?

"Blood," I said immediately. "Or semen? Dirt? Or sand from the beach. Maybe she was dragged up to the house from the beach." I thought about that for a second. "That doesn't make sense."

"No, it doesn't. But I won't reject any wild theories just yet."

As I reached for an olive, I suddenly remembered something else that might be important. "Okay, I've got a wild one for you."

His mouth curved into a smile. "Of course you do. I can't wait."

"Did you happen to hear about the rat we found the last time Mac and I went out to the mansion?"

"I did. Some of your guys were talking about it at the pub one night. There was a lot of laughing, and the consensus was that your rat was barely big enough to be seen with the human eye. But you insisted on having the place exterminated, anyway."

I sniffed. "If you've seen one rat, you've got to assume there are a few hundred more hiding somewhere. And that many rats can work like an army. They were planning an attack to defend their home. And, in my defense, it wasn't small. It was a great big ugly rat." I was exaggerating again, but I still wasn't comfortable admitting how teensy-weensy the thing had actually been. A rat is a rat. "And, besides, I use a no-kill exterminator. They trap rats and mice and raccoons and rabbits and remove them before tenting the place for termites."

"Are you kidding? A no-kill exterminator?"

"I'm not kidding. Well, they do kill termites and carpenter ants—any bugs that destroy wood. But the rodents are trapped in cages and driven out to the mountains, where they're set free." And, yes, I suspected that the rats would come scurrying back to town, but my hope was they wouldn't remember their previous address.

He scratched his head. "Now I've heard everything." He grabbed his pen. "I'd better get the name of your exterminator. He might've seen something while he was out at the house."

"Good idea." I gave him the name of my guy, then grabbed a cracker. "Over the past fifteen years, though, do you think those rats could've eaten Lily's clothing? Could they have chewed through any sheets and towels left lying around?"

He thought about it as he reached for another chip. "As far as I know, rats will eat anything. Frankly, they might've eaten parts of her flesh, too, if they could reach her inside the dumbwaiter shaft. We may never know."

I grimaced. "Thanks for that visual."

"It's disturbing, but entirely likely." He shook his head. "But back to the question of clothing. Even if rats did eat away at it, I think there would still be some remnants. But I'll discuss it with the medical examiner. He'll know more about rats' eating habits than I do."

Gathering up my nerve, I said, "Okay. So why are you talking to me about all of this?"

He sat back in his chair, but before he could speak, Tiger took the opportunity to hop up onto his lap.

I started to get up. "I can take her if you'd rather not hold her."

"I don't mind at all." He stroked her soft fur, looking perfectly content.

"She doesn't mind, either, clearly." I shook my head at my presumptuous, flirty pet, then glanced down to see Robbie gazing up at me with a hopeful expression. Robbie's problem was that he was too polite—not that I was complaining. Tiger, of course, had no such issues.

"Okay, come on." I patted my lap, and the sturdy little dog jumped up and made himself comfortable. "So, what were you going to say?"

"The reason I wanted to talk to you," Eric began, "is because I'm worried that this case has gone completely cold. Evidence has a way of disappearing after this many years. The cops working the case have retired, died, or moved away. Memories fade, so it's going to be hard to find anyone who can shed new light on what happened."

"That's true."

"You knew Lily and Sean and Amy. You knew who their friends were and what they were like in school. You heard the rumors about their parents."

"Yes, but half the people you work with in the police department went to school with them. We all knew the Brogan kids. I mean, I'm pleased that you trust me to answer your questions, but you're always telling me that you play by the rules. So why don't you talk to someone in the department? Why don't you ask Tommy? He knew the Brogans."

Eric absently scratched Tiger's neck, and the pushy little cat stretched up, demanding more.

"You know Tommy," he said with a shrug. "He likes everyone. He's not objective enough and he's not as insightful as you are." Eric quickly held up his hand. "Before you say anything, I'm not trying to be harsh. Tom's a great guy, but he himself admitted it's true. He's the one who told me I should talk to you."

"But I like everyone, too," I protested weakly. Okay, nobody on the face of the planet was as nice as Tommy—which was why it was so hard to understand why he had married Whitney, but that was a different story. I wasn't sure why I objected to telling Eric what he wanted to know. Was I afraid I might hurt Sean? *Maybe*.

Eric grinned. "I'm sure you like everyone, but you also have a healthy awareness of people's attitudes and of the dynamics that go on between different groups. You know the folks in this town better than anyone I've met here. You're part of the social fabric of Lighthouse Cove. And your memory is sharp."

"It is?"

"Yeah."

I sighed, because he was right about me. "Okay, so what do you want to know?"

He checked his notes. "Lily had a boyfriend. Did you know him?"

"Oh yeah. I knew him."

"See? Right there," he said, pointing directly at my face.

I frowned. "Right where? What?"

"You wriggled your nose."

"No, I didn't." I touched my nose. "I don't wriggle."

"Yeah, you do. And that little wriggle tells me you didn't like the guy." He grinned and clicked his pen. "So give me the scoop on him. What's his name?"

"Oh, all right." It wouldn't hurt to give him some details. They were fresh in my mind after my run-in with Cliff at the market. And just thinking about him brought back the anger and fear. "His name is Cliff Hogarth, and you're right: I don't like him. But it has nothing to do with Lily."

"Let me be the judge of that. Why didn't you like him?"

I sighed again and reached for a sip of water. I realized the anger was still so fresh, I could barely swallow. "Because he's mean, pushy, vain, and obnoxious."

"You're talking about him as though he still lives here."

"He does. He moved away, but now he's back."

Eric made a note on his pad. "So, what's his story?"

"Cliff dated Lily most of their senior year, but I never got the feeling she was serious about him. I hope not, anyway, because he's horrible. He left town at some point. Let me think." I shut my eyes and pictured the scene back in high school. "He must've left right after graduation."

"And when did he come back?"

"A few months ago."

Eric glanced up, his eyes narrowing. "A few months ago?"

"Yeah. Pretty big coincidence, right?"

"Is it?"

"Maybe not." Those were the same thoughts I'd had earlier, after Cliff had accosted me, but I'd been too freaked-out to think clearly. Now, talking to Eric, my thoughts were starting to solidify. "Maybe Cliff heard through the grapevine that the town had finally sold the lighthouse mansion. If he was Lily's killer, he would've kept tabs on the place, right? He would want to get back here and make sure that the police didn't find anything that incriminated him." I gave Eric a hard stare. "I told you he's mean and pushy, but now I realize that's putting it mildly. He's downright malicious. I wouldn't be one bit surprised to find out that Cliff Hogarth killed Lily."

Chapter Four

"That's quite an accusation," Eric said in a mild tone.

"If you knew him, you would agree it's justified." I lifted my shoulder in a half shrug. "Maybe it's unfair of me to accuse him, but I told you what a toad he is. I kind of wish you'd arrest him on general principle."

He met my gaze. "You said he was obnoxious, pushy. Give me some examples."

I thought back to the months before Lily disappeared. "Even though he was dating Lily, it was a well-known 'secret' that he was always cheating on her. He liked to hit on other girls, including me. The thing is, he wouldn't give up. And the more you said no to him, the more he pushed. Maybe he thought he was so ultracool that the girls would eventually give in and go out with him." *He couldn't have been more wrong,* I thought.

"Did you ever give in?"

"No, never. I kept telling him to buzz off. Everyone in school knew I was dating Tommy."

"Right. High school sweethearts."

"Yeah, that was us for a while." I wasn't about to go into the angsty history of my relationship with Eric's second in command. "Anyway, back in those days, Cliff worked every summer for a local builder. Not my dad, by the way. And once he left for college, he didn't return for more than a decade." I frowned in thought. "You could probably get the precise dates from him. Because you'll be talking to him, right?"

"Yeah."

"Good. So, anyway, Cliff moved back recently, maybe two months ago. He was telling everyone he missed the California weather. I mean, given that he was living in Chicago, that story could be true. But I doubt that's why he really came back. He's been going around town, letting everyone know what a big-time successful businessman he is, after making millions in Chicago. I think he came back to rub everyone's nose in the fact that he's rich now."

"From construction?"

"Not exactly. He made his money by flipping foreclosures. Which is a perfectly legitimate way to make money, as far as I'm concerned. But it wouldn't surprise me to find out he was underhanded about it."

"Have you seen him around town? How do you know he's still the same person he was back then? Maybe he's changed."

I groaned. "Oh, please. He's so much worse. I saw him less than an hour ago at the market and he acted like a complete psycho." I took a breath and realized I was still reeling from the run-in. "Cliff doesn't even try to hide the fact that he wants to screw over all the local contractors, especially me. He's trying to move in on our jobs and steal our crew members."

This had been bugging me since the day Cliff moved back to town. I mean, if things were so great in Chicago, why would he come back to a town as small as ours? He probably didn't like being a little fish in a big pond like Chicago. In Lighthouse Cove, he could be a big fish in a little pond. Maybe some bigger Chicago fish chewed him up and spit him out, forcing him to swim back to my tiny pond. Something was definitely fishy about the whole situation. *But okay,* I told myself. *Enough with the fish metaphors.*

"He's actually made offers to your guys?" Eric asked.

"Yes, in the beginning. But not lately." I scowled. "My guys are too loyal to leave me, or so they say. But several of my friendly competitors have had their crews poached. And another thing Cliff has done is gone behind my back to talk to some of the homeowners I'm working with to see if he can move in on my jobs. It's a small world around here and all the local contractors know each other. They've told me the same thing. It's a sleazy way to build a business."

"Yeah, it is," Eric said, staring thoughtfully at his notepad.

"And I can't blame the guys on the crew. Like I said, my guys have always been pretty dedicated to working for me, but if they were offered a lot more money, why wouldn't they take the job? That's life, right? But it sucks."

"It sure does," Eric murmured.

"I have too much work to do every day without having to deal with a poacher in my territory." On a roll now, I leaned forward, elbows on the table. "And not only that, but Cliff Hogarth is an arrogant sexist and, frankly, when he first started his business, I think he deliberately homed in on my job sites and my crew members in particular."

"Why would he do that?"

"I'm going to sound paranoid, but I think it's because I wouldn't go out with him back in high school."

Eric looked doubtful. "That does sound extreme."

"I know. But every time I see him, he acts like a vicious bully. What other reason could there be?" I flopped back in my chair. "He's vindictive and childish and he's bugging me to death. I wish he would get over it and go away."

"You sound frustrated." Eric continued writing notes for another minute.

"I'm more than frustrated. He told one of my guys that it must be hard to work for a woman because everyone knows they can't do the same work as a man, but then they expect to make all the same money."

Eric wrote it down. "That's sexist, all right."

"You think?" I shoved a strand of hair back off my forehead. "Look, my father taught me to do every single job his men could do. He told me that power wasn't the answer to everything, and showed me ways to finesse things when I couldn't get it done through sheer brute strength."

"Your dad's a smart man."

"And he's a good man." And then, because I knew Eric wouldn't want to take my word for it when it came to Cliff's attitude, I gave him the names of two other contractors who'd been having the same problems with Cliff that I'd had.

"Do you know where Hogarth is living right now?"

"He's staying at the Inn on Main Street. Word has it that he's running up big tabs, buying meals and drinks for anyone he meets. He's the big spender now, trying to impress everyone. I don't know why. Maybe it's because he didn't have a lot of money in high school. But I refuse to feel sorry for him."

Eric kept writing. "You mentioned that you ran into him at the market earlier. Something happen?"

"Nothing out of the ordinary," I said lightly. When he simply glared at me, I decided I'd better tell him the whole story. "Okay, in a nutshell, he threatened to put me out of business. He told me that by the time he was through with me, I'd be begging him for a job."

Eric glanced up slowly. "You're kidding."

"I wish I was. He grabbed my arm and—"

"He grabbed you?"

"Yeah. I guess he thought I wasn't paying enough attention to him. And that's when he said all that stuff about destroying my business."

"Has he threatened you before?"

"Yeah." I told him about the time Cliff approached me at the pub and what he'd said.

Eric rubbed his jaw, clearly agitated. "He actually referred back to the way you treated him in high school?"

"Yes. And I swear I hardly ever said anything to him in high school. Just had to finally tell him to buzz off, or I'd tell Tommy."

"And Hogarth said he could make life miserable for you. Did anyone hear him say it?"

"No. The bartender was too far away and there was music playing, too."

"Those are some pretty ugly threats."

I gazed at my hands, willing them not to shake. "I know."

"Don't get mad, but I've got to ask this."

"Go ahead." I had a feeling I knew what he wanted to ask.

"Did you threaten him in any way or say anything that would egg him on?" He held up his hand before I could speak. "It won't condone what he did, but I want to have all the facts."

"I understand." I fiddled with a cracker. "I might've called him a few choice names, like *jerk* and *clod*. And when he followed me outside the pub and said what he said about walking home in the dark, I told him that if he didn't want to be found dead in a ditch, he'd leave me alone."

Eric considered for a moment. "That sounds like something you would say."

"Can you blame me?"

He didn't answer, but asked, "Did he touch you that night? Hurt you?"

"He didn't hurt me, but he scared me," I admitted. "He grabbed my arm a bunch of times. This afternoon in the market I thought he might punch me."

I could see Eric's jaw tighten. "And you said he's staying at the Inn on Main Street? I'll have a talk with him."

"I'd feel better if you just threw him in jail."

"We'll see how it goes."

I gritted my teeth. "I hate to sound like a tattletale, but—"

"Shannon." He reached over and squeezed my hand. "All you did was report a legitimate threat to your well-being. I don't like that happening in my town. So let me take it from here."

"Okay." I took a deep breath. "Thanks."

"No problem." Eric flipped a couple pages of his notepad and read what he'd written. "So, if you don't mind, I'd like to go back to high school."

"Good idea."

"So, what was the story between Hogarth and Lily? You said they dated. For how long?"

"From what I remember, they were together maybe six months during their senior year."

"Were they dating when she disappeared?"

I'd already thought about this question. "It had started to cool down. Lily was hearing rumors about him cheating. But they still must've been involved, because I heard that the police interviewed Cliff."

He wrote it all down, then glanced up at me. "This may seem like an odd question, but let me ask it anyway. Do any moments stand out in your mind from that time? Anything at all that might've struck you as odd in the days and weeks before and after Lily disappeared?"

I thought about it for a minute. The memories were still spinning around and I had to concentrate. High school girls were known to dwell in fantasyland sometimes, and I was no exception. I didn't want to tell him anything that wasn't absolutely true.

"This might not have anything to do with anything," I said, "but if nothing else, it'll give you some insight into the way girls think. And once you start interviewing Lily's girlfriends, you might want to take the things they say with a grain of salt. Because it all happened a long time ago."

"Thanks for the warning. Go ahead."

"My girlfriends and I were obsessed with Lily's disappearance. She was like a celebrity to us because, first of all, she was a senior and she was beautiful. She had the lead in the school play and she could sing. And she was smart, too. So, after she disappeared, my girlfriends and I would sit in the cafeteria and spin new stories, come up with different ideas of what might've happened. Did someone lure her away? Was she kidnapped? Did she tumble over the cliff into the ocean? Did she fall in love with a traveling soldier? Did they run off and get married?" I glanced at him. "That last one was Jane's idea, because even back then, she had a romantic soul and believed in love that lasts through time. The rest of us quickly blew off that scenario."

Eric grinned. "You have to appreciate Jane's good heart."

"I do," I said, smiling. I'd known Jane Hennessey forever. We'd been best friends all through school and we still were. She owned Hennessey House, the newest, most elegant, most *romantic* bed-and-breakfast in town. She and Eric were good friends, so I knew he could relate to what I'd said. "Naturally, I was the one who kept pushing the notion of foul play. I was forever coming up with elaborate, gruesome theories of what had happened to Lily. Even with her problems at home, I couldn't imagine that she would simply leave town on her own." I fiddled with my napkin. "I also had several clever conspiracy theories that revolved around all the cutest boys in school."

He laughed. "Naturally."

"I guess we were being ridiculous. But here's the weird thing, and it probably doesn't have anything to do with Lily. But you asked about moments that stand out in my mind and this is one of them. There was one girl who went a little too far with the obsession and caused a scene in the school cafeteria."

He sobered. "What happened?"

"She accused an innocent boy of hurting Lily. Of course it wasn't true, but his reputation suffered. She wasn't part of our group, but she occasionally tried to join in. Her attempts always seemed to fall flat."

"What was her name?"

"Ophelia Hawkins. She was sort of a needy type. I felt

sorry for her, but I have no idea what she was thinking when she accused Bernie. Maybe she thought her accusation would make her more popular. Whatever her reason, I blame myself for her freaking out."

"But you don't think Ophelia had anything to do with Lily's disappearance."

"Oh no, not at all. But you were asking for odd moments." I paused to remember the day it all happened. "She wasn't evil. She was just sort of sad."

"Kids are impressionable," he said, staring at the page. "Can you give me the names of some of Lily's friends?"

I named five girls I knew had been in Lily's crowd, including her best friend, Denise Jones. I also named three boys that hung out with Lily and her friends. All of them still lived in town. "There were plenty of others. Lily was really popular."

"I'll probably collect more names as I talk to these people."

We sat in silence for a long moment, until Eric closed his notepad. He reached for his glass of water and took a sip. "That boy in the cafeteria. The one who was falsely accused."

"What about him?"

"What's his name?"

"Bernard, but we all called him Bernie. Bernie McHugh."

"Is he still living around here?"

"No. His family moved away that summer, but I still wonder about him." And I continued to regret the small role I'd played in turning his world upside down.

An hour later, I left the house to meet my guys for dinner at the pub. Mac spotted me leaving the house and I invited him to join us. A good thing, because he helped make the atmosphere lighter than it would've been otherwise. He kept us entertained with stories of how he'd researched all sorts of scary stuff for his famous Jake Slater thrillers. Since Mac had been a Navy SEAL himself, he knew what it was like to be in a helicopter hovering a few hundred feet above the ocean and have to scramble down a rope to rescue a beautiful woman.

"Sadly, I never rescued a beautiful woman, but Jake Slater does it all the time," he said.

We laughed, and I could tell that Sean was enjoying himself. That was all that mattered tonight. I wanted him to remember he had friends who cared about him and who didn't want him to be alone and sad. After the waitress brought our orders, Wade invited Sean to stay with his family for a few days.

"Come on, you guys," Sean said, smiling wryly. "I'll be fine. I'm not going to flip out or anything."

"Promise?" I said.

He chuckled. "Yeah."

"Besides, you already flipped out a long time ago," Billy joked.

"Very funny."

To change the subject, Wade and Johnny pestered Mac to tell them more of his daring exploits.

As we dined on fish and chips and burgers, Mac spun a story about another group of Navy SEALs sneaking behind enemy lines somewhere in the Hindu Kush, the mountain range that formed the border between central Afghanistan and northern Pakistan. He had us laughing and shaking our heads at some of the tricks they pulled as they hiked toward their target. Then the story took a sudden dark turn as the men were set upon by knife-wielding Pashtun warriors. The SEALs fought back, but they'd been caught by surprise and it was touch and go for a while.

We were on the edges of our seats as Mac recounted the action.

I kept an eye on Sean as Mac spoke, because his emotions were so clearly reflected on his face. Laughter at first, then wide-eyed amazement, but as the tale turned more frightening, Sean appeared to check out. He looked dazed and no longer reacted to anything Mac was saying. His eyes glazed over and he stared at nothing in particular.

When Mac finished, I elbowed Sean lightly. "You okay, Sean?"

He jerked as if I'd woken him from a deep sleep.

"Oh, wow." He blinked and shook his head. "Sorry. I zoned out there. Maybe I should go home."

"No way," I said. "You haven't finished your dinner."

"Yeah, I'm not ready to call it a night yet," Wade said.

Sean took a deep breath and let it out slowly. "Okay."

"Sorry the story got a little violent there," Mac said.

"Hey, no problem," Sean said, rubbing his temple. "I was just . . . remembering stuff."

"What kind of stuff?" Mac asked, not willing to let it go. Maybe it would help Sean to talk things through with Mac and the guys.

"Grim stuff," Sean muttered. "Really ugly stuff my dad said when I got back from juvie. You know, after Lily left." He sucked in another deep breath and his cheeks expanded as he exhaled slowly. He glanced around the table and then looked directly at me. "I think my father killed Lily."

*   *   *

After dinner at the pub, Mac and I convinced Sean to telephone Eric. The chief needed to know that Sean thought his father had been capable of killing Lily. Even if there was no evidence to support it, Eric could use every possible piece of the puzzle to work with as he sought to solve this crime.

It wasn't as though Sean was betraying his father. That ship had sailed a long time ago. The man was dead and gone. And maybe it was unfair of me to say so, but good riddance.

Mac and I followed Sean home and stayed with him for moral support while he talked to Eric on speaker-phone. I was surprised to hear Sean sounding cool, calm, and clear as he pointed out his reasons for believing the worst about his father. Besides his father's violent temper and history of abuse, Sean remembered something specific that his father had said after Lily disappeared.

"When I told my dad that I wasn't going to give up until I found Lily, he said, 'Don't bother. Where she's gone, nobody will find her.'"

"Your father told you that?" Eric said, sounding shocked.

"Yeah. He was pretty drunk when he said it, and I demanded to know what he meant. But he brushed me off, just said, 'She's gone to hell.'"

Eric paused, and I figured he was writing it all down. "Did your father ever talk about the lighthouse mansion or say anything else about Lily's disappearance?"

"I always had the feeling he knew something," Sean said. "But no matter how many times I tried to bring up the subject, he refused to mention her name ever again."

"Why didn't you tell me this before?" Eric asked.

Sean winced and glanced at me and Mac as he spoke.

"To tell you the truth, I didn't remember until Mac was telling this story tonight about the Pashtun warriors fighting with knives."

"Sounds interesting," Eric murmured.

"Yeah, it was," Sean said. "So, my father owned a really old Vietnamese knife with a sheath made from buffalo horn that he mounted on the wall like it was some kind of art piece. He said he stole it off a dead Vietcong soldier, but I didn't know whether to believe him or not." He shook his head in bewilderment. "Sometimes he would get drunk and take the knife and just hold it. Every so often he'd sharpen it and then run his thumb along the blade until he drew blood. He always said his days in Vietnam were the best of his life, which is pretty screwed up, if you ask me."

"Some guys miss the camaraderie or the sense of purpose," Eric explained briefly.

"I guess," Sean said. "So, anyway, when Mac told the story, I remembered my dad and that knife. He was holding it, stroking it, when he said those words about Lily. I'd completely blocked that memory until tonight."

The next day, Eric telephoned to tell me that the medical examiner had just called to verify that it was indeed Lily's body—or, rather, her skeleton—that we'd found in Mac's new home, thanks to dental X-rays received from Lily's childhood dentist.

"That was fast work," I said.

"That's how I like things to move," Eric said. "By the way, I'd appreciate it if you'd keep this information to yourself. Even though Sean was fairly certain the body was Lily's, we haven't told him or his sister, Amy, the news yet, so I'd like to talk to them first before the whole town finds out."

"I won't say a word."

I hadn't slept well the night before and didn't sleep well that night, either, thanks to visions of poor Lily being cooped up in the dumbwaiter all these years. And I still felt so bad for Sean, who had dedicated half his life to finding his sister, only to discover that she'd never even had the chance to leave town.

I woke up Wednesday morning feeling groggy and out of sorts. But when I remembered what day it was, I jumped out of bed, knowing I needed to be wide awake and perky, even if I had to fake it.

It was Career Day at my old high school and I would be talking to students about my job every hour from nine until three o'clock. I'd done it the past four years in a row and it was always fun. The kids were attentive and asked lots of great questions, and it always felt especially good to have some of the girls sign up for a summer job on my crew.

I just wished I were feeling a little more energetic. I'd spent the past two nights tossing and turning, continuing to relive that moment when Sean had told us that his father might have murdered his own daughter. Sean had looked so sad and I couldn't blame him. Even though the man had been a cruel monster when he was alive, he had still been Sean's father.

I shook off the memory and took a long shower, then poured myself two full cups of coffee to sip while I dried my hair, put on some makeup, and dressed in my usual attire of jeans, henley shirt, denim jacket, and work boots. After chowing down on my own homemade version of a breakfast burrito, I fed my furry kids and made sure their water was fresh before heading for my truck and driving to my alma mater.

Fifteen minutes later, pulling a small dolly that held my heavy-duty pink tool chest filled with all my pink tools, along with my laptop computer and briefcase, I walked into the main corridor of Lighthouse Cove High School. It was bizarre to smell the same smells, see the same colors and sights, hear the same sounds. But they weren't really the same, were they? How could they be after fifteen years? What was definitely still the same, though, was that feeling I always got, that odd mix of nostalgia for the good old days and sheer relief that I didn't have to repeat them.

I'd felt this way the last time I was here for Career Day. The reality was that the school hadn't changed a bit. But I had. At first I wondered if things looked smaller because I was taller. But no, I hadn't grown an inch since graduation. Maybe I'd just gotten used to living in a bigger world.

The decibel level was earsplitting, with kids everywhere, talking as they gathered around open lockers or whispered in corners. They walked in pairs or in groups and there was a lot of laughter, a few shrieks, some high-pitched whining. Two boys ran through, dodging in and out and around the clusters in order to make it to a class before the bell rang.

Some kids were outfitted in colorful stripes and prints; some in severe, unrelieved black; some in camouflage. Most of them carried backpacks, like my friends and I used to. Watching them, I had so many mixed emotions. It was so normal and yet so foreign. It was another world.

I made it to the classroom where I'd be spending my day. I peeked through the door's cloudy reinforced-glass window before walking into the room and setting my pink tool chest on the floor by the front desk. There was nobody else in the room yet, so I took a minute to glance around at the green blackboards in front and the wall of corkboard along the side, almost completely covered in flyers and photos and posters of upcoming events.

They no longer used individual desks in this room, but utilitarian rectangular tables designed to seat two students. These were arranged in three rows that curved around the front of the room. The curve gave it all a friendly touch, but the plastic chairs looked too small and too hard to be comfortable.

The classroom floor was made up of multicolored linoleum squares that I was certain hadn't been updated in the more than ten years I'd been gone.

The windows would've been more cheerful if they hadn't been covered in old, industrial-strength venetian blinds. I would ask to have them opened once the sun was no longer glaring down on this side of the building.

"Thank you for that scathing review, Ms. Hammer," I muttered to myself. What was I expecting? The Ritz-Carlton? Ignoring the room's decor, I pulled my bullet-point list of topics out of my purse and studied it for a few minutes, until the door opened and a woman wearing a dark orange blazer over black pants and a black-and-white-striped top walked in. She was about forty and wore her brown hair in a chic ponytail. Her brown eyes were bright and focused, and I would bet she didn't miss much of anything in her classroom.

"You're our Career Day speaker." She set her briefcase down and reached out to shake my hand. "I'm Judy Cummings."

"Shannon Hammer."

"You're the contractor," she said, studying me. "What a fascinating job. And you're so lucky, you're allowed to hit things with hammers all day and get rid of all your frustrations, right? You must be very well adjusted."

I laughed. "I can loan you a hammer, if you think it'll help. For pounding nails, I mean."

She laughed along with me. "Oh, believe me, I'm beyond help."

As I positioned my laptop on Mrs. Cummings's desk to use for my PowerPoint presentation a little later, the door flew open and a dozen noisy, laughing teenagers poured into the room at once. They stared openly at me as they made their way to their seats. Over the next two minutes, ten more kids walked in.

"Don't let them see your fear," Judy whispered.

I chuckled. "I carry a hammer, remember?"

The bell rang and we got started. I began the usual way, with the story of how I got started working in construction. After my mom died, my dad began bringing my sister and me to his construction sites because he didn't want us being raised by babysitters. The guys on the crew took us under their wings, bought us pink hard hats, pink tools, and little pink tool belts of our very own with which to play and build fun stuff, like boxes and a doghouse and a wagon.

When I took over my father's business five years ago after he suffered a mild heart attack, Dad bought me a celebratory gift of a rolling pink tool cabinet, along with a full set of pink Craftsman tools. They were just as well made and effective as regular tools, but since they were pink, the guys on my crew didn't walk away with them.

The girls in class enjoyed that detail.

I talked about a few specific jobs and showed a cool PowerPoint slide show of the evolution of my friend Jane's new bed-and-breakfast, which slowly changed from a rodent-infested nightmare to an elegant show-case. I told them that while it was hard work, there were both immediate and long-lasting rewards.

My talk was impressive, if I did say so myself.

The boys always enjoyed hearing about construction work in general, but I liked to think I won the girls over with the pink tools and the comment that pounding nails and hauling lumber was a great way to tone one's upper arms. That line usually prompted one of the boys to shout out, "Show us your muscles."

"Sign up for a summer job with my crew and you'll see them every day."

If all that wasn't enough to sway them to give it a shot, I always added a line at the end that the money was good, too.

I'd given three hour-long presentations and still had a small group of teenagers surrounding me, asking more questions, when Judy announced, "We've got to close the classroom and get to the cafeteria, or you won't have a chance to eat lunch."

I smiled at the kids. "Okay, that's it. But if you have any more questions, take one of my business cards and send me an e-mail."

Most of them grabbed a card, and they slowly dispersed. Once they were out of sight, I let my shoulders sag.

"They suck the wind right out of you sometimes," Judy said. "But I haven't seen them so enthusiastic in weeks, so it's all good."

"Thanks." I knelt down and returned my tools to their proper drawers in the tool chest, then slid my business cards into the pocket of my briefcase. "You're going to lock the classroom, right?"

"Absolutely," she assured me. "Your tools and laptop will be safe."

"Thanks." I stood and grabbed my purse. "Okay, I'm off."

"Enjoy," she said, walking me to the door. "I've got to run a quick errand, so I'll meet you back here in about forty-five minutes."

"It's a deal." I took off down the hall, headed for the cafeteria to grab a sandwich.

"Is it really Shannon Hammer?"

I whirled around to see who was talking. "Mr. Jones!"

"No, it's Brad."

We both laughed and I gave him a hug. How could I not? He was still the cutest teacher in school, even after all these years. "How are you?"

"I'm harried and hungry," he said. "You?"

"About the same."

"Come on, I'll walk you to the cafeteria."

Bradford Jones had been my absolute favorite teacher back in high school. I wasn't alone; Mr. Jones was everyone's favorite, and not just because he was by far the best-looking teacher on the faculty. He was also the nicest, most thoughtful man. All of my friends had huge crushes on him. He taught biology, and there was always a waiting list to get into his classes.

Nowadays the two of us were friendly because he and his wife, Denise, had hired my construction company to remodel their kitchen a few years ago. During the job, he insisted that I call him Brad, but I just couldn't. Instead I continued to call him Mr. Jones, and we always had a good laugh about it.

"How's Career Day going?" he asked.

"I love it. I always have a good time."

"That's a great attitude. I've got Dr. Kersey talking to my classes."

"He's my doctor," I said as we walked toward the lunchroom.

"Denise's, too. He's a great doctor and a good guy, but his presentation is a little too intellectual for some of the kids."

"They don't seem to have that problem with me," I said, and was pleased to hear him laugh again.

If I hadn't been watching him, I wouldn't have seen the minuscule change in his expression from cheer to dismay. At least, I thought that's what I saw. A half second later, the unhappy look was gone and he wore a bland smile, and I wondered what had happened.

"Hi, Brad!"

Ugh. Now I knew what had changed Mr. Jones's mood. It was Whitney Reid Gallagher, my oldest, worst enemy from high school. She and her posse of rich, snotty girls had taken great pleasure in tormenting me about my wild hair, my clothing, my construction-worker fingernails, and anything else they could harp on.

"What's she doing here?" Whitney said, looking me up and down as her face wrinkled in disgust. It wasn't a good look for her, even though I had to admit that Whitney was a very pretty woman. At least she had that one thing going for her. Two things, if you counted her luck at being married to Tommy.

I turned to Mr. Jones. "What's she doing here?"

He refused to make eye contact and it sounded as if he was choking on a laugh.

"I happen to work here," Whitney said.

Working? "I know you can't be teaching," I said. "So what're you doing?"

"If it's any of your business, I coach the cheerleading squad twice a week."

"Oh." That actually made sense, since she'd been a cheerleader during our senior year. "That must be fun. Good for you."

As usual, Whitney was overdressed for the job, in stilettos, skinny jeans, and a sleeveless pink-and-lime-green sequined top. If that wasn't enough, she was carrying pom-poms in the school colors of navy and gold. Somehow it worked for her.

I glanced down at my own casual outfit and gave a mental shrug. What could I say? This was my daily uniform.

"You look great, by the way," Brad said, grinning at me.

I beamed at him. "Thanks, Mr. Jones." He had just earned my lifelong gratitude.

I watched Whitney seethe, and beamed even more.

Sadly, though, she wasn't about to stomp away from the best-looking man in the building. And even though my stomach was starting to growl from hunger, I didn't want to leave him alone with her.

"How are you, Brad?" Whitney asked, turning her back on me. "How's Denise?"

"She's fine. She's working today."

"She's so dedicated to the nursery."

"Yes, she is."

"By the way, Brad," Whitney said. "Did you hear they found human bones in the lighthouse mansion?"

"What?" He looked from me to Whitney. "Is that true?"

"It's true," she said, her head bobbing affirmatively. She looked inordinately proud of herself.

"That . . . that's awful."

Her eyes lit up. "I know. Shannon's the one who found them. Again. Honestly, she spends so much time with dead bodies, she should have gone to work at a cemetery or something."

Mr. Jones gave me another horrified glance.

I frowned at Whitney. Why was she talking about this in front of Mr. Jones? Anyone who knew him had to know about his weak stomach for that kind of thing. Back when I had been demolishing his kitchen, he refused to watch, for fear we might find something living behind the walls. And when I had tried to show him the petrified squirrel we discovered, he'd cringed and hurried from the house.

Besides that, Brad's wife, Denise, had been Lily Brogan's best friend in high school. I was afraid Brad might turn green if he heard the news about Lily from bigmouth Whitney.

"Tommy says it was the most gruesome thing he's ever seen." Whitney looked positively giddy. "And that's not even the best part. You'll never guess."

"Whitney," I said in warning.

She shot me an evil look but kept talking. "They found a MedicAlert bracelet, too."

I knew what she was doing. She was showing off to Mr. Jones and the rest of the world, trying to prove that she knew more about what was found in the lighthouse mansion than I did. Because Tommy had obviously told her I was there.

"Whitney," I said again.

"What?" she snapped.

"Tommy wouldn't want you talking about a police case."

She planted her hands on her hips. "How do you know what Tommy would or wouldn't want?"

"Okay, let me rephrase that. *Chief Jensen* wouldn't want you talking about it."

Those must've been the magic words, because she immediately began to pout. "You think you know everything."

"Not everything, but I do know that Chief Jensen swore us all to secrecy. So if something leaks out, I'll be sure to let him know who was talking about it."

"You're a little snitch, you know that?"

"And you don't know when to shut up."

She glowered, and I knew what it meant to have someone shooting daggers at me. But I didn't care. She shouldn't have been talking about the bones.

Whitney tossed her hair back and turned, deliberately ignoring me as she grabbed Mr. Jones's arm to get his attention. "Listen to this, Brad," she murmured. "They think the bones were—"

His cell phone rang at that moment and he held up his hand to stop Whitney.

Saved by the bell, I thought.

"Hello?" Mr. Jones said, and smiled. "Hi, honey. Everything okay? What?" His smile disappeared and he shot me a look of pure fear. "I'll be there in ten minutes."

"Is Denise all right?" I asked. "Is she hurt?"

"The police just arrived at my house," Mr. Jones whispered, his face turning paler by the second. He turned to Whitney. "They think the remains of the body they found in the lighthouse mansion were Lily Brogan's."

Chapter Five

"I hope you're happy," Whitney snarled, as we watched Brad Jones dash toward the exit.

"Of course I'm not happy," I said. "He's really upset."

"Exactly. I was just about to tell him it was Lily, but you wouldn't let it go. I could've warned him if you hadn't butted in." Hands at her hips, she shook her head and gave me a look most adults reserved for very stupid children. "You always have to be so high-and-mighty, sticking your nose in other people's business."

What is she talking about? "I'm not high-and-mighty. I just don't think you should be talking about an active crime investigation."

"What. Ever. The fact is, Brad and Denise are really good friends of mine. I trust them. Brad wouldn't have said anything to anyone else."

"That's not the point."

"It's exactly the point. I wanted him to know that Lily was out of the picture so Denise wouldn't have to worry anymore."

"Worry about what?"

She sighed heavily, as though it was such a burden

having to explain things to me. "About having to be friends with Lily again. You know, in case she ever came back to town."

I shook my head, hopelessly confused by her. "Denise and Lily were best friends all through high school. Why wouldn't they be friends again?"

"I don't expect you to understand," Whitney said, glancing around to make sure she wasn't being overheard. "But it was always obvious to some people that Denise had a lot more class than Lily."

I gaped at her. "How would you know? You never even met Lily." Whitney hadn't moved to town until our junior year, and Lily had been gone by then.

She waved off my protest. "But I know her brother, Sean, and he's not exactly the most cultured person in the world. And didn't their father spend time in jail? I mean, they were practically poor."

She said that last word in the same tone most people would say *Ebola*.

I had to grip my hands together to keep from slapping her for talking about Sean that way. I wanted to defend my friend, but at the same time I knew that trying to explain myself to Whitney was as useful as trying to empty the ocean with a sand pail. "Who cares?" I said. "Lily was smart and generous and kind. Maybe that meant more to Denise than money."

She rolled her eyes. "Oh, please. You're so naive."

Why was I arguing with this woman? Whitney had no concept of the idea of friendship. It was all about money with her. If you had enough money, you had status. Class. Denise's family had money; Lily's didn't. So how could they possibly be friends?

I checked my watch and almost groaned out loud. I no

longer had time to get a sandwich. I was going to starve, and I laid the blame directly on Whitney. "Never mind. I have to go back to work."

"Work? Where are you working?"

I pointed down the hall. "Room 117."

She looked baffled. "Is there a leak in the pipes or something?"

"No." *You blockhead,* I thought, then felt a wave of remorse for calling her names, even under my breath. She couldn't help being what she was. Though it would've been nice if she could just stay home and not subject the rest of us to her blockheadedness. "It's Career Day."

"Okay, but why are you here?"

"Because it's fun. I've done it for five years now."

"But . . ." She shook her head, honestly dumbstruck. "Who would want your career?"

I had to walk away before I smacked her. But after taking two steps, I stopped and said, "People who want to make a whole lot of money—that's who."

She grasped for something snotty to say, but came up lame. "Well, money isn't everything."

I choked on a laugh. Her chin jutted defiantly, but even she knew she was being ridiculous. We'd already established that money meant everything to people like her.

I turned away. "See you around, Whitney."

"You should do something with your hair."

All the way back to my classroom, I imagined myself stuffing those pom-poms down her throat.

At the end of the last session, I thanked Judy Cummings for a fun day and then hoisted up my tool chest—why did it feel heavier at the end of the day?—onto the dolly, along with my laptop and briefcase, and trudged down the hall and out the door. I'd had a good time—no, thanks to Whitney—and I felt great. I'd given out my entire batch of business cards and had twenty-eight names on my list of teens who wanted to interview for one of our four paid internships over the summer. The internships were fun, sort of like being at summer camp, except no canoes or campfires.

We taught our interns the right way to use all the tools, even power tools. And then we put them to work, sometimes painting a room, sometimes helping raise a wall or hammering drywall. Over the years, several of our interns had gone on to work full-time in construction or related fields. A couple of guys ended up going into plumbing, another started his own masonry business, and one boy wound up entering college to study architecture, inspired after spending a summer with my crew.

Thinking about how enthusiastic the kids were today reminded me of Whitney's stupid comments earlier. I wished it wasn't true, but I still found myself shocked and offended by her statements.

I'd known her ever since she moved to Lighthouse Cove at the beginning of our junior year. Her family used to spend summers here, and her parents decided it would be a good place to raise their children. And it was. But Whitney had been miserable. Apparently, she'd had really cool friends back in her San Francisco suburb that no one in Lighthouse Cove could come close to matching for awesomeness and style.

My friends and I had tried to reach out, but Whitney refused to have anything to do with the kids she referred to as townies. Even though by then she, too, could've been considered a townie by kids who'd arrived more recently. Eventually she became friends with some of the other privileged girls whose parents had also chosen to move into the beautiful Victorian-style homes built along the Alisal Cliffs. Whitney would've been appalled to discover that her parents and those of all of her snooty friends, the ones who'd insisted on living in homes built by the best construction company in Northern California, were the ones responsible for making my father a wealthy man.

I shook my head as I crossed the central quad and headed for the senior-class parking lot, where I'd been assigned to park my truck. To this day, I didn't quite know what I'd done to make Whitney hate me so much. Was it because I'd had the audacity to offer to be her friend, as though she were some yokel from nowhere? Or did it have more to do with the fact that Tommy was my boyfriend? But even after she'd won him over by sleeping with him and getting herself pregnant—something I had not been willing to do—she continued to hate me. Her digs were always personal and usually had something to do with my construction-crew wardrobe. I was a mess, she said. I dressed like a boy. My nails were too short. My hair was hideous. That last one was especially funny to me, because Tommy had always been crazy about my hair.

I didn't understand her contempt until years later. I boiled it down to a complicated mix of jealousy over my relationship with Tommy—the nicest, cutest boy in school and the star quarterback on our football team—and suspicion over my easy acceptance of my place in our small-town society. I'd grown up believing that everyone was my friend, and until Whitney showed up that had always been true. She especially hated my oddly buoyant personality that allowed me to bounce back from every sling and arrow she hurled at me.

It had taken Tommy tearfully explaining that Whitney

was pregnant and they were getting married for me to face the ugly reality of Whitney Reid's determination to hurt me, but I finally got it.

Eventually I learned to avoid her and, except for those rare moments like today, when I was forced into a face-to-face interaction, her anger wasn't something I dwelled on anymore.

But in a small town, it wasn't always easy to avoid her. We crossed paths regularly. I'd even saved her life twice, but still got no respect. That was because she'd considered it my fault that she'd been in danger in the first place. She was wrong, of course, but why would I ever expect her to face the truth?

"Shannon!" someone shouted.

"What?" On the edge of panic, I whirled around to see who it was. I'd been so involved in my mental rant that I thought Whitney had followed me out to the parking lot. Talk about paranoia! But it was only Ms. Barney, the school principal, waving at me. I tried to calm my thundering heartbeat as she approached.

"Hello." I made sure the dolly wouldn't roll away and moved to greet her and shake her hand. "How are you, Ms. Barney?"

"I'm dandy," she said, jovial as always. "I heard you had a good Career Day."

"I did. The students were great. They had lots of smart questions and really good comments."

"I'm glad to hear it." She pointed toward the parking lot. "Well, the school board should be making their decision any day now."

I smiled. "You must be getting tired of waiting."

"You think?" She laughed. "Let me walk with you to your car."

We made small talk as we went. Ms. Barney had become our high school principal at the beginning of my senior year and I had always liked her. She was a fair, no-nonsense administrator who seemed to genuinely enjoy working with students. But beyond that, she'd won my heart a few years ago when she hired my company to build a small extension onto her living room. She wanted a cozy reading room with floor-to-ceiling bookshelves and a fireplace.

Since we already had a working relationship, it wasn't surprising when, about three months ago, she had called me into her office to tell me about a new construction job that the school board was about to open up for bidding by local building companies.

That day, she had asked me to walk with her out to the senior parking lot, where she'd stopped and gestured at the crumbling, faded blacktop before us. "Pretty soon this will be a brand-new solar-paneled parking lot with a shiny new blacktop surface and space for at least five times more cars than we have now. The school board is taking construction bids and I'm hoping you'll submit one. I would love it if they chose your company to do the job."

I'd been pleased that she thought my company was capable of something like that. "It sounds interesting and I'd love to have the work, but I have to confess we haven't done a solar-panel job like that before."

"That doesn't matter," she'd confided, then gone on to explain why. "The solar-panel company has already been chosen. They sent a designer and a team of engineers to do a site analysis and survey last month."

"So why would you need me?"

"The company recommended that we find a reputable local contractor to repave the surface of the lot and help with the installation of the canopies and the panels. They'll have their own electrical engineer and a full crew, along with a project manager on-site to supervise the entire project. And they'll take care of all the testing and maintenance."

She pointed to a swath of pressed gravel that formed a wide walkway leading to the track field fifty yards away. "The plan is to tear up all of this old blacktop, along with the landscaping all the way to the tennis courts and halfway to the track field."

"That's a big area." I pointed to an incline covered in agapanthus. "You'll lose a lot of those plants."

"We'll transplant them to other areas around the school." She flashed a broad smile. "So it's a win-win. We plan to expand the lot to seventy-two total parking spaces."

"Wow, that's a lot."

"Yes. We'll need three double canopies to cover seventy-some cars. The solar panels on top of the canopies will eventually generate enough power to run the entire school all year round."

"That's amazing."

"I know. And a few of the posts will have hookups for electric cars, too. And get this," she added. "The canopies are configured with gutters down the middle that can harvest rainwater to use for irrigating the student gardens, the football field, and all of the landscaping."

"Wow. You've covered all the bases. That sounds fantastic."

"I'm getting excited just talking about it." She'd glanced at me. "So, are you interested in the job?"

I had scanned the parking lot and the surrounding school grounds, thinking quickly. The way she'd explained it, I figured it wouldn't be as complex a job as I'd first thought. Basically a lot of digging, building supports for those canopies, and laying down blacktop. And even though all of that had little connection to my specialized field, which was new-home construction and Victorian-home renovation, it wouldn't matter. My guys and I could handle it.

The job sounded unique and interesting, and I liked the idea of involving my company in a high-tech project like this. It would be a good thing for both the school and the community, as well as for Hammer Construction.

"I'd love the chance to bid on it," I'd said.

"Wonderful." She'd reached into her satchel and handed me a manila envelope. "Here's the company's bidding form. I'm bound by school-board regulations to obtain at least one other bid, and I've already heard from three others that they'd like the chance to bid, too. But, truth be told, I'd prefer to work with you."

"I'd like that, too," I said, but I knew the rules. "How much time do I have to submit my offer?"

"The sooner the better, naturally, but I can give you up to one week."

I could envision working several late nights doing research into the solar-tech industry in order to feel competent enough to bid on the job. "I'll try to finish it by the weekend."

"Let's make it Monday."

That would give me five days to work on the bid. I could do that. "Okay. How about if I swing by your office Monday morning with my completed offer?"

"Perfect." She'd thought for a moment. "Call my office before you make the drive, will you? I want to be sure I'm here to personally accept it."

"I really appreciate your confidence in me."

"You've proven yourself more than capable of handling anything thrown your way," she'd said, smiling with an assurance I wasn't sure I felt. "Now we just have to make sure you get the job."

I'd gone home that night and begun the process of bidding on the job. Since the bid would be presented to the school board, a local government agency, there were a lot of hoops to jump through.

I spent an hour studying the solar company they'd hired to do the work. I was impressed by their Web site, and even more so with the testimonials written by their clients. By the time I shut down my computer for the night, I was determined to get this job.

My father had taught me that while my good reputation was essential in obtaining any job, my skill at presenting a winning bid was just as important. It helped to have all the details in hand before starting the bidding process. I gathered as much information as I could, but since I'd never worked with companies that installed solar panels specifically, I would have to rely on my own past experiences and do the best I could with the facts and figures I already had.

The solar company, as contractor, had provided its own customized bidding form for me to fill out. On most jobs I was dealing with an individual homeowner, so I usually created my own forms. In a way, this was easier. But I was still determined to present an organized and realistic summary of the job I wanted to win.

On the front of the form, I included information about myself and my business, my professional qualifications, and a few references from satisfied homeowners who had previously agreed to sing my praises. Much of that information was available on my own company Web site, but I included a few new quotes and details I hadn't had a chance to upload yet. I wrote down my contractor's license number and those of my crew members.

The solar company had attached a table with a long list of every job they expected the subcontractor to perform. There was a column for me to fill in my cost estimate and another column in which to justify that cost. In other words, how much labor I expected to employ and what sorts of supplies would be needed, plus a reasonable markup for my profit. The last column was my time estimate, where I gave my best guess as to how long each phase of the job would take.

I went down the list, filling in my estimates. I allowed some flexibility in case of unexpected costs or delays. My goal was to give good value, not price myself out of the job or, worse, lose money.

It took me three extremely late nights, reworking numbers and man-hours, to finish the bid. Even though she'd allowed me more time, I really did want to get it to Ms. Barney before the weekend.

Once I'd completed the bidding forms, I made a copy for myself and placed it in a new file folder I labeled LIGHTHOUSE COVE HIGH SCHOOL PARKING CANOPY. As I put the original bid into a business envelope with Ms. Barney's name on the front, I wondered who my competition might be.

The following morning I had called Ms. Barney bright and early and she'd told me to stop by anytime, so I drove straight to the high school to drop off my envelope. Before I'd handed it to her, I'd removed the completed form and taken out my pen.

"I'm writing down the time I gave it to you," I explained, "in case the company has any questions."

"Good idea," she said.

Yes, it was. In rare instances when two contractors came in with the exact same bid, the contract would be awarded to the one who submitted theirs first. And that's why I'd stayed up so late those three nights, finishing the paperwork. I wanted to beat the competition and get this job.

Now, almost three months later, Ms. Barney and I were standing at the edge of the small crumbling parking lot again.

She shook her head in dismay. "It still shocks me to realize how interminably slow the school board can be when it comes to making decisions like this."

"Everyone has an opinion, I guess."

"Of course, and it's like pulling teeth to get a consensus." She clasped her hands together. "But I'm happy to say that they've promised me they're ready to choose the construction company and they'll let me know the result this week."

"Hurray," I said. "You must be thrilled about that."

"I'll believe it when I see it, but I wanted to give you a heads-up. I've still got my heart set on your winning the job."

We reached my truck and I turned to her. "Whether I get the job or not, I want to thank you for considering me, Ms. Barney."

"What can I say? You're the best." She patted my shoulder. "Keep a good thought, and with any luck, I'll be calling you this week with good news."

I was bowled over by her enthusiasm and trust in me. "I'll keep my fingers crossed. Thanks again."

As I drove home, I tried to tamp down my excitement at the possibility of winning the job. But I couldn't help it. I was as competitive as the next guy, and after all the work I'd put into drafting the bid, I'd be bummed if I didn't get the job.

I'd forgotten all about my mental tirade over Whitney until I got home. Then I remembered, and it reminded me of two things: one, that I was starving, and two, that I hadn't gotten my nails done in weeks.

The connection to Whitney and my nails was obvious. To me, at least. Whitney and her crowd used to criticize my raggedy fingernails, among everything else. Working on construction sites, I always figured my shabby nails were an occupational hazard, but I'd discovered a way to do something about it. So from one angle, I had the Mean Girls to thank for my appreciation of the mani-pedi experience.

I called on my way home to see if Paloma, the goddess of manicures, was available and, miracle of miracles, she was. My stomach was still growling—again, thanks to Whitney—so I took a quick detour into the Yummy Burger drive-in and gulped down a burger and milk shake. Then I drove home and ran inside to change into something more casual. Within minutes, I was walking the three blocks to the town square, where Paloma had her shop.

Two hours later, I awoke in a fragrant, waxy haze. I was still sitting in the massage chair at Paloma's, having been fluffed and massaged and buffed to a fine sheen. The image of Whitney had vanished from my consciousness, and it wasn't until I was strolling home that I even recalled that phone call Mr. Jones had received from his wife, Denise, earlier that day. I pictured his distraught expression and wondered if they had recovered from the shock of being questioned by the police in a murder investigation. I hoped so.

I'd known Denise Armstrong—now Denise Jones— my whole life. We'd always been friendly, though not especially close, because she was a few years older than I. But I liked her. Her family owned a small chain of upscale nurseries up and down the Northern California coast, and I did all my garden shopping there. They made their own mulch, and it was the best I'd ever used.

Denise had been Lily's best friend from as far back as I could remember, and for that reason alone I liked her. I figured her only flaw was that she was now friends with Whitney. Sadly, that was enough to make me question the woman's judgment, but the fact that she'd had the good taste to fall in love with and marry the wonderful Mr. Jones mitigated things somewhat.

Back in high school, my friends and I were shocked when we heard the news that Mr. Jones had married Denise barely a month after she graduated from high school. It was the biggest scandal ever. Well, besides Lily's disappearance a few months before. Denise was only two years ahead of me and my friends. And Mr. Jones was a teacher! They had been very discreet, though, and nobody had ever suspected a thing. That might've made it even more shocking than it would've been had we been gossiping about them all along.

In the end, we girls reluctantly accepted the fact that the match was a good one. Mr. Jones was just a few years older than Denise, after all, and they made a very cute couple. We finally had to admit that we'd only considered the marriage a scandal because we were all so jealous of lucky Denise.

It was dark by the time I got home and let myself in through the kitchen door.

A loud bark greeted me and I saw Robbie shivering deliriously at the sight of me. I set my purse down on the table as Tiger, purring loudly, wound her furry body around my ankles.

"Hello, my darlings," I crooned, stooping down to give each of them a hug and then tussle and pet them. "I'm excited to see you, too. Did you miss me? Of course you did."

Robbie barked twice.

"Yes, my fingernails are pretty, aren't they?"

He barked again, as if to say, *Get real. Feed me.*

"I know, I know, it's dinnertime." I gave him one last scratch behind his ears and stood. "I promise I won't let you starve."

I chuckled at my own conversation as I grabbed their empty water bowls. At the sink, I rinsed them out and filled each with fresh water.

Robbie and Tiger sat patiently until I set the bowls back down at their respective dining spots. They lapped up water as I took their food bowls and doled out their small evening meals.

While they nibbled at their dinner, I thought about making a salad, but I wasn't hungry after chowing down on that burger a few hours ago. I did pour myself a glass of wine, though, because I deserved one after the day I'd had.

As I took my first sip, I heard a heavy *thump-thump* sound and glanced out the window. It was Mac Sullivan, wearing a black leather jacket, dark jeans, and boots, jogging down the garage stairs.

"Wonder where he's going looking so darn hot?" I

asked myself aloud, then felt foolish. Especially since my knees had gone a little weak at the sight of him. But honestly, what woman would blame me? The man was ridiculously handsome.

Tiger bumped up against my leg and I leaned down to pick her up. I was so lucky to have a cat who was willing to snuggle with me once in a while.

"I know what you're thinking," I murmured as I buried my face in her soft fur. "You're thinking that if Mac's so great, why was I semiswooning the other day when Chief Jensen was sitting right here at the kitchen table?"

Tiger just purred, obviously used to my reading her mind.

It's a good question, I thought. Did it matter that I found both men so darned attractive? I didn't think so, and I wasn't going to worry about it. Not yet, anyway. Neither of these two friendships had developed into anything serious . . . yet. I was happy just to have them around to talk to and flirt with.

Mac and Eric had become friends, although they weren't at all alike. Mac was definitely the friendlier of the two, which had been a surprise at first. As dangerously dark and edge-of-the-seat thrilling as his novels were, I hadn't expected to find that he was actually an easygoing, fun-loving guy. I enjoyed spending time with him because he was open and honest. He liked to talk and laugh and go on adventures. And in case I hadn't made it clear enough, he was absolutely gorgeous, with dark hair and midnight blue eyes. I'd already been halfway in love with him before I ever met him, thanks to his amazing photograph on the backs of his books.

Eric, on the other hand, had a dark side. I sometimes wondered if he'd been hurt badly in the past, because he was so circumspect when it came to talking about himself. He was tall and blond and had the world's greatest smile—when he allowed anyone to see it, which was rare. Most of the time, he scowled. Still, there was something to be said for the tortured-hero type.

I set down the cat and watched her shake herself off and stroll away to the comfort of the living-room couch. I wiped down the kitchen counters, emptied the drying rack, and filled the coffeemaker for the morning.

My mind drifted back to my life before the two men moved to Lighthouse Cove. I hadn't been out on a date in almost four years, for good reason. Ever since high school, I just hadn't had a lot of luck with men. After my shattering breakup with Tommy, I'd withdrawn for a while. I spent most of my time working on construction sites or gardening. I had girlfriends, and I felt as though my life was full enough without a boyfriend around to mess up my mind.

The pitiful fact was that, until recently, I'd had exactly two dates since the breakup with Tommy, both of which were disasters. One guy turned out to be gay and the other one turned out to be a felon. I figured the universe was telling me to avoid men, and I was happy to take its advice.

But a few months ago, I reluctantly decided it was time to dip my toe back into the dating pool. I agreed to go out on a blind date set up by the ever-matchmaking Lizzie. The date ended very badly, with the guy trying to attack me on the beach. Sadly, his life ended badly, as well, a few days later, when he was murdered in the basement of a house I was working on.

"Wow, grim memories," I muttered. Where had those awful thoughts come from? Shaking my head, I finished my wine and went upstairs and got ready for bed. Rob-bie and Tiger both jumped onto the bed to join me, and I switched on the television to catch a few minutes of one of my favorite old sitcoms. I needed a good laugh after rehashing my pitiful dating life. The three of us fell asleep within minutes.

Early Thursday morning, as I was drinking my second cup of coffee, Ms. Barney called. "You got the job! You won the bid. I'm so happy."

"Are you kidding?" I said, not quite believing my luck. "That was so fast."

"Well, it's been three months," she said with a laugh. "But I know what you mean. We were just talking about it yesterday."

"I'm completely thrilled."

"Good. Me, too. If you're available, why don't you swing by my office in the next two hours? We can sign some forms to make it official."

"I can be there by ten."

I arrived on time and we gave each other a quick hug before I sat down to sign some boilerplate waiver forms. She handed me a tentative schedule for completing the work on the parking lot. I thanked her again for the op-portunity and she gave me a high five.

I walked out to the hall, chuckling to myself and men-tally scanning the list of job sites I needed to visit that day, when I was stopped in my tracks. Halfway down the hall, Police Chief Jensen and Tommy Gallagher were walking into the counselors' offices.

Without thinking, I scurried down the hall to see if I could talk to Tommy. He would tell me what the police were doing here. Was this about Lily? Of course it was.

So who were they here to question? Were they going to arrest anybody?

By the time I reached the doorway leading to the offices, the short inner hall leading to the clerk's counter was empty. I glanced around, wondering which of the three counselors' offices they'd entered, but I wasn't about to knock on each of the doors to find out. Maybe I'd be able to catch up with Tommy in the next day or so to get the scoop.

Back in the main hall, I took a quick look at the brass plate on the door. It listed the three high school counselors who had offices down that hall, and I saw a name that sent chills up my spine: DARREN DAIN. So he was still working here, still giving bad counsel to the poor students assigned to him. Thank heavens there were two other counselors to choose from—a good thing, since the school enrolled almost five hundred students from all around the county.

"I can't believe it," I muttered. Darren "Dismal" Dain had been the world's worst counselor, even back in my day. There was no way he'd improved, because besides being a stupid man and a bad counselor, he was a condescending prig who hated teenagers. I'd had the bad luck to be assigned to him when I first started high school. I couldn't count the times he'd ridiculed me for thinking I could ever make a living working in construction. He thought that with all my hair, I should consider going to beauty school and becoming a hairdresser. I could just picture Whitney and her pals having a field day with that news. I mean, the man was a clod. I remembered leaving school in tears one afternoon when he pulled me into his office to tell me I should wear a dress once in a while so the boys wouldn't be so turned off by me.

What kind of a creep said that to a teenage girl, especially when that girl worked a construction job every afternoon with her dad? My father finally had to complain to the principal, and I was reassigned to Mrs. Sweet, whose personality fitted her name. I still sent her a Christmas card every year.

Why would Ms. Barney continue to allow Dismal Dain to counsel students? Did school counselors get some kind of tenure? Maybe he was blackmailing her. There was no other reason I could think of. The man was a horror show. There had to have been hundreds of complaints by now.

I glanced up and down the hall and realized it wouldn't be smart to be caught snooping around here, so I walked away.

I didn't know which office Eric had gone into, but his visit must have had something to do with Lily. Which meant that one of those three counselors had to have advised Lily all those years ago. And on the off chance that she'd been stuck with Dismal Dain, I fully intended to visit Eric that afternoon to let him know why that despicable man belonged right at the top of his suspect list.

Chapter Six

I reached my truck, still flipped out about Dismal Dain. It had been almost fifteen years since I'd been stuck with him. I had to think that in all that time he must have been warned at some point to clean up his act. I hoped he'd been forced to take sexual-harassment training and psychological counseling so he no longer came across like the sexist troglodyte he'd been when I knew him. One could always hope. But the real issue with him went deeper than that. Dain's real problem was that he hated people, especially teenagers. I wondered just how bad his own school counselor had been to steer him toward a career working with the very people he most despised.

I drove through town on my way to my friend Emily Rose's new home, the former Rawley mansion, where several of my guys were already at work. Sean would be assigned there for the time being, until we could get back inside the lighthouse mansion. Although now that I thought about it, it would be better to switch him with Douglas. I doubted Sean would want to work every day in the place where his sister's remains had been found.

As I stopped at the light across from the Cozy Cove

Diner, my cell phone rang. I clicked the button on my Bluetooth and said hello.

"Shannon? It's Teddy calling." Teddy Peters was head of the Planning Commission and an old friend of my father's.

"Hi, Teddy. What's up?"

"It's Aldous again," he said, his tone apologetic. "Do you have time to come by the office this morning? I need your help talking him down off the ledge."

"Off the ledge? Is he about to . . ." Was Aldous threatening to kill himself? The Planning Commission's offices were on the first floor of City Hall. Could he really hurt himself?

"No, no, it's nothing like that," he rushed to add. "But I just ran into him in the hall and he's all riled up again. He's still got that bug up his bum over the lighthouse-mansion rehab and he won't let it go. Can you talk to him?"

I didn't resist rolling my eyes, since no one was there to see me. From the first day I'd met with the Planning Commission to discuss Mac's proposal for a few modest changes to the mansion, Aldous Murch had questioned my ideas and had worried aloud whether I would destroy the town's beautiful old landmark. Never mind the part about insulting me professionally and hurting my feelings on a personal level; he was just plain wrong. I'd tried at least ten times—no exaggeration—to go over the blueprints with him, but he would just shake his head, grumble that I didn't know what I was talking about, and stomp off.

"Is he there right now?" I asked.

"Yes. I swear he's going to have a heart attack over this thing if he doesn't calm down."

"We don't want that, but I'm not sure I can do anything to help. We've gone around and around on this issue."

"I know, but I'd appreciate your coming by if you can."

"I'll be there in ten minutes."

"Thanks, kiddo."

As I drove to City Hall, I thought about the best way to handle the crotchety old man. Aldous was at least eighty-five years old, and besides his long-held seat on the Planning Commission, he also ran the town's Historical Society. He had been one of the original group of coastguardsmen stationed at the lighthouse mansion during World War II, when there was a constant threat of Japanese submarines along the coast. So, to be fair, no one in town had a more vested interest in making sure the lighthouse mansion maintained its historical integrity than Aldous. But the fact that he doubted my ability to do my job was upsetting. The man knew me. Knew my work. I was trying to be thoughtful of his age and his concerns, but all this arguing was starting to annoy me.

I tracked down Teddy in his cramped office and knocked on the open door. He glanced up. "Oh good. You're here."

"I wouldn't get your hopes up. He's not going to listen to me. He never has."

"That's funny, because he complains that you're the one who won't listen."

"He would never have pulled this attitude with my father," I muttered, disgusted with the old guy.

"You're partly right, and I'm sorry. But, truth be told, your father would've dragged Aldous over to the pub for a beer and they would've hashed it out."

"Well, even if I invited him to the pub, he wouldn't

show up. And that's the crux of the problem. He doesn't trust me because I'm female, and that little detail isn't going to change anytime soon."

Teddy chuckled as he led me down a long hallway and into the large mahogany-paneled meeting hall. He gestured toward the old man sitting in a chair at the massive conference table, his back toward us. He didn't see me standing at the door.

"Just go talk to him," Teddy whispered.

"I'm willing to do this for you, Teddy, but please don't blame me if nothing changes." I walked straight across the room and right up to Aldous, who flinched when he saw me. "Hello, Mr. Murch."

His eyes narrowed. "Are you here to admit your mistake?"

"What? No." He really was losing it. "I'm here because the other commission members told me you have something to say to me."

He shook his finger at me as though I were a misbehaving ten-year-old. "I drove out there, and the place is covered in yellow construction ribbon. You can't start the project until you tear down the stairway."

"It's not construction ribbon," I said sharply. "It's crime-scene tape. We found a dead body inside the house."

His eyes blinked and his hands shook. "A . . . a body? You found her, then? On the staircase?" He worked his jaw back and forth and rubbed his hand over his mouth a few times, clearly uneasy. "No. Not on the staircase. The body was . . . We . . ." He blinked again and continued to mumble, but I couldn't understand him.

I regretted my outburst. Aldous was an old man and obviously couldn't take that kind of shock. But he'd said something about a body. Had he been around when Lily was killed?

"Aldous, do remember seeing someone hanging around inside the lighthouse mansion? A girl, maybe? Someone who didn't belong there?"

He stared at me for a few long seconds, as if he didn't know me. A moment later, the haze cleared from his eyes and he was glaring at me again. "You need to tear down the staircase."

My shoulders sagged a little. Hearing him say the same words he'd been repeating for the past two months made me want to run from the room. In the beginning, I had worried that Aldous's protests over the sale itself and the plans for renovation would cause Mac to back out of the deal. That worry had passed, thank goodness, but now I was concerned that his mind was slipping.

The problem was that just when I was about to feel sorry for him being nonsensical, he would turn all cantankerous about the mansion because he'd lived there once upon a time and he considered himself an expert. He was also a stickler for the most obscure Historical Society rules and procedures, which he'd probably made up himself.

I wanted to be kind to the old man, but he had tried my patience to the limit. I decided to take a different tack. I pulled out the chair next to him and sat down. "You've been friends with my father for years and he taught me everything he knows. Don't you trust him?"

"This isn't about your father."

"Of course it is. He entrusted his company to me. Now it looks like you don't trust me to do a good job on the mansion and you're letting everybody in town know about it. Are you trying to ruin my business?"

I caught the distress in his expression as he leaned back away from me. "I'm not ruining your business."

"But you're bad-mouthing me around City Hall," I explained. "What if some homeowner gets wind of it? Do you think they'll ever hire me?"

"Now see here, young lady." He wagged his finger at me. "I have nothing but respect for you and your father, and your business is doing just fine. My concern is with the lighthouse mansion."

"That's my concern, too."

"Good. Then we're agreed."

I frowned. "Okay."

"So, you'll admit that you're wrong about the blueprints."

"What? No." I shook my head to clear it. "No. I have the very latest version of the architect's prints and I've done a complete walk-through of the house. The blueprints are correct."

He threw his hands up. "Then it'll all be ruined."

And we were back to where we'd started. This was the same argument I'd been having with him for weeks. And I didn't even understand what his problem was. Aldous had claimed there were other blueprints for the mansion and I had the wrong set. But I'd gone back in the Planning Commission archives and checked the original version against the more updated set and they were exactly the same. I'd followed them as we did our walk-through the other day. The blueprints I was using were correct. I didn't know any other way to explain that to the old man.

"Chimney," he muttered, mindlessly scribbling squiggles on a piece of paper. "There's no chimney."

"There are four chimneys," I said quietly.

He shot me a heated look. "How many staircases?"

"One."

His jaw clenched so tightly, I thought he might break a tooth. I hated to see him so angry. I sighed and reached over to take his hand in mine. I could feel every one of his fragile bones and his thin, crepey skin. I wondered how much longer he would live, and I was suddenly afraid this fight would be the death of him. I wanted to end our argument right here and now. "Mr. Murch, I don't want to argue about this anymore. All I can do is promise, on my father's honor, that I will make you proud of the job I do on the lighthouse mansion."

His lips shook slightly as he spoke. "I believe you, dear."

"And anytime you want to come out to the mansion and see what we're doing, you're always welcome. I'll even drive you out there myself."

His smile seemed a little sad. "I'll take you up on that offer one of these days."

Was that an admission of my ability to do a good job or had he just given up the fight for now? I didn't have a clue, but I wasn't about to go another round with him.

"I'm available anytime. All you have to do is call me." I squeezed his hand once more before letting it go. Giving him an encouraging smile and a nod, I stood and walked away. I didn't know whether to laugh or cry as I left the meeting hall. I felt bad for Aldous, but I couldn't do anything to fix a delusion from the past that had no basis in reality.

I made a quick detour to Teddy's office to let him know that Aldous seemed willing to call a truce for now. "I can't tell you if he'll feel the same way tomorrow, but he didn't want to argue anymore. Maybe I just wore him out."

Teddy shrugged. "I guess that's something. But I'm afraid the old guy still has plenty of rant left in him."

"I suppose you'll call me if he gets going again."

"You bet I will," he said cheerily.

I shook my head and walked out of his office.

I finally made it to Emily's house and walked in on the organized chaos of a full-blown rehab. A ladder was perched under the chandelier medallion in the foyer. A dozen five-gallon drums of paint were lined up along the stairwell, along with clean paint rollers, a couple of roller extensions, and a stack of paint trays. Streaks of different colors were slashed across the wall of the dining room, where Emily was testing which ones she liked best. Splotched drop cloths covered every inch of floor space. Blue painter's tape masked the edges of all the windows.

"Hey, boss," Johnny said from atop the ladder. He wore a baseball cap backward to protect his hair from flakes of dried spackle as he patched up a thin crack that ran half the length of the narrow room. If the crack had been any wider, we would've had to use drywall compound, because spackle was likely to dry unevenly and eventually crumble and fall out of a large crack. For a small one like this, I thought we were safe with spackle. It went on more smoothly without having to be sanded, and it dried quickly.

"Good job, Johnny."

"Ceiling should be ready to paint anytime."

"Has Emily chosen the colors she wants in here?"

"Yeah, about six different times."

I laughed. "She's having an adventure."

"She's cool," he said, grinning.

Emily had surprised us all a few months ago when she

announced that she'd purchased the old Rawley mansion. She'd heard the rumors that the place was haunted but laughed it off, especially since the asking price for the home had been drastically reduced based on those rumors. Little did she know that the ghost of Mrs. Rawley would indeed turn out to be her new roommate.

Nobody had believed me when I'd claimed to have seen the ghost once years ago, when my friend Jane and I had been trick-or-treating. I'd dared to peek through a window and had seen a woman sitting nearby writing a letter and crying. I didn't realize she was a ghost until she started to fade and I could see right through her!

I didn't dare mention it to Emily at first, but then I didn't have to, because as we started working on the house, Mrs. Rawley made her presence known in some startling ways: shaking chandeliers, moaning and groaning, flying paint cans. Ever since we'd discovered her old diary buried behind a wall, though, she had eased up on the spirited antics. Emily insisted that the ghostly presence was comforting.

Things felt peaceful as I walked through the house, checking on the work we'd done so far. I tracked down Sean and Douglas in the kitchen, where they were removing the old sink in the butler's pantry.

"Hey, guys," I said.

"Hi, Shannon," Douglas said, grunting as he lifted his end of the heavy cast-iron sink. They set the thing down on the linoleum and stood, breathing heavily.

"That weighs a ton," Sean said, wiping his forehead. He looked at me and smiled, but I could tell by the sad look in his eyes that he wasn't himself yet. And who could blame him? "Where have you been all morning?"

I grinned. "I ran over to the high school to sign the waivers for the senior-parking-lot job."

"Did we get it?" Douglas asked.

"Yes. I'll work up a schedule as soon as I hear from the solar company."

"That's awesome, boss," Sean said, and this time his smile reached his eyes.

"I think it will be. And you know I always like trying something new and different."

"This will be different," Douglas agreed.

Sean stuck his cap on his head. "Ready to move another sink?"

"Let's do it," Douglas said.

"Wait, Sean," I interjected. "Can I talk to you for a minute?"

"Sure." He glanced at Douglas. "I'll just be a minute."

"No problem," Douglas said. He grabbed a half-filled bottle of water and chugged it down.

I led the way to the kitchen door and we walked outside.

"What's up, boss?"

I quickly zipped up my down jacket to keep the cold March wind from turning me into an icicle. The sky above us was crystal blue, but out along the horizon, dark gray clouds loomed once more. The air practically snapped with the smell of ozone and salt. I didn't need a meteorologist to predict it would be raining by sunset. I turned and faced Sean. "I saw Chief Jensen at the school this morning, going into the counselors' offices."

He thought about that and I saw the exact moment when the light dawned. "He wants to talk to Lily's high school counselor."

I crossed my arms. "That's what I figured."

Sean's placid expression turned to a glower. "That's good. That makes sense. I just hope he kicks that jackass in the behind for the things he told Lily."

I asked the question carefully. "Exactly which jackass are you referring to?"

He glared at me. "Who else? Dismal Dain."

"Okay." I sighed. "I figured it might be him."

"Did you know him?"

"I was assigned to him when I was a freshman, but he was so awful, my father finally protested and I got switched to Mrs. Sweet."

"You're lucky you had a father who cared." Sean scuffed his boot against the cement foundation. "Lily, not so much."

"Dain was horrible," I said, remembering the man's mortifying advice as clearly as if I'd heard it an only hour ago. "He was an impossible combination of stupid and arrogant and hateful."

"Tell me about it."

So I did, relating some of the highlights of my conversations with Dain. By the time I was finished, Sean was laughing again.

"He thought you should be a hairdresser? That's priceless. The guy's a moron."

"I know." I brushed my hair back self-consciously.

"Oh, come on, boss. You've got great hair."

"And a lot of it."

"Maybe that's how he came up with the idea. He sure didn't bother to get to know you, because if he had, he would've realized that you've been working construction since you were a kid and you're good at it besides. The guy didn't have a clue how to do his job."

A gust of wind swept by and I pulled my collar close to my neck to keep warm. "He should've been fired years ago. I still can't believe he's still there."

He shook his head. "Me neither."

"He must be blackmailing somebody on the school board or something. There's no way he could've lasted this long otherwise."

Sean chuckled. "That's one explanation. I don't know how they can justify paying him an actual salary to dole out such bad advice."

"Do you have any idea what kind of stuff he told Lily?"

"Oh yeah." He sniffed in disgust, crossed his arms over his chest, and leaned back against the side of the house. "Remember how Lily had the lead in the school play?"

"Sure. I used to watch her every night while I was building sets. She was so talented and beautiful."

"She was a good student, too, despite all our problems at home. She was determined to win a full drama college scholarship, but she made the mistake of mentioning that to Dain."

"What did he do?"

Sean gritted his teeth. "He laughed in her face."

I blinked. "Are you kidding?"

"He actually called her a fool. Told her to give it up and get real." Sean scraped his hands through his hair in frustration. "I'll never forget it. I found her in tears one afternoon, and she told me Dain had told her to stop with the foolish notion of college. He said her home life was so bleak, she'd never get any academic support. I guess that much was true."

I squeezed his arm. "You supported her, Sean. And so did Amy."

"Yeah, we did." He shoved himself away from the

wall and paced a few feet back and forth. "Dain said that besides not being smart enough, she had too much flamboyant theatrical style—I'll never forget those words. And he said that no reputable college would want her on their campus."

"That is incredibly harsh and unfair and wrong. And flamboyant theatrical style? What in the world was that supposed to mean?"

"I have no idea. The only time she was theatrical was when she was onstage. She always dressed conservatively. My mother would have a fit if she walked out of the house showing any skin. So I have no clue what he was talking about."

I was fuming on Lily's behalf. "How rude of him to say that no reputable college would want her. She could've gotten a drama scholarship anywhere. Or an academic one, if she wanted to." I pounded my fist into my hand, unable to do anything to help the situation. "I would love to throttle him."

"I'd like to do more than that," Sean muttered. "And here's the kicker. Dain told Lily she was better suited for work as a shopgirl."

"A shopgirl? That was it?"

"Yeah."

"Who uses that kind of term? It sounds like something out of a Dickens novel." I thought about it. "Did he say what kind of shop?"

"No. It didn't matter to him—that's the point."

I shook my head. "Maybe if Dain had his way, Lily and I would've gone into business together. We could've opened a beauty shop."

Sean managed a laugh. "Because you both have hair, right?"

"Right. At least he credited Lily with some ability to run a business."

We talked for another few minutes. Sean told me that after Lily talked to Dismal Dain, she never mentioned her goals to anyone again. Only a few other people already knew she was trying for a scholarship, including Sean, who always tried to encourage her despite his own troubles at home.

I squeezed his shoulder. "I'm going to call Eric and find out what Dismal had to say."

Sean hesitated. "You don't know for certain that he's the guy they were looking for."

"Who else could it be?"

He nodded thoughtfully. "Yeah, it's got to be him. I wonder how the chief found out about him being Lily's counselor."

"Probably from Denise."

"He talked to Denise?"

"Yeah, he went by her house. Mr. Jones left school in a hurry to be with her."

"Oh, man. That's a drag." He lifted his shoulder in a helpless shrug. "But she was Lily's best friend, so it makes sense. I've talked to her a bunch of times over the years, you know, when something new came up that I thought might finally lead us to Lily. But Denise never really knew anything."

"That's too bad."

"So, what're you going to say to the chief?"

"I'm not sure yet. But I wouldn't put it past Dismal to lie to Eric about Lily, so I want to set the record straight about what a miserable counselor he was."

Sean grabbed my arm. "Whatever happens, Shannon, whatever you hear, I want you to tell me the truth."

"I will, Sean." I grabbed him in a hug. "Don't worry. We're on the same team here."

"Okay." He let go of an anxious breath. "I know. I trust you. Thanks."

Instead of calling Eric on the phone, I decided it would be more effective to talk to him face-to-face. So while the guys took a lunch break, I drove over to the police station in hopes of finding him in his office. Instead, I ran into him on the sidewalk outside the glass double doors leading into the station.

"Shannon? What're you doing here?"

I almost laughed. He didn't look suspicious exactly, but I could tell he was wary. "Do you have a minute?"

He checked his watch. "Barely. What's up?"

"I saw you at the high school this morning."

There was that scowl I'd grown so fond of. "What were you doing there?"

I gave him a pleasant smile. "I had a meeting with the principal to sign some papers."

"Papers?"

I almost laughed at his wary tone. "Yes. I bid on a school-construction job and just found out this morning that I got it."

"Hey, great. Congratulations."

He sounded genuinely happy for me—and very relieved, probably because it meant I wasn't there to investigate Lily's murder. I joined him as he walked toward the parking lot where his SUV was parked.

"Anyway," I said briskly, "I saw you there, of course, and I noticed you walking into the counselors' offices."

I watched his jaw clench. "What's your point, Shannon?"

I reminded myself that it was his job to be distrustful and tried not to take his attitude personally. "Remember how you asked me to give you some background information on the people who were around when Lily was in school?"

"Yeah."

"Well, when I saw you, it stirred a memory of someone who was a really bad guy."

"And who was that?"

"One of the counselors. Darren Dain. Lily had him as her senior adviser."

"How do you know that?"

"Sean told me. And I had him, too, for a brief period. He was a real creep. I was assigned to him my freshman year and he said some awful things. And I know he gave Lily some really stupid advice, too. They should've fired him a long time ago."

"So, you think I should arrest him?"

My eyes widened. "Can you?"

"No," he said flatly. "Giving bad advice doesn't make him a killer, Shannon."

"Neither does extinguishing kids' hopes and dreams, but he did that, too."

We reached his car and he pulled out his keys. "I appreciate your passing along that information."

He reached for the door handle, but I blocked his way. "Look, my main point in coming to see you was to let you know I wouldn't be surprised to find out that Dismal lied about Lily. So if you want the truth, you should talk to me or Sean. That's all I'm saying."

Eric breathed in and out and seemed to relax a little. Nodding, he said, "I appreciate it, Shannon. And if it means anything, Tommy agrees with your assessment of

Dain. But that still doesn't mean I'm going to throw him in jail."

"Oh, I forgot that Tommy was assigned to him, too."

Eric leaned his elbow against the driver's door. "Yeah. His advice to Tom was to open a tune-up franchise."

"Oh, my God." I had to laugh. I'd never had a chance to hear what Dismal had advised him to do with his life. But that was more proof that the counselor was totally off base on everything. If he'd known Tommy at all, he would've realized that Tommy didn't know squat about cars. In fact, I was the one who used to change his motor oil. I gave Eric a sheepish look. "If you think that's bad, he . . . he told me I should wear a dress more often and . . . and open a beauty shop."

He did a double take and then his eyes narrowed. "That's the dumbest thing I've ever heard."

"Exactly."

He held up his hands in mock surrender. "You've convinced me. I'm going to arrest him right now."

"Thank you," I said, laughing weakly as he jumped into his car and started the engine. But as he pulled out of the lot, my smile faded. *Darn. I really, really wish he wasn't kidding.*

Chapter Seven

I spent the rest of the day scraping wallpaper off the living room walls at Emily's house. It was the best kind of job to do whenever I wanted to forget everything. Like the fact that Dismal Dain would not be spending the rest of his life in jail. I just couldn't get Eric to take the evil man seriously.

While wallpaper removal was the perfect job to zone out on, it was also the worst task of all when it came to rehabbing a house. This was especially true of Victorian homes, which were built in an era when wallpaper was worshiped and often applied to walls in every room in the house—and occasionally on the ceilings, as well.

Back in the day, when it came time to redecorate a room, instead of scraping off the old wallpaper, an owner would simply cover over the existing wallpaper with a new pattern. It was just easier. So 150-some years later, when I'd come along to renovate a place, there might be as many as six layers of wallpaper to remove. But even if there was only one layer and it came off easily, the glue residue would often remain on the wall in sticky, streaky, gooey brown globs. That was when we'd start pulling out our hair in frustration.

There were a number of different methods for removing wallpaper. Some people believed in good old vinegar and water. Some might add a portion of fabric softener to the mix. Some swore by scrapers or sponges. Any or all of these might work for a small job.

Douglas had grown up working construction jobs with his father, and his preferred method of removal was to use an industrial-strength garden sprayer that he filled with equal parts hot water and fabric softener. He'd spray a wide section of the wall with the liquid, wait about five minutes, and then start scraping. Often a sheet would peel off in one large swath. Once the wall was dry, he would go back and scrape off the glue.

The trick with spraying all that water was to not allow the liquid to sit too long before removing the wallpaper. Victorian walls were constructed of lath and plaster, and if that much moisture seeped into the wall and sat there for too long, it would damage the plaster.

For big jobs, I'd found the steamer method worked best. My father had invested in a heavy steamer that rolled and swiveled around on casters and had a large stainless-steel plate that was lightweight and easy to use, even for an eight-year-old. The heating element and the hot water were contained inside a fully insulated tank, so Dad never had to worry that I might accidentally burn myself.

One secret I'd learned early on was to start steaming at the bottom of the wall and work my way up. This was because as you steamed the wallpaper, water would drip down the walls and onto the floor. If you started at the top, you'd wind up kneeling in mushy, gluey paper when you reached the bottom of the wall. It also helped to stuff old towels along the floor edges.

Once you were finished, it was smart to apply a primer before painting the wall; even if you couldn't see it, there always seemed to be some residual glue left on the wall, and the primer helped conceal it.

Because of the mind-numbing nature of wallpaper removal, my guys and I always took turns so that no one got stuck doing the entire job him- or herself. We were each assigned a separate room on a separate day, and that way we shared the pain. I was all about equal opportunity on every level.

When Emily arrived home at six o'clock, I was still working. The guys had all gone home, but I was there, all alone, completely wrapped up in the job.

"Shannon?"

"What?" I flinched a little, which told me how zoned out I'd been. And since zoning out had been my purpose all along, I figured I'd succeeded. "Hey, Emily."

"You're still working?"

I stared at the wall and the progress I'd made, then back at her. "I guess I am. But I'll clean up and get out of your way." I climbed down the ladder, picking curly pieces of wallpaper slivers off my shirt and tossing them into the large trash bag nearby.

She gazed around the room. "You've gotten so much done."

"Yeah, I just decided to go for it."

With a smile, she said, "You look tired."

"What every girl wants to hear," I said, and laughed. "But, yeah, I really am tired. And annoyed. Mostly annoyed."

She set her purse and a small grocery bag that held a

pretty bouquet of flowers on the utility table we'd set up near the foyer archway. "Who or what has annoyed you?"

I waved the question away. "You don't know him and it's not worth talking about."

"Of course it is. Come and have a glass of wine with me."

I hesitated, then said, "Well, I can hardly refuse an offer of wine."

She walked into the butler's pantry. "Oh, the boys pulled out the sink."

I unplugged the steamer and began to clean up the crimped and twisted bits of old wallpaper. "You can still use the main one, right?"

"Oh yes. It's not a problem. They're just moving ahead so quickly."

"I wish it was quicker, for your sake."

Emily Rose, despite being ten years older than me, was one of my dearest friends and a member of my inner circle. There were five of us who met regularly to console each other and laugh and plan and scheme. Emily had moved to town from Scotland years ago with her fisherman boyfriend, who was later lost in a tragic accident at sea.

Her new tea shop, along with many of her new friends in town, had sustained her through the hardest days. Emily had lived in the apartment over the shop until recently, when, out of the blue, she decided to buy this old house. Now I couldn't wait to complete the job and have her finally feel settled.

I joined her in the big unfinished kitchen as she pulled a bottle of chardonnay from an old, temporary refrigerator and poured two glasses. We sat at the small café table she'd moved into the kitchen.

She handed me a glass. "Now take a sip or two and then tell me why you're annoyed."

I must've been ready to talk, because once I started, I couldn't seem to stop. I told her all about finding Lily's bones and how the discovery affected Sean. I gave her a brief history of my high school years and how kind Lily had been to me. I told her—ranted, really—about Dismal Dain and his historically imbecilic advice to students. I gave a quickie recap of my Career Day successes and my delight in having been chosen to construct the new high school parking lot. By my second glass of wine, I was compelled to mention Whitney's idiocy, on general principle. By that point Emily was laughing, and I suppose I was, too. Even though there was very little that was funny about the events of the past few days.

My light mood faded quickly and I sighed. "It was so frustrating for Sean to realize that poor Lily never left town. She was lying dead and alone in the lighthouse mansion all this time. It's sad and creepy."

"I'm so sorry for Sean," Emily said.

"Me, too. He's spent so many years searching for his sister and waiting for her to return. He was simply shattered by the news."

Emily took a sip of wine, then asked in a gentle tone, "But don't you think, Shannon, in a way, it must be a relief for him to finally know the truth?"

It was hard to admit she was right. "I suppose so. That doesn't mean I'll stop bugging Eric to find the killer."

"Is it possible that she wasn't murdered?" she asked cautiously. "Perhaps it was an accident."

"It's conceivable, but how did she get inside the dumbwaiter?"

Emily thought for a moment. "Was she hiding from someone?"

"Maybe. But where did her clothes disappear to? And what about that awful mattress? Was she living there? Escaping from her parents for a while? Was she with someone?"

"There are too many questions," Emily admitted.

"And not enough answers, as usual."

"At least Eric is asking your advice this time. That must feel good."

"It does," I said, feeling a glow that probably had more to do with the wine than with Eric's approval. "Although it's sad that he wouldn't arrest Dismal Dain when I suggested it. So I guess that means he won't be hiring me as an expert consultant anytime soon."

Emily chuckled. "Dismal Dain sounds like a dreadful person."

"He is that."

Emily got up and poured glasses of water for us both, and we changed the subject to other things, namely Mrs. Rawley's ghost, who was relatively quiet these days.

"Unless Augustus stops by," Emily said. "Then she starts swinging on the chandeliers."

Augustus Peratti, or Gus, as I called him, since I'd known him forever, owned the best auto shop in town. He was a gorgeous, sexy Italian who'd been attracting women like bees to honey since the first grade. A few weeks ago, Gus had stopped by to see Emily, and Mrs. Rawley's ghost went crazy. The chandelier began to swing and lights flashed on and off all over the house. Gus even lost consciousness for a few seconds, but quickly recovered. Several of us witnessed it with our own eyes and had no explanation for the phenomenon until Mrs. Rawley's diary was recovered shortly afterward. In it, she confessed that she had been in love with Gus's great-grandfather all those years ago, but her parents had forbidden her to marry him. She must've recognized him in Gus, because she went a little crazy when Gus walked into the house. Since then, she'd been as calm as could be.

The really odd aspect of the story was that Gus was supposed to bring Emily's car to her tea shop that day, not to Emily's new house. But somehow he'd been compelled to show up at the new place instead. Had the ghost actually conveyed that message to him clairvoyantly? We would never know.

"So the chandeliers still swing when he comes here?" I chuckled. "I shouldn't be surprised. Gus has had that effect on women his whole life."

Emily laughed and slapped my arm. "Very funny. Seriously, though, I think it's so nice of Augustus to come by to visit Mrs. Rawley."

"Are you sure he's not coming by to visit you?"

"Oh no," she protested. "He's just being nice, and I couldn't be happier. He really does seem to have a calming effect on her."

"Calming, really? The woman is making the chandeliers swing."

She bit back a smile. "To tell the truth, they only sway a bit."

I wasn't ready to drive home yet, so I walked around the house with Emily while she pointed out other areas she'd like to have fixed whenever I had the time to fit her into my schedule. We made a plan to get together with the girls sometime in the next week, and an hour later, I was ready to drive the eight long blocks to my home.

As I carefully pulled the truck into the driveway, I was pleased to see Mac standing there.

"Are you on your way out?" I asked after climbing out of the truck.

"No, I just got home and saw your headlights coming, so I thought I'd wait for you." He wrapped his arm around my shoulder and it felt so warm and so right, I almost froze in fear. I couldn't get attached to Mac—I just couldn't. The man was a bachelor millionaire who dated supermodels and celebrities. But could I fling his arm off my shoulder? No. Actually, I snuggled even closer to him as we walked through the gate into the backyard. My only excuse was that the wind had picked up and it was too darn cold to bear it alone.

"I haven't seen you in a few days," he said. "Is everything all right?"

"Sure," I said casually, then reconsidered. "Well actually, it's been weird, with the mansion closed until further notice and Sean dealing with his sister's death and Eric showing up at school to talk to Lily's horrible high school counselor."

"Whoa," he said. "That's a lot of stuff going on. And I want to hear every last detail, but I can tell you've had a long day. Would you like to have dinner sometime this weekend?"

"I'd love to," I said, shoving all thoughts of blond supermodels to the far regions of my brain.

"Good." He walked me to my kitchen door and waited until I unlocked it, then kissed me on the cheek. "Sweet dreams, Irish."

First thing Friday morning, Ms. Barney called again. "The head engineer from the solar company wants to meet you this afternoon at two o'clock. Are you available?"

"I'll be there. Your office?"

"Let's meet out at the parking lot. That way you don't have to walk back and forth across campus."

"Perfect. I'll see you then."

"Just one more thing, Shannon." She hesitated, then said, "It's about one of the other bidders for the job."

I didn't like the tone of her voice. "Is there a problem?"

"Sort of. When I told him we were going to go with your company, he didn't take the news well. He told me I'd be sorry, and to watch out for you because you liked to cut corners."

"What?" I stared at the phone. "Are you kidding? I've never cut corners in my life."

"I know that, dear, and I wish I were kidding, but I'm not. He also said . . . Well, it doesn't matter."

"Oh yes, it does. What else did he say?"

She hesitated, then added, "He said you were lazy and probably wouldn't finish the job."

"Oh my God." My stomach began to churn, and I had a feeling I knew where all of this was coming from.

"I know it was just sour grapes," Ms. Barney said, "because you're the best worker I've ever dealt with. I just wanted to warn you that you seem to have an enemy out there."

"Can you tell me who it is?" But I already knew. "Never mind. It was Cliff Hogarth, wasn't it?"

"Yes," she said, surprised that I would know. "He was very unpleasant. I got the feeling from the way he talked that you two had had some other run-ins."

I paced back and forth across the kitchen, unable to

sit still after hearing Ms. Barney's revelation. "We have, I'm sorry to say. He's tried to poach some of my crew members and bad-mouthed me to a few of my clients."

She considered my words for a moment. "Didn't you go to school with him?"

"He was two years older than me, but he asked me out a few times. I said no."

She groaned. "Oh, Shannon. This can't be about that."

"I'm afraid it might be."

"Oh, dear. I'm sorry." She let loose a heavy sigh. "I never thought I'd ever have to say this to anyone, but please watch your back."

"I will. Thanks, Ms. Barney."

I hung up feeling drained. It was barely eight o'clock in the morning and I had a full day of work ahead of me, but I wanted to crawl back into bed and hide from the world.

"No," I said out loud, causing Robbie to bark in response. "Sorry, buddy." I picked him up and hugged him tightly, then set him back down. After gulping down the rest of my coffee, I carried the mug and my empty cereal bowl to the sink.

No, I refused to crawl back to bed. Instead I wanted to go find Cliff Hogarth and smack him upside the head. I wouldn't mind if Eric threw him in jail, either. What a conniving creep.

Hmm. I wondered if I could file a complaint of some kind. What Cliff had said and done crossed the line into slander, and I wondered if I should just sue him. But maybe the best thing to do was track him down, get in his face, and let him know I wasn't going to put up with his nonsense anymore.

Once I'd straightened up the kitchen, I sat down and

called Wade, then conferenced in Carla to let my two foremen know that I'd be meeting the engineer that afternoon to discuss the new job. I asked Wade to join me at the school for the meeting, since he had experience laying down blacktop.

"I'll be there," Wade said.

"You want me to work any of it?" Carla asked.

"Let me see what their schedule is first," I said. "I think I'll start the job and then maybe pass it on to you, Carla. I want all of us to get some experience with these canopies they're setting up, because as soon as companies around town see what's going on, there's going to be more and more demand for alternative-energy construction. We might as well get all the experience we can."

"I agree," Wade said. "We've done rooftop gardens and greenhouses, and we did the windmill farm out by the Zen center."

"Hey," Carla said, laughing. "You might have to change the name of the company to Green Hammer."

"I like that," I said, feeling better. But my mood didn't last long, as I related Ms. Barney's warning about Cliff Hogarth and his slurs against me and the company. "Can you guys keep your eyes and ears open in case you hear anything else?"

"He's a joke," Wade said derisively.

"A dangerous joke," Carla amended.

"I can't afford to take it as a joke," I admitted. "And, for some reason, the fact that he said what he said to Ms. Barney, my old high school principal"—I rubbed my arms—"that's more disturbing than anything else."

We spoke for another few minutes, and I promised I'd call Carla later to tell her how the meeting with the engineer went.

I wished my father was in town, but he was working at my uncle Pete's winery out on Highway 128. They were building an addition onto the modern barn that housed the massive, stainless-steel, temperature-controlled tanks. This was where the wine sat and fermented before it was transferred to oak barrels.

Uncle Pete's winery had grown more popular in recent years, as had all of the wineries in the Anderson Valley. He'd purchased another ten acres of vineyards a few months ago and now he needed extra space to add a few more tanks.

I had promised to drive out there some weekend and help with the construction. Uncle Pete had agreed to make homemade pasta while I was there. It sounded like a pretty good trade. And it wasn't exactly a hardship to drive the distance, since the Anderson Valley was barely ten miles east of Lighthouse Cove.

When Dad wasn't helping Uncle Pete or traveling to some fishing hole somewhere, he parked his RV in my driveway, and I got to see him anytime I wanted to. I could've used some commonsense advice from him right about now, because I was feeling pretty low. Thanks to that slimy snake Cliff Hogarth.

I supposed I could call him, but Dad rarely had his cell phone turned on. No, I would have to go out there and see him in person if I wanted to talk.

Tiger curled herself around my ankle and I smiled, amazed at how well my animals could sense my moods. "I'll snap out of it," I said. "Don't worry about me."

Despite my words, Robbie perched himself in front of my feet and whined until I picked him up and let him comfort me.

After a few minutes of quiet, I whispered, "No, I don't

like that guy either. But don't worry. Everything will be okay."

Just as soon as I sued Hogarth for defamation. Or maybe I'd just go ahead with my original plan and smack him upside the head, preferably with a two-by-four.

That afternoon, I met with Josh Martin, the engineer from SolarLight, the company providing the solar canopies for the school parking lot. He had scruffy hair and a nice smile and wore horn-rimmed bifocals. I would describe him as a good-looking nerd. He wore a navy sports coat with a wild red Jerry Garcia tie I recognized from one that Lizzie bought Hal a few years ago. I liked Josh immediately, maybe because of the tie.

Ms. Barney was there, too, and one of the school board members, Bob Heath. Wade arrived a few minutes after me, and I was glad to have someone else on my side in case I missed anything.

Josh handed each of us a thick, dark blue folder that contained several of the company's glossy brochures as well as pages of specs and a precise timeline for the work to be completed. The brochures contained numerous photographs of the architecturally appealing canopies, showing a streamlined design that consisted of a long V-shaped panel held in place by thick, fifteen-foot-tall steel posts that would cover two rows of twelve cars each, for a total of twenty-four cars. The school had ordered three of the canopies, so the total number of cars that would be able to park in the lot would be seventy-two.

"The theory behind our product is a simple one," Josh explained. "Asphalt and concrete parking lots and pavements cover much of our country, especially in the cities.

These surfaces retain heat and create what scientists call the urban heat-island effect. Our canopies offer an easy solution to the problem by providing shade to cool the ground surface and the individual cars parked there."

"That's pretty simple logic," Bob said. I could tell that despite the board's having approved the expenditure, he was hoping to be convinced further.

"It might sound like mere convenience to provide shade for your students' cars," Josh continued, "but consider this: the Department of Energy has determined that parking in the shade actually has a positive effect on the environment. That's because when a student gets in his car at the end of the school day, he won't have to switch on the air conditioner to cool off, thus increasing fuel efficiency for the life of the car."

"Never thought of that," Bob muttered.

"Additionally, the design includes a gutter system that collects rainwater and directs it to a ten-thousand-gallon tank that will be concealed beneath the parking lot surface. That water can be used to irrigate the fields and landscaping across the campus, as well as being available for various nonpotable uses within the buildings, thus reducing your water and power bill."

"What kind of nonpotable uses?" Bill asked.

Josh nodded. "Good question. Mainly things like flushing toilets, hosing down the floors of the cafeteria or the locker rooms, laundering gym towels—that sort of thing. Part of our service includes the installation of pipes that run from the tank to wherever you have a use for the water."

"That's brilliant," Ms. Barney said, clearly anxious to sway Bob Heath.

"I like to think so," Josh said. "Now the panels themselves generate a lot of energy, of course. We've estimated that your canopies will eventually generate enough power to cover forty-five percent of the school's needs for an average school year."

"Forty-five percent is pretty darn good," Bob mused. "But this stuff sure costs a lot to install."

"The costs are going down every year, but, yes, that is the major sticking point. But here's the thing: we estimate that with the power and water you save, you'll have made your initial investment back within four years. We've already contacted your local water and power company to get your new system hooked up to its grid. All things being equal, you could start saving money on your bill immediately. But realistically, it'll take time. A few months, usually. If you have any problems, you'll contact us."

Bob shrugged. "Sounds fair."

"In addition to all that, the panels will also serve as a power source for any hybrid or electric cars parked in the lot. I counted eight hybrids in the lot today, and within the next five years, that number is expected to triple. So this will provide your students with a welcome perk." Josh paused, then managed to smile and make eye contact with each of us before adding, "And besides all that good stuff, let's face it: these canopies look really cool."

"They sure do," Bob muttered.

We all chuckled and nodded in agreement. Because they really did.

Once Bob and Ms. Barney left, Josh and Wade and I had a long discussion about the construction process. First we would regrade and level the surrounding area to provide enough space to park seventy-two cars, plus an entry wide enough to allow cars to enter and exit at the same time. We would excavate deeply enough to make space for the ten-thousand-gallon water tank that the company would provide. We would install pipes leading from the gutters to the tank and from the tank to specific hoses for irrigation, and other pipes leading to the main building, for nonpotable uses.

We would set the thick steel posts in six feet of concrete and embed them into the blacktop.

And while my guys and I would do most of the work, it would all be supervised by several members of the SolarLight team. I was very happy to hear that they'd be around, because this would be my first experience installing solar canopies and I wanted to make sure it was done right.

"Man, that was interesting," Wade said as we walked back to our cars. "And this job is going to be a lot more complicated than I thought."

"I got an idea of the scope of the job from the bidding forms," I said. "But you're right. It's going to be a lot of work. We can handle it, though. I'm excited to get started."

He grinned. "Yeah. Me, too."

"Hello, Shannon."

I glanced in the direction of the voice. "Hey, Mr. Jones."

He looked exhausted, and I suddenly pictured him rushing out of the building the other day to go home to the police.

"How are you holding up?" I asked. "How's Denise?"

"She's been a real trooper, even though she cried for a while. She and Lily were such good friends." He rubbed his neck, looking discomfited. "I was pretty flipped out, though. I can't tell you how weird it is to see a couple of cops sitting in your living room, interviewing your wife."

"I can imagine." Except for the wife part, I could totally relate to his dilemma, but I didn't mention that. "Chief Jensen is a great guy, though. He'll get to the bottom of things. And I'll bet Denise was a big help to him. She told him about Mr. Dain, right?"

"Yes," he said, looking a little dazed by my fast talking. "She told him that Darren—er, Mr. Dain—was Lily's advisor. I hope he was able to help the police."

"I hope so, too." Although I doubted Dismal would have anything worthwhile to say.

Mr. Jones seemed to realize he was in a mood and physically shrugged it off, and flashed me a cheery smile. "So, what brings you back to school again?"

"We're rebuilding the senior parking lot," I said. "By the way, have you met Wade Chambers? He's my foreman, so you'll probably see him around here a lot."

The two men greeted each other and shook hands.

"Hi, Brad."

The three of us turned to see Whitney approaching, and my spirits took a nosedive. Instead of greeting me, she looked from Wade to Mr. Jones and gave me a look of puzzlement. She was so transparent, I knew she was trying to figure out how I rated the company of two such good-looking men.

"Hello, Whitney," Mr. Jones said, and gave me and Wade a quick, forced smile. "Nice meeting you, Wade. If you'll excuse me, I've got to go run an errand. See you all later." And he was gone.

"He didn't have to leave," Whitney said, pouting as she watched Mr. Jones run to his car.

Wade grabbed my arm. "We've got to go, too. Remember, Shannon? See you around, Whitney."

I almost laughed. My big tough foreman looked scared to death. I didn't blame him. Whitney was in predator mode.

"Shannon, wait," Whitney said.

I stopped and turned around.

"I'm glad I ran into you," she said.

I stared at her. "Are you talking to me?"

"Of course, silly," she said, giggling.

Giggling? Had hell frozen over? Whitney didn't giggle. Not around me. I was more suspicious than ever, and I gripped Wade's arm like a vise. No way was he leaving me here to face her alone.

"What is it?" I asked.

"I wanted to let you know that I've hired a contractor to redo my powder room," she said blithely. "And I'd like you to deliver the blueprints of the house to him."

"But . . ." Nobody else had ever worked on Tommy's house but me. Ever. My first reaction was confusion. "I always do the work on your house."

"I know, but just this once I'd like to make a change. You don't mind sharing with someone new, do you?"

I was so furious, I could barely speak, but I managed to squeak out a word. "Who?"

She smiled brightly. "Cliff Hogarth."

Chapter Eight

My breath caught. I tried to remind myself that Whitney wasn't really as awful as I sometimes painted her to be. But then there were times like this when the woman was truly Satan's spawn.

I had to swallow a few times before I could respond, and even then my voice sounded raspy and slow, like I'd caught the plague or something. "Cliff can get the blueprints himself from the Planning Commission."

"Of course he can," Whitney said reasonably. "But he's been away from town so long that he doesn't know all the ins and outs and all the right players. And since your father built the house, I know you can get ahold of them so much faster than he could. Would you mind?"

"My father built the house," I murmured, staring at my hands. "And I do the work."

"I know, but—"

I looked up at Whitney. "That's how it's always been."

She tossed her hair back. "I know, Shannon. But Cliff is an old friend, so I wanted to help him out. You can understand that, can't you?"

"If Cliff wants a favor from me he can ask me himself," I told her, and kept to myself the part about how I'd do him a favor when hell froze over.

"Well," Whitney answered with a tiny wince that didn't cause any nasty frown lines between her eyebrows. "He probably would, but he told me he's worried that you're feeling threatened by him being back in town."

"You should ask yourself why I might feel that way," I said. I might have said more, but, thankfully, Wade dragged me away from her before I could snap her skinny neck like a twig.

I hated that she sounded so sensible when I came across like a petulant child.

I'd never had a true homicidal thought, but around Whitney, all bets were off. The more I stewed over how she'd tried to manipulate me, the more enraged I grew. Sure, maybe she only wanted to help Cliff, but she was earning extra bonus points for screwing with me.

"Get the blueprints, huh? When pigs fly." My breath was coming fast and heavy, like a prize bull catching sight of the flashing red cape of a bullfighter. It wasn't a pretty analogy but it worked for my current situation.

Wade grabbed the keys from my hand and opened my truck door. "It'll be okay, boss." He gave my arm a light shake. "You need to chill out."

"I've always done the work on Tommy's house," I explained haltingly. "That was the deal my dad made when he sold it to him."

"Your dad sold the house to Tommy?"

I nodded, not sure why I'd never mentioned that fact to Wade. Dad had been both owner and builder of many of the beautiful Victorian-style homes that studded the dramatic Alisal Cliffs. He'd always been fond of Tommy, even though he'd broken my heart when he dumped me,

so Dad had given him a good deal on a lovely home. One
that Tommy couldn't really afford at the time.

At first I'd been horrified that my own father had
gone behind my back to help Tommy, but in the end, I
was glad he did. I wanted Tommy to be happy—I really
did. Just not with Whitney.

"We don't need the work, boss," Wade said.

"You know it's not about the work or the money. It's
about Cliff Hogarth. He's a bloodsucker, going after my
clients behind my back. And Whitney's so clueless, she
doesn't get that he's manipulating her. Meanwhile, she
turns around and tries to do the same to me."

"You're right," Wade said calmly. "But you can't do
anything about it right now."

"I can't hunt him down and punch him in the nose?"

He smiled. "Not right now. You're too flipped out. You
need to get in your truck and leave. Go home and pour
yourself a glass of wine. Or go visit your girlfriends. Do
something. Just let this go for now. We'll deal with it
later."

"Oh, God." I felt so powerless and that wasn't like me.
I was a fighter. But right now, I was just plain tired.
"Okay, I'll go home for now. But we'll find a way to get
back at him."

"Yeah, we will." Wade gave me a comforting hug and
rubbed my back. "We will."

I stopped by the house to feed Robbie and Tiger and
play with them for a few minutes, but I knew I was too
agitated to stay home alone. Wade was right about visiting friends. I needed a friendly face. I ran upstairs to grab
a warmer jacket, then drove over to Hennessey House,
my friend Jane's elegant new bed-and-breakfast, hoping

she would have some time to spend with a friend in need. Namely, me.

Jane and I had been BFFs since we were babies. Her uncle had lived next door to me until recently. We were the same age and had gone from first grade to senior graduation together. She knew all the players, especially Whitney, although Jane had never been the target of as much scorn as I had. Probably because she hadn't been Tommy's girlfriend.

I walked inside the massive Victorian B and B and found Jane sipping wine in the well-appointed front parlor, surrounded by her guests. She was describing some of the restaurants on the pier to them, but looked up when I entered the room.

"Shannon."

"Sorry if I'm interrupting."

"No, no, your timing is perfect." She glanced at her guests. "This is Shannon Hammer, the friend I told you about. The one who renovated my B and B."

One of the women gasped in delight. "Oh, you did the most fabulous job. We travel a lot, but I've never been in such a gorgeous home before. The Victorian details are fantastic."

"Jane chose all the furnishings," I said. "I just hammered and painted and all that stuff."

Jane laughed. "She's being far too modest. Believe me, the place would still be a shambles if Shannon hadn't been around to whip it into shape."

Jane handed me a glass of pinot noir, and I sipped it while she spent a few more minutes making small talk with her guests. We both made suggestions about the best places to shop in the town square and the easiest, fastest route to get to the Anderson Valley wine country.

I had to admire my friend, who certainly looked the part of elegant innkeeper with her hair swept back in a French twist and her understated makeup. She wore brown silk trousers and a simple white silk shirt with a pair of Kenneth Cole brown flats. I knew the brand because I had the same pair in my closet. Gold earrings and a thin gold lariat completed Jane's outfit.

Finally she excused herself and latched onto my arm as we left the sitting room. We walked down the hall to the kitchen, where Jane grabbed a small tray and filled it with a basket of crackers, a plate of cheese, and a bowl of olives. Then she practically dragged me up the stairs and into the sitting room of her private suite.

She opened a bottle of wine from her small stash on the shelf, poured two glasses, and handed me one.

As soon as I sat down on the love seat, she said, "What happened to you? You look terrible."

"Sadly, you're not the first person to notice."

"Really?" She sat in the chair across from me.

"Yeah, Emily said something similar yesterday. I guess I should appreciate your honesty."

"Don't be a dolt. You always look ravishing, but I can tell something's wrong. Spill it."

I took a serious gulp of wine and grabbed a few crackers. Then I unloaded on my best friend and told her everything, starting with finding Lily's bones and dealing with Sean's pain. I went into my long interview with Eric and how I ran into Mr. Jones. I ranted on about Dismal Dain and my hope that he would spend time in jail. And I ended with my feelings of horror at the thought that Whitney and Cliff Hogarth might be in cahoots.

"You've been busy," Jane said mildly, relaxing in the overstuffed chintz chair.

"That's one way to spin it," I said with a sheepish smile. "Switching topics, I saw Emily last night. She seems pretty happy in her new house."

"I ran into her at the market a few days ago. But let's not change the subject just yet."

"But I'm so tired of whining about me."

"Have you talked to Tommy?"

I had to think about it as I took another sip of wine. "Not since I saw him at the mansion on Monday. Why?"

She leaned forward, resting her elbows on her knees. "Shannon, Tommy would never renege on the deal he made with your father. Whitney has no such scruples, unfortunately. Her problem is that she's so self-centered, she doesn't even realize how much she's hurting you."

"No, my pain is just a happy consequence."

She reached out and squeezed my hand. "Talk to Tommy."

"I hate to be a snitch." I grimaced at the memory of Whitney accusing me of being that very thing.

"Oh, please." Jane brushed my words aside. "Who cares? This is a good-faith contract between Tommy and your dad we're talking about here. The fact is, Whitney's pulling something on you, and Tommy needs to fix it right away." She grabbed her wineglass. "So think about it. There must be all sorts of reasons why you'd be at City Hall and happen to run into Tommy in the parking lot. And when you see him, you can be the snitch you always wanted to be." She took a sip of her wine. "Besides, if the work is done on his house and you're not there, don't you think he'll notice?"

I laughed, but Jane was right. City Hall shared a parking lot with the police department. It would be easy to track down Tommy and pretend I just happened to be passing by. But what would I tell him? I didn't want to whine to Tommy about Cliff Hogarth. There had to be a way. . . .

Then a simple yet brilliant idea struck. I jumped up from my chair and did a little happy dance. "I know what I'm going to do. Yay! Thank you." I leaned down and squeezed her knees. "You're a genius."

"I am," she said, grinning. "And someday you'll tell me all about your diabolical plan."

"I will, I promise. I need to think it through first, but it'll work—I'm sure of it." I sank down into the chair and sighed contentedly. "I feel so much better now."

"Good." She finished her wine. "I'd feel better, too, if we went out for pasta."

The next morning was Saturday, and I worked for a few hours at Emily's house, scraping more wallpaper off the living room walls. I think the stuff was alive and reproducing in the night, because I never seemed to make much progress. But I didn't really care. Basically I just needed more time to think, and lately wallpaper was my go-to drudge work that gave me the opportunity.

At noon, I took a lunch break and drove to the police department, taking a chance that Tommy might be working that day. At the front counter, I asked the desk officer if Tommy was around. "You bet, Shannon. Just have a seat."

A minute later, Tommy walked out and greeted me with a hug.

"How are you?"

"I'm great. I came by to drop off the blueprints."

He looked around. "What blueprints?"

"The ones for your house," I said with every strand of innocence I possessed. "I've got them out in the car."

"Why?"

I batted my eyelashes virtuously. "Because Whitney said Cliff Hogarth would need them to do the work on your powder room."

"Cliff Hogarth?" His eyes narrowed. "Powder room? Wait. Aren't you doing the work?"

"Not that I know of."

"Well, huh." He scratched his head. "Hmm. Okay, I guess I was supposed to ask you when you'd have time to do it, but . . . shoot. With everything that's happened since finding the skeleton and all, it must've slipped my mind. But you'll do it, right?"

"You know I'd love to. But Whitney told me she hired Cliff to do the job. That's why he needs the blueprints."

Tommy clenched his jaw. He hated conflict, so I knew he was aggravated. "Shannon, we only work with you. Whitney must've forgotten. I'll talk to her."

I patted his arm. "It's totally understandable that she'd forget, what with all she has to do every day."

"I know," he said, relaxing slightly. "She never stops."

"You're so lucky." I pulled my keys out of my purse. "Okay, I'll be happy to do the work. Just let me check my calendar and I'll get back to you with some dates when we can meet to discuss exactly what you'd like to have done."

"Great. Super." He shoved his hands into his pockets. "Thanks, Shannon. I'm sorry about the mix-up."

"No problem, Tommy. I'll talk to you later." I gave him a big hug and a loud, smacking kiss on the cheek and walked out smiling. With any luck, Whitney would hear all about that kiss.

An hour later, back at Emily's, I held the steaming iron against the wallpaper and thought about Tommy and his reaction to the news that his wife had tried to hire Cliff Hogarth. Tommy was possibly the mildest-mannered, most happy-go-lucky person I'd ever known, so seeing him react with even that small amount of negativity was a rare sight.

And I didn't feel a single ounce of remorse for manipulating the situation toward my own ends.

Why should I? Yes, Tommy would try to read Whitney the riot act, but she would make up some excuse and wind up wrapping him around her little finger all over again. But that didn't mean she would get her way when it came to hiring Cliff as their new contractor. Tommy and my father had shaken hands on the deal all those years ago, and Tommy was too honorable a man—despite Whitney—to ever go back on his word.

Besides, I thought, *this isn't even about Tommy and Whitney. This is about getting back at Cliff Hogarth, who has apparently decided it would be fun to ruin my life.*

Sunday morning, our town Festival Committee met at my house to put the finishing touches on the St. Patrick's Day parade and Spring Festival scheduled for three weeks from now. We had tried to find another day to meet, but the festivities were fast approaching, and this Sunday was the only time we were all available.

I made everyone happy by serving bagels and cream cheese with a pretty platter of fruit.

Lighthouse Cove was becoming famous for its festivals and parades. We had something scheduled every month, and the whole town got involved. Last year Jane and I had volunteered to work on the committee, already comprised of Ellie Stewart, Pat Miles, and Sylvia Davis, all of whom we'd known for years. The five of us had been having so much fun putting the events together, it didn't feel like work at all.

That is, until Whitney and her equally annoying friend Jennifer decided to join the committee a few weeks before the Valentine's Day Festival. They had done what they could to sabotage our efforts, but hadn't succeeded and had finally quit. It was a happy day when we no longer had to deal with their abrasive personalities.

"We've got eight vendors that plan to sell green beer in the town-square park," Jane said.

"Eight?" I exclaimed, a little shocked.

Ellie laughed. "Is that all?"

"The park isn't that big," Pat said. "But I guess green beer is a tradition."

Jane went down her list. "Let's go over what we've got for the kids."

Planning events for St. Patrick's Day was a little trickier than some other celebrations, since the main purpose of the holiday seemed to be to get drunk and stay that way. But our committee was tasked with making all the festivals family- and kid-friendly. Some months it was more of a challenge than others.

I raised my hand. "Emily has offered to make a big batch of green soda. Either that or she can do green tea. Not the healthy stuff. I mean, really green."

"I like the idea of green tea," Ellie said.

"Me, too," Pat said, waving her hand. "I'll bet I can get one of the vendors to make green lemonade, too."

"Okay, green lemonade and green tea," Jane said. "Sounds perfect for anyone who doesn't want beer."

Ellie leaned in. "There's always water, too."

"Okay, we're covered on the beverage front."

"We've got a green cotton-candy truck coming," Ellie said. "They'll park on the street. They also make green popcorn."

"Yummy." Sylvia studied her notes. "And, by the way, I just received those five hundred green bowler hats in the mail. We'll hand them out along the parade route."

"That'll be perfect," Jane said.

"And shamrocks," Ellie added. "They're on sticks and you wave them like little flags. I think there's a couple thousand of those."

"Emily's tearoom staff is also making green mini cupcakes," I said. "And we've got all of our usual food vendors returning. So there'll be hot dogs and ribs and the usual fare."

Sylvia reached for a strawberry. "We'll also have the face-paint lady and a puppeteer for the kids."

"Okay, good," Jane said. "Moving on. I've got the pep squad set to decorate the fire trucks Friday afternoon."

"Hopefully there won't be any fires," Pat murmured.

Ellie raised her hand. "Um, I've got a new entry in the parade, if you all don't mind. It's a skateboard brigade. Twelve boys will skateboard along the parade route, and at the end they'll have a double ramp set up where they'll do lots of tricks."

"That sounds like fun," I said.

Jane frowned. "I don't want them to hurt themselves."

Ellie chuckled. "Since one of them is my son, I agree with you. He swears they'll be fine. First of all, they'll be padded to the hilt, and I'm making them all wear helmets. Plus we'll surround the ramps with that bouncy rubber stuff, so there shouldn't be any injuries. I'll have the other parents sign our general release, so we should be okay on all fronts."

"You'll take care of that?" Jane asked.

"Absolutely."

"Sounds like they'll be safe enough," Jane said with a sigh, and wrote something down. "And, personally, I think they'll be a big hit."

"Me, too," I said.

Jane continued scanning her clipboard for another few seconds, then looked up. "How about if we put the skateboarders in the parade right after the cheerleaders?"

"That's probably not a good idea," Ellie said quickly. "I wouldn't trust my son not to torment one of those cute little cheerleaders."

"Good point," Jane muttered. "I'll put them after one of the marching bands instead."

"I'll make sure they're all dressed in green with the hair combed and ready to go," Ellie said.

Sylvia piped up. "We've got the veterans lined up to go first, and the classic-car club members coming at the end."

"Are they okay with going last this time?"

"They love it," Sylvia said. "The crowd will be able to follow them to the parking lot, where they'll show off their low-rider stuff for everyone."

"Okay. On to the advertising," Jane said, nodding at Pat.

"I've been to every store and restaurant on the town square," Pat said. "The restaurants all plan to offer a St. Patrick's Day special and the stores will push a few sales items. The town square retail association is running ads in this Sunday's paper and next week's, listing every business that's offering a deal. We should have quite a nice turnout."

Jane stared at her list for a long moment, then looked up at us. "I think we're ready."

Sylvia grinned. "We're ready."

After the girls left, I went outside to the garden and walked around, studying my plants, examining pots, checking for bugs, and pruning here and there. I made a list of everything I wanted to buy at the nursery. And I mentally planned out my conversation with Denise. Once I spoke to her, I wanted to be able to tell Sean what was going on. I just hoped Denise would be willing to talk to me about Lily.

"Hello, Irish," Mac said.

I gazed up at the balcony, where he stood outside his apartment, looking dark and dangerously handsome in a T-shirt, jeans, and socks. "Good morning, Mac."

"You look thoughtful. What're you doing?"

"I'm making a list."

"Making lists is one of my favorite things to do," he said, grinning back at me.

"I'm about to go to the nursery. Do you need anything while I'm out?"

He leaned his elbows on the railing. "Since I asked you to go out with me sometime this weekend, why don't I go with you now?"

I smiled. "Why don't you?"

He raised his arm in a victory gesture and I laughed. I don't know how he did it, but I always felt happier when he was around.

He went inside his place to grab his wallet, shoes, and a jacket, and was back outside in seconds, locking his door and bounding down the stairs.

I met him at the gate and he grabbed my hand. "This feels like an adventure."

"It will be—I promise."

We took my truck because I'd be able to fit more bags of soil and plants in the back.

I drove east to Highway 101 and then headed north.

"I've never been to the nursery out here," he said. "Haven't had any reason to yet. I guess once I move, I'll want to get into landscaping."

"You'll love this place."

"Maybe they'll help me out. I like the look of lots of plants around the yard, but I'd rather pay someone else to do it for me." He glanced over at me. "I know I sound like a lazy slug with my first-world problems."

I laughed. "I'm not judging. If you don't love gardening, you shouldn't do it. The reason I do it is because I love it."

"And I love watching you in the garden," he said, reaching over and squeezing my hand.

I felt myself blushing. "You're sweet."

"No, I'm not. I told you I'm a slug."

"And lazy," I reminded him. "Don't forget lazy."

He laughed and I grinned at the sound of it.

We chatted for six more miles, until I turned off the highway and wound my way up the hill to the Gardens. I parked the truck, but before Mac could open his door, I grabbed his arm. "I should tell you, I have an ulterior motive for coming here today."

"Excellent," he said, rubbing his hands together. "Tell me all about it."

I gave him a quick explanation of what had happened at the school when Mr. Jones got the call from Denise about the police arriving to interrogate her.

"So her family owns this nursery?"

"Yes."

"And you want to grill Denise if she's here."

"I'll hardly be grilling her," I said, objecting to the word *grill* even though, okay, it was fairly accurate. "We'll just talk."

"Tomato, tomahto," he said. "It'll be fun to watch either way."

I rolled my eyes. "I'll probably end up saying nothing."

"Whatever happens, I'll follow your lead." With a wink, he jumped out of the truck. "Wow. Great view from up here."

It was true, and I rarely stopped to notice. Now I took a long moment to gaze at the coastline spread out before us. The lighthouse was in plain view, of course, but I could also see the dark red roof of the mansion next door.

"What's that pagoda-looking thing over there?" he asked, pointing toward a small structure with an Asian-style roofline a mile or so down the highway.

"It's a Chinese temple and museum, one of the oldest buildings in the county. It was built by a group of Chinese immigrants who constructed the railroads during the gold rush."

"For real? Is it open to the public?"

"Absolutely."

"I've got to go there."

"You should. It's a peaceful place. And really tiny."

"So much to see." He gestured toward the nursery entrance. "Let's go check things out."

"Let's."

He pushed open the wide wooden gate and let me lead the way into a tangled, rambling garden of beautiful colors and amazing plants. The nursery meandered up the hillside and stretched out over ten acres. There were hidden ponds and a babbling brook or two along the way.

"Oh, man. This place is cool," he said. "I like the way everything seems overgrown and the plants blend into one another."

"It looks overgrown, but it's actually well planned. Each plant complements the one next to it. Isn't it beautiful?"

"I would love to look at something like this every day."

"You could hire one of their landscapers to design your new property."

"I just might do that." He turned his head one way and the other, checking out everything.

Twenty feet inside the gate, we came to a stop and stared at three different pathways. I turned to him. "Which way do you want to go?"

He grinned. "This really is an adventure. Let's go this way."

We headed off to the left, and a few hundred yards later found ourselves in the middle of a wild English garden. Slender foxglove and gladioli wavered in the slight breeze. Yellow bearded irises contrasted with graceful stalks of blue delphiniums and fat pink peonies. In the middle of it all was a brass sundial surrounded by lavender and rosemary.

Twenty yards farther along the path, a jumble of rocks had been pressed together to create the semblance of a terraced hillside. Moss-covered stone steps led up to a koi pond. Beyond the pond, hedgerows separated this area from one of the other gardens.

"I kind of want to live here," Mac said. "It's like some sort of hippie fantasy land."

"Next time we come, we'll take the path that runs along the creek. It feeds into a lily pond, and you would swear you're in a fairy tale."

"*The Frog Prince*?"

"That's the one," I said with a laugh. "I always expect to see a big, fat toad hop up and start talking."

We strolled for another few minutes.

"Why are there three separate paths?" he asked.

"They each showcase different types of plants and flowers. For instance, closer to the pond, there are grasses and tropical plants. The third path features a lot of cacti and succulents. It's got a real Zen feeling to it."

We walked in silence for a few minutes. Mac stopped to look at a statue of Buddha perched in the middle of a verdant mound surrounded by ferns and cyclamen.

"I get a lot of inspiration when I come here," I said.

He nodded. "I can see why."

We rounded a small copse of bay laurel trees and I grabbed his arm to stop him, pointing toward the woman digging up a withered azalea a few yards ahead.

"That's Denise," I whispered.

"Go for it," he murmured.

I didn't know why I was so nervous. Probably because I had no plan and no idea what to say. I took a deep breath and tried to school my features, whatever that meant. "Hi, Denise."

She whipped around, clutching her shovel, until she recognized me. "Oh. Hi, Shannon. You snuck up on me."

She chuckled self-consciously and added, "I haven't seen you in ages."

"I know. I was here a few weeks ago, but it must've been your day off."

"Probably. I do get them once in a blue moon." She pulled off the Australian-bush-style canvas sun hat she was wearing and brushed a few strands of her light brown hair off her face. "Everything going okay with you?"

I shrugged. "It's been a weird week."

"You're telling me." She seemed to brace herself as she gripped the long handle of her shovel. "I heard you were at the mansion when they found Lily."

"Yeah. It was pretty bad." I glanced at Mac. "This is Mac Sullivan. He's the one who bought the lighthouse mansion."

"Nice to meet you. I've read all your books."

"I appreciate it, thanks. Nice to meet you, too."

She pulled off her right glove, wiped her hand on her jeans, and reached over to shake his hand. "Sorry if I got dirt on you."

"I don't mind at all," he said. "Your garden is fantastic."

She beamed a smile. "Thank you. We love it."

"So, I guess you've talked to the police," I said, plunging forward.

"Yeah." She shook her head, looking a little dazed. "Not a fun experience."

"I know what you mean," I said. "No matter how innocent you are, their mere presence makes you wonder if you did something wrong."

"That's exactly how I felt." She chuckled ruefully and added, "You would know about that, I guess."

She was referring to my recent involvement in several

murders and Eric's suspicions about me. And while I hated to think about those circumstances, I was willing to use them to get Denise to talk. "I know all about it. But the police would never suspect you."

"Right. Chief Jensen said I could be a lot of help to him, so I just tried to think back to that time and told him everything I could remember."

"I talked to him, too. All I could remember about Lily was that you and she were such good friends. She was lucky to have you."

"Thanks, Shannon." Denise sniffled, obviously getting a little choked up. She pulled out a tissue and blew her nose delicately. "It's still a shock to me. I spent so many years feeling angry and worried and confused. I couldn't understand how Lily could leave when she had everything going for her. I mean, it seemed so selfish somehow."

"I knew her a little," I said. "Not like you did, of course. But when she disappeared, I took it so personally. And it hurt."

"Exactly." Denise struggled to gulp back tears. "Do you remember how she had the lead in the school play our senior year? And she'd applied for a bunch of scholarships because she was determined to escape those parents of hers and make a good life for herself."

"That's what Sean told me."

"I felt betrayed. Abandoned." Denise stared up at the sky, lost in thought. Finally, she said, "And now to find out that she never left. I feel so awful for thinking all those things about her. That she was only concerned about herself, or that maybe she just gave up on everything."

"I remember thinking, *How could she run away be-*

fore the Spring Festival? Her understudy had to take over her role in *Grease*."

Denise nodded. "I was so mad at her."

We stood in silence for a long moment until I said, "If you ever need to talk about anything, I'm around."

"You're sweet, Shannon. I really appreciate it."

"Did you know the police talked to Mr. Dain?"

Her eyes darkened and her lips tightened with resentment. "Good. Maybe they'll arrest him."

"Was he your counselor?"

"No, thank goodness. But he was Lily's." She grabbed the shovel handle and thrust the steel cutting blade over and over into the soft ground, as though she were attacking the dirt. "I could kill him for the things he said to her."

Once Denise and I were finished talking, I had to shake off the sad vibes and get down to the business of shopping. I bought three heavy bags of potting soil, six colorful pots with bases, a new trowel, a pair of gloves, and a dozen four-inch containers of herbs I planned to keep inside, next to my kitchen window, until the weather turned warmer.

Mac had a long talk with one of the landscapers and set up an appointment to meet at the mansion the following week. Then he bought a hardy outdoor plant for his balcony table and a few herbs for his kitchenette. "They'll keep the place smelling nice," he said.

We paid for our purchases and used a flatbed cart to carry them out to the truck.

"It's always a good time with you, Irish," Mac said, as I drove back to town.

I shook my head in frustration. "We didn't get any information from her at all."

"Yeah, but it was interesting to see her working that shovel blade."

"I was mesmerized," I admitted.

"I'd hate to be on the receiving end of that anger."

"I know." I stared thoughtfully at the road. "I'm not sure she realized what she was doing."

"Maybe not. But if this guy Dain goes missing, you'll know who to call."

"I don't blame her for hating him." I confessed what Dismal Dain had advised me back in my freshman year. After Mac had a good laugh, I told him Dain's horrible advice to Lily.

"No, that's impossible," he said, shaking his head in disgust. "He sounds like the very opposite of a counselor." He stared out the window for a few seconds, then back at me. "You've described a caricature. He doesn't sound human. I know you're not kidding, but I find it hard to believe someone like that is still employed."

"You're not the only one," I muttered.

"No wonder Denise wanted to kill him," he mused. "As if being in school and trying to figure out who you are, who you want to be, aren't hard enough. I can understand why she was pounding that shovel so intensely now."

I shivered at that image, and we spent the rest of the drive in silence.

Once we got home, Mac helped me carry the heavy bags back to my potting shed behind the garage.

"I promised you dinner," he said as we walked back to the patio. "How do you feel about grilling steaks here instead of going out?"

"That sounds great. Much better than going out."

"Good. I'll run up to the store and get everything we

need." He pulled me closer and wrapped his arms around me. "I had a good time at the nursery."

"I did, too."

He lifted my chin with his fingers and kissed me.

"There you are!"

We were both startled enough to jump away from each other. I turned to see who had spoken.

The girl standing at my open back gate was very beautiful and very young. And very blond, naturally. She wore a short black leather jacket, faded denim jeans, and boots. And she was grinning ecstatically at Mac.

Mac looked completely flummoxed. "Callie?"

I exhaled slowly, feeling myself deflate. Another blonde? And could she be any younger? What was with this guy? And what was with *me* for buying into his act again?

"I guess dinner's off," I said stiffly. "Have a good time with your 'friend.' See you around." I walked away quickly and crossed the patio to my kitchen door, feeling like a complete idiot.

"What? Wait. No. Shannon!"

I didn't stop; just kept climbing the steps. I had to get inside before I said something I would be sorry for later.

"Uncle Mac?" the blonde said. "Aren't you glad to see me?"

I blinked and turned to take a second look.

Uncle Mac?

Chapter Nine

"Callie is my sister's daughter," Mac whispered while his niece locked up her bicycle.

I had sort of figured that out in the nick of time. "Do you know what she's doing here?"

"I don't have a clue."

I was almost afraid to ask, but I went ahead. "Does your sister know she's here?"

His forehead creased with concern. "Callie, does your mother know you're here?"

She averted her gaze. "Um, not exactly. I thought we could maybe call her together."

"So she'll yell at me, not you?"

She bit her lip. "She probably won't yell at you, Uncle Mac."

He gave her a cynical look. "Who are you trying to kid?"

"I guess you're right." Callie sighed. "She yells at anyone who's got to tell her bad news."

That doesn't sound good, I thought. Had this happened before? Did the girl run away from home often? And where did she live? Close enough that she could ride her bike to Mac's garage apartment, apparently. So why hadn't I heard about Mac's sister and her daughter before now?

"Okay." Mac pulled out his cell phone. "No time like the present to get yelled at."

"Wait," Callie said, grabbing Mac's arm. "Here's the thing. She's in Brussels."

"Brussels." Mac repeated the word and stared at his niece as if he hadn't understood her. "As in Belgium? As in Europe?"

"Yeah. She's working on a trial over there." Callie checked her wristwatch and calculated. "And it's, um, about midnight there."

He glared at the teenager. "So if I call her, I'm going to wake her up."

"Yeah. So are you sure you don't want to wait until morning?"

"No," Mac said brusquely. "Because when it's tomorrow morning in Brussels, it'll be the middle of the night here."

She grimaced. "Oh yeah."

"I'd rather wake her up than have her wake me up." He winked at me, letting me know he wasn't quite as frazzled by all this family drama as he seemed.

"Let's go inside," I said. "It's warmer and you'll be able to hear the phone call better."

"Good idea," Mac said.

Callie lifted her backpack, and once she was in my kitchen she set it against the far wall.

I pointed to the table. "Have a seat."

"You have a dog," Callie said when Robbie presented himself to her. "What a cutie."

"His name is Robbie and he's really friendly."

"Can I hold him?"

"Sure. He loves the attention."

"Okay." She sat down and patted her knees. Robbie hopped up onto her lap and gazed adoringly at her. "Oh, he's so sweet."

"He sure is," I said, smiling. Anyone who liked my pets was okay with me. "Would you like a glass of water?"

"Yes, please."

I poured three glasses and handed one to Mac, who stood leaning against the counter. He gave me a ragged look that I interpreted to mean, *Holy Pete. I wasn't expecting this.*

I rolled my eyes and shook my head. All I could think was, *The weirdness continues.* I wouldn't be surprised by anything at this point.

I gave Callie her water and sat down at the table. Tiger, not to be outdone by the dog, immediately leaped onto my lap and made herself at home.

"How long has your mom been gone?" I asked Callie as I sipped my water.

She calculated in her head. "It's been about ten days."

"And you've been home alone all this time?"

"Oh no," she said, stroking Robbie's back. "Karl and Mavis are there."

Mac filled me in. "Karl and Mavis work for my sister."

"Like housekeepers?"

"More like bodyguards," Callie said offhandedly. "Mavis cooks, too. Karl's in charge of the grounds and he drives my mom to work."

I stared wide-eyed at Mac. *Wow, more things I didn't know.* The man was a constant surprise. "Your sister lives on an estate with bodyguards?"

Mac shrugged. "It's complicated. And it's not exactly

an estate; just a few acres, but big enough to need a small staff. And her job is sort of odd. So, bodyguards."

"Where do you live?" I asked Callie.

"Bel Air. That's sort of next to Beverly Hills."

"Right. I've heard of it." No wonder Callie carried that sense of entitlement with her. Children of wealthy parents sometimes had it ingrained within them. It didn't make her a bad person, just ... entitled. I realized I couldn't even tell her age, and I wondered if she was still in school.

And how did she get from Bel Air to Lighthouse Cove on her bicycle?

"How old are you, Callie?"

"Sixteen, but I'm practically seventeen."

"In six months," Mac pointed out casually. "That doesn't quite qualify as *practically*."

"But I'm mature for my age."

Mac chuckled, but left it at that.

"Is Callie short for something?" I asked.

She smiled. "It's short for Calla Lily."

"That's pretty."

"I like it. It's different. My mother was a flower child."

"When she was young," Mac added. "She grew up to be a shark."

A little confused, I turned back to Callie. "Are you still in school?"

"Um." She cast a cautious glance at her uncle, who was watching her every move. "Well, that's the thing."

Mac raised one eyebrow. "*That's* the thing? Exactly *what* thing is *that* thing?"

She made an exasperated sound. "Uncle Mac, you're being weird."

"Uncles are supposed to be weird," he said, as if that

explained everything. It didn't, of course, and I expected him to revisit her comment about *that* thing shortly. And if he didn't, I would. Because now I was desperate to know what *that* thing was.

Mac still hadn't made the call. I figured he wanted to hear Callie out completely first.

"What does your mom do, Callie?" I asked, although I was fairly certain I knew.

"She's a lawyer."

Just as I suspected. "Thus your shark reference."

Mac grinned.

"So she's a lawyer. That sounds interesting." I sipped my water. "What kind of law does she practice that takes her to Europe?"

She pursed her lips in thought. "I'm not sure this is exactly right, but she calls it *white-collar crime*."

"So her clients are businessmen?"

"Well, sort of, but not exactly." Callie scratched behind Robbie's ears and sent my little dog into spasms of ecstasy. Whatever else happened here today, my dog was seriously in love. "I mean, I suppose they have white collars, but they're more like war criminals and drug kingpins than actual businessmen. And she worked with some mafioso guys a few years ago. And there was that gang member a while ago. Remember him, Uncle Mac?"

"Oh yeah."

I blinked. Mac walked over and stood behind me, gave my shoulders a comforting rub, then reached down to take hold of my hand in his. I clutched his hand tightly and contemplated the fact that he had a sister and a niece who dealt with dangerous criminals.

"So," I said, trying to sound casual. "I'll bet that's a really intense job."

Callie nodded. "She does a lot of yoga."

I could feel Mac's arms shaking and knew he was laughing. This was the strangest conversation I'd ever had with anyone.

"How did you get here, Callie?" I asked, still clutching Mac's hand.

Her eyes brightened. "I figured it out all by myself. Did you know there's no direct route from LA to here if you're not driving a car? So basically, I rode my bike from my house to the Culver City Metro station and took the Metro to Union Station in downtown LA. I got a ticket on the Coast Starlight train to Oakland and from there, I transferred to the Capitol Corridor train to someplace called Martinez and then I got on the bus to Ukiah."

I was sort of impressed. This was one determined, very smart girl.

I didn't want to look at Mac because I knew his eyes had to be bulging out of his head. His sixteen-year-old niece had been wandering around the train stations in downtown LA, Oakland, and Martinez? Fascinating.

"Once you get to Ukiah," I said, prompting her to continue, "it's pretty easy to take a bus to the coast."

"I was going to do that, but since I had my bike on the train with me, I found this really cool app with some great bike routes. So I ended up riding along Highway 253 to Highway 128. And I ended up here."

"That's a long ride."

"Yeah. I didn't really realize how long it was when I decided to go that way. I mean, I passed other riders on the road, but it's kind of lonely. But I just kept riding."

Mac shook his head, then looked at me. "Do you know that area?"

"Yeah," I said. "I've ridden along Highway 253 a few times. It's a tough ride through the hills, but the scenery is beautiful."

It could actually be treacherous and some areas were indeed desolate, but Mac didn't appear ready to take in that much reality. He seemed to be trying to control his breathing. I couldn't blame him.

"It was so much fun," Callie said, sounding younger than she had before. "I like to ride my bike."

"Yeah, me, too," I said, fascinated by her ability to switch from worldly teenager to happy kid in the span of a sentence or two.

"So, how did you find me?" Mac asked.

"That was the easiest part. When I rode into town, I just went into a store and mentioned your name and asked directions." She leaned in closer, as if to share a secret. "Uncle Mac, are you aware that a bunch of people around here know where you live? Isn't that weird for you?"

"Not anymore," Mac said. "That's how it is living in a small town."

She smiled at him. "Do you have a lot of friends?"

"I'm getting to know more and more people and they're all good folks."

"That's so nice." Her voice was wistful now. "In our neighborhood, nobody really talks to anybody because we all live behind these really high walls, so you can't even see the houses. But here I saw people sitting on their front porches and that looked like fun, too. I miss seeing you, Uncle Mac, but I'm glad you're happy."

"I'm happy about that, too, and I'm glad you're here." He held up his phone and wiggled it. "But I think we've procrastinated long enough. I'm going to make the call."

"Okay." She bent over and buried her face in Robbie's scruffy neck, almost as if she could hide from her mother.

"I hope this goes through," he muttered, and pressed a button on his phone. He paced around the kitchen, waiting for the call to go through, and after a few long seconds he stopped and stood at attention. "Lauren? It's Mac."

He paused for a long moment, then said, "Yeah, sorry to wake you up, sis, but it's important." Another pause. "Listen, Callie showed up here a little while ago. She's fine, but it looks like she's going to stay with me for a few days until you get back to town."

Callie looked pale now. She stared out at nothing and continued to pet Robbie. I felt sorry for her and began to wonder where her father was. Neither she nor Mac had mentioned him.

"School? What about school?" His eyes narrowed in on Callie as he listened to his sister. "She's suspended? Ah. Nice of the principal to text you."

Callie winced but kept her gaze on Robbie, not daring to make eye contact with her uncle.

Mac held the phone away from his ear and I could hear Callie's mom yelling from halfway across the kitchen. Belgium had never seemed closer. Both Mac and Callie looked a little shell-shocked by now.

"Maybe she can go to school here," I said.

Mac gaped at me, then suddenly grinned and held up his thumb.

Callie, on the other hand, glowered at me.

I could hear her mother saying something but couldn't understand the words. Mac nodded. "Yeah. Her name is Shannon. She's my contractor. And my landlady." He winked at me. "Yeah, she's suggesting that Callie go to school while she's here." Lauren said something, and Mac replied, "Yeah, it's a darn good idea. She's really smart like that."

There was another long pause while Callie's mother spoke at length.

"I'll talk to the school on Monday," Mac said. "When do you get home? Wow." He nodded. "Okay. Be careful. I'll keep in touch. Bye, sis."

We were all silent for a few long moments.

"That seemed to go well," I said, then watched as Mac and Callie began to laugh. "So . . . it didn't go well?"

Mac came back around and squeezed my shoulders lightly. "It went as well as could be expected, I guess. My sister is a force of nature, but she agreed that your idea is the perfect solution. Thank you." He leaned over and kissed my cheek.

Callie grumbled.

"Sorry, kiddo," he said, "but it's the best way to keep you here. Otherwise, your mom'll send Karl up here with the limo and take you back home."

"I don't want to go home with Karl," she whined, sounding a little like a spoiled brat for the first time.

"Yeah, yeah, you can dial back the attitude," Mac said easily, pulling out a chair and sitting down next to his niece. "Karl and Mavis do their best."

"I know."

"Look. You can stay here for a while, at least as long as your mom is gone. But if you're going to stay, you'll go to school. That's the deal."

"Do you know how long she'll be gone?" I asked.

Mac shot me a look that said plenty about what he thought of his sister for leaving a sixteen-year-old girl home alone with "bodyguards." He finally said, "It's always hard for Lauren to gauge how much time these things will take."

"I can imagine." And I would try not to judge the woman for making difficult choices.

Callie sighed as though she carried the weight of the world on her shoulders. "A new school. Where I don't know anyone. Are you sure that's necessary, Uncle Mac? Maybe you could homeschool me."

Mac snorted, and I couldn't help laughing. Callie was grinning, too, as if this was one of those family jokes they'd chuckled over before. It was lovely to see that Callie had a good sense of humor, just like her uncle. Gallows humor, it seemed to me, but at least they were laughing.

"Hey, you'll like it here," Mac said. "Everyone is friendly. It's no big deal. You'll go to school, you'll meet some nice new kids. Might even learn something."

"Kids aren't nice," she muttered darkly.

I frowned at Mac and saw him clench his jaw. "They'd better be nice to you, or I'll kick their butts."

"Oh, Uncle Mac," she droned, drawing his name out to four syllables. "You just don't understand."

"Oh, Ca-a-a-al-lie," Mac replied in a high-pitched falsetto. "I feel your pain."

She giggled and the tension was broken. For now.

"Let's take a walk to the pier for dinner," Mac suggested, and gave his niece's cheek an affectionate tweak. "And you can fill us in on how you managed to get suspended."

While Callie used my powder room to wash her hands and freshen up after her long trip, Mac paced the kitchen.

He looked a lot more worried than he had a minute ago when Callie was sitting in the room.

"I'm so sorry," he said, shaking his head. "I had no idea she was on her way up here."

"That's obvious. You don't have to apologize."

"What am I going to do with her?" he muttered.

"If you'd like her to stay in the second garage apartment, I have no problem with that."

"But she won't have any supervision."

"I hate to say it, Mac, but I doubt she has much of it at home, either."

"It's that obvious, huh?" He rubbed his forehead, clearly puzzled as to his next move. "At least if she's in the other garage apartment, she'll be right next to me. I can keep an eye on her. Probably."

"If you want to supervise her more closely, you could both move into Jane's bed-and-breakfast. She has a couple of suites with two bedrooms attached to a sitting room. But that seems like a drastic move."

"Yeah, it does. Callie's basically a good kid," he said, sounding a little desperate to convince me. "She'll probably be okay here."

"Of course she's a good kid," I said, patting his arm. He seemed so discombobulated, and I couldn't blame him. "She's smart, too. Made it all the way here, didn't she? She came to you because she doesn't want to be on her own, Mac. So, let's just move her into the second apartment. She'll appreciate having her own space, and she's not going to sneak out and go anywhere. She loves you, so she'll comply with your rules."

"Yeah, I guess you're right."

I hesitated, then added, "And if she wants to spread out a little, she's welcome to use my kitchen or the rest of the house, for that matter. That goes for you, too. I know this is stressful for you."

"That's generous of you, Irish." He wrapped his arms around me and held on. "I'm not sure what to say."

"Just say you'll buy me a yacht when this is all done. And maybe something with diamonds."

He laughed, just as I'd hoped he would. "I've got to tell you, this is about the weirdest thing that's happened to me in a long time. My niece doesn't usually track me down and show up unannounced."

I gazed up at him and smiled. "I believe it. You looked pretty shocked to see her." I wasn't about to mention my own reaction when I first saw Callie at the gate.

"*Shocked* is putting it mildly," he said, then chuckled sheepishly. "You know, I've faced down enemy gunfire and been ambushed by insurgents, but none of that ever stunned me as much as Callie did this afternoon. I love her, but what do I know about taking care of a teenager? Nothing."

I believed it.

On the short walk to the pier, Callie began to sound more and more like a normal teenager as she bounced from one topic to another. "I can't believe I'm actually feeling excited about starting school in a new place. Okay, I wasn't, but now it's sort of like an adventure, right? I mean, nobody knows me here. I can be whoever I want to be."

With her arms open wide, she spun around in a circle.

Mac shook his head and laughed at her antics. "I've got an idea, kiddo. Why don't you just be Callie?"

She lifted her chin proudly. "That's exactly who I intend to be, Uncle Mac."

"Good." He grabbed her in a one-armed hug. "I like her the best."

We turned at the corner and headed west toward the pier. From here we could see the sun turning into a hot orange ball on the horizon. The deep blue sky was splashed with streaks of coral and fuchsia as the earth moved toward sunset.

"That sunset is so cool—wow. And isn't it cool how we can just walk to the pier? What'll we get? Pizza? No. Fish? That'll be better, because riding my bike all that way made me really hungry and protein would probably be best for me. So, fish." Callie turned to me. "I totally love your hair. Do you color it? Are those extensions? Do you curl it?"

I smiled at the mile-a-minute conversation and the abrupt change of subject. "No. It's all real and all mine."

"You're so lucky," she said. "My hair is so boring. Maybe I'll dye it red while I'm here."

My chin dropped. *Is she kidding?* "Don't you dare dye it another color. Your hair is beautiful."

"You sound like my mom," she said amiably.

"I'll take that as a compliment."

"Oh, you should," Callie assured me. "She's really smart and pretty. Don't you think, Uncle Mac?"

"She's a knockout," Mac agreed, "and so are you."

Callie studied me until I began to feel like a smear on a microscope slide. Finally, she said, "I can tell you're really smart."

I raised my eyebrows. "I like to think so."

"She is," Mac said, but Callie ignored him.

"What do you do for a living?"

She was making my head spin with her rapid-fire

switching of subjects, but my job description rolled off my tongue with little effort. "I'm a building contractor specializing in Victorian-home renovation and repair."

She stopped walking and stared at me. "Wait. You build stuff? Like houses and stuff?"

"Yes."

Her mouth hung open. "That's the coolest thing. I've never met anyone who does that. Like on the DIY Network? I totally love those shows. I, like, watch them all the time. You could do a show on their channel, I bet. Can I watch you work sometime?"

"Uh, sure. Maybe on the weekend."

"Oh, my God. I would love that."

"Keep moving, kids." Mac nudged her forward and we continued to stroll toward the pier.

I hesitated to mention it, but finally said, "My sister has a show on the DIY Network. It's called *Concrete Facts*."

"Are you kidding?" she shrieked. "With Chloe Hammer and Dirk Bodette, right? I love that show! Is Chloe your sister?"

"Yeah."

"Oh, wow. She's so smart and funny, and they're so cute together."

"Aren't they?" Everyone loved Chloe and Dirk. Everyone except Dirk's wife.

"Their show is a real public service," Callie said earnestly. "I mean, they actually help people avert disaster."

"That's sort of the point of the show." My sister, Chloe, had been trained by our father, just like me. Her television show was important to her. She felt as if it gave her the opportunity to really help people.

"But wait," Callie said, frowning. "Chloe has blond hair. How come?"

I would've considered the question rude coming from anyone else. "Her hair was strawberry blond when she was young, but the red faded away and she's been a blonde ever since." I used to be really jealous of my sister's hair, but I liked mine just fine now.

"She's beautiful."

I smiled. "I think so."

"So are you." Callie laced her arm through mine. "I'm so glad you're my uncle's girlfriend."

"Oh." I frowned, unsure of how to respond. What in the world was I to Mac? I was a friend, for sure, but what else? "I'm really not his—"

"We're going to a fish restaurant, right, Uncle Mac?" she asked, completely ignoring my hesitation.

"Yeah."

"I hope they have scallops."

"They do."

"I love scallops," she confided happily, and squeezed my arm. "Isn't this the best day ever?"

I offered to call Ms. Barney over the weekend to let her know that Callie would be enrolling in the high school temporarily on Monday. Mac was uncharacteristically nervous about the whole procedure and I couldn't say I blamed him. So I agreed to go along with him and Callie on Monday morning. That's how I found myself once again walking down the hall of Lighthouse Cove High toward the principal's office.

Ms. Barney had already contacted Callie's principal in Bel Air to let him know she would be attending here for the next two weeks or so. I had warned her that Callie had been suspended, so it wasn't a surprise. We'd managed to squeeze the truth out of Callie over dinner the night before. She'd been suspended because she'd locked another girl in a gym locker after the girl snapped a picture of Callie taking a shower and posted it on a social-media site.

Once the shock and horror wore off, Mac and I both agreed that the world was a much different place than when we were in high school.

Ms. Barney gathered up all the forms Mac had filled out and stuck a big paper clip on them to keep them together. "Callie, I'm assigning you to Mr. Jones's homeroom class. I'll take you there now, if you'd like me to."

"Yes, please, ma'am," Callie said, clearly nervous. She shifted her backpack that I'd filled with various office supplies the night before.

"I guess we'll be going," Mac said, "unless you need anything else from me."

"No," the principal said. "I think we've got all the forms and information we require."

She and Mac shook hands and Ms. Barney said, "Thank you so much for coming in with Callie. And if you ever want to be a guest lecturer, our creative writing students would love to hear all about the life of a thriller author."

"It would be my pleasure," Mac said. "Maybe when my next book comes out."

"Wonderful," she said, winking at me.

I grinned at Ms. Barney, who was too sharp to ever let an opportunity pass her by.

"And thank you so much for bringing Callie to Lighthouse Cove High," she added. "We're lucky to have her."

Callie beamed, and I wanted to hug the older woman for making the teenager feel welcome.

"Behave yourself," Mac said, giving Callie a tight hug. "Play well with the other kids."

"Uncle Mac," Callie said. "You're so silly."

"I love you, kiddo," he whispered. "Call me for a ride home."

"Okay."

"See you later, Callie," I said, giving her a hug.

She hugged me back. "Thanks, Shannon."

Mac grabbed my hand and pulled me out of the principal's office before we both burst into tears. As we walked down the hall to the exit, he exhaled heavily. "Jeez, why do I feel like I'm deserting my five-year-old at her first kindergarten class?"

"I feel the same way." He pushed open the door and I walked outside onto the steps. "But she's in good hands with Ms. Barney and especially with Mr. Jones. I should warn you that she'll be in love with him by the end of the day."

"Oh, great." We crossed to the quad and walked toward the parking lot. "I'm not having the birds-and-bees talk with her."

I laughed out loud. "Something tells me she's way ahead of you there."

"Yeah. And that's just sad."

Mac had decided to let Callie stay in the second garage apartment, but, strangely enough, Callie wasn't all that thrilled to have her own private space.

Earlier that evening, the three of us had spent an hour in my kitchen, talking about Callie's first day at school. She could barely stop talking about Mr. Jones, just as I'd warned Mac. Then uncle and niece went off to dinner at the pub and I stayed home to get some paperwork done.

My kitchen doorbell rang about nine o'clock. I was already in my pajamas and about to bundle up on the couch and watch a couple of shows before going to bed. I checked through the window to see who it was, then opened the door.

"Do you mind if I watch television with you?" Callie said. "I mean, unless you're going to bed."

"Not yet," I said. "Come on in."

"It weird," she said as she curled up in the opposite corner of the couch from me. "I'm always alone at home and it doesn't bother me. But here I'd rather be with other people."

"That's not weird. You're in a strange place, and the garage apartment is basically set up to be a hotel room. It's not the coziest place in the world."

"Oh, it's wonderful—I don't mean that. I guess after going to all this trouble to be with Uncle Mac, I kind of want to ... well."

"You want to be with Uncle Mac."

"Yeah. And you, too. Do I sound like a big baby?"

I felt bad for her. Callie was hungry for family and the kind of cozy home I had growing up. I didn't know enough about Mac's sister to make any judgments, but it sounded like her career was high pressure. With that stress and the traveling she had to do, it wasn't surprising that she didn't make it home often. And two bodyguards didn't make for much of a warm family setting.

"Not at all," I said. "You sound like you want your family around."

"I guess so."

The show began, and we were quiet until the commercial break. I muted the TV and turned to Callie. "So, tell me more about school. Did you like your classes?"

"Yeah. I did. And Mr. Jones is amazing, as I already mentioned."

"More than once."

She laughed. "And I had lunch with a couple of girls. Ms. Barney asked them to hang out with me, but they didn't seem to mind. They were nice. Normal."

I smiled. "We're pretty normal around here."

She pulled the blanket tighter **around** herself. "They told me something creepy, though."

I frowned, hoping they hadn't **told Callie** something that might have offended her. "What'd they say?"

"They said that there was some girl who died a bunch of years ago and that they just found her bones in my uncle's new house."

I couldn't lie to her. "Yeah, that happened."

"That's so terrible." She rubbed her arms as though she were cold, but I figured she was shivering from the story the girls had told her.

"It happened a long time ago. You don't need to worry about it."

"But it happened at Uncle Mac's new house. Don't you think that's awful?"

"I do, Callie." I made a quick judgment call and decided to tell her the truth about Lily. "I knew the girl who died. And I was there the other day when they found the bones. And, yeah, it was awful."

Her eyes widened. "You knew her? Who was she?"

"A friend from school. She was really sweet and very talented. And really pretty, too. We all thought she ran away because her dad was such an awful man. But apparently she didn't run away."

Callie frowned and I could see she was thinking about all of this and getting more and more upset. "That's so sad. How will Uncle Mac live out there, knowing that someone died inside his house?"

"How well do you know your Uncle Mac?" I asked lightly, hoping to defuse her fear. "You must know that he loves all that macabre stuff. In fact, he's thinking of writing an article about the bones for a magazine."

She smiled a little. "That does sound like Uncle Mac. Okay, I won't **worry** about him too much, then."

The program started up again and the conversation ended. When the show was over, I offered to let Callie stay with me in the house if she didn't feel comfortable in the garage apartment. "I have a couple of bedrooms upstairs and there's a big bathroom, too."

"Thanks, but I'll be okay in the apartment." She slipped her feet back into her shoes and stood. "Uncle Mac is right next door and he might miss me."

I chuckled and stood, too. "I know he would definitely miss you."

I walked her out of the house and up the stairs, just to make sure she felt safe. Then I gave her a hug and waited on the balcony until I heard her door lock. "Sweet dreams."

Mac's door opened and he glanced out. Despite a serious case of bedhead and drowsy eyes, he looked completely awesome and outrageously attractive in boxers with no shirt. "Hey, Irish."

"Hi, Mac. Callie and I were watching TV. I just walked her back to her room."

"Thank you, sweetheart," he whispered. "G'night."

Tuesday morning, I was mooning around the kitchen, thinking about Mac's words the night before. He'd never called me *sweetheart*. Did it mean anything? Probably not. He'd been half asleep, after all. Truth be told, he'd been more like three-quarters of the way asleep. So I would be stupid to believe the endearment had come from his heart. The word had, nonetheless, given me a cozy feeling that kept me warm all night.

"Does that make me a fool?" I asked Tiger, as the pretty orange cat wrapped herself around my foot. I picked her up and held her close, listening to the sound of her intense purring.

I went with *yes*. "Yes, I'm a fool," I muttered into Tiger's soft neck. And, *yes*, I had better things to do than flounce around the house, worrying about such dumb things. Today was the first day on the parking-lot job. I needed to be fully awake and alert.

The phone rang loudly and Tiger jumped out of my arms. Robbie barked, as if demanding to know who was calling so early. I agreed with him.

I grabbed it before the noisy thing could ring again.

"Hello?"

"It's Chief Jensen," he said gruffly, then softened his tone. "I mean, it's Eric. Hi, Shannon."

"Hi, Eric." I held the phone between my ear and shoulder and poured myself a second cup of coffee. "What's up?"

"Can you . . . that is, are you available for a consultation?"

I smiled at the difficulty he seemed to have when asking me for help. "Of course. Did you want to come over?"

"No. I need you to come to police headquarters. The sooner, the better."

Chapter Ten

Eric was on the phone when I arrived at his office. He looked annoyed and stressed-out and he was pacing back and forth along the wall of windows on the west side of the room. When he saw me, he gestured toward one of the visitors' chairs that faced his desk.

"We don't have the budget," Eric said, then paused to listen to whoever was speaking on the other side of that phone call. "Right. It would be pretty dumb to order DNA tests for every male in town over the age of thirty."

DNA tests? Who was he talking to?

"That's right," Eric said. "We'll have to take it on a case-by-case basis, depending on the evidence."

Eric listened for another minute, then said, "Yeah, thanks, Jay. Keep me posted." When he hung up, he looked fried.

"Who was that?" I asked.

"Medical examiner."

"Everything okay?" I was sitting on the edge of my seat, ready to jump up and run out. "Should I come back later?"

"No, I need to talk to you right now."

"Okay." I scooted back in the chair and waited while he stared out the window for a moment. The view seemed to calm him down, because when he turned around and walked back to his desk, he was breathing easier and it looked like maybe his blood pressure was falling back to normal. But maybe he was just faking it.

"What's going on, Eric?" I asked. "How can I help?"

He scowled. Not at me in particular, but at the world in general. At least, that's what I chose to think, and I refused to take his bad mood personally.

"I really wish I didn't have to involve you," he said, still standing at the edge of his desk.

"I know, I know," I said briskly. "I've heard it all before. You hate to trust me, but you have to. Blah, blah, blah, whatever. So, look," I said, holding up my hand like a Girl Scout. "I swear myself to secrecy. On my honor, what's said in this room will stay here. Like that Vegas commercial. What happens here in the jail stays in the jail. You called because you need my help, so let's talk."

I could see him biting back a smile. That was a good sign. Maybe he wouldn't arrest me for being flippant to the lawman. I couldn't help it, though. I was tired of his constant reminders that I wasn't trustworthy. Because I was! Oh, sure, I'd discussed a few aspects of the case with Jane and Emily. And Mac. And Callie, too, now that I thought about it. But I hadn't disclosed any deep dark secrets.

He sat in his chair and said without warning, "Lily Brogan was pregnant."

It was like he was speaking in tongues or something. Or maybe I just didn't want to believe it. "Wh-what did you say?"

"Lily Brogan was pregnant when she died."

"Oh." I had to concentrate on breathing because it felt like I'd had the wind knocked out of me. "Oh my God."

"We should've found out sooner, but the medical examiner's office deals with cases coming in from three different counties. So he's always backed up."

"But . . ."

He finally seemed to notice that I was stunned and upset by the news he'd just dropped. "Sorry, Shannon. The thing is, the medical examiner found a tiny skeleton in with Lily's bones."

Chills skittered down my spine and the hair on my arms stood up in horror. Tears welled, too, but now wasn't the time to get weepy. Still, my heart hurt for Lily and her baby and the future they would never have. "Oh no."

"Oh yes," he said. "Jay estimates that Lily was at least three months pregnant."

"Three months?" I wrapped my arms around my stomach, as though I could protect myself from the tragic news. "That's terrible."

"Yeah." He stared at the wall behind me. "Jay said the baby's skeleton was still mostly cartilage, although bone was beginning to form at the joints. Knees, elbows, some teeth. It was about three-point-five inches long."

His tone was eerily matter-of-fact but I knew he was hurting inside. I imagined a tiny skeleton three-and-a-half inches long and felt my spirit grieving. "Why are you telling me this?"

Through gritted teeth he said, "Because I need you to think harder, think back to that time, and give me the names of every single man Lily was involved with three months before she died."

"Okay." I nodded as if in a fog. "Okay. Wow. Well,

we've gone over most of the people I remember. I told you about Cliff Hogarth."

"Shannon, don't give me his name just because you don't like him. Was he truly involved with Lily or not?"

"I already told you he was." I said it more petulantly than I meant to, but I didn't like how he was getting in my face.

"Okay. Sorry." He held up his hands in surrender as a way of acknowledging that he was being pushy. "Really, I'm sorry. I'm a little . . . well, this whole thing has blown up in our faces, and I'm angry—really angry—about it."

"I don't blame you. I'm currently in shock, but I'll be moving toward angry any minute now."

"You might want to hurry up," he said curtly. "This case was unfortunate to begin with, but it just turned really ugly. Frankly, I was hoping to write it off as an unfortunate accident or misadventure, but the fact that Lily was pregnant makes me think somebody wanted to get rid of her and the baby. And that spells murder."

"Oh, God." I rubbed my stomach, feeling sick. Poor Lily. If only she'd had an understanding parent at home, she might've been able to get through this with family support. Instead she'd had only Cliff to lean on—if he even knew. Or if the baby was even his. Either way, I couldn't see him being any help at all.

I knew instantly that it wasn't fair to blame Cliff. At least until there was more evidence against him. But in my book, he was a big enough creep to have killed Lily and her unborn child. So until further notice, he was number one on my suspect list.

"So, that's why you were talking about DNA tests."

Eric's eyes narrowed. "There you go, paying attention again."

Whether he was kidding or not, his response made me laugh. "Yeah, it's an irksome little habit of mine. So I guess this means the ME was able to extract the baby's DNA, and now you're going to want to run a DNA test on whoever you think is the father."

"You've got the basics right there," Eric said. "So, can you think of anyone else, any other male who was friendly with Lily? Maybe you saw her talking to some guy and it didn't register at the time, but now it makes sense? Anyone, Shannon. I'm willing to grasp at straws to nail this guy."

"I'm thinking." I hated to name names off the top of my head, but that was what I was here for. "Okay, I'm just going to call out every male who was around at the time. Doesn't mean I think he's guilty, okay?"

"Noted." He grabbed a pen and clicked it open. "I'll write down the names."

"Okay. So there's Sean, of course, and his father, Hugh. And there's Cliff and his buddy, Jason. I forgot about him before. Jason moved away years ago. They hung out with a bunch of other guys, but I can't think of any of their names. They were older than me."

"Okay."

"And there were all the guys in the play with her." I thought for a moment. "Bart Bockner played Danny, the lead."

"He still living around here?"

"He's not in Lighthouse Cove anymore, but I think he lives maybe ten or fifteen miles away. Tommy might know all these guys and where they live. And there were a couple of stagehands who were friendly with Lily." I gave Eric the names of everyone I could remember seeing on a regular basis in the drama club. "I guess you could add the drama teacher, Mr. Peterson. He and Lily were always talking together because he was directing the play. I think he's still teaching."

"Good to know."

I shrugged. "And as long as you have Mr. Peterson, you might as well add all the other teachers in school. There's Mr. Delgado, Mr. Jones, Mr. Carver. And let's not forget Dismal Dain. I know you already talked to him but I'll bet he's worth another shakedown."

He glanced up. "Shakedown?"

I smiled. "Just wishful thinking, I guess."

"Do you even know what *shakedown* means?"

I broke out in a grin. "Not really, but I'm hoping you'll shake him silly."

Eric shook his head. "Dream on. Anyone else?"

I threw my hands up, exasperated. "Everyone I went to school with is a possibility. I mean, Hal Logan went to school here. He was in Lizzie's class and they're both five years ahead of me. But Hal might've known Lily. And there's Billy. He's on my crew and went to school with me and Sean. And there's Tommy. And Gus."

"Wait. Are you talking about Hal Logan, your friend Lizzie's husband? And Gus Peratti at the auto shop?"

"Right. We were in the same grade."

"And Tommy," he said flatly. "Your former boyfriend and my deputy chief."

I gave him a pointed look. "You asked for the names of guys who went to school with Lily and me."

"I did. But I'm more interested in any guys who were actually part of Lily's circle. We can't go around accusing the whole school."

"But you asked," I grumbled, then shook off my mood. "Okay, you can erase Tommy and Hal and Billy and Gus off the list. And Sean, too, as far as I'm concerned, but I know you have to at least consider him. Of course, he already agreed to your DNA test, so you've already proven he's innocent, right?"

Eric didn't answer, just gave me one of those looks that told me I'd ventured into unwelcome territory, so I moved along with my theories. "Cliff, on the other hand, is a definite suspect. And his buddy Jason, too, although I don't know how you'd track him down. Mr. Dain is another definite, in my humble opinion. Bart and the other actors in the play were with Lily almost every night for three months leading up to the Spring Festival. They should all be investigated. Not that I'm telling you how to do your job."

"Thanks," he said dryly. "Besides Bart, how do I get the names of the other actors? Do you have a year-book?"

"I do, but you'd be better off looking at the playbill for that year. They're all on display in the glass case outside the theater auditorium. And they'll have not only the actors, but the A/V guys and the prop guys and stage-hands and carpenters. Not that a carpenter could ever be the bad guy."

"Of course not."

"I'll be working at the school tomorrow," I said. "I could get the programs for you."

He smiled for the first time. "No, thanks, but I appreciate the offer." He set down his pen and sat back in his chair. "So, you got the job at the school."

"Yes. I'm excited about it. My crew and I are expanding and resurfacing the senior parking lot and erecting solar canopies."

"Really smart idea."

"I think so, too." I stood to leave, then remembered something. "Why don't you ask Denise Jones for some names? She would know if Lily was ever with one special guy." I didn't mention that I knew he'd already talked to her. It couldn't hurt to ask her again, right?

Eric's jaw clenched even tighter than before and I stepped back in shock. "Oh, my God. Denise is a suspect?"

"I didn't say that."

"Interesting," I said.

"Nothing is *interesting*, Shannon," he said flatly. "Don't you have someplace to be?"

I grinned. "I do. But before I go, maybe I should mention that I was out at the nursery on Sunday and I talked to Denise."

"Why?"

It wasn't easy, but I managed to keep from rolling my eyes at the very question, not to mention his tone. "Because she's a friend and she works at the nursery where I've been buying plants for most of my life."

"Okay, just checking."

I sighed. "You're a suspicious guy, aren't you?"

"Comes with the job."

"Understood. Anyway, Denise and I were talking about Dismal Dain and the horrible stuff he told Lily. And Denise got so angry, she started pounding and hammering her shovel blade into the dirt. I don't think she realized what she was doing, but it was weird and kind of violent."

"What's your point?"

I shrugged, unwilling to admit that I didn't really have

a point. "I just thought she seemed capable of killing someone with that shovel of hers. And she really hated Dismal Dain, so you might want to keep an eye on him."

He gazed up at me. "I thought you hated him, too."

Darn, he had me there. "I guess I do. But I wouldn't kill him with my shovel."

"I'll make a note of that."

I drove over to the high school as quickly as traffic would allow. Wade had promised to fill in for me until I could get there. I didn't want the SolarLight people to think I was shirking my duties the first day on the job.

On the way, I thought about Lily and the sad fact that she was pregnant when she died. She must've been so frightened and alone. Or was she? What if she was happy to be pregnant, but her own father was furious to find out? Could Hugh Brogan have tracked her down and killed her for being promiscuous?

Or what if Cliff's friend Jason was the father of Lily's baby and Cliff was jealous? Jason was a good-looking guy back in high school. So Cliff could've killed Lily and then killed Jason, but not right then, since I remembered that Jason was still living in town until he left a few years after high school. Who knew where Jason was living now? Or if he was alive at all?

It was a ridiculous theory, but I liked it, along with a bunch of others I could dwell on and refine later when I had nothing better to do.

My head was spinning as I pulled into my temporary space in the faculty parking lot. I had to think about my attitude toward Cliff. I really didn't like the man and wanted him to be guilty of all sorts of transgressions. But wishing didn't make it so. Especially since Eric was scrupulous to a fault about following the rules and playing by the book. He would rely on the evidence to show him who was guilty and pay no attention at all to my pithy declaration that Cliff Hogarth was a big, fat creep.

I climbed down from my truck cab and spotted Wade and two other men walking on the path that led from the senior parking lot to the track field. Wade turned and saw me and waved as I approached. He introduced the other two men as company engineers, and we all shook hands.

For the next hour and a half, we walked the anticipated perimeter of the new parking lot, pointing out grading and other issues. The size was going to be impressive. Unfortunately, it would take up every bit of the landscaping and walkways to the very outer edge of the track field. The new southern perimeter would leave only a few feet of pathway between it and the tennis courts.

I was so glad Wade had agreed to be the point man on this job. His background was in engineering, and he had more hands-on experience than I did with grading and leveling land for pouring concrete and asphalt surfaces. I'd done plenty of smaller projects around town, but it would be dumb of me to pretend I knew more than I did, rather than handing off the job to the most qualified person. And I prided myself on being smart.

Ms. Barney joined us as we were taking down the final measurements, just in time to approve everything. "I went over the numbers with the original team from Solar-Light," she said. "I'm not concerned about the landscaping that borders the track field or the tennis courts. It's more important to get the parking situation worked out."

"I'm always happy to lay down more asphalt," I assured her. "And you did say you were moving a lot of the flowers and plants to other areas, right?"

"That's right," she said, nodding. "Unfortunately, our students and parents will complain a lot more about the lack of parking than the lack of pretty flowers."

"I guess I see their point."

"The students will still have our beautiful front lawn to enjoy," she said, "so I'm willing to sacrifice a little back here. And as long as you leave a narrow path around both sports areas, we'll be okay."

"It's a deal," I said, smiling.

That afternoon, while Wade, Carla, and I were meeting to juggle crew assignments, order supplies, and line up our asphalt subcontractor, my cell phone rang.

I saw Eric's number and was almost afraid to answer it, wondering what new horrors the police chief intended to pass along. But I braced myself and said hello.

"Hey, Shannon," he said, his deep voice sounding so much calmer than earlier today, thank goodness. "Forgot to mention when you were here that Mac's house is no longer a crime scene. You and your guys are free to start work there whenever you want."

"Thank you so much, Eric." We chatted about nothing in particular for another moment; then I hung up and shared the news with my foremen.

"It's about time," Carla said. "I know you're anxious to get back to work there, and Mac must be champing at the bit."

"That's for sure," I said, relieved to know that Mac's lighthouse mansion was finally on the road to becoming a real home for him. "I'll call him as soon as we're finished here."

*   *   *

That night I invited Mac and Callie over for pasta and salad. Mac brought a bottle of wine. Callie had sparkling water—her favorite beverage, she said—and we toasted to the future success of the lighthouse-mansion rehab.

Robbie and Tiger were banished to just beyond the doorway, as usual. It was for everyone's own good, because anytime I had other people helping to prepare food in the kitchen, the little ones would invariably trip someone up in their relentless quest for food droppings.

They were hardly starved for attention, though, since Callie darted over to pet them every other minute.

"Uncle Mac started writing that article today," she said. "The one about the bones."

I turned and gazed at Mac, who was stirring the red sauce in the big pot on the stove. "So you sold it."

"I did," he said with a grin. "They won't actually print it until everything's been resolved. I wouldn't want the story to sway a jury."

"No," I agreed. "But I bet it helped sell it when you told them that the scene of the crime was your own house."

"It definitely sealed the deal," he said, grinning. "I love all the macabre aspects of finding bones in the basement and I plan to play it to the hilt. I mean, what all-American, hard-boiled mystery author wouldn't be intrigued by the fact that his new house turned out to be a grisly murder scene?"

I glanced at Callie. "See what I mean?"

"I know. He's totally *not* creeped out about the bones. It's weird."

Mac laughed shortly, but then sobered. "Please don't get me wrong. The real story centers on Lily Brogan.

What brought her to the mansion? Who were the important people in her life? And who was responsible for killing her? She was a beautiful young girl who died tragically. I'd like to make the article a sort of homage to her, but I didn't know her. You did, Irish. So I'm wondering if you'll consent to my interviewing you."

I stopped slicing tomatoes to gaze at him. "Me?"

"Yeah, you. Sometime in the next few days, if you have time, I'd like to sit down and talk with you."

"About Lily?"

"About everything that was going on back then. Not only at the high school, but all over town. The news, the politics, the gossip. I need some local background. I plan to do plenty of research and due diligence and talk to others, including the police, but I figure you know the history of just about everyone in town."

"Well, not everyone."

He gave me an indulgent smile. "You know the people Lily knew."

I thought about Eric and what he would say about this. It was easy to conjure up an image of the police chief scowling at me, and it wasn't pretty. I was always happy to help Mac, but since Eric had taken me into his confidence, I would have to walk a very thin line.

"I'd be thrilled to help you," I said.

Mac had been watching me and now he grinned. "But you had to think it through for a minute. How come? Is it because of Sean?"

"He's part of it." I set three long green onions on the wooden surface and began to slice them into thin rounds. "But also I've sort of been doing the same thing for Eric. You know, giving him some background on who was around back then."

Without asking, Callie pulled a knife from the drawer and joined me at the chopping block to start cutting up the cucumber I'd picked that afternoon.

I beamed at her. "Thanks, sweetie."

"You're welcome. It's not fair that you're doing all the work."

"I don't mind at all, but it's always more enjoyable with others around."

"Back at home, I don't get to help in the kitchen, and I totally love cooking—or trying to, anyway. So this is fun for me."

Not to be left out, Mac grabbed a head of fresh romaine, broke off the leaves, and washed them in the sink. Moving in next to me, he tore the leaves into smaller bits and added them to the salad bowl.

"Would you feel uncomfortable sharing the same information with me that you shared with Eric?" he asked.

I thought about it and concluded that all I'd really given Eric were names of people who'd been around back then. Names that Mac could find by himself, if he had a week to scour old yearbooks in the library. That would be a waste of his time. "No. I'll be happy to share the information with you."

"Did Eric reveal any confidential police evidence to you?"

Boy, did he ever, I thought, then frowned at Mac. Was I transparent or what? "Why do you ask?"

"Because you seemed troubled at first, and if it's not about the information you gave him, then I'll bet it's about the confidential stuff he told you."

I had to play back what he'd just said twice before I understood it. "Okay, yes. You're right."

"So now I understand your initial hesitation. Believe me, I won't ask you to betray Eric's confidence."

"Good, because I wouldn't do it."

He grinned. "That's okay. I'll just talk to Eric about it."

"Fine, but please don't tell him I said anything. Just leave my name out of it. He already has enough of a problem trusting me."

Mac laughed and slung his arm around me. "Don't panic, baby. I'll keep your secrets, just as you're keeping his."

"Thank you." With him smiling down at me and his arm around my shoulders, it felt . . . cozy. Warm and wonderful. I really did enjoy spending time with Mac and, let's face it, he wasn't hard to look at.

"Besides, I don't know what his problem is. You're the most trustworthy person I've ever met."

I stared at him for a long moment. "Thank you."

He touched his glass to mine. "No. Thank *you*."

Callie had been gazing back and forth at Mac and me, until she looked as if she were at a tennis tournament. "You two just had the most totally grown-up conversation I've ever heard. You didn't yell or anything, and you ended up agreeing with each other."

"That's what grown-ups do," Mac said, winking at me.

"I don't think so," she said, looking a little confused. "Karl and Mavis mostly just grunt and swear around each other. Unless I'm in the room, and then they pretty much clam up."

Mac tried to hide his amusement. "They have their own special way of reaching consensus."

I turned away from both of them to make up the dressing for the salad. I could barely breathe after hearing Mac call me . . . what he'd called me. *Baby*. I exhaled slowly. It didn't mean anything; just another one of those words of endearment people tossed around. But then to hear him say he thought I was trustworthy? That was better than a declaration of love. Especially after enduring Eric's suspicions for so long.

Was I blowing it all out of proportion? Was there something wrong with me? Why would having someone say he trusted me mean so much to me? Wouldn't I rather be adored for my looks or my intelligence or my business savvy than my trustworthiness? It sounded so dry.

But it wasn't dry at all. Trust was important.

The water was about to boil over, so I set those questions aside for the time being. Eventually I would have to figure out just how much Mac Sullivan meant to me and what I planned to do about it. If anything.

I stirred the linguini into the boiling water and listened to Mac and Callie teasing each other. Their voices faded to the background as I went back to pondering my strange love life—or lack thereof. If I were being truthful, I would admit that I'd recently considered taking things with Mac to a new level. But as I gazed at his niece now, I saw that my rather shaky plan would have to be put on hold.

Callie was a sweet girl, but she was going to be a handful for as long as she was staying with Mac. He was completely responsible for her right now, and I knew that it scared him to death like nothing else ever had. Okay, maybe not *scared* as in *terrified*, but he was at least worried. And he should be. Taking care of a teenager was going to be a lot of work, and I wasn't all that sure Mac was used to having to share his time.

I gazed at Callie's big blue eyes and the long blond

hair streaming down her back. The boys at school had to have fallen halfway in love with her by now. That would be a challenge for any parent—or uncle, in Mac's case— but doubly so for one with a beautiful girl like Callie. No wonder he'd expressed so much worry the other night.

What am I going to do with her? he'd probably wondered. *I love her, but what do I know about taking care of a teenager?*

And suddenly, in my mind's eye, I was staring at Lily's face. She had been a beautiful girl, too, and half the boys had been in love with her, as well. What a difference it might have made if her parents had been there for her, supervising her dates more carefully and worrying over where she might've been spending the night.

Time flipped back to the present. What would happen if there was someone like Cliff Hogarth in one of Callie's classes? What if he developed an interest in Callie? Would she be able to distinguish the creeps from the good guys? Sometimes it was hard to tell. What if she ran into trouble? What if some smooth-talking boy lured her to some dreadful place, like the deserted lighthouse mansion? I hated to think of anything happening to Callie. And I hated to think that my beloved little town might have more tragedy in store for it.

I blinked and noticed Mac and Callie staring at me.

"Where'd you go?" he asked, amused.

"Sorry." I grimaced. "Guess I zoned out for a minute."

"It's because you work so hard," Callie said sympathetically.

I busied myself with dressing the salad and putting the bowl on the table, then turned and smiled. "Speaking of work, I'll be working at the high school every day for the next week or so. That means I'll be able to give you a ride in the mornings and drive you home each night."

"That'd be great, Shannon. Thanks!"

Callie was happy, but Mac was looking at me like I'd gone a little crazy. I didn't care. I knew Mac would be there for her, and so would I. And nothing was going to happen to her on my watch. Not in my town. Never again.

Chapter Eleven

Early the next morning, I spent some time on the phone with Carla and Wade, reconfiguring our crew once again in order to work around my new obsession. Namely, Callie. For the next five days, I would be working with Wade, Sean, and Douglas on the parking-lot project. Carla would be swinging from site to site, mainly supervising the lighthouse-mansion crew and two of our other big rehab jobs. We had several smaller jobs, as well, and Carla would make sure they were completed by one of the other guys within the next week or so.

"I was thinking," I said. "I might work on the parking lot in the mornings and shoot over to Mac's or Emily's place in the middle of the day to help out for a few hours. I just need to be back at the high school by four-ish."

"Sounds good, boss," Wade said.

Was he placating me? Was I turning into an eccentric diva? I hoped not. I was just a little obsessed with Callie's safety, but it would pass. As soon as she was back home with her bodyguards.

"The thing is," I said, "I hate to shuffle the guys around at random. So if you think someone is happier doing one job rather than another, we can take that into consideration."

"Don't worry about it, Shannon," Carla said. "The guys are happy to do whatever needs doing. I think it's important that both you and Wade are at the school during the first few days of the project. SolarLight should know how concerned you are about getting it done right."

I smiled. "Thanks, Carla. You give the best pep talks."

"That's because they come from the heart."

"You can't see me," Wade said, "but I'm rolling my eyes right now."

"No, I can't see you," Carla said. "But I can hear them rolling in their sockets."

"That counts," I said.

"You bet," Carla said. "Okay, I've got my tablet ready. Let's go over priorities at Mac's place."

I checked my own list. "Normally we'd start with the basement, but I'm a little concerned about doing anything down there yet. We never inspected it the day of the walkthrough, so let's leave it alone for now."

"I'm more than happy to wait," Carla said, her tone somber.

The image of those bones scattered on the basement floor flashed through my mind. I shuddered and tried to shake off the memory so I could concentrate on the notes I'd made on my tablet. "Okay, since the kitchen is a complete remodel, let's start in there. You can tear out all the cabinets, take the walls down to the studs, and get rid of the linoleum, but leave the dumbwaiter alone for now. I want to maintain the integrity of the shaft and the inner workings until we know if Mac wants to replace it or not."

"Don't touch the dumbwaiter," she murmured as she

wrote down instructions. "Sounds good. Kitchen'll take us a day or two, at least."

"And we talked about widening the kitchen door and putting in French doors, but don't do anything yet. I'll ask Mac if that's still what he wants. Since the house turned into a crime scene, we haven't gone back and firmed up all the work he wants done."

"I understand. Should we do anything with the exterior?"

"Sure." I scanned down the list and also checked the photos I'd taken. "One of the guys can remove all the shutters. We've got a couple of broken ones on the back windows, but they'll all have to come off eventually. We'll want to scrape and sand them all before we paint."

"Shutters," Carla murmured, and wrote it down on her list.

"The chimney on the north side of the house is missing some bricks. I'm not sure why, so could you inspect it for possible earthquake damage? I'm afraid we might have to take down the whole thing and rebuild it according to the new regulations."

"Might as well plan on that, boss," Wade said.

"Yeah." I made another note. "Oh, and, Carla, if you get a chance, can you check the windowpanes on the solarium for any cracks or other damage?"

"Got it."

"And we'll want to get rid of that tacky latticework covering the underbelly at some point. And a number of planks on the porch are rotted. But you guys won't get to that this week."

"We might not pull them up, but I can do an inventory of the ones that'll need replacement. I'll also check the balusters and handrails."

"Can you measure the balusters while you're there? They looked a little too far apart to me."

"I'll check them."

Some states had laws that required balusters to be less than four inches apart, and I abided by that. Four inches was the approximate size of an infant's head, and I didn't want any babies getting their heads stuck inside the porch railings. Not on my watch.

I scrolled down my list. "There's a root cellar around the side of the kitchen. No idea what's down there, but if you can convince one of the guys to explore it, let me know what he finds."

Please, no more bones, I thought, but didn't say aloud.

"You got it," Carla said. "I think all of this will keep us busy until you can get back out there."

"I really appreciate it, Carla," I said. "Hey, Wade, I'll see you in a little while."

I ended the call a few seconds later, in time to see Callie standing outside my kitchen door, ready for school. Mac waved from the balcony as we took off in the truck. He had been willing to have me drive Callie back and forth only because I was going to be working at the school anyway. But he didn't want me to feel obligated. For now, his plan was to write in the mornings and be available after school for Callie.

I figured after a few days the poor girl would start complaining about all the attention I was giving her, but until that happened, she seemed to be enjoying my company. We chitchatted and laughed all the way to campus.

I smiled as I parked the truck. This arrangement was going to work out just fine. At least I thought so, until we split up at the senior parking lot. I was crossing the blacktop to meet Wade when I happened to turn to watch Callie heading toward the main school building. From out of nowhere, two boys approached her.

"Oh my God. No," I said, and waved my hands in the air, as if I were shooing away flies. "No. Get away from her."

Wade had joined me by then and started laughing. "What is wrong with you?"

"Me? Nothing's wrong with me." I pointed toward Callie. "It's those boys."

"They look perfectly normal," he said, staring after the animated threesome.

"They always look normal from afar," I grumbled, then forced myself to focus. "Let's get to work."

The next day I left the job site early to meet my girl-friends for lunch at the Scottish Rose, Emily's tea shop on the town square. Jane Hennessey, Lizzie Logan, and Marigold Starling were already seated at a table in the charming back room when I arrived at the restaurant.

"Sorry I'm late," I said as I gave each woman a hug.

"You had to come the farthest," Jane said. Her B and B was only three short blocks from Emily's shop.

"Besides, you're not really late," Lizzie said, patting my shoulder. She and her husband, Hal, owned Paper Moon, a book and paper shop that faced the town square, a few doors down from the tea shop. "It's only five minutes past noon."

"I hope you can take time to relax and chat," Marigold said in her usual gentle way. She and her aunt Daisy owned the beautiful Crafts and Quilts shop, also on the town square. Many of the handcrafted toys and quilts she sold were made to order by her Amish family and friends and shipped out to her from the Pennsylvania countryside.

"It's our busiest time," Emily explained, after setting a teapot down in the center of the table. "So please just enjoy yourselves and I'll try to swing by to catch up on things as I can."

Lizzie grabbed her hand. "We need to meet at some-one's house next time so Emily doesn't always have to miss the latest scoop."

"Don't worry about me," Emily said lightly. "Just take note of all the juiciest gossip and fill me in when I come back around."

"I think Shannon's got the latest news," Jane said, reaching for the teapot to pour for everyone. "Why don't you start with the lighthouse mansion and go from there?"

"Oh my God, Shannon," Lizzie whispered. "We heard it was Lily Brogan."

"Did you know her in school?" I asked. Lizzie was five years older than me and had been my babysitter when I was little.

"Barely," she said. "She was younger, so our paths didn't cross much. But I knew the family."

Jane frowned. "Yes, the family wasn't a happy one."

"Tell me about them," Marigold said. She had been raised back east in the Amish world and had moved to Lighthouse Cove years ago to live with her aunt. So even though she hadn't grown up locally, she'd been here long enough to know many of the people we were talking about.

I gave her a brief history of Lily, Sean, and Amy and what they'd gone through as the children of a violent father and an alcoholic mother.

"That's just tragic," Marigold said. "Sean is such a nice man. He comes into the store sometimes to buy toys and gifts for his niece and nephew."

"Amy's kids," I said, nodding.

"Yes. The kids are adorable. They've all been in the store once or twice, as well. I'm sorry for their loss."

"I'm really concerned about Sean," I said. "He spent so many years holding on to the hope that Lily would return one day, and now to find out that she won't? Well, he's been through the wringer. I don't want him to become disheartened and give up on life. I wish there was something I could do."

"I could set him up on a date with a nice girl," Lizzie said.

We groaned as a group. Lizzie was at it again, wanting everyone to be as blissfully happy and married as she was. And while all of us could admit to wanting that someday, going on countless blind dates was not the way we chose to get there.

"Lizzie, a date isn't the answer to everything," Jane said.

"But it'll get him out of the house," she said. "It'll expand his horizons. He'll take a shower. Wear nice clothes. Get a haircut. Okay, go ahead and laugh, but simple activities like these are good for people. They civilize us. And if you're worried about him getting depressed, the first thing you've got to do is get him out of the house."

"You're probably right about that," I conceded. "But you need to be careful who you set him up with. I mean, to all of us Sean is adorable and big and strong and smart and charming, but let's face it: right now, he's not at his best. So you've got to wonder how desperate a girl would have to be to date a miserably unhappy construction worker."

Lizzie's forehead furrowed at that. "Okay, let me think about this."

"So, Shannon," Marigold said. "I haven't heard yet how you found the body."

"It wasn't really a body," I said, and winced. I quickly checked the nearby tables to make sure nobody was listening in. "It was just bones. Mac and the guys and I were doing our walk-through of the lighthouse mansion to see what work needed to be done." I held up my hand. "Everybody swallow their tea before I go on." I waited for a moment. "Okay, I opened up the dumbwaiter door, and the sudden updraft caused the rotted pulley mechanism to snap. The bones fell three floors to the basement."

"What are you saying?" Marigold whispered.

I gritted my teeth. "Her body had been inside the dumbwaiter all this time."

Jane had already heard the story, but she still looked pale.

Marigold blinked repeatedly. "Oh, my goodness."

"I don't trust dumbwaiters," Lizzie whispered, shaking her head.

"I beg your pardon?" Emily said. "Are you calling one of my staff a dumb waiter?"

We couldn't help but laugh. Lizzie hastened to explain herself as Emily placed two three-tiered trays of tea sandwiches, scones, and pastries on the table.

"This looks beautiful, Emily," Jane said. "Can you sit for a half second?"

"I've actually heard all about Shannon's dreadful discovery," she said, giving my shoulder a light squeeze. "So I'll let you enjoy your lunch and be back around shortly."

She started to walk away, but stopped abruptly. I heard her gasp, and I turned to see what had caught her attention. That's when I noticed that Gus Peratti, my auto mechanic and Emily's ghost whisperer, had just walked into the shop. I smiled and waved at him, but he didn't acknowledge me.

Every other women in the place saw him, too, and half of them were waving to no avail.

He wore a tight black T-shirt that showed off his tanned, muscular arms, along with faded jeans and scuffed boots. He was all male and rugged, and looked completely out of place surrounded by the feminine, mint-green walls of the tea shop.

I watched him approach Emily and heard him ask, "Can I see the kitchen now?"

"Of course." Frowning, Emily led the way, and the two disappeared behind the swinging door.

"I wonder what that's all about," Jane said. She'd grown up with Gus, just as I had.

"Maybe something mechanical is wrong with one of her appliances," Lizzie suggested.

We all reached for another round of sandwiches and chatted some more as we ate. I told them about Mac's adorable niece, Callie, and they all wanted to meet her, so I promised to arrange a barbecue one of these days. Then the conversation drifted to the problem of Cliff Hogarth moving back in town.

"Cliff Hogarth is a bad apple, Shannon," Lizzie said between bites. "Try to avoid him."

"I'd love to, but he keeps bad-mouthing me to people I care about. I don't know how to handle it."

"He's such a blowhard," Jane muttered.

"I wonder if there's some way to get him to leave me alone." I turned to Lizzie. "Was Hal a friend of his?"

"No, Hal can't stand him."

I sighed. "Hal has good taste."

"I know Cliff is a jerk, but he was always nice to me," Jane admitted.

I frowned at her. "I can't remember. Did he ever ask you out?"

"No, never. I guess I was always too wrapped up in books for him to notice me."

"You're lucky, but I'll bet he did notice you."

"He was probably intimidated by you," Lizzie said. "You're tall and blond and beautiful. You probably scared him to death."

Jane waved away Lizzie's explanation, but I thought it was spot-on.

"You know," Jane said, "I have my weekly hotel-association lunches at the Inn on Main Street. I've noticed him in the dining room a few times. If I see him again, I'll strike up a conversation and find out what he's up to."

"I'd appreciate anything you can find out," I said.

The kitchen door swung open and Emily stumbled out, giggling. She fiddled with her skirt, and her face was so uncharacteristically flushed, it was obvious to all of us that Gus must've just kissed her silly.

Gus sauntered out of the kitchen and went directly to the front door, not making eye contact with anyone. As he left, Emily busied herself at the front counter, clearly trying to pull herself back together.

"Oh, how romantic," Jane sighed.

"He is so handsome," Marigold whispered.

Emily deliberately avoided our table while she bustled from one guest to the next and back and forth from the kitchen, carrying dishes or bringing out new teapots.

"Her face is still red," Lizzie whispered.

Jane smiled. "She looks so happy."

Yes, Emily was practically glowing, and my girlfriends seemed to be thrilled for her. I didn't say anything, but I was worried. If she fell for Gus, he could break her heart. He was gorgeous and sexy and had always had a reputation with the ladies. He was also ten years younger than Emily was. I didn't want him to hurt her.

Jane whispered, "I wonder how long this has been going on."

"I think it just started a minute ago," I guessed, and told them what Emily had said about Gus coming by to visit the ghost of Mrs. Rawley. Emily had refused to believe that he might be stopping by the house to see her. But now I wondered, *Did Mrs. Rawley's spirit somehow bring Gus and Emily together?*

It was a ridiculous notion, but I liked the thought of it, anyway.

A few minutes later, another waitress approached to clear our dishes and take our money.

"What happened to Emily?" Lizzie asked.

"She's not feeling well," the waitress said, and quickly changed the subject. "I hope everything was to your liking today."

"Wonderful as always," Marigold said, and popped the last mini cheese Danish into her mouth.

We waited for the server to leave and then we stared at one another.

"Do you think she's too embarrassed to talk to us?" Lizzie wondered.

"That won't fly," I said, taking a last sip of tea. "She's got to know that the longer she puts off telling us, the more we'll hound her."

Lizzie laughed. "As she would do for any of us."

Jane leaned closer. "If she's smart, she's on her way home to jump in the sack with Gus."

Marigold fanned herself. "And I know for a fact that Emily Rose is a very smart woman."

When I got back to the high school parking lot, the guys had already begun to break the old asphalt apart. The SolarLight technician handed me a powerful set of headphones, because the noise of the equipment was incredibly loud. My guys were operating jackhammers, while the SolarLight team had brought in a really cool hydraulic hammer attached to a backhoe loader. Tomorrow, SolarLight would bring even more heavy equipment to the site and begin loading and hauling away the old asphalt.

Once the old area was completely cleared, we would excavate a hole deep and wide enough to contain the large underground water tank that would store the runoff from the canopies. Then, with guidance from the engineers, we would dig six-foot holes in which the thick steel canopy posts would stand. The posts would be encased in a three-foot-thick concrete base. At every step, the company's engineers and experts would be configuring the electrical grids and solar panels to provide both battery-charging stations and outdoor lighting.

Once the posts were erected, we would begin leveling the soil and layering the aggregate materials that would make up the base beneath the outer asphalt surface. In anticipation of our subcontractor's laying down the asphalt, SolarLight had brought in an asphalt paver—a massive piece of machinery—to press the hot asphalt mix down into the base layer until the surface of the lot was smooth and even.

Sadly, the company had also brought its own drivers to operate the heavy machinery, so my crew and I had to assist on the ground. Even so, it was always fun to work around these monstrous machines and watch how they could tear the earth apart and put it back together again.

"Hey, boss," Sean said when the hydraulic-hammer operator took a break and we could all hear ourselves think again. "You ought to buy one of those monsters for the company."

"Oh, sure. And I suppose you're offering to operate it?"

"Absolutely." He flexed his muscular arms for me. "I could rock that thing."

"I'm sure you could," I said with a grin.

"Think about it, boss. It's an awesome machine."

"It's noisy, anyway." I was thrilled to see Sean's good mood returning more and more with each day. Good, hard work helped, although he'd had some setbacks and I expected him to have many more. Every so often I would catch him staring off, and I wondered if he was thinking of Lily. I was still worried that he wasn't getting out much. I hated to think of him sitting home alone every night, berating himself and wondering what he could've done to save his sister's life. "So, what's up, Sean? How're you doing?"

He kicked a pebble away with his steel-toed work boot. "You might as well know, I talked to Chief Jensen a little while ago."

"Eric was here?"

"No, he called me. Said he was checking my dad's arrest file and was disappointed to find no DNA on record."

I had to think for a minute. Hugh Brogan had been in and out of jail for years and he'd died only a few years ago, so why didn't they have his DNA on record?

"Did he say why he wanted it?" I couldn't imagine

Eric confiding in Sean that his sister had been pregnant when she died, but who knew? Would Eric actually ask Sean if he thought his father was capable of raping his own daughter and then killing her when he found out she was pregnant?

It was a horrible possibility, and I hated even the remote chance that Sean might have to deal with it.

"You remember I told him that I thought my dad was capable of killing Lily?"

"Yes."

"So Eric said he would look into every possible scenario and let me know what he found out. But now without my dad's DNA ... it's like he's hit a wall." Sean shrugged helplessly.

"Do you have anything that might contain his DNA?" I asked.

"That's what Eric wanted to know. I've tried to think of anything of his I might've held on to, but I don't have a thing." He shoved his hands into his pockets. "I got rid of everything in his house before I sold it. Believe me, nothing he owned had any value, sentimental or otherwise."

"I understand." I squeezed his arm in sympathy and tried to see all of this from Eric's perspective. "You've already submitted to DNA testing, right?"

"Yeah."

"Well, at least you'll be cleared of any wrongdoing. That's all I care about right now."

He smiled. "You just don't want to lose an able-bodied worker to do your bidding."

I grinned, pleased that he was able to find something to joke about amid all the unhappy stuff. "That's right, so get back to work."

"Yes, Your Boss-ship." He backed away, bowing.

I walked away happy.

All afternoon, as the guys and I worked together to break up the asphalt, I marveled that Sean's sense of humor was still intact. But according to Wade and Douglas, Sean had turned down several of their offers to meet for drinks or dinner after work. That worried me. If he was avoiding friends and spending evenings alone, was he growing more depressed? It was hard to tell his real feelings from just seeing him at work, because it would be natural for him to put up a good front around his boss. I wondered what I could do to help him out, but couldn't come up with anything. And the earsplitting noise of the hydraulic hammer wasn't helping me think.

Later that afternoon, I saw Callie waiting at our usual meeting spot. "Ready to go?"

"Would you mind if I stayed at school a while longer?" she asked. "I met a girl in one of my classes who's starring in the spring play. She said I could come by to see the rehearsals, and she'll take me home later. If it's okay with you, I mean."

"That sounds like fun. Mind if I tag along?" I quickly added, "I won't hang out with you, but I'd love to see what they're doing."

"Sure," she said, surprising me. "And we can hang together if you want. I don't care. Let's go."

I tried to convince myself that I wasn't tagging along solely because I was worried about Callie. I really did want to see how the rehearsals were going. I especially wanted to see if the carpentry crew was as good as they were when I was in charge.

That was my story and I was sticking to it.

On the way to the theater building, I texted Mac to let him know we'd be home a little later than expected. We reached the stairs leading to the auditorium just as the door opened and Whitney walked out.

"Oh, great," she said. "Way to ruin my day."

"Callie, you go on inside. I'll be just a minute." There was no way I was going to put up with Whitney's insults in front of Callie.

"Are you sure?" Callie asked. She was frowning at Whitney, and I wanted to hug her for sensing danger. Not that I was in any real danger, but Whitney was definitely not a friend. I was impressed that Callie had recognized it instantly.

"Sure," I said easily. "I'll see you inside."

"Okay." She jogged up the stairs to the door. Swinging it open, she disappeared into the building.

"Who's that?" Whitney asked, her voice free of disdain for once.

"A friend. Why?"

"She's cute. Is she a student?"

"Yes," I said with caution, wondering why she wanted to know.

"Does she want to try out for the cheerleading squad?"

I decided to cut Whitney a tiny bit of slack, only because she'd said something nice about Callie. "She'd probably enjoy it, but she's a temporary student visiting from out of town, so she wouldn't be a good choice for the squad."

"Oh. Too bad." Whitney started to walk away, then stopped. "Oh, and just as I suspected, you had to go and snitch to Tommy about me hiring Cliff."

"I didn't snitch," I said calmly. "I was just dropping off the blueprints you asked for, and Tommy didn't know what I was talking about. So it's your own fault for not getting your story straight with him."

"Well, it's really unfair and selfish of you to keep Cliff from doing one teensy job in my home."

"You're remodeling a bathroom," I said. "That's not a teensy job. But that's not even the point. Tommy and my father had a business arrangement."

"Whatever. I just wanted to do something nice for Cliff, and it figures you'd get in the way." She sighed. "Do you even remember him from high school? I was sooooo in love with him, it was crazy."

"Funny, I thought you were in love with Tommy."

"Of course I was," she snapped. "But Cliff kept asking me out. I actually think he was in love with me."

"Gosh, I'm really sorry to get in the way of all that love." I wanted to hurl. Better yet, I wanted to tell her that Cliff had asked out almost everyone, including me, numerous times. Even better, I wanted Whitney and Cliff to go jump off a real cliff.

I said a hurried good-bye and dashed up the steps and into the auditorium. I found Callie sitting on the aisle halfway down from the stage and slipped into the seat next to her.

The teenage girl on stage was singing "Do-Re-Mi" from *The Sound of Music*. She was really good, very theatrical and very pretty, although she appeared to be wearing a short blond wig to look more like Julie Andrews in the movie. It looked unnatural, but she probably didn't want to cut off her hair just to play the role.

Callie leaned over and whispered, "Isn't she great?"

"She is."

The kids playing the Von Trapp children were good, too. I would have to inform the festival committee that we had a hit on our hands. The spring play coincided with the town's spring festival, so it always drew a good crowd.

A minute later, the song ended and the director clapped her hands. "Good job, everyone. Much better, Sarah. That was beautiful." She consulted the tablet she held. "We'll break for five minutes, then rehearse scene seventeen next."

"Come meet Sarah," Callie said to me, and I followed her up the aisle to the stage. Her actress friend waved and came over to the edge.

"You made it," she said.

"I'm so glad I did," Callie said. "Oh, my gosh, Sarah, you're so good. I'm so impressed. This is my friend Shannon. She's a contractor. She's the one who's building the new parking structure. Don't you love her hair?"

"Hi." We shook hands and the three of us chatted for a quick minute, until the director came over to say something to Sarah.

"This is Ms. Matthews," Sarah said. "She's the best drama teacher ever."

"Hello, Ms. Matthews," I said.

Ms. Matthews smiled indulgently as I introduced myself and Callie. Sarah beckoned Callie to join her a few yards away so they could have a private conversation, leaving me to talk to the drama teacher. I liked her. I guessed she was in her early thirties, close to my age. She was pretty, with dark hair and eyes, and she wore neatly pressed jeans and a long striped sweater.

"I give you permission to call me Lara, by the way," she said, her eyes sparkling with humor. "I'm one of those mean teachers who insists on being called by their surname."

"I think that's so much better."

"Me, too. It helps tap into that innate fear of grown-ups every teenager has."

I laughed out loud; you had to have a sense of humor to teach high school. "Have you been working here long?"

"It's been three years now. How about you?"

"I'm a building contractor. I'm putting in the new parking structure out by the tennis courts."

"Oh yes. Everyone's excited about that."

"It's really innovative, all solar-powered, and it'll collect water, too, and save lots of money. But don't get me started."

She laughed. "So, have you seen *The Sound of Music* before?"

"Only a few dozen times. I love it."

"I'm glad. I played Maria in high school and again in college. I've always loved the music."

I studied her a little more closely. "You have the look of Maria."

"You mean nunlike?" she asked, laughing.

I laughed, too. "Not at all. But you do look like you can handle a bunch of wild children."

"Definitely," she said with a smile. "Even though I have none of my own, I do an excellent job of wrangling other people's teenagers. And pets. I have several of those. No husband, luckily. Not yet, anyway."

I chuckled. "You'll be thrilled to know that I was the head carpenter when I was going to school here." I pointed toward the back of the stage. "That looks like one of the flats I built the year we did *Grease*."

"You did good work," she said. "Do you want another job? We just lost our head carpenter to the varsity baseball team."

"Oh no. Can one of the other kids step up?"

She looked around to make sure we weren't being overheard, then whispered, "They're not the most talented group I've ever worked with."

I winced, because really stage decoration had as much as acting to do with the success of a play. "Sorry about that."

We chatted for another minute, until it was time for her to call the kids back to the stage. "Nice talking to you, Shannon."

"You, too, Lara. I'll see you at the play." As I walked out of the theater, a brilliant idea began to form in my mind.

Chapter Twelve

"Are you sure you don't mind?" I asked, as Sean and I crossed the high school campus after work the following Monday. "It would just be for a few weeks, until the play is over. My friend is a little worried that things won't get done in time."

"I don't mind at all," Sean said. "It'll get me out of the house a few nights a week."

"That's really generous of you."

And clever of me, too, I thought, but it wouldn't do to crow too loudly.

Sean held the door for me and we walked into the auditorium, down to the edge of the empty stage, where I looked around for Lara Matthews. "She must be here somewhere," I muttered.

"Break's over, guys," Lara shouted as she walked out onstage, staring at her tablet. "Come on. Shake a leg. I need the Von Trapp kids front and center to rehearse 'So Long, Farewell.' Everybody onstage."

She glanced down and noticed us when I waved. "Shannon? You're back. Are you a glutton for punishment?"

"Hi, Lara," I said, smiling. "I came up with a solution to your carpenter problem. This is Sean, one of the guys on my construction crew. He's willing to help out your carpenters for a few weeks, if that works for you." I turned to Sean. "Sean, this is Lara Matthews."

They stared at each other for a moment; then she stooped down and stuck her hand out. "Welcome to the show, Sean."

He shook her hand, grinning. "Nice to be here, Lara."

Lara gazed at me. "Wow, you make good things happen."

I shrugged modestly. "Just want to make sure the carpentry crew shines."

That night, flush from my brilliant introduction of Sean to Lara, I walked down to the pub to pick up a celebratory burger for dinner. As I was about to place my order, Eric walked in.

After greeting me, he asked, "Are you meeting someone?"

"No, I was going to get something to go."

"Why don't you join me?" he said.

"I'd love to."

The waitress showed us to a booth along the far wall and took our drink orders. I was willing to admit it was not a hardship to gaze across the table at him. "You come here a lot, right?"

"Yeah. This and the wine bar are pretty much my go-to places when I don't feel like cooking."

"Mine, too," I said. "But I might be a little prejudiced when it comes to the wine bar."

"True—your uncle owns the place. But I can speak objectively. And I say it's the best Italian food around."

"On behalf of Uncle Pete, I thank you."

We both smiled. Everyone knew my uncle owned the wine bar. It was officially known as Bella Rossa, but more commonly was referred to as the wine bar on the square.

As soon as our drinks were served and we'd ordered our food, I said, "Anything new on the crime-fighting scene?" and had the pleasure of watching him scowl.

"You just asked me that to watch my blood boil, right?"

"No, but that's a delightful side benefit."

He shook his head and glanced around. "I'm not about to tell you anything while we're sitting here, but I will say that we're not much farther along than we were when I saw you in my office the other day."

"I'm sorry to hear that." I glanced around, too. The booth was one of the most secluded in the pub, but I still thought it best to lower my voice. "I spoke to Sean. He said you didn't find what you were hoping for."

He knew what I was talking about and nodded somberly. "It's too bad. On the other hand, I'm not sure if those tests would've proved much, anyway."

The DNA tests, I guessed. "You mean, because the mother's genetic code and her father's would be too similar to discern?"

He was scowling again, but it was still sort of fun to talk to him cryptically.

Eric leaned over to whisper, and he was so tall that he almost reached my ear. A good thing, because what he said next was totally confidential. "The real problem is that the tests won't be conclusive, no matter what. It's got something to do with the genealogical pattern of chromosomes descending within the patrilineal line vis-à-vis the matrilineal line."

"Translation, please."

His laugh was short and humorless. "That's a direct quote from the medical examiner. Bottom line is, it's not worth our time and money to test Hugh Brogan's DNA."

In my head, I decoded what he'd told me. That Lily's DNA was too close to her father's DNA for anyone to tell if the baby was his or not.

With a sigh, I said, "I think it's for the best." When he looked puzzled, I lowered my voice to a bare whisper and scooted closer. "If I were Sean, I would hate to know that my own father had raped my sister, then killed her when she got pregnant."

He grimaced but had no comment.

"Because that's basically what you're trying to prove by testing Hugh's DNA, right?" I sat back. "And that's just too horrific a scenario to contemplate."

He gazed at me for so long that I started to wonder if I had food smeared on my cheek or something.

"You know, Red," he said, "for a civilian, you're pretty darn smart."

I clutched my chest dramatically. "Oh, be still my heart. That may be the nicest thing you've ever said to me."

He was grinning now. "I know. Don't get used to it."

"Ah, that's better. The earth has returned to spinning around its axis."

The next day, all went according to plan. I drove Callie to school, and we walked together until we reached the parking-lot construction site; she kept going to the building.

Several hours later, it was getting close to lunch and I had just turned off the jackhammer to relieve the relentless shaking of every bone in my body. I usually let the guys work that particular piece of machinery, because even though I had rather awesome upper body strength for a woman, I couldn't match Sean's or Douglas's ability to hold and control the machine.

It made me wonder if Sean's idea of buying—or, better yet, renting—a hydraulic hammer for jobs like this would be a more reasonable idea all around. It would save wear and tear on my guys because, let's face it, jackhammers were brutal on anyone's system. I could protect them from the noise level by requiring them to wear their headphones, and I was a regular maniac when it came to wearing protective eye gear, but what could I do about the body-jarring effects of the machine? I usually mitigated things by setting a time limit and making the guys switch jobs so that no one man had to suffer for hours at a stretch.

Naturally, my guys loved using the jackhammers, although if given a choice of sticking with those battering machines or switching to one of those gigantic hydraulic hammers that the SolarLight guys were operating, I'd bet they'd go with the big hammer.

As I set the jackhammer back in its portable carrier, I saw Douglas coming toward me with purposeful strides.

"Hey, Douglas. You going to lunch?"

He pressed his lips together, looking like he was thinking about something, then blurted, "Cliff Hogarth has offered me a lot of money to go work for him."

I almost choked on my own breath. It was as if he'd kicked me in the stomach. My head began to spin and all I could do was nod distractedly. "I see. Okay. Thanks for telling me."

Before he could make excuses, I walked away. I didn't want to hear how much more money he could make or whatever else Hogarth had promised him. As soon as I was far enough away that he couldn't see me, I started running all the way to my truck. I was sick to my stomach and out of breath by the time I got there. Douglas had worked for me for five years. He was a part of my family. "But he's not your family," I muttered angrily as I fumbled for my keys.

My eyes were hot with unshed tears, but not for long. As soon as I got inside the truck, I slammed the door and locked it, then laid my head on the steering wheel and started to cry. After a minute, I lifted my head and wiped away the tears. All I needed was for someone to see me and tell Cliff Hogarth that he'd made the girl cry.

I didn't even know if Douglas was going to take the job with Cliff, but I couldn't imagine him turning down a huge raise, either. I paid fair wages, but Cliff was clearly not above bribing my guys.

"I hate him!" I shouted, and pounded the steering wheel really hard, wishing it were Cliff Hogarth's head.

"Ow! You idiot." That hurt. I had to shake my hand and flex my fingers to make the pain go away. I didn't need to break my hand on top of everything else.

I looked around the parking lot, knowing I had to get out of there before someone came along who knew me. Without thinking too hard, I realized where I had to go. I shoved the truck into gear and took off toward Main Street. I pulled into the closest parking space and stormed over to the inn.

In the restaurant, the hostess smiled. "Do you have a reservation?"

"No." I pushed past her and spied my target across the elegant dining room. He sat at one of the power tables in front of the wide plate-glass window that overlooked Main Street, the pier, and the ocean beyond. He wore another expensive black suit and his hair was perfectly coiffed, as usual. All in all, he was buffed and polished to precision, and looking at him, one would never guess he'd ever soiled his soft hands working on a construction site. He was dining with my friend Dave, another local contractor. Wasn't that just dandy?

As I stomped closer, I had a vague thought that it would probably be a good idea to calm down first, but that was impossible. I was incensed. This confrontation had been too long in coming, and now I was a runaway train, ready to collide with my worst enemy.

"Cliff Hogarth," I said crisply, and marveled that my tone was relatively modulated.

"Why, it's Shannon Hammer." He actually looked surprised to see me, and that just infuriated me more. "You know Dave, don't you?"

"Of course I know Dave. I've known Dave for years." I turned to Dave. "Hello, Dave. Nice company you're keeping."

"Hi, Shannon." Dave had the good grace to recognize my wrath and avoided direct eye contact.

Cliff gave me a smarmy smile. "We'd invite you to join us, but . . ." He glanced around. "I'm afraid there's no room for another chair."

"I wouldn't join you if you were the last man on earth. The poisonous stench you give off would ruin the excellent food here." I edged closer so he could hear every word I said. "I am sick of you bad-mouthing me to my clients, stealing my workers behind my back, and trying to undermine my business. If you don't back off immediately, I will make you sorry you ever showed up in this town again."

He chuckled and tried to appear blasé, but I could see his neck turning red. "Is that a threat?"

"No, that's a promise."

"Oh yeah?" he said cockily. "Good luck with that."

I leaned over his table and jabbed him in the chest for emphasis. "And good luck surviving a slander lawsuit, you creep."

And then I turned and walked out of the place.

Back in my truck, I had to breathe deeply. The initial rush of fury was gone and I was crashing precipitously. I glanced around and realized I was parked where anyone in town could see me, so I had to get away from there.

I turned on the engine and started driving. I went east to Highway 101 and then drove north. A few miles later I exited, and it was only then that I realized I was headed toward the nursery. And that was a good thing. I could wander the pathways and stare at pretty flowers for a while and maybe bring my heart rate down a little.

I walked for twenty minutes and finally sat down on a worn burl bench in front of a miniature waterfall that had been created by redirecting part of the brook to spill over a short wall of slate bricks. It was a charming sight, but it was the sound of the water babbling and gushing that most appealed to me. It was a happy sound, and it drowned out my own voice repeating itself over and over in my head.

That's a promise.

You creep.

I covered my face with my hands. It had been stupid of me to verbally attack Cliff Hogarth in public like that. But what else could I do? I had endured his direct assaults as well as the shadowy rumors of certain malicious comments from him. I had brushed off Ms. Barney's concerns after Hogarth berated her and slandered me. And I'd barely tolerated Whitney's idiocy over the guy. But now he was trying to take Douglas from me and it was suddenly very personal.

The whole town knew what Cliff was up to, so there was no point in pretending otherwise. So, really, what had I done that was so bad? I'd stood up for myself, my crew, my business. I'd showed everyone that I wouldn't roll over and play dead for a low-life interloper like Cliff.

I could rely solely on my own good reputation to see me through this crisis, or I could hire a lawyer and sue Cliff. If I chose to go the way of a lawsuit, I wondered how much damage I might've just done to my case by confronting him personally. I supposed there was only one way to find out. I pulled my tablet out of my purse and made a note on my calendar to call our business lawyer tomorrow and find out.

I put away the tablet and began walking farther down the path, wandering among the plants and greenery. I'd done this before, of course. Gardens had always soothed me, ever since I was a little girl and my mother, Ella, who was a botanist, had taught me all about gardening. I could still picture her laughing as I tried to grow green beans up the side of the house.

"Oh, dear." I had to stop and concentrate on the feathery leaves of a nearby willow tree. Thinking of my mom often brought me close to tears. And memories of my mother's death reminded me of Lily's kindnesses. I desperately blinked back the waterworks. Today had already been overly emotional for me and I really hated to cry. It turned my eyes red and my face puffy, besides clogging up my head and making me feel like a sad little five-year-old.

"You look so lonely."

I flinched at the sound and looked behind me. "Hey. Hi, Denise."

"You okay?"

"Oh, sure. I'm not really lonely, just hiding. And destressing."

She smiled. "This is a great place to do both."

"I know. It's so beautiful here."

"It is." She gazed around. "Sometimes I wonder how my life would've turned out if I had traded my garden tools for a briefcase. There was a time when I actually had to make that decision."

"I think you made the right one," I said, brushing my fingers over the wispy strands of pink pampas grass growing along the path.

"I like to think so," Denise said. She moved her rake in and around the nearby bushes, extracting dead leaves and weeds. "If you've got something on your mind, Shannon, feel free to vent. I figure anything said out here stays out here."

I laughed lightly, recalling that I'd said almost the same thing to Eric a few days back. *What happens here in the jail, stays in the jail,* I'd assured him.

"I guess it might help to talk it through," I said.

"Go right ahead. Pretend I'm not here if it helps any."

"No, I don't mind talking to you. Especially since you know the players."

"Now you've stoked my curiosity."

I smiled. "Okay. So one of my favorite crew members—well, they're all my favorites, really. I've been working with the same guys for years now and they feel like my brothers, you know? Anyway, one of them just told me that Cliff Hogarth offered him a lot of money to quit my company and work for him."

"I'm so sorry. That's just wrong."

"It's very wrong, mainly because he only did it to harass me." I told her about the slanderous statements he'd made to Ms. Barney and others, and I was about to complain about Whitney, too, when I remembered that Denise and Whitney were friends.

And speaking of friends, it just occurred to me that since Cliff had dated Lily, maybe Denise had been friends with him, too. *Oh, boy. I should've kept my mouth shut.*

"I probably need to stop talking," I said. "For all I know, you and Cliff are old pals."

"Believe me, we're not," she rushed to say. "I've always thought he was a scumbag."

"I never liked him, either, and now it's worse than ever."

Her eyes narrowed as if she were searching back to a certain moment in the past. "Cliff was always a troublemaker. Always pushing people's buttons. He pushed Lily's plenty of times, and sometimes I hated him for it."

"He's sure been pushing mine," I muttered.

"And, frankly, don't you wonder why he came back to town?" Denise leaned on the rake handle and squinted up into the sun from beneath her gardening hat. "I mean, he got here, and within a month you'd all found Lily. It makes me wonder."

So I wasn't the only one who had questioned the timing of Cliff's return to Lighthouse Cove. Why *had* Cliff come back? And why now?

"But now I can see that I'm feeding your anger," Denise said, "and I don't like to do that."

I smiled. "Then let's change the subject. How are you and Brad doing? How's the kitchen working out?"

"You know, we love it." She talked about how Brad— Mr. Jones—loved cooking now that they had a wonderful, state-of-the-art kitchen. "Before, he would never even boil water, but now he's always experimenting with new, amazing recipes, like short ribs and chicken piccata and lots of yummy sauces, you know? And it's all because of our kitchen. So thank you. You did a fabulous job."

Laughing, I said, "Well, I fished for that compliment, but thank you. I'm glad it makes you happy."

"The only thing we need now is a few kids running around the house."

I grinned. "Are you planning a big family?"

"I would love three or four, but Brad thinks two would be plenty." Denise smiled, but it didn't reach her eyes. "Of course, we haven't had much luck in that area yet."

Her happy tone had completely faded. I tried to think of something encouraging to say, but all I could do was reach out and squeeze her arm lightly. "But you will. I know it."

"I hope so. It's funny. Back in the day, after we realized we were in love with each other, we were hesitant to rush into having kids. It didn't seem right. Because of Lily, you know? But now . . ."

"I understand, and I'm so sorry you're having problems now. But you're both such good people, I know good things will happen for you."

"Thanks, Shannon." She took a deep breath. "I guess

we'll see how it goes." She shook her head as if to shake away the melancholy and changed the subject. "What about the lighthouse mansion? How is that job coming?"

"We just got back in there, after it was declared a crime scene for a week. And it's going to be beautiful. I'm hoping I can talk Mac into joining the House and Garden Tour in May. It would be great to open the place to the public for a day or two once we've finished the rehab."

"That would be fun," she said. "I'd love to see it. It's in the perfect spot, isn't it? Right there where the break-water and the lighthouse and the beach and the cliffs all come together. I always loved walking along the rocks when I was little."

"Me, too. My dad used to drive us out there. Remember when there were sand dunes between the road and the beach? We used to slide down them and pretend we were surfing."

"Of course I remember. They're mostly sand mounds now."

"Sand dune-lettes."

We both laughed. It was nice to reminisce with someone who'd grown up experiencing the same joys.

"You'll laugh at this," I said. "The first time I walked inside the mansion, I barely made it to the kitchen before this tiny white rat came skittering across the floor. I went screaming out of there. It's so embarrassing to think about."

She laughed. "I don't mind little white rats. It's the ugly big gray ones that freak me out."

I moaned. "I'm just a wimp."

"I wasn't always good with rats, but I got used to having the little white ones around when Brad and I got married."

I was confused at first, then realized what she was talking about. "Oh yeah. The first time I ever saw a white rat was in Mr. Jones's biology class. It freaked me out then, too."

"He's still got them in the classroom."

"It's nice to know some things never change."

My arms were covered in goose bumps by now, after all this talk about rats. "I hope you got used to them. Didn't you have to take them home when school was closed for vacation?"

Denise made a face. "Not at first. Brad knew how I felt about the little critters. Darren Dain always took them home." She rolled her eyes. "Doesn't that just figure?"

The name was an instant buzzkill. "Mr. Dain? Dismal Dain, the world's worst guidance counselor? He took care of the rats?"

She just laughed and nodded.

"Wow. That makes perfect sense," I said, as the goose bumps returned. I shook my head at the thought of that horrible little man communing with rats. But, then, who else would put up with him all summer besides a bunch of squirmy rodents?

By the time I left Denise at the Gardens, I felt so much better. I would still call the lawyer in the morning, but at least I wouldn't continue to suffer from that awful sick feeling in my stomach. It had faded sometime during my friendly conversation with Denise.

Unfortunately, I couldn't forget that one moment

when she confessed that she and Mr. Jones had tried to have children but hadn't succeeded yet. They were still so young, though, so I refused to give up hope. I smiled at the image of Mr. Jones holding an adorable little baby in his arms.

My smile faded when I pulled into my driveway and saw Douglas pacing up and down my walkway. I was tempted to back up the truck and drive off, but that would be cowardly. Besides, maybe he'd decided to turn down Cliff's job offer. I almost laughed. Why would anyone turn down more money? I gathered my work stuff and my purse, determined to listen to what he had to say for himself. And then I would pour myself a big glass of wine. I thought I deserved it after the day I'd been through.

Taking a deep breath, I jumped out of the cab and slammed the door shut. "Hi, Douglas," I said, as breezily as I could muster, knowing that after this last confrontation, I wouldn't see him at work again. I braced myself for that unhappy certainty as I strolled toward him.

"Shannon, where did you go?" He raked his fingers through his hair, something he'd been doing constantly, if his scruffy, disheveled hair was any indication.

"I took a little drive. What's the problem?"

"What's the—? Are you kidding? You just took off before I could even tell you that I would never quit you to take a job with Hogarth. None of us would. Why would you think that? You're the best boss I've ever had, and Cliff is a jackass. Everyone in town knows that."

"They do?"

"Yes. Believe me, I wouldn't work for him on a bet. You have nothing to worry about where he's concerned." Douglas gave me a wary smile, as if half-afraid I might bolt again. "I'm just really sorry you were so upset. It's all my fault. If you want to dock me, go ahead, because I didn't get much work done this afternoon. I was too worried, thinking you might be at the bank, cutting off my paycheck or something."

"Come here," I said, and pulled him close for a hug. After a long moment, I let him go. "Thank you for telling me all that. And I'm glad you told me that Cliff approached you about a job. It's good for me to know those things."

"God, you scared the crap out of me. I thought you were so mad at me."

"I'm not mad. Not at you. And I'm sorry I scared you. I scared myself a little, too. But that's over now, and I'm delighted that you aren't quitting."

After he left, I went inside and poured that glass of wine I'd promised myself. I sat on the couch with Robbie and Tiger crowding me on both sides and thought about what Douglas had said. Mainly the part where everyone in town knew that Cliff was a jackass and he wouldn't get many jobs after his bad reputation became more known. If only that were true.

Tiger climbed onto my lap and I relished the warmth. I reminded myself that Whitney had tried to hire Cliff, so not *everyone* in town felt the same way Douglas did. But despite Whitney's moaning about her *love* for Cliff, chances were excellent that Whitney had only hired him to bug me.

I'd always been able to get along with my competition, although I had to admit I'd had my share of adversaries when I first took over my father's business. Strangely enough, not everyone took kindly to a woman running her own successful construction company. But until Cliff came back to town, we had all managed to live in relative peace and harmony. Now the peace had been shattered, and I didn't know what to expect next.

The phone rang early Wednesday morning and I had to run out of the bathroom with my toothbrush in hand to grab it.

"Hello?"

"Shannon."

"Lizzie? What's up?" I glanced at the clock by my bed. "For Pete's sake, girl. It's barely seven o'clock. Is everything okay? Are the kids okay? Is it Hal? What's wrong?"

"Everyone here is fine, Shannon, but you'll never guess."

"You're right—I won't. So just tell me."

"Cliff Hogarth is dead."

Chapter Thirteen

A half hour later, after taking the shortest shower on record and dressing for work, I paced around my kitchen, wondering what to do. Cliff was dead, and my head was about to explode from the guilt of having yelled at him mixed up with burning curiosity. How had he died?

In the midst of all that, Lizzie called back.

"I'm sorry, Shannon!" she moaned over the phone. "Cliff isn't dead after all!"

"What?" I stared at the phone, shaking my head. "What are you saying? What happened?"

"Hal heard on the police scanner that Cliff was dead, but the report was wrong," she explained. "According to Hal's friend Steve over at the medical center, Cliff is clinging to life in the intensive-care unit."

"We can talk about Hal's obsession with the police scanner later." I slid into a chair and had to grip the kitchen table to take it all in. "Tell me what happened to Cliff."

"He was hit in the head with a shovel."

A shovel?

My mind was about to spin off into hyperspace now. I

had a sinking feeling that I'd seen the shovel she was referring to.

"Who hit him?" I asked, afraid I already knew the answer.

"Denise Jones."

I gripped my stomach. The past hour had been like a roller-coaster ride, with Lizzie calling three times, first to tell me that Cliff was dead, then to tell me that she wasn't sure, and finally, just now, to say that he was alive. Honestly, I didn't know whether to throw a party, have a drink, or pray. The good news was that whatever had happened to Cliff Hogarth, I didn't have anything to do with it, thank heavens. But now I was worried about Denise. She'd admitted to me that she'd hated Cliff, but I wasn't about to mention that to Lizzie or anyone else. Not yet, anyway.

"Tell Hal to toss that police scanner in the trash," I grumbled. "This isn't the first time they've jumped the gun with the wrong information."

"I've begged him to get rid of it," Lizzie said. "But he enjoys listening to it. He works so hard, I want him to have his hobbies. I just hope he's not living vicariously through it."

"I'm sure he's not." I sighed. Hal Logan was the most sensible man I knew. He balanced out Lizzie perfectly. "He probably just likes to keep his finger on the pulse of things around here." I took a last gulp of coffee and re-filled my cup with more. Not that I needed more of a jolt than I'd already received from Lizzie's numerous phone calls.

"Lately, the town has been hopping with action," Lizzie said. "Hal feels like he's right in the middle of it all, thanks to the scanner."

I could picture Hal getting excited about the latest buzz over the scanner. Lizzie's husband was a darling man and he loved his wife to distraction—which was how Lizzie justified her relentless attempts to set us all up on blind dates. Their kind of true love was out there for all of us.

But I digressed.

"Tell me every detail, Lizzie."

"Okay, but I don't want you blaming Hal for thinking Cliff was dead. It's the EMT's fault for reporting that news in the first place."

"Okay, but—"

"It took a while for them to report that they were able to revive Cliff. And now they say he's clinging to life."

Clinging to life is a heck of a lot better than dead, my guilty conscience assured me. Because, yes, I felt horribly guilty. Call me a hypocrite, but I was praying that Cliff Hogarth would survive. I'd ranted and raged in his face yesterday at lunch—in front of witnesses—and then later on to Denise. And over the past month to anyone who would listen, really. Even Chief Jensen had been subjected to my fuming tirades about Cliff.

I frowned at the thought. I was usually so even-tempered, but now I was tempted to sign up for anger-management classes.

"I've got to get Callie to school," I told Lizzie, after taking a look at the clock. We hung up and I grabbed my stuff and went running outside to meet Callie.

I was surprised to see a sleepy-headed Mac waiting with his niece. "Do I have news for you," I said as he pushed open the gate and we walked to my truck.

He pulled open the passenger's door. Callie settled inside the truck and immediately started texting her friends.

Mac glanced at me from across the truck bed. "I think I might have bigger news."

"So you heard that Cliff Hogarth almost died?"

"Yes. How'd you hear about it?"

"Lizzie called me." I told him about Hal hearing it on the police scanner, and about the multiple phone calls from Lizzie. "So now he's clinging to life."

Mac nodded. "Yeah. He'll probably make it."

"I'm glad, I guess."

"You guess?" he said with amusement.

"Sorry. Yes, sure, I'm glad."

He studied me. "What's going on, Irish?"

I fiddled with the zipper of my down vest, feeling foolish. "I . . . I sort of threatened him yesterday. In public." I waved the incident away. "But I wouldn't. I mean, I didn't follow through. I'm not a violent person, despite my occasional rant."

"Of course you're not."

I smiled at him. "Thanks. So, how did you hear about Cliff?"

He circled around the truck to stand closer to me so we could speak more quietly. It was still early enough to wake up some of our neighbors. "You know I've been doing ride-alongs with the police to research my next book, right?"

My eyebrows perked up. "Oh, of course. So, you were with Eric? You must know everything. What happened?"

Mac looked pleased by my enthusiasm. "We were just about to head back to the police station when we got the call that Cliff Hogarth had been hurt."

"Where was he?"

"He was out at that nursery you took me to."

"I wonder what he was doing out there."

"He went to talk to Denise Jones."

"Why?"

"Brace yourself."

"Oh no. Please don't tell me they were having an affair."

"No." Mac looked over his shoulder, clearly making sure that Callie was paying no attention to us. Of course, she wasn't. A teenager with a phone couldn't care less what adults were doing. "He was trying to blackmail her."

"Wh-what?" I felt my jaw drop. I knew Cliff was a horrible human being, but blackmailing Denise? "Are you kidding?"

"Nope."

"Oh my God. Poor Denise!" I paced in front of the truck. What could he possibly have on Denise? *Not the point right now, Shannon,* I told myself. "Cliff is so awful. Just when I think he can't stoop any lower, he goes there. So, what happened exactly?"

"Denise was working late," Mac said, setting the scene. "She had just dug out some old flower beds and was rolling the trash barrels out to the parking lot to be emptied in the morning. She was about to lock up the place when Hogarth showed up to talk. Apparently she didn't like what he had to say, because she ended up bashing him in the head with her shovel."

I had to lean against my truck to keep from falling over. This was all so hard to believe. Even though Denise and I had both voiced our sincere disgust with Cliff Hogarth, and even though I'd noticed how viciously she'd been pounding that shovel against the ground that time I'd been at the nursery with Mac, I still couldn't picture Denise being so angry that she'd attack someone badly enough that they were now clinging to life. "I can't believe it. I'd just visited her a few hours earlier."

"Did she have her shovel with her when you were there? Because that thing is lethal."

Immediately I felt obliged to defend my friend. "*Any* shovel is lethal, not just Denise's. And if Cliff was trying to blackmail her, she must've hit him in self-defense." I frowned, imagining it, then tried to brush it off. "Besides, she didn't kill him. He's still alive. So, really, he's lucky, because he clearly had it coming."

Mac's eyebrows went up. "I think I like this tough-girl streak, Irish."

I could feel my cheeks heating up at my bloodthirsty tone. "Is Denise okay?"

"She was hysterical," Mac said. "I'll try to remember everything she said, but it got complicated."

"Oh, dear."

"Denise told Eric that Hogarth kept goading her about paying him money to keep quiet—she never would say what it was exactly—and she finally got so angry, she started to swing at him with whatever she had. It happened to be the shovel. Hogarth was able to grab it and they tussled." He shook his head and lowered his voice. "He pushed her down and lifted the shovel to hit her. She thought she was about to die, but at the last second she was able to roll out of the way and scramble to her feet. He got distracted by that and it gave her time to grab the shovel back and bash him over the head."

"Wow. She's really strong."

"I know. I saw those arms of hers, remember? Anyway, she said she finally managed to swing the shovel blindly and nailed him in the head. He dropped like a big tree."

I pressed my fingers against my mouth. I was shocked,

of course, but also horrified for several different reasons. "Poor Denise. Sorry, I just can't bring myself to say *poor Cliff*. I know I shouldn't speak ill of the nearly dead, but it's hard to pretend I feel bad for him."

Mac raised an eyebrow.

"Okay, nobody deserves to be hit with a shovel, but he clearly provoked her. Pushed her to the limit." I slapped one hand on the truck fender. "Heck, he had me pushed until I was a raving lunatic just yesterday. He has a gift for rubbing people the wrong way."

"Sounds like it." Mac checked his wristwatch, then covered my hand with one of his. I appreciated the show of comfort and solidarity. "Denise is being interrogated by Eric right now, so I guess he'll have to figure out whether it's all justifiable or not. My guess is that she'll be released."

"I hope so."

"Think about it," he said. "By the time she actually hit him with the shovel, it was a case of fighting for her life."

My mind narrowed in on one thing. "This must have something to do with Lily's death."

His eyes lit up and he gave my hand a squeeze before letting go. "Of course it does. Let's discuss."

I had to laugh. Mac loved tossing around murder theories. It was more grist for the mill. Or research for his books. "Okay," I said. "Why would Cliff be blackmailing Denise? She was Lily's best friend."

"Keep talking," he said.

"So you never heard what it was about?"

"Nope."

Bummer, I thought. I'd have to theorize some more. "Okay. What if the two of them had been fooling around behind Lily's back?"

"Which two?"

"Cliff and Denise." I made a face. "I can't believe she would ever be interested in him, but it could happen. So what if . . ."

"What if . . . ?" he prompted.

"Well, Cliff could've been threatening to tell Mr. Jones." I frowned at that idea. "But if they were having an affair back in high school, it's all in the past. Why would Mr. Jones care? This is weird."

"Weird and wonderful," he said, energized. "Let's take Callie to school, then come back home and I'll interview you some more. This will be more great background for my article."

I sighed, torn between obligations and having fun. "I'd love to, but I really have to work for a few hours. But I can come home at lunch and we can talk then. Does that sound good to you?"

"I'll be waiting."

I drove Callie to school and talked to the guys for a while. They had everything under control with the parking-lot demolition, so I jogged back to the truck and drove out to the lighthouse mansion to work with Carla and her crew.

Carla greeted me with a look of puzzled concern on her face.

"What's up?" I asked. "Is something wrong?"

"Aldous Murch was here when I arrived first thing this morning."

"Aldous? Did he drive himself?" I hoped not. The man was in his eighties and a little too fragile to be driving his own car.

"He said he took the Northline bus."

"The bus? Was he looking for me?"

"No." Her forehead creased in worry. "That's the weird thing. He stood right here on the front porch and shouted that the truth needed to come to light. Then he pushed me out of the way, marched into the house, and started climbing the stairs. He had to stop on every step to catch his breath and was worn out by the second floor."

"I hope you convinced him to go back downstairs."

"Since he couldn't breathe, it didn't take much convincing. But while he was on the second floor, he walked back and forth down the hall, stopping at every doorway, mumbling about something. 'It's here somewhere,' I think he was saying. And he kept coming back to the stairway, kept staring up toward the attic."

"The attic?"

"Yeah. I finally asked if he wanted me to look for something in the attic for him."

My stomach started its nervous twitching again. "What did he say? Did he leave something up there?"

"He wouldn't tell me," Carla said. "He continued to mumble to himself, so I finally called his daughter, and she drove out to pick him up."

"Good." I shook my head, befuddled by Aldous's strange behavior. What was he looking for? And why was he staring up at the attic?

Those questions led me to wonder, *Did Aldous know Lily Brogan fifteen years ago? Had he seen her hiding out in the lighthouse mansion?*

"Oh, God." Was it possible that Aldous had something to do with Lily's murder? Impossible. But I couldn't let it go. Fifteen years ago, Aldous would've been in his late sixties. Maybe he was frail now in his eighties, but he would've been a strong man back then. Strong enough to pick up a woman and shove her inside a dumbwaiter? My mind started spinning at the thought. It wasn't possible, was it?

"Absolutely not," I muttered immediately. I was grasping at straws. But a tiny niggling doubt remained.

After all, from the very beginning when Mac first bought the mansion and then applied to the Planning Commission to rehab the place, Aldous had been dogging the process. Was the old man more concerned about the house itself or what we might discover inside?

There was only one way to find out. I would have to track him down and have a conversation with him. For now, though, I was here and ready to work off some of these worries with good, hard labor. I glanced at Carla, who still looked anxious. "Don't worry," I said. "I'll talk to Aldous."

"Okay, good. Thanks, Shannon."

"For now, let's go over the stuff you guys have been doing all week."

"Sounds like a plan. Let's start out here." We circled the front porch, and she pointed out the items on my list they'd taken care of. "We've taken down all the shutters. I'm storing them up on the porch because it keeps threatening to rain."

"Good thinking." Two dozen pairs of shutters were neatly piled under the front window. Also, a number of wooden planks were chalked to indicate that they needed to be replaced.

"This header will have to come down, by the way," she said, reaching up to slap the head beam that ran between the two main posts that stood on either side of the front steps. "Water damage."

"Yeah, I had that on my list. The roof over the porch

is warped, so I know water's been leaking into those beams for years now."

"That's the downside of having a two-hundred-year-old house next to the ocean," she said, shaking her head.

"Sad but true." I pulled out my tablet and consulted my handy list of projects. "Did you get started on the kitchen yet?"

"Sure have," she said. "Let's go inside."

We walked through the foyer into the dining room and pushed open the kitchen door. The sink and the entire counter and the cabinets above and below it were gone. "I had the guys put the old cabinets in the garage for safekeeping until you're ready to do something with them."

"Thanks," I said. "I'd like to salvage them somehow. Maybe Mac has some ideas of ways to use them. The wood is so beautiful."

Carla gestured toward the tools leaning against the wall where the sink used to be. "I've got a sledgehammer and a pickax sitting here, just in case you feel like attacking something."

I laughed. "How did you know?" I crossed the room and lifted the ax. "Tell me what to work on next."

She pointed to the other side of the room. "That pantry closet needs to come down. It's all yours. Billy and I can start tearing apart the mudroom."

"Sounds like a plan." I stared at the south end of the kitchen, where a floor-to-ceiling pantry had been built out from the wall, taking up half the space on that side of the room. On the wall next to the cabinet was nothing but a faded, boxy outline, indicating that an old refrigerator had once stood there.

The wood cabinet was old and had been picked apart

from the inside by termites, so I had no intention of salvaging any of it, except to use as kindling.

I slipped on my safety goggles and did a few practice swings before I slammed the ax into the side of the pantry. Splinters and chunks of wood went flying. I continued swinging until the doors and sides of the pantry were scattered in pieces across the floor.

I could feel my muscles thrumming, and I don't know why the thought came to me, but I remembered that Denise Jones had strong arms, too. Swinging an ax or a sledgehammer—or a shovel—every day could do that for you.

The entire pantry had been attached to the wall by one-by-two-inch wood slats. I used a regular hammer to claw off the slats, and part of the wall came off with them. I wasn't concerned, because we would have to take the entire room down to the studs, anyway.

But instead of the usual layer of lath beneath the surface plaster, there was a sheet of old drywall. I knew drywall had been around for almost a hundred years; that wasn't the problem. It just didn't match the rest of the walls of the house, which had been constructed using the traditional lath and plaster. Had this wall been built later?

Since we'd be rebuilding it anyway, I used the pickax to dig through the drywall and break it up. But instead of finding two-by-four studs beyond the drywall, there was only empty space.

"What in the world?" It was too dark to see anything, so I tore down more of the drywall and then grabbed the big flashlight from my tool chest.

"How's it going?" Carla asked, strolling over to my side of the room.

"We've got a little mystery in here," I muttered, shining the light through the hole I'd opened in the drywall. I really hoped I wouldn't find another body. Or rats. *Please not rats.* I stepped back to give Carla room to look. "Can you see anything?"

"What's back there?" She peered into the space for a long moment. "Huh. Looks like a staircase."

"Oh, my God." A tingle of excitement mixed with fear shot across my shoulders and down my arms. "It *is* a staircase."

I grabbed the sledgehammer and slashed away at the rest of the wall. Carla used her gloved hands to tear off a few chunks and toss them on the floor.

Within minutes, we were able to step through the wall and get a closer look at the impossibly narrow, rickety set of stairs that led up to a second-floor landing and then continued up to the third floor. I could see from where I stood that the landing came to an abrupt end at a blank wall. There was no doorway. The entire staircase had been completely blocked off and enclosed by walls.

"This must've been the servants' stairs," Carla marveled. "I don't understand why they would cover them up."

"I don't, either," I said, gazing at the dark wooden bannister that wobbled when I touched it. "But I owe Aldous Murch an apology."

The guys and Carla were happy to clean up the remains of the demolished pantry while I drove back to town to track down Aldous and tell him what we'd found.

I stopped at the Planning Commission offices first, but he wasn't there. One of the secretaries came over to the counter and said, "You'll probably find him strolling somewhere between here and the Historical Society office down on the square."

I decided to walk the same route and finally caught up with him. He was seated on a park bench in the tree-lined grassy center of the town square. His head was bowed and I wondered if he was dozing.

"Hello, Mr. Murch," I said.

He blinked and sat up straighter. "Well, hello, there. I haven't seen you in a while, young lady." He coughed to clear his throat.

"I've been pretty busy. But I heard you were out at the mansion, and I was wondering if you needed any help looking for something."

"I didn't . . . I wasn't. . . ." His lips curled down in a frown. "I forget what I was looking for."

I sat down next to him on the bench. "Maybe this will help you remember." I held out my tablet so he could see the photograph I'd taken.

He stared at it for over a minute and finally looked up at me. I was shocked to see tears blurring his eyes. "I told you," he whispered.

"You did." I felt terrible that I hadn't taken his word about the staircase. Especially when it seemed to mean so much to him. "I'm sorry I didn't believe you. You were right. We found this staircase behind the kitchen wall." I slid my finger across the screen and showed him the next photo. "Beyond the stairs we found a little room with this small fireplace. But this whole area was completely closed off on all three floors. And you can't see this chimney from the outside of the house, so they must've taken it down, brick by brick."

"It was the servants' parlor," he murmured, and curled arthritic fingers around the edges of the tablet.

"But why did they close it off? They even went to the

trouble of changing the blueprints so nobody knew it was there."

He pressed one hand against the bench seat and seemed to brace himself before speaking. "A young girl was attacked on those back stairs." He took another breath and kept talking. It was painful to listen to him struggle for words. "She was a sweet girl, and pretty. Betsy was her name. They hurt her, you see. Badly. She wasn't the same after that."

"Did they punish the person who hurt her?"

"No," he uttered in disgust. "She would never say who did it, but we knew. We knew."

"You couldn't do anything about it?"

"Not without her testimony. Frankly, even if she'd testified, they never would've prosecuted the evil man who did it. The navy decided to close off that dangerous passageway rather than discipline the man who did those horrible things."

I patted his arm. "I'm so sorry."

Aldous shot me a sideways glance. "The man was untouchable back then. He was a high-ranking officer. The one who did all that bad stuff. You understand."

"I'm afraid so." The navy wouldn't want to risk receiving negative PR over one insignificant housemaid.

"I'd like to say times have changed," he said, "but they haven't, have they?"

"Some things are changing," I said lamely, unable to think of anything that would make him feel better.

He reached over and I felt again the crepe-paper-thin skin of his hand as he patted mine in sympathy. "Perhaps you're right, dear. Things do seem to be changing. Altogether too fast sometimes, if you ask me." He pursed his lips tightly, and then slowly he seemed to make a conscious effort to smile. I wouldn't have been surprised to find out it was the first time he'd done so in months.

"It's good you uncovered those stairs," he said. "Betsy deserves to be remembered, not shut away behind walls and deaf ears."

I got a chill, but he was right. Finding the stairs would allow us to shine a light on the past.

"My offer to show you around the mansion still stands," I said. "Whenever you'd like me to drive you out there."

"I appreciate that. And thank you for showing me the pictures, Shannon, dear. I've got to admit, I thought I might be going a little senile for a while there."

"Not you, Mr. Murch," I said, chuckling. "Not you."

On my way home, I stopped to visit Lizzie at Paper Moon on the square. "Any word on Cliff?"

"Let's go get a latte," she whispered. We both waved to Hal, who smiled and shooed us off. "I can take fifteen minutes."

We didn't speak as we walked three doors down from her shop to the coffeehouse, where I bought two lattes. We found a quiet corner and sat to talk. Lizzie took a sip first and then said, "Cliff is still in intensive care but not quite as critical as earlier."

"Have you heard if they arrested Denise or not?"

"I haven't heard, which is sad, because why have a stupid police scanner if you can't get the latest updates?"

"Why, indeed?"

I filled her in on everything Mac had told me about Denise bashing Cliff with the shovel and the interesting detail of him trying to blackmail her.

"Blackmail?" Lizzie repeated. "What could she have possibly done that would cause someone to blackmail her?"

"I can't figure it out. Is it something that happened back in high school or is it more recent?"

"I wonder if it has something to do with Lily."

"That was my first guess."

"I'll talk to Hal. He might know something."

"Okay, and if you see anyone else who might have a clue, ask them. I want to know what the heck Cliff was thinking."

"And we don't know if Denise has been arrested," she said. "I hope they let her go."

"Me, too," I whispered. "It sounds like Cliff would've killed her if he'd had the chance."

I walked Lizzie back to the store and drove toward home. We had both promised to call each other first thing if we heard anything. Because that's how our small-town world operated.

It bothered me that Cliff had told Denise something so outrageous that she'd taken a lethal swing at him. I supposed the story would leak out eventually, so I would just have to wait. Patience, sadly, was not my greatest virtue.

When I got home, I dashed up the stairs that led to the apartment over the garage to look for Mac. After a few seconds of my pounding on the door, he answered, looking as though he hadn't slept all night. He wore a ratty old T-shirt with holes, an ancient pair of cargo shorts, and flip-flops. Despite all that, he looked ridiculously sexy.

"Are you working?" I asked, recognizing his usual writing attire.

"No, because someone was hammering on my door so loudly I couldn't concentrate." He said it with a gleam in his eye, so I didn't feel too awful for interrupting.

"Sorry, but I have to talk to you."

He swung the door open. "Come in. Talk to me."

The large studio apartment was neater than I'd thought it would be, given that Mac was in writing mode. Yes, his desk was a mess, but that was to be expected. The king-sized bed was made, though, with all the pillows stacked in an orderly fashion. The small dining table in front of the bay window held only a thin vase with a sprig of flowers from my garden.

"What's up?" he said.

"There's a secret room behind the kitchen wall with a fireplace and a staircase going to the second and third floors," I told him.

He pulled out one of the chairs next to the table. "Sit. Breathe."

I plopped down, realizing for the first time how fast my heart was beating. It was no wonder. I had discovered a secret room!

Mac pulled out the other chair and joined me at the table. "So, Aldous had the right of it after all."

"Yes, and I felt so bad. I tracked him down a while ago to show him pictures and tell him about it. He had tears in his eyes, and it almost broke my heart."

"Can I see the pictures?"

"Oh yeah." I pulled my tablet out of my bag and handed it to him.

As he gazed at the photographs, I related the entire story to Mac, of poor Betsy's attack on the back stairs and the cover-up that followed. When I was done, Mac took my hand and we sat in silence for several long minutes.

"I admit I'm fascinated by the hidden staircase," Mac said. "But its history is so dark, I wonder if the whole thing should be walled up again."

"You should look it over before you decide, of course. But maybe you could hang a plaque in there. And maybe your story could be a tribute of sorts to Betsy." I shrugged, feeling a little silly for telling a bestselling author how to write. "Or not, if that isn't your style."

He squeezed my hand. "I'd like to think I have it in me to do her justice."

"Oh, Mac." I rewarded him with a bright smile. "I know you do."

Eventually the subject changed back to Lily. Mac brought his computer over to the table and typed rapidly as I told stories of those days back in high school. I switched to Denise's attack on Cliff and conjectured here and there, wondering if Denise had been sleeping with Cliff and speculating on which other girls Cliff might've been dating. I knew he had asked me out, and Whitney, too. But not Jane. So who else had Cliff Hogarth been interested in? Did he make some girl so jealous that she stalked Lily and killed her? And what about the present day? Was Cliff spreading lies about other people besides Denise? And me? I'd almost forgotten my desire to sue him for slander. The lawsuit would have to wait until he was healthy enough to be dragged into court.

I told Mac what Denise had said about Dismal Dain and his weird attraction to Mr. Jones's biology rats. I told him more about Sean and Lily's father, and wondered aloud if Hugh Brogan had had something to do with

Lily's demise. I didn't mention her pregnancy or anything else that Eric had told me in confidence. I knew that detail would be revealed eventually and it would be important to Mac's article. But for now he had enough ghoulishly useful information to begin setting the scene for Lily's death.

I drove back to school to finish up the day with my parking-lot crew. As I watched the backhoe scoop up big chunks of asphalt into its loader, Whitney approached. I braced myself for her latest insult, but she was too shaken to verbally abuse me.

"What's wrong with you?" I asked.

"I'm just so upset about Cliff." She sniffled into a tissue, seeming genuinely distraught. "Just when he was getting his life back together, this had to happen. It's not fair."

"Well, if you really want to be fair, you must admit he had to have said something pretty awful to Denise if she was driven to try to hit him like that."

Whitney uttered a sound of contempt. "It figures you would have no sympathy for him."

"Hey, I'm glad he's not dead. But my real sympathy is for Denise. And yours should be, too. I thought you guys were good friends!"

"We are! Of course we are," Whitney insisted. "But Cliff's the one in the hospital."

"I'm sure Tommy told you the whole story. Denise was fighting for her life when she finally hit him."

"Whatever. I still feel for Cliff," she said. "And if Denise hadn't confessed that she hit him, I would suspect you. You hate him and I don't know why. Wait. Yes, I do.

It's because you're jealous because he liked me so much."

"Oh my God," I muttered, and started to walk away. But I couldn't let it go. I just couldn't. I turned around and said, "The way you've been yammering on and on about how much you like Cliff Hogarth and how he was always asking you out, and how you wanted to give him a job at your house? It makes *Tommy* look more like a suspect than I could ever be. So think about that."

Her face turned pale. She opened her mouth to speak but nothing came out.

I couldn't have asked for a better reaction, so I spun around and walked away as fast as I could. It wasn't often I managed to get the last word in with Whitney and I wanted to enjoy the moment.

I kept walking and ended up at the main school building, staring up at the double doors leading inside. I didn't want to walk back to the parking lot and take a chance on running into Whitney again, so I walked up the stairs and into the building. Maybe I would stop in and say hello to Ms. Barney.

But once inside, I leaned against the door and sighed. I didn't know why Whitney was so determined to defend Cliff when she was supposedly such good friends with Denise. I had to think it was only because of me. Tommy refused to hire anyone else to do the work on their house but me, and Whitney didn't like that one bit. She wanted Cliff. Or anyone else, for that matter. Anyone except me.

And that was too darned bad.

"You look like you're hiding from someone."

I turned around and smiled. "Hello, Mr. Jones."

"Hello, Shannon." He glanced out the window. "Who are you hiding from?"

If only I could tell the truth, but instead I continued to smile and told a small fib. "I'm waiting for someone, but it looks like they'll be late." My smile faded as I realized what he'd been through today. "Is Denise okay, Mr. Jones? I'm so worried about her."

"She'll be fine," he said somberly. "She's home, resting."

"Home? Oh, I'm so glad. I thought the police might . . . Well. I'm glad she's home."

"You thought they might arrest her for attacking that blackmailing scumball?" He touched my arm. "I'm sorry for that. Pardon my language. It's not very charitable of me. But no, she's not being arrested. The police believe she hit him in self-defense. And fortunately Hogarth is still alive, so we'll have to wait and see what happens."

I'd never heard him utter a harsh word before, so I knew he had to be upset. "If she needs a character reference, I'll be happy to talk to Chief Jensen." I gave a slight shrug. "Not that I'm anyone special, but every little bit helps."

"That's not true. You're very special, Shannon. And I appreciate it." He gave me a tired smile, and I thought how hard this had to be on him. "I'll let you know if we need any extra help."

"Okay." I gazed out the window again. "Well, I guess I'd better go back to work. Maybe my friend meant to meet me at the parking lot. That's where I can usually be found most days." Another fib, but I didn't feel bad about it.

"I have a free period, so I'll walk with you." He pushed open the door and we strolled down the stairs together. The wind had picked up and I zipped my vest closed.

"I was going to stay home with her," he said, "but Denise told me to go back to work because I was driving her crazy. I think I'm more nervous than she is."

"I don't blame you. It must have been terrifying to hear what happened."

"Yes, that's the perfect word for it." He shook his head as if to shake off the bad vibes and gazed around at the beautiful campus. "You're making excellent progress on the parking lot."

"It's coming along pretty well."

"It's nice to see Sean Brogan hard at work every day," he said. "He always says hello."

"He's a great team player," I said, pushing my wind-swept hair off my face. "I'm lucky to have him on my crew."

"The Brogan children overcame a lot of obstacles," he murmured. "Their father was a real brute."

"Did you ever have to deal with him?" I asked.

"Oh yes," he said, his eyes narrowed in thought. "I had a few run-ins with Hugh Brogan. The man was a true bully. He considered his children his property, his chattel, really. He refused to take advice from anyone else."

"You tried to talk to him?"

"Yes, about Lily." His jaw tightened. "It didn't go well."

"I'm so sorry."

"Me, too." He stared across the greenbelt and I wondered if he was looking into the past. "I just . . . I just wish Lily had been given the chance to get that scholarship and go to college as she'd always dreamed of doing."

"I wish she had, too. She was so smart and talented, she could've done anything she wanted with her life."

"True." Mr. Jones checked his wristwatch and sighed. "I'd better get back to the classroom."

"Thank you for walking with me. Please let Denise know that my thoughts are with her."

"I will." He smiled. "Thank you, Shannon. It's always great to talk to you." He turned and jogged back to school.

I came home from work a grungy mess, covered with dirt from head to toe. I jumped into the shower to wash my hair and scrub myself clean, and when I'd dried myself off and put on fresh clothes, I felt so much better. I was filling the animals' bowls with water and wondering what to do about dinner when the doorbell rang and I ran to answer it. "Eric, hi. What a surprise."

"Hello, Shannon." He was leaning against the porch railing, looking casually gorgeous in his distressed-leather bomber jacket. "Was there something you wanted to tell me?"

"Me? I don't think so."

He took a step closer and said, "Something about a conversation you had with Cliff Hogarth?"

Understanding dawned. "Oh, that."

"Yeah, that."

I held up both hands in a sign of capitulation. "I can explain."

"I'm all ears."

"Okay, look. My crew guy Douglas had just told me that Cliff had offered him a bunch of money to leave me and go work with him. And I freaked out. That was the last straw. I was going to read Cliff the riot act, so I tracked him down to the Inn on Main Street and told him what I thought of him."

"An eyewitness says you threatened him."

"Maybe a little."

Eric shook his head. "So where'd you go after that?"

"I, um, drove out to the Gardens and talked to Denise." I frowned. "Why? We just talked. I didn't do anything wrong."

"I didn't say you did. I just have another question or two." He glanced over my shoulder at the front door. "May I come in for a minute?"

"Oh, sure." I held the door open until he was inside, then shut it securely. "Would you like something to drink?"

"No, thanks."

I gestured toward the two chairs by the bay window. "Have a seat. How can I help?"

He took off his jacket and tossed it on the couch before sitting down, then pulled a small notepad from his pocket and opened it. "I wanted to know if Denise Jones said anything to you yesterday that made you think she might have a grudge against Cliff Hogarth."

"A grudge? But you can't think she actually planned to hit him. He attacked her. She bashed his head in self-defense."

"We only have her word that it happened that way."

I squeezed my eyes shut and tried to remember our conversation, then looked over at him. "I won't pretend we didn't talk about Cliff, because I drove straight from my confrontation with him to the Gardens, where I ran into Denise."

"Why did you go to see her?"

"I didn't. I just went to stroll around the Gardens. It's pretty and peaceful out there, and I go sometimes when I need to think or unwind. And I needed to do both yesterday."

"So you walked around for a little while and then you ran into Denise?"

"That's right. I wasn't going to say a word about Cliff, but we got to talking and I ended up telling her what had happened. She basically admitted that Cliff was always a troublemaker, even back in high school. He was always pushing people's buttons."

"Guess he pushed a few of yours."

"You could say that. Denise agrees with me that Cliff's timing is interesting. Why did he suddenly move back to town barely two months before we discovered Lily's body?"

"Did she think the two events were connected?"

"She did. And I've been thinking about this. Cliff was in real estate. He could've heard that the lighthouse mansion had been sold and that someone would be moving in soon. He knew Lily's body would be discovered and he decided he'd better be nearby when it happened."

"Did Denise say that?"

"No. I'm saying it now to you. It's just something to think about." I glanced at him. "Also, just so you know, all the time I was talking to Denise, I was thinking I'd have to call and tell you everything she said."

He was scribbling rapidly. "But you didn't."

"You didn't give me a chance." He shot me one of his looks, and I quickly added, "It's only been a day since I was out there talking to her. So much has happened since then, I've lost track."

As he wrote something down, I added, "Did Denise tell you we talked?"

"She mentioned it."

"So you were hoping I'd corroborate her story."

I got another of his looks.

"One thing you should know," I continued, "is that I was the one ranting about Cliff, not Denise. She was the one who calmed me down and changed the subject. She didn't want to feed my anger, as she put it. So we talked about cooking. And rats. Nothing that would interest you."

He raised an eyebrow. "You talked about rats?"

"Mm-hmm." I smiled. "We talked about Dismal Dain and how he used to take care of Mr. Jones's biology-class rats during school vacations. Just one more disturbing aspect of Mr. Dain's odd personality."

A little while later, after Eric left, Callie went to the library with her girlfriends—and, yes, they were actually going to the library to study, she insisted. Mac and I stayed home and grilled steaks. We had potatoes baking in the oven, and while I prepared a salad, we talked more about Aldous Murch and his tale of the housemaid who was assaulted.

"With Betsy's sad story and the discovery of Lily's bones, I might have to bring in a coven of witches to cleanse the place," Mac said.

"Not a bad idea," I replied.

"So, you are the hero of the hour," he said, holding up his wineglass in a toast. "Despite all the grisly details, I think congratulations are in order. You broke through that wall and found a whole new section of the house. That's amazing."

"It's an uncomfortably small section, but yes. It has a parlor with a fireplace, and there's a narrow staircase going up to the second floor. It's a hazard right now and I wouldn't trust anyone to walk on it, but once it's been reinforced, you can use it as a back staircase."

"Cool. Good work, Irish." He reached over and clinked his glass against mine for a second time. "Cheers."

"Thanks." I sipped my wine. "I think Aldous was happy."

"That's even better than plain old good work. That's awesome work."

I smiled at his accolades. "Thanks, Mac."

"And now I have even more history and mystery to add to my article. This is amazing."

And he doesn't even know the true motive behind Lily's death, I thought. But he would. The truth about her pregnancy would have to be revealed before long. Otherwise, a murderer would go free.

Chapter Fourteen

I spent the next day at the lighthouse mansion, where I continued to demolish Mac's kitchen. It felt darn good to be destroying things—in a constructive way, of course.

Carla joined in the fun and together we managed to pull out the heavy cast-iron sink and set it outside the kitchen door. I'd hired a forklift to carry the heaviest stuff over to the Dumpster a few dozen yards up the road. This sink, on the other hand, would be taken directly to my truck. I planned to restore it and use it in another lucky house—or, at the very least, I'd refashion it to use as a quirky planter in my garden.

"Hey, Shannon," Carla said, trying to get my attention over the hammering and pounding.

"Yeah." I set down the sledgehammer and grabbed my water bottle. "What's up?"

"I've been thinking about the dumbwaiter," she said, and rapped her knuckles against the old sliding door. "I think we'd be smart to go ahead and refurbish the internal mechanisms, replace the tray, and make sure the trolley system is operating. And then Mac can make his decision about the style of the outer frame any time he wants."

I stared at the dumbwaiter wall. The shaft itself couldn't be enlarged without damaging the structural integrity of the wall, so Mac would have to live with the dumbwaiter size as it was. And as far as I knew, the size was fine with him.

"Good idea," I said, taking a long sip of water. "I'll stop by the hardware store tonight and order the parts we need."

After that, I got caught up in the demolition until Carla reminded me that it was quarter to four.

"Oh, shoot. I've got to run." I put my tools away and grabbed my jacket and purse. "See you tomorrow."

"Have a good one, boss."

"You, too." I ran to my truck, drove over to the school, and parked, just as the digital clock on the dashboard hit four o'clock. I jogged over to check out my guys' work on the parking lot while I waited for Callie.

I waved to Wade. "It's starting to look better around here."

"We've cleared most of the asphalt, as you can see." He swiped his forehead with the back of his hand. "Tomorrow the geotech team will be back to test the subsurface and make sure the conditions of the soil deep beneath the asphalt are stable and good to go."

The geotechnical engineers were an important part of the whole picture. They'd already determined there were no soil issues around the perimeter, and now they would decide if the soil under the existing site would play nicely with the aggregate layer the company planned to lay down. That layer would be followed by the asphalt base layer and finally the asphalt surface layer. If it wasn't compatible—if there was, say, too much clay or too much iron—they would add more of some other mineral until everything was copacetic.

It was a complicated process and I didn't pretend to know exactly how they came up with their formulations. I was just glad they were paying attention.

"I'd hate to sink that water tank into the earth," I said, "and find out later that some corrosive element down there had eaten right through it."

"Exactly," Wade said. "The SolarLight people won't let that happen."

"They are a really smart bunch," I said.

"Yeah. I hope we can work with them again."

I smiled. "If Ms. Barney has her way, the school board will eventually turn all the parking lots solar and probably some of the outside lunch areas."

"I like it," he said, grinning.

My phone buzzed and I excused myself to check it. There was a text from Callie saying that she would be a few minutes late. She was still talking to her homeroom teacher.

I glanced up at Wade. "I think I'll walk over to the school and meet Callie."

"I'll get back to the cleanup, then. See you later, boss."

I headed for the main building, hoping I'd run into Callie on the way. Then again, if I made it as far as the classroom, I'd be able to say hello to Mr. Jones. I was curious to find out how Denise was doing.

On the way, I thought about Cliff, still clinging to life in the hospital. What would happen when he recovered? Would he go back to being a jerk or would he be chastened? Everyone would know that he'd tried to black-mail Denise, who was a beloved lifelong resident of

Lighthouse Cove. How would he be able to face anyone? Never mind; I knew the answer. He would bluster and lie his way through, because that was what he'd been doing since high school.

By the time he'd finished, Cliff would have Denise looking like some chainsaw-wielding serial killer from a B movie.

And thinking of Cliff made me wonder for the umpteenth time why or what, exactly, he'd been trying to blackmail Denise over.

I didn't run into Callie out on the walkway, so I kept going to Mr. Jones's homeroom class. The door was closed, so I peeked inside through the reinforced-glass square. Mr. Jones sat at his desk in the front of the room and Callie stood talking to him.

She looked so pretty in a simple blue sweater and jeans, with her long blond hair worn in a single braid down her back. Mr. Jones, as always, was sweet and handsome and interested in whatever she had to say. But I was most struck by the look on Callie's face. If I had to put a name to it, I'd call it adoration.

Strange, but I was almost afraid to interrupt their conversation. I went ahead, though, and knocked on the door and walked inside. "Hi, you two."

"Hello, Shannon," Mr. Jones said.

"Hi, Mr. Jones." I gazed at Callie. "Are you ready to go, Callie?"

She winced. "Shannon, I'm so sorry. I should've texted you again. I'm going to stay for rehearsals and hang out with Sarah for a while. Uncle Mac said he'd pick me up in a few hours. Do you mind?"

"Not a bit," I assured her, then turned to Mr. Jones. "I hope Denise is feeling better."

"She is, and she so appreciates your thoughtfulness."

"I'm glad." I smiled, feeling oddly awkward. I wasn't sure what it was that made this moment feel a little peculiar. It wasn't just seeing the way Callie was looking at him. It was more than that. But since I couldn't put my finger on it, I just took a deep breath and let it go. "Okay, I guess I'll see you both later."

They waved, and I turned to leave the classroom just in time to see Dismal Dain standing across the hall, staring straight into the classroom at Mr. Jones. Or was he looking at Callie? He wore an ugly glower, and it didn't matter which of them he was looking at. Either way, it wasn't a good thing. Dain's mouth was sullen and his eyes were dulled by bitterness. Maybe it was my imagination, but he looked a lot like one of those rats he was so fond of.

I glared back at him. There was no way I would allow that spooky excuse for a counselor to stare at Mac's niece with such animosity. And I was worried for Mr. Jones, too. I wondered if Dain made a habit of staring at Mr. Jones like that. Finally Dain gave a scornful sniff and skulked off, leaving me to wonder what was wrong with his mind.

Was he jealous that the students liked Mr. Jones? I certainly hoped he didn't intend to "counsel" Callie anytime soon.

I glanced back and realized that Mr. Jones and Callie hadn't even noticed Dismal was watching them. Brad Jones was so in tune with his students, but I wondered if he had ever noticed the counselor staring at him from across the hall.

By the time I got to my truck, I was feeling antsy and out of sorts and not ready to call it a day. I was worried about Callie because of that look I'd seen on Dismal's face. The man was like a cautionary tale about the scary neighbor down the street whose house was always dark and whose yard was covered in dead plants and trees. Your parents always warned you not to venture too close. . . .

And there went my imagination again. But, honestly, how creepy was it that he was standing there glaring at Mr. Jones and Callie? Very creepy, indeed! High school seemed to be even more of a soap opera than I remembered. As for Dismal, it was hard to shake off the miasma that seemed to follow him around like a dark cloud and envelop everyone else in the vicinity.

I stopped at a red light and glanced over at the passenger's seat. There was my tablet with my list of things to do. And that reminded me of the one thing I hadn't done. I'd promised Carla I'd order supplies for the dumbwaiter tonight, but I'd completely forgotten to get the measurements I needed.

I made a U-turn and drove the short distance out to the lighthouse mansion. Despite its many twists and turns and wide curves, the three-mile drive north relaxed me and took my mind off of all the people who had been in my face lately. Like Mr. Dain and Cliff and Whitney. Although, to be fair, I had been in Cliff's face as much or more than he'd been in mine, only because he seemed just as happy to stab you in the back as face you head-on.

Since I was wearing my Bluetooth, I gave Mac a quick call to let him know I'd seen Callie briefly. I didn't mention Dismal Dain's odd presence in the hall.

"Where are you?" he asked.

"I'm driving out to the mansion to get a few measurements. Then I'm stopping at the hardware store to pick up some things."

"Any chance we can have dinner together later? I had a craving for pasta, and the red sauce is cooking as we speak."

"I am very fond of red sauce, as you know."

I could almost hear him grinning over the phone. "And I'm very fond of you."

"Oh." I was surprised and happy and bashful all of a sudden. "Well, likewise."

He chuckled and the sound was amazingly intimate. "Be careful out there, Irish. Hurry home."

"Okay." I disconnected the call and sighed. Maybe when Callie went back home, he and I could take up where we'd left off. Wherever that was.

I turned onto Old Lighthouse Road and bumped along over the potholes and cracks for a quarter of a mile until I reached the big house at the end of the road. There were still a few cars parked over by the massive, towering lighthouse, so I figured it was still open for business a while longer. Perhaps some tourists were up at the top, enjoying the sunset. I envied them.

Standing outside of my truck, I breathed the sea air and let my gaze sweep across the water. A few sailboats skimmed the surface, but the water was turning choppy, with white froth slapping into the air. I heard the waves pounding at the rocks beyond the lighthouse and it sounded like a heartbeat, with its comforting, steady rhythm.

For some reason, the air here felt cleaner than in town, even though my house was only a few blocks from the shore. Maybe it was the fact that there were no stores and streets in the way. Out here, there was nothing standing between me and the immense ocean.

I crossed the wide, scruffy lawn and unlocked the door.

It was getting dark, and I flipped on a few lights as I made my way back to the kitchen to examine the dumbwaiter. The counters were gone, so I set my tablet and purse on the floor and pulled out my pocket tape measure.

As I measured the space and made a list of the hardware we would have to replace, I was careful not to look down into the basement below. It still gave me chills to think of Lily's bones lying there. Instead I forced myself to study and admire the interior design of the dumbwaiter. I loved quirky Victorian contraptions like those, and Mac's mansion was filled with them. I was determined to renovate this house so beautifully that Mac would never connect death and murder to his new home.

Being Mac, though, he would clearly relish those very things I was trying to gloss over.

I leaned farther into the dumbwaiter shaft to measure the panel on the far side of the opening. I froze when I thought I heard something.

I pulled my head out of the chamber and the sound disappeared. I wondered if I had imagined it.

I stuck my head back inside the shaft and heard it again. Something was scraping against an interior wall of the house. Was it being amplified inside the dumbwaiter?

"Oh, God." I pulled out and stood up straight. I couldn't hear anything out here, so I poked my head back into the dumbwaiter shaft and heard it again.

Darn it, why had I come back here alone? Why weren't any of my crew working late today? I was suddenly leery of being in a place I'd known my whole life. And I didn't like the feeling.

Had a new family of rodents moved into the house? I trembled at the thought. Then again, maybe it was only a tree branch brushing against the outside wall or the roof.

I stood up straight and tried very carefully to hear the sound again. But there was nothing. I heard it only inside the dumbwaiter, so I stuck my head inside the thing again. And now I could hear the distinct murmur of a human voice.

I wasn't alone in the house.

More shivers flitted and leaped over every inch of my skin, covering me from the top of my head to my ankles. Truly, I could feel my ankles shaking. I had chills on top of the shivers, and now I had a choice of running screaming out of there or investigating whoever else was inside Mac's house with me.

If anyone had been watching me, I knew what they'd be thinking: I could also call the police. But if I dragged Eric out here for nothing, I'd look crazier than he already thought I was.

But if I didn't drag Eric out here and something happened . . .

I compromised and sent a text to let him know where I was and that I was checking out some odd noises. He could make the next move.

I had already run screaming out of the house once before when I saw that tiny rat a while ago, so call me cuckoo, but I was determined not to leave until I found out what was going on. I wasn't sure if the noises had come from upstairs or from the basement, but I felt safer checking upstairs first.

I tiptoed across the foyer and quietly climbed the stairs, unsure if the talking had come from the second floor or the attic. *It had to be the second floor,* I reasoned, because I really didn't want to go all the way up to the attic. That made a perfect kind of sense to me. *Didn't it?*

As I got closer to the top of the stairs I could hear the

mumbled words growing louder. Prepared to run at any second, I took a tentative step onto the second-floor landing and was shocked to see someone down the hall by the laundry chute.

"Aldous?"

The old man jolted, then turned and grinned at me. "Shannon! I was looking for the spot on the second floor where the old staircase would've been and couldn't find a trace. They walled over the doorway. Did a good job, too." He held up what looked like an old backpack. "So, I was looking around up here and I found this. It was stuck in the laundry chute."

It took me a full minute to catch my breath from being frightened half to death. "Aldous, what're you doing here all alone? How did you get here?"

"My granddaughter has some friends visiting and she brought them up here to see the lighthouse. I hitched a ride, but I couldn't make the climb up to the top of the lighthouse. So while the girls went exploring, I wandered over here. The back door was open, so I figured, *What the heck?* Thought I'd take a look around."

"All righty." Relief flooded through me. My intruder was no more than a curious old man who had vivid memories of this house. But my breath remained stilted as I led the way downstairs to the kitchen, where the lights were brightest and we could see exactly what he'd found in the chute.

"I guess you saw the kitchen demolition in progress," I said.

"Sure did," he said, looking around. "It's a real mess you've got here, Shannon. I hope you show me what it looks like when you've worked your magic on it."

"Promise. Okay, let's see what you've got." I turned on the light that had once shone over the now-departed sink, and he held up the backpack. I unlatched the wide front pocket and pulled out a school notebook.

"Must be some kid's," he said.

"Yeah." But I already knew whose it was as I flipped the notebook open. The first page was covered in doodles and flowery writing that looked like a young girl's. Here and there on the page were hearts drawn around the initials BJ and LB.

"Lily Brogan," I murmured. But who was BJ? I mentally scanned the list of boys who'd been in school with Lily and couldn't think of anyone with those initials. And suddenly my heart stuttered in my chest. Not a boy. A man. And a teacher. "Brad Jones."

"What's that?" Aldous said.

"Nothing," I said, my voice a hoarse whisper. "Sorry, Mr. Murch. I was just thinking out loud."

And I hated what I was thinking. *It doesn't have to mean anything,* I tried to convince myself. Every girl in school had had a crush on Mr. Jones. There had to be a dozen girls who'd encircled their initials with his when doodling in notebooks. We all imagined ourselves walking down the aisle with him.

But Lily had gone missing. Lily had been pregnant. And Lily had drawn little hearts with Mr. Jones's initials on her notebooks. It couldn't be true, could it?

But no matter what I told myself, I knew it had to be true. Brad Jones had to have been the father of Lily's baby.

Now that I accepted that thought, I kept remembering little clues, little things that had happened lately. Mr.

Jones had known that Lily had been trying to get a scholarship. He'd talked about it just the other day when he mentioned that her father had been such a bully.

Sean had told me that Lily had refused to tell anyone about her dream of college after being discouraged by Dismal Dean's remarks. Had Mr. Jones known about her dream before Dean did?

I suddenly knew why I'd had that peculiar feeling when I saw Callie talking to Mr. Jones earlier. It was the look of teenage worship on her face. I'd seen that look so many times over the years whenever I saw Mr. Jones talking to a teenage girl.

I was reminded of a day back in high school when I happened to see Lily talking to Mr. Jones in his classroom. But rather than an artless, adolescent crush, the look on Lily's face had revealed so much more. She had looked positively radiant, mature, and deeply in love. And I knew now, as surely as I knew my own name, that Lily had been pregnant with Mr. Jones's child.

Not that those few minor facts alone were the reason I believed what I did. But added to all that was the fact that Cliff Hogarth had tried to blackmail Denise. It made me wonder if Cliff had known that Brad Jones was the father of Lily's baby.

But how did Cliff even find out that Lily was pregnant? Did she tell him? I couldn't imagine she would.

Putting those thoughts aside, I returned to the backpack. Opening the main pocket, I could clearly see a flimsy blouse and a balled-up pair of jeans. There were possibly shoes and socks and underwear beneath the jeans, but I didn't want to disturb the contents any more than I already had.

"Mr. Murch," I said, "let's go find your granddaughter and get you back to town."

"That would be swell, Shannon." He rubbed his stomach. "I'm getting a little peckish, now that you mention it."

For me, that red sauce Mac had promised didn't sound quite so appetizing anymore.

Once I dropped off Mr. Murch, I swung by the police station to see Eric. He didn't seem surprised that I was bringing him a key piece of evidence.

"Mr. Murch found it stuck in the laundry chute," I said, holding up the backpack.

He frowned. "The laundry chute would empty into the basement."

"That's my assumption, although I haven't inspected it well enough to make sure."

"I'm surprised."

"I know," I said, smiling. "I've been slacking off."

"Don't worry about it," he said. "We'll take it from here."

Eric decided another search of the lighthouse mansion could wait until the next day, since time wasn't really a factor anymore. So all day Friday, the police conducted an intensive search of Mac's house. They called in the county crime-scene specialists, who combed through the backpack and notebook and other odds and ends Lily had carried with her. They searched the attic for even more evidence, but didn't find much.

Inside the dumbwaiter they found traces of blood.

In the laundry chute they discovered minute threads

that had caught on the wooden surface. The threads could've come from any material that had ever been sent down the chute, but the specialists would run tests to see if any of them had come from Lily's backpack.

Eric's comment the night before about the chute leading to the basement made me wonder if Lily's killer had debated whether to drop her body down the chute, as if she were nothing more than a sack of laundry, or simply stuff her into the dumbwaiter. Obviously, he had decided on the dumbwaiter. The thought that someone could be so cold-blooded that they would leave her in that place alone, in the dark, and walk away made me sick.

Mac and I had a delightful and very interesting pasta dinner Friday night. Callie popped into my kitchen to tell us she was home from her girlfriend's house and, thankfully, that glow I'd seen on her face while she'd been talking to Mr. Jones was mostly gone, and she had morphed back into a normal teenage girl.

Once she went up to her room, I asked Mac, "Did Eric tell you why the police were searching your house all day?"

Mac gazed at me as he sipped his wine. "I think you probably know why."

I grimaced. "I do, but I don't want to break any confidences."

"Then I'll let you off the hook. He told me that Lily was pregnant with Brad Jones's baby."

My shoulders sagged in relief. "I was dying to tell you, but I just couldn't."

He smiled. "I think it's admirable that you can keep a secret, but I obviously need to work on my coercion skills."

"No, you don't," I muttered.

That made him grin, but he quickly sobered. "Brad seems like a nice guy, but hasn't anyone expressed concern that Lily was underage when she got pregnant by her teacher?"

"That bothers me a lot," I admitted. "But I remembered that Lily had been held back a year in grammar school, so she was eighteen years old when she was a senior. Don't get me wrong—I'm not excusing Brad. But, officially, she was an adult."

He nodded thoughtfully, then thanked me for taking him into my confidence.

"I would've told you everything sooner because I trust you," I said. "But I just couldn't break Eric's confidence."

"I appreciate you saying you trust me, because I feel the same about you."

"Thank you." And after hearing myself say it out loud, I realized it was true. I trusted Mac completely. "So Eric told you all about the backpack and notebook we found in the laundry chute?"

"Backpack? Notebook?" His eyes widened and he grinned. "I know nothing. Tell me. Hold nothing back."

"That's how we found out it was Brad's baby." I told him what Aldous had found in the laundry chute and how I'd seen those hearts all over her notebook and figured out that Mr. Jones was the father of Lily's baby.

"Wow," Mac said. "I remember looking into the laundry chute. I should've investigated it more thoroughly."

"I was thinking the same thing. We might've saved a lot of time and avoided some problems if we'd just cleaned out the laundry chute."

*   *   *

Saturday, while the police and crime-scene specialists continued to work at the lighthouse mansion, I took a few hours to drive out to Uncle Pete's winery to visit him and my dad. I had talked to Dad on the phone briefly the other night, and he reported that the barn was almost finished. They would be rolling two huge new tanks into the space soon, and Dad would finish the construction project and go fishing for a few days before heading back to Lighthouse Cove.

Uncle Pete's business had more than doubled in the past few years, so there was always something new to see at the winery. I parked my car under a shady tree and walked around until I found my dad in the barrel room. It was dark and cool, and Dad was in the process of moving one of the heavy oak barrels over to make room for another.

"Dad? Should you be lifting that by yourself?"

He stood up and grinned. "There's my girl."

My heart fluttered at his greeting. He had always called me his girl. I rushed over and gave him a big hug.

"Missed you, honey," he murmured.

"I've missed you so much."

"Hey, what's wrong? What's going on?" He frowned as he studied my face. "Did something happen? Someone hurt you?"

"No, it's just been a weird time."

Dad grabbed two wineglasses and walked over to a barrel. He removed the cork and stuck a long glass tube—sometimes called a thief—into the small hole and siphoned off some wine for each of our glasses.

"That's convenient," I said.

Dad chuckled, and we walked out of the dark barrel room into sunshine. Scattered across the wide patio between the winery tasting room and the fermentation barn were picnic tables and small seating areas. After our eyes adjusted to the light, we found a picnic table and sat down across from each other.

"Spill the beans, honey," Dad said. "If you need me to come back to town, I'll do it."

"No, I can fight my own battles." But I wasn't so sure that was true when it came to fighting Cliff Hogarth and his slanderous comments. I told Dad all about Cliff's horrible remarks about me and our various run-ins. I concluded with the fact that the guy was now in a coma and laid out in some hospital bed because he'd tried to blackmail Denise.

"I hate to say it," Dad said, "but it looks like the guy got what was coming to him."

"It's awful to think that way, but I agree." And in retrospect, my problems weren't all that bad.

I filled Dad in on all the grim aspects of Lily's death and the investigation, omitting the truly grisly details of the baby and the backpack. He was especially intrigued by Aldous Murch's connection to the mansion.

"A hidden room with a staircase? That's right out of a mystery novel," Dad said.

"I know." I laughed.

He wasn't laughing, though. "I think I'd better cancel my fishing trip and stick closer to home. At least until Lily's killer is discovered."

"I'll be fine, Dad. I've got Mac right next door and Eric is just a phone call away. You've been working so hard out here. You need a vacation."

"Okay, I guess I can trust Mac and Eric to look out for you. But I want you to call me at the first sign of trouble."

"I promise."

Uncle Pete joined us then, and we spent the rest of the afternoon laughing and sipping a number of different wines. The two men gave me a tour of the new fermenting area and showed off their construction skills. We wandered through the vineyards, and later Uncle Pete served us a pasta salad that almost caused me to swoon.

I drove back to town, feeling so much better and more relaxed than I had in days. And I was looking forward to the day when Dad would park his big old RV in my driveway again.

Sunday morning I joined Lizzie and Hal and their adorable kids, Marisa and Taz, for a ten-mile bike ride down the coast. We stopped for a late breakfast at a funky old seafood diner we'd been going to forever.

"Lock up the bikes," Hal told the kids. "I'll get us a table."

Eleven-year-old Taz was happy to do it, and unwrapped the bike chain from around the seat of his bicycle. As he wound it through all five of the back wheels, his thirteen-year-old sister, Marisa, rolled her eyes and checked her phone.

Lizzie grabbed my arm and we followed her tall, lean, adorable husband up the old wooden steps to the front door and inside. The smells of bacon and syrup were instantly overwhelming, and we both grinned.

"I miss coming here," she said. "I'm having the waffles."

"I might do French toast."

"Ooh, good choice," she said. "And bacon."

"Naturally." I glanced outside. "Marisa is so beautiful, Lizzie. And Taz is going to be taller than Hal."

Lizzie peeked over my shoulder. "I can't tell you how

much I regret buying her that stupid phone, but what can you do?" She sighed. "She's still a good girl, but the hormones are starting to kick in. I expect her to turn into a monster any day now."

"You've been saying that for two years," I said, laughing. "But she's still very sweet."

"Thirteen going on twenty-five," Hal said, joining the conversation. "Come on, we've got a booth over here."

As we crossed the restaurant, Lizzie said, "I want to hear all about Lily and Sean and Mac and everything that's been happening with you. I feel like we haven't talked in weeks." She frowned. "Even though I just saw you the other day for fifteen measly minutes."

"And we were with the whole gang at the tea shop and it's hard to get a word in edgewise sometimes."

"True." We sat at a big round booth by a south-facing window, and from there we could see the entire coastline. The day was clear and sunny with a brisk offshore breeze.

We all ordered coffee or hot chocolate and juice. When the waitress rushed off to get our beverages, Lizzie pounced. "Now tell me everything that's going on. I don't get out much."

Hal shot me a grin. "That's why I bought the police scanner, babe. So we can keep up with the latest."

I had to laugh.

Hal quickly added, "Sorry about Wednesday morning, by the way. Sometimes they tend to jump the gun."

"No worries," I said. "Although it freaked me out a little."

"Yeah. Me, too," he admitted.

I turned to Lizzie, who was sitting next to me. "You're going to be very pleased with me."

"I am anyway, but why? What happened?"

"I played matchmaker the other day."

She gasped and clutched her hands to her chest. "I'm so proud."

With a laugh, I said, "You should be. I think I did a pretty good job."

"Tell me all," she said, bouncing in her seat. "Who, what, when, where, how."

"Sean," I said.

"Oh, excellent."

I proceeded to tell her about the drama teacher who needed a carpenter and so on, and so on.

"I'm so excited for him. And for you. I hope it works out." She took a quick sip of orange juice. "And if it does, I never want to hear any grief from you again."

Yikes. Seeing the determination in her eyes, I wondered if maybe I should've kept my accomplishment to myself. I sipped my coffee and changed the subject. "So, have you heard from Emily?"

"I left her two messages and finally had to hunt her down at the tea shop. At first she denied everything, but I hounded her."

"That's my girl," Hal murmured.

Lizzie grinned. "And guess what. She told me that the day we were all having lunch at the tea shop? That's the first time Gus ever made a move."

"I kind of thought so at the time," I said. "But, wow. Things looked pretty hot and . . . hmm." I glanced at the kids and tried to find a subtle way to say what I was thinking. "They looked like they might've been together before."

"I know," Lizzie murmured. "But she insisted they hadn't."

I thought about it and finally admitted, "I'm worried about her."

"Why? She looks so happy."

"I don't want him to hurt her."

Lizzie frowned. "Gus is a lot younger than her. And he does have a reputation with the ladies."

Marisa snickered. "You mean he's a horn dog."

Lizzie scowled. "Marisa!"

Her daughter shrugged, and Taz giggled. It was Lizzie's turn to roll her eyes.

"You know I think Gus is wonderful," I said. "But Emily is sort of fragile, don't you think?"

"She looks fragile," Hal said, "but she's probably a lot stronger than you give her credit for."

"I hope so."

"OMG, Mom!" Marisa cried, then whispered dramatically, "It's MacIntyre Sullivan!"

I turned in time to see Mac and Callie walk inside and glance around. Mac waved when he saw us and said something to Callie. Her eyes lit up and she rushed over to the booth, while he stayed up front and spoke to the hostess.

"Hi, Shannon!" she said. "What're you doing here?" Then she gazed around the table at the Logan family and flashed them all a friendly smile. "Hi, I'm Callie, Mac's niece."

"Callie," I said, "these are my friends Lizzie and Hal and Taz and Marisa."

There was a buzz of greetings back and forth until Mac finally joined Callie and more cheeriness was exchanged. Marisa was strangely silent and seemed in awe of the older girl.

"We've got a table right over here," Mac said to Callie.

"Okay. It was really nice meeting you all." Callie smiled at everyone and then homed in on Lizzie's daughter. "Marisa, I love your bike shirt. If you want, maybe after breakfast we can talk some more."

Marisa's eyes widened and her head bobbed in agreement. "Okay, yeah."

"Cool," Callie said, and walked away with her uncle.

Lizzie's eyes were bright with unshed tears as she turned toward me. "That was so sweet of her. She is remarkable."

"She really is," I said, glancing fondly at Callie's back.

Late that afternoon, I was exhausted but happy after all of the riding and laughing and eating. I sat on the couch, watching an old movie with Tiger and Robbie, and started to doze off. A loud knocking on the back door startled me awake.

I hurried into the kitchen and saw through the window that it was Mac, and I opened the door with a smile. "Hi, what's up?"

But he wasn't smiling. "Hey, Irish."

"What's wrong? Is it Callie? Come in." I grabbed his hand and pulled him into the kitchen. "Talk to me."

"It's Cliff Hogarth," he said somberly, taking my hand in his. "Somebody walked into his hospital room an hour ago and killed him."

My phone rang before I could say a word and I ran to answer it. Mac followed me.

I stared at him, stunned, as I picked up the phone. "Hello?"

"You'll never guess," Lizzie said.

"Yes, I will," I said, feeling numb. "Cliff Hogarth is dead."

*   *   *

I couldn't sleep. I didn't think I would ever be warm again despite the extra blanket I'd thrown over me and the socks I wore and the long knitted scarf wrapped around my neck. My cat was cuddled up beside me and Robbie slept at the foot of the bed, and I was still shivering. I couldn't help it, after hearing the details of Cliff's death.

Earlier that night, after we got the ugly news, Mac and Callie had stayed for dinner. None of us wanted to be alone, so I had thrown together meat loaf, mashed potatoes, and a veggie casserole. I didn't mind that the meal was constantly interrupted by phone calls from Lizzie and Hal, who wanted to share the latest police-scanner buzz and theories and gossip.

Finally, Mac called Eric directly. The chief grudgingly confided certain details Lizzie and Hal hadn't heard over the police scanner.

"Someone took advantage of a quiet Sunday night at the hospital," Mac said, after he hung up from talking to Eric. "They had a bare-bones staff on duty, and I guess it was easy for the killer to slip unnoticed into Cliff's room."

"What did they do?"

Mac took a quick bite of mashed potatoes before answering. "The investigators think the guy tampered with his IV tubing."

"You mean they disconnected it?"

"No, they injected another substance into it."

I grimaced. "Do they know what it was?"

"They're not willing to say until they run more tests, but I'm pretty sure they'll find some type of liquid rat poison or cyanide."

I cringed at the word *cyanide*. It sounded like something out of the Cold War. "Where would anyone ever find cyanide?"

He shrugged. "Rat poison. Pretty common to find some brands that contain cyanide."

"So why do you think it's cyanide?"

"I recognize the symptoms."

"Of cyanide poisoning?" But of course Mac would know the symptoms. He was always researching new and exciting ways to kill people.

"Yeah," he said. "The nurse thought Hogarth was suffocating, so she tried to clear his air passage. But it was no use. His entire body was shutting down, one system at a time. He was dead within minutes."

By Monday morning, the news of Cliff Hogarth's murder was on everyone's mind. The entire town seemed to be holding its collective breath, worried sick that someone else might die. I was pretty sure the killer had specifically targeted Cliff and didn't plan to go on a killing spree, but after tossing and turning all night, I wasn't feeling strong enough to bet money on it.

I had hated Cliff Hogarth and I'd wanted him to go away, but I couldn't ever wish such a horrible death on him. And to have it occur in a hospital? A place where people were meant to feel safe? It was doubly upsetting.

Mac, of course, was thriving on all the grisly news. I forgave him his buoyant joy, though, because he'd never met Cliff or any of the other players, for that matter. And I had a feeling he just might win a Pulitzer for the article he was writing, given all the macabre details he'd been able to gather from this gruesome case.

Eric's reaction was the complete opposite of Mac's,

naturally. He was frustrated and angry that another person had been killed on what he considered his watch. He redoubled his team's efforts to scour the evidence and find a connection between Lily Brogan's death fifteen years ago and Cliff Hogarth's murder yesterday.

Work always helped change my mood, so I attacked it with gusto. I was digging up the last remnants of asphalt around the edges of the old parking lot when Ms. Barney arrived at school. She greeted everyone on the crew and then pulled me aside to talk.

"Are you all right?" she asked.

I nodded, then admitted, "I'm a little shaken up."

"I thought you might be," Ms. Barney said, and that was when I remembered that she had been subjected to Cliff's innuendos when she hired me for the parking-lot job.

"I guess it's natural that everyone is looking over their shoulders," I said. "But I'm pretty sure Cliff was the only target. He made a lot of enemies in a very short time."

She sighed. "I know you weren't friends with him, but the news was still so shocking."

As I walked with her across campus, we shared what little we each knew about Cliff's death. She had heard the same basic story that Eric had told Mac. Apparently Cliff's killer had taken advantage of a slow afternoon at the hospital with not many staff members on duty. Later that night, someone had reported a pair of scrubs missing from the locker room in a size that would fit a normal-sized male, whatever that meant. There were no actual suspects so far, but having been on the receiving end of Cliff Hogarth's vitriol, I figured there were probably plenty of folks who were *not* mourning his loss.

All the anxiety over Cliff's death had made me forget about Lily for the moment. But now I was unsettled all over again by the fact that Mr. Jones and Lily might've been a couple all those years ago. Unfortunately, I couldn't share that news with Ms. Barney, because so far it was just a supposition I'd deduced from reading Lily's notebook.

Once Ms. Barney and I had exhausted the subject of Cliff's death, we kept our chitchat light, talking about what we'd done over the weekend and about school and the town and this and that. She insisted again that she planned to add more solar canopies around the campus, and I assured her once again that I would love to get the job.

"I hope we can make that happen," she said as we approached her office.

"Good morning, Ms. Barney."

We both glanced up and saw one of the school secretaries standing by the door to the principal's office.

"Hello, Helen," Ms. Barney said.

"Sorry to interrupt," Helen said, "but you have a phone call."

"Who is it, Helen?"

The secretary was about to speak when the double doors at the far end of the hall were flung open and Eric, Tommy, and a small phalanx of cops came marching into the school.

Eric walked straight up to Ms. Barney and spoke in a low voice. "I've got a warrant for the arrest of one of your teachers. I'd appreciate if you would call him out into the hall and leave the students inside the room while we speak to him."

Her face turned white, and I was afraid mine matched hers.

"Are you sure this is necessary while school is in session?" she asked.

"I'm afraid so."

She walked him a few yards down the hall, away from the group of secretaries, who were watching everything from her doorway. "Who do you want to see?"

Eric lowered his voice. "Bradford Jones."

Someone screamed behind us. We all turned and saw Helen, who had been following closely behind Ms. Barney. She quickly whipped around and raced back into the office.

And I knew the news would move faster than a bullet train around town.

"Eric, why?" I asked.

He pulled me to the side of the hall, where his men wouldn't hear me freaking out. I understood that Mr. Jones and Lily had had an affair, but standing here in the light of day, with Eric about to arrest him, I just couldn't believe that the teacher I admired and thought I knew so well could be a killer. "It's impossible."

Eric's jaw twitched. "You don't know that."

"But I know him. And I refuse to believe he killed Lily."

Ms. Barney approached us, looking very worried. She pointed down the hall. "He's in room 124."

Eric nodded. "Thank you, ma'am."

I grabbed his arm. "Please, Eric. Don't do this. He's not guilty. He can't be. He loved her."

He looked down at me and frowned. "Shannon, the evidence is overwhelming."

"What evidence? An old notebook? All that proved was that Lily had a crush on him, just like every other girl in school. But even if they had been together, it doesn't mean he killed her. Don't tell me you found his bloody fingerprints somewhere."

Eric glanced around to make sure we weren't being overheard. "Shannon, Jones was the father of Lily's child. She wrote it down in her notebook."

I swallowed hard. "But he's a good man. I refuse to believe he would hurt her."

"He was her teacher." Eric was speaking carefully, slowly, as he would to a very young child. Any other time I might have been insulted. "She was his student. They had sex. She told him she was pregnant, and he knew his career would be over if anyone found out."

"You don't know that. Maybe he was happy with the news. Maybe someone else was angry. What about Cliff? He was her boyfriend. Wouldn't he be furious to know she'd been with someone else? I think that would drive him crazy. He's always had a lot of rage boiling inside him." I had a sudden thought. "And he was trying to blackmail Denise! Cliff must've found out that her husband was the father of Lily's baby."

"Those are all good points," Eric admitted. "But the very fact that Cliff tried to blackmail Denise makes it even more likely that Brad Jones killed him."

"That is so unfair," I said. "Brad Jones is kind and thoughtful and . . . and squeamish! He could no more kill someone than fly to the moon."

"If he's innocent, he'll be free to go. But I have enough probable cause to take him in for questioning."

I glanced up and down the hall at the gathered officers. Lowering my voice even more, I said, "You've come here with six police officers to drag Mr. Jones out in handcuffs. You're treating him like he's a mass murderer.

It's going to ruin his career. Can't you at least wait until after school is out?"

"Trust me to handle this, Shannon."

I stared at him for a long moment and then nodded and stepped back. What else could I do? I couldn't spin around on the floor and throw a temper tantrum and embarrass myself—and Eric—in front of his officers. But I wanted to, darn it. Because I knew Brad had to be innocent.

Okay, I didn't actually *know* he was innocent, but how could he be guilty?

Ms. Barney had been standing off to the side, and Eric nodded at her. She looked so unhappy, but she dutifully slipped into the classroom and closed the door. Thirty seconds later, she emerged with Mr. Jones right behind her.

"Thank you," Eric said to the principal, who nodded grimly.

Tommy crossed the hall and stood in front of the classroom door, probably to keep any curious students from sneaking out.

Mr. Jones glanced from the police chief to Ms. Barney to me. "What's going on?"

Eric pulled a pair of handcuffs from his back pocket. "Bradford Jones, I have a warrant for your arrest in the murder of Lily Brogan."

Brad stared at him in horror. "What? Are you serious? No! I didn't kill Lily. I loved her. We were going to be married."

"You can tell me the whole story down at the station," Eric said quietly.

"The station? But I didn't . . ." His gaze darted around

the hall until he found me. "I swear I didn't hurt Lily, Shannon."

"I believe you," I said, and prayed I was right. But then I quickly brushed the doubts away. There was no way Brad Jones could ever hurt anyone. I was sure of it.

Brad stared at the handcuffs and straightened his shoulders. "Those won't be necessary, Chief Jensen. I'll go with you."

Eric took a moment to decide the best way to proceed, then simply took hold of Brad's arm and led him down the hall and out the door. Tommy and the other cops followed behind, and I, being no fool, joined them.

They got Brad seated in the back of the patrol car. The officer at the wheel had just started the engine when a silver truck careened into the parking lot and skidded to a stop. Denise jumped out of the cab of the truck and ran toward the patrol car, screaming, "No!"

Eric and another officer tried to waylay her but she was too quick for them. She grabbed the back-door handle of the car and tried to yank it open, but it was locked. "Let him go!"

"Ms. Jones," Eric shouted. "Step away from the car."

The driver jumped out of the patrol car and tried to pry her hand off the door handle, but Denise had adrenaline and panic on her side. He couldn't budge her.

"Everybody step back!" Eric yelled, clearly annoyed with the breakdown in order. "Ms. Jones, calm down!"

Denise whipped around. "I did it! Arrest me. I killed Lily. I—I was jealous of her and Brad, so I killed her."

Eric's gaze narrowed in on her. "Ms. Jones, are you confessing to the murder of Lily Brogan?"

Her eyes widened in fear and confusion. "Yes. No. Yes, I did it."

"Oh, Denise," I said. "You didn't kill Lily."

"I did, too," she insisted.

Eric nodded at the driver, who jumped back into the patrol car and took off before Denise could throw herself in its path.

She whimpered as Brad was taken away. "He didn't do it."

"Did you want me to arrest you, Mrs. Jones?" Eric asked.

"Yes. Arrest me, not Brad."

"Are you just saying that to protect your husband?" he asked.

"Well, somebody has to!" she cried.

"Do you think your husband is guilty?" Eric asked softly. "Is that why you're doing this?"

"Guilty?" She looked aghast. "No. Brad couldn't hurt anyone."

"Why was Cliff trying to blackmail you?" I asked, then winced at the furious look Eric gave me.

Denise answered anyway. "Cliff thought Brad killed Lily, and threatened to tell the police if I didn't pay him fifty thousand dollars. But he was wrong," Denise said, and turned to Eric. "And so are you, Chief Jensen. Brad didn't kill Lily. He loved her."

Eric shot me another quick glance, then stared intently at Denise. "You admit your husband was in love with Lily Brogan?"

"Yes," she said, as some of her frenzy began to fade. "I was Lily's best friend, so I knew how they felt about each other. They were in love and she was going to have his baby."

"So you knew she was pregnant?"

She sighed. "Yes, of course I did. I was the one who

used to cover for her so she could meet Brad at the mansion."

"But, then, how did you and Brad get together?" I wondered aloud.

"We had something in common," she said softly. "We both loved Lily. When she disappeared, we were both heartbroken. I guess it brought us closer together."

"If you loved your friend Lily so much, why would you kill her?" Eric wondered.

Denise's mouth opened, but she couldn't come up with an answer.

"You did just confess to killing her," Eric reminded her.

She blinked, then gazed at me beseechingly.

All I could do was change the subject. "Why did Cliff think that Brad killed Lily?"

That snapped her back to attention. "Oh. Cliff had dated Lily briefly, but he got it into his head that there was more to the relationship than there really was. He was pushing her to sleep with him, but why would she? He was cheating on her the whole time, so why did he think she owed him anything?" Denise shook her head in disgust. "But he kept harassing her, until she finally insisted that he leave her alone. She told him she was seeing someone else."

This sounded way too familiar. Cliff had always thought women should fall at his feet.

"He didn't believe her," Denise continued, "so he started following her. Apparently, according to Cliff, he followed her out to the mansion one night and saw her with Brad."

I gave Eric a meaningful look. "So Cliff knew he could find Lily at the mansion."

"I heard what she said, Shannon."

"Just making sure," I muttered. Because if Cliff had wanted to hurt Lily, what better place to do it than the remote lighthouse mansion?

Denise ignored our banter and kept talking. "So, recently, when Lily's body was found, Cliff put two and two together and came up with five. And that's when he tried to blackmail me."

"Because your family has money," I murmured.

"Right," she said, disgusted. "Brad's always been a schoolteacher, so he was hardly a target for a blackmailer."

Eric scowled. "But now Hogarth is dead, so nothing adds up."

Denise looked completely lost. I wanted to give her a hug, but I knew Eric would growl at me.

"Ms. Jones," Eric said, "I would appreciate your coming down to the station for an in-depth interview. Assistant Police Chief Gallagher will escort you there."

I looked around to find Tommy and noticed that a small crowd of secretaries and teachers was standing at the top of the stairs, near the door to the school hall. They had seen everything, from Brad Jones being taken away in a squad car to Denise arriving and creating a scene. Now I felt even sorrier for her.

Among the crowd on the stairs, I could see Ms. Barney, watching. Thankfully there were no students, but Dismal Dain was there, smirking as usual. I felt a chill at the sight of him.

Eric watched as Tommy walked over and gave Denise's arm a gentle squeeze. "Come on, kiddo."

Denise gazed at Tommy, someone she'd known her entire life, and her eyes filled with tears. "Hi, Tommy."

"I'll meet you there, Tom," Eric said, and walked to his SUV.

As soon as Eric got into his car, I came up and gave Denise a hug. "It's going to be okay. I know you and Brad are innocent."

"But Brad . . ." She broke into sobs, and I felt helpless.

"You're making a fool of yourself, Denise."

Tommy and I turned at the sound of an irritating new voice, and the chills I'd felt before turned to cold fury. Dismal Dain had moved closer to eavesdrop. He wore a cheap brown suit and his now-famous sneer. I'd never had such an urge to slap someone in my life, but I wanted to smack him so hard, I had to force myself to clutch my hands together. The man was an arrogant little worm, and I hated the thought of him gloating over Denise and Brad's difficulties.

And then I remembered the way he'd stared at Callie the other night and it made my stomach twist into a hard knot.

Denise wiped her tears away and glared at Dain. "Just go away, Darren. This is none of your business."

"It's very much my business when a colleague acts like an idiot. Brad's behavior reflects poorly on all of us."

As Dain was speaking, Tommy turned around and muttered something into the walkie-talkie clipped to his shirt.

"You've always been jealous of Brad," Denise said.

"Jealous!" Dain laughed and the sound was slightly maniacal. "Why? Because he got that little slut pregnant?" He shook his finger at Denise. "Don't make me laugh. It was only a matter of time before they caught him."

"Before who caught whom, Mr. Dain?" Tommy asked.

Dain hesitated for a moment, then said, "Before the

authorities caught Jones. He was having sex with a student. It's about time he was disciplined."

"How do you know that?" Tommy asked.

Dain stared at Denise as if he were aiming his words right at her. "I saw Jones with that girl. I know what they did together."

"Are you saying you saw Brad Jones having sex with Lily Brogan?" Tommy asked quietly but pointedly. At that moment, I saw Eric approach and stop a few feet behind Dain's back. Tommy must've used his walkie-talkie to alert the chief to come back and hear Dain's accusations.

Way to go, Tommy, I thought.

"Your friend was a slut," Dain said, still speaking to Denise. "And your husband was weak. Always so weak. And delusional, too. Do you know he filled out scholarship applications for her? As if she would ever be anything but a whore."

Denise rushed forward, ready to claw Dain's face, but Tommy grabbed her and held her back. She struggled to get loose, but Tommy had strength and experience on his side.

"Your emotions rule you, just as they rule your husband," Dismal taunted. "He couldn't keep his hands off of Lily. And then he killed her."

"How did you know about the scholarships?" I asked.

"Mr. Dain, did you see Mr. Jones kill Lily Brogan?" Tommy asked, his voice calm, in complete control. Unlike me. I was so furious I could hardly breathe.

"I know what was going on," Dain said.

"You don't know anything," Denise muttered.

"How did you know that Brad was helping Lily with her scholarship applications?" I asked again.

He sniffed in my direction, as though I weren't important enough to speak to him. "I know who applies for scholarships," he finally explained. "Back then, they all had to come through me to get the forms."

Dain homed in on Denise again. "Don't you think I knew he was filling them out for her? What a foolish waste of time. He was pathetic, and she made him worse."

"Just shut up about Brad," Denise said. "He's stronger than you will ever be. And Lily was smarter than you'll ever know."

"But where did you see them sleeping together?" I asked, trying to divert him.

He flashed me another derisive look. "I saw them at the lighthouse mansion."

I exchanged a quick look with Eric, who took another step closer to Dismal Dain. "Did you follow them out to the lighthouse mansion, Mr. Dain?"

Dain whipped around, saw Eric standing there, and seemed to realize his mistake. "No. No, of course not."

"Liar." Denise pointed at Dain. "You did. You followed them and you watched them. You're nothing but a pervert."

"Why would I care about either of them?" he said scornfully. "They were both beneath contempt, especially the girl."

"You're the contemptible one," Denise said. "If I find out you had anything to do with Lily's death, I'll make sure you suffer the same way she did."

Dain turned to Eric, cutting her off. "I don't have to stand here and listen to this drivel."

But Denise wasn't finished. "As soon as the police find Lily's diary, we'll know who killed her."

Dain frowned, then waved his hand brusquely, dismissing her. "I have work to do." He began to walk away toward the main building.

"Mr. Dain," Eric said sharply. "Stop right where you are. I'm taking you in for questioning in the murders of Lily Brogan and Cliff Hogarth."

Before Dain knew what was happening, Tommy circled around and grabbed his arm.

"This is an outrage," Dain said, as sweat began to bead on his forehead. "I demand to see my lawyer."

"No problem," Eric said. "Tell him to meet you at the police station."

Eric and his team questioned Dismal Dain for hours that night, but his lawyer insisted they couldn't hold him unless they had enough evidence to support their claims that he had something to do with Lily's death. They didn't. Not yet, anyway. So Dain was let go.

Denise was also sent home after a few hours, but Brad was held for two long days before they allowed him to leave. Basically his lawyers argued that Lily's flowery words about Brad in her notebook did not constitute enough evidence to hold him. Faced with the team of expensive attorneys Denise had hired to defend her husband, Eric had no choice but to let Brad go with a warning not to leave town.

A few days later, I called Denise to check in, see how she was doing, and ask if she wanted to get a cup of coffee sometime.

"Let's meet this afternoon," she said. "I owe you for helping me tag team Dismal Dain the other day at school. That little rodent."

"I didn't do much, but I was glad to see Eric drag him off to the police station."

"Me, too."

She had already ordered me a café latte and was waiting at a table when I walked into the coffeehouse.

"Thanks," I said, joining her. "How are you doing?"

"A little better than when I last saw you," she said. "I can't stay long. I have a doctor's appointment this afternoon."

"Hope it's nothing serious," I said, attempting to keep things light.

"It's a fertility specialist," she confessed. "I told you we've been trying to have kids, right? But after all these years of putting it off, I'm concerned I might've waited too long."

I grabbed her hand. "You're still really young, so I hope not. I'll keep a good thought for you."

"Thanks."

I took a sip of my latte. "Did you hear whether Mr. Dain confessed or not?"

She waved away the question. "He'll never confess, but I would bet a million dollars he killed Lily. I could see it on his face."

"I could, too. He was so contemptuous of everyone, but especially Lily." I contemplated my coffee cup. "For a while, I thought maybe Cliff had done it. He was so awful."

"You're right." She scowled. "Between Cliff Hogarth and Dismal Dain, it's hard to say who was worse."

We sipped our drinks for a full minute before I said, "Did you ever consider that Mr. Brogan might've done it?"

She pressed her lips together in frustration. "Yes. Hugh Brogan was completely capable of killing Lily. When she disappeared, I wondered if he knew she'd been hiding from him at the mansion. I mean, if Cliff and

Dain could follow her out there, Mr. Brogan could've, too."

"Do you think we'll ever know the truth?"

"I hope so. I'd like someone to pay for killing my friend."

We sipped our coffees in silence for a moment, and then I ventured a question. "How did Lily and Brad get together in the first place?"

There were tears in her eyes, but she began to smile as she told the complete story, filling in some of the blanks for me.

Lily had been desperate to get away from her parents, and Mr. Jones had been a sympathetic listener. Lily confided that she wanted to try for a scholarship, and Brad did everything he could to encourage her.

"I knew the exact day when Lily and Brad fell in love," Denise said. "By then the three of us were best friends. I loved them both so much."

Lily was vulnerable and so beautiful, and she and Brad grew very close, very fast. The pregnancy took them off guard. But they were both thrilled and planned to get married after graduation.

"I was going to be the godmother," Denise said with a sad smile.

"Did the three of you start going to the lighthouse mansion together?" I asked.

"Not exactly. I'd heard about it from one of the old hippies that used to come to the Gardens," Denise explained. "It had been used as a crash pad back in the sixties. So I told Lily about it, and sometimes I would drive her out there so she could hide from her father. Usually after he'd beaten her silly."

I shivered. "What a horrible man."

"He really was," Denise said. "When she disappeared, Brad and I both thought her father had done something to her. Brad went out to the mansion to look for her, but didn't find her. I thought maybe her father had hurt her so badly that she'd finally run away. I thought I would hear from her eventually." She shook her head in helpless frustration.

"When Brad and I heard that Lily's remains had been discovered, we wondered if maybe she died from a fall." Denise gripped her coffee cup. "We never imagined that someone had followed one of us out there and then waited for his chance."

"It's too terrible to contemplate," I said. "And I hate to say it, but it's starting to sound like her father might have been the one who killed her."

"She must've been so frightened," Denise murmured, her cheeks damp with tears.

Clearly we were both struck by the horror of what Lily had gone through in the last minutes of her life. We continued drinking our lattes in silence.

"Just one more question," I said, breaking the quiet. "You told Dain that Lily had a diary. Was that true?"

She grimaced. "I didn't realize the police had already found her notebook. That's where she wrote down all of her thoughts."

I didn't have the heart to tell her that the notebook had given the police all the evidence they needed to take her husband in for questioning. I doubted there was anything in the book that would incriminate Dain, but I prayed there was nothing else that would further condemn Brad Jones.

I had a crew of six working on the lighthouse mansion the next day. I wanted to do a big push to finish up the kitchen demo and start work on the basement beams. When Mac and Wade and I finally got the chance to walk through the basement for the first time, we were surprised to find many of the crossbeams and posts were in fairly good shape, despite years of abuse from ocean spray, offshore breezes, and the usual termite infestation that occurred in houses built near water. Despite their decent shape, though, Mac and I decided to replace all of the crossbeams and the posts, not only to give his new house a fresh start, but also to guarantee that those crucial load-bearing beams had a long, healthy life. They would be supporting the weight of the entire house, after all.

By four o'clock most of the crew had left and it was just Carla and me finishing up in the kitchen. I felt a sense of accomplishment when all three layers of linoleum were ripped up and thrown outside. But now the subflooring was exposed, and I was surprised the entire floor hadn't buckled or that one of us hadn't fallen through to the basement. The one-by-four slats that made up the subfloor weren't level, and some of the slats were missing altogether. Of the ones that remained, many were warped.

The old pipes running every which way along the walls of the kitchen were in bad shape, too, with several of them tied and nailed to the strips of lath to keep them in place.

"We have our work cut out for us in here," Carla said.

I gazed around at the exposed walls and floor. "I'll say."

"Are you ready to leave?" she asked, checking her wristwatch. "I've got to pick up Keely at ballet practice."

I smiled. Her five-year-old daughter, Keely, was on her way to becoming a prima ballerina. "You go ahead.

I'm going to take a quick look around the house and make a priority list of things to do tomorrow."

"Okay." She picked up the small red toolbox she always brought with her. "I'll see you in the morning."

"Thanks, Carla."

After she left, I wandered from room to room, making a list of projects that needed work. I was struck again by the number of doors in the place, and how most of them were in disrepair and needed restoring or replacement. Some had been cut short at the bottom edge. I'd seen this in other Victorian homes and it was because the owners—or in this case, the navy—had installed new carpeting that was too thick to allow the doors to close. So instead of replacing the carpet or replacing the door, they would simply saw off four or five inches. Naturally, that would create a whole other set of problems to deal with.

I had a feeling these doors would be a project for years to come. I wondered if Mac would be happy to see me showing up every other month or so to work on a door in some room. I smiled at the thought.

I was kneeling down to check the flue in the secret servants'-quarters fireplace when I heard a creaking sound coming from the front of the house. It was dark out, almost six o'clock, and I wondered who was coming by this late. Mac, maybe?

"Hello," I shouted. "Mac?"

No one responded.

I heard another creak and that one sounded like it was over my head. Was someone on the second floor? Now I had to wonder if Aldous had returned to the house.

I stood up and listened for another creak. I couldn't

say if it was a good thing or a bad thing, but nobody would ever be able to walk around this house without the owner knowing there was someone else inside. Every floorboard and door creaked or groaned when it was moved or walked upon. I would be able to fix some of them, but right now I just wanted to know who else was in here with me.

"Hello?"

Again there was no answer. And that was when I felt a shiver of doubt. Lily had died in this house. And so had an innocent serving girl named Betsy. I didn't want to be the hat trick.

And with that disturbing thought hovering in my head, I pulled out my phone and texted Eric.

"At Mac's place. Someone is prowling around. Help!"

I rolled my eyes at the cryptic message, knowing Eric would blow a gasket. But I hit Send anyway. Then, just for good measure, I texted the same basic message to Mac.

Footsteps sounded on the subfloor of the kitchen and I knew my visitor was getting too close. I burrowed into the space between the brick fireplace and the wall. It was barely a foot wide but I squeezed in there, trying to hide from whoever was stalking around. It couldn't be a friend. He or she would've shouted out a greeting right away.

The footsteps grew softer, and I pictured the intruder walking toward the service porch at the far end of the kitchen. Maybe he or she would leave the house through the kitchen door and I would be able to come out of hiding. I felt ridiculous.

A door creaked open, but I could tell it wasn't the door leading outside. No, it was the sound of the basement door opening. But who would be crazy enough to go down to a cold, dark basement all alone?

Sure enough, I could hear the light pounding of footsteps on the wooden stairs leading down to where Lily's bones had been found. I wondered, *Is this person returning to the scene of the crime?*

But the basement hadn't been the scene of the crime. I assumed that the real crime had occurred in the third-floor attic, where Lily apparently had been killed and shoved into the dumbwaiter shaft.

So who in the world was down in Mac's basement?

By now I was a trembling mass of nerves. I had to do something. If the prowler stayed downstairs for a few minutes, I could run to the front door and reach my truck before he or she made it back upstairs.

I pushed myself out of my hiding place and tiptoed toward the front hall. But the wooden floor of the servants' room was so old, it creaked even louder than the subflooring in the kitchen. I had no choice but to keep going, especially when I suddenly heard the sound of feet pounding up the basement stairs.

"Oh, God!" I careened around the corner into the wide front hall, forgetting about the ladder folded up against the wall. A dozen sample cans of paint were stacked nearby, along with rollers and folded tarps. My hip bumped into the ladder and threw me off balance. All I could do as I fell was try to protect my head from banging into anything else.

"Well, well, aren't you graceful?"

I hated to be trite, but the sound of that voice had the exact same effect as fingernails scraping on a chalkboard. Every nerve ending in my body clenched as I glared up at him.

"What are you doing here?" I asked, pushing the ladder aside and dragging myself up off the floor.

Dismal Dain sniffed as though he'd caught a whiff of something unpleasant. "Not that it's any of your business, but I misplaced something the last time I was here."

I hated to show weakness, but I was forced to rest my hand on the wall to steady myself from the fall. "The last time you were here," I said slowly. "You mean, the time you came out here to kill Lily?"

He bared his teeth. "You think you're clever, but you're nothing. You're as useless and stupid as she was."

I was so sick of him. "You like thinking you're smarter than everyone else, don't you, Mr. Dain? But clearly you're not. Otherwise you wouldn't be here, desperately trying to find something you should've taken with you fifteen years ago."

"Nobody will miss you," he said softly, and that was when I saw the tire iron he was holding.

With any luck, Eric or Mac would be here in the next ten minutes, but that wouldn't be soon enough. I had to think fast, or I'd be another victim. I had to keep Dismal Dain talking. I suddenly remembered something Denise had said to him the other day, about Lily keeping a diary. I knew she meant the notebook, but did Dain know that?

"You came out here to find Lily's diary, didn't you? I don't think you'll find it."

"I'll find it," he insisted, swinging the tire iron as he spoke. There was no doubt he intended to kill me.

"W-were you in love with her?" I asked.

He snorted. "In *love*? With a whore? Don't be ridiculous."

"Okay, maybe you weren't in love, but you wanted her, right? She was beautiful." I was grasping at straws, but he had to have felt something for Lily. Otherwise why would he have followed her all the way out here those many years ago? "Did you try to get close to her during your counseling sessions? Did she turn you down? Were you jealous of Mr. Jones?"

He tried to ignore my accusations, but his nostrils were flaring and I could tell that my words were getting to him. "I told you she was a whore. She wasn't just having sex with Brad Jones, you know. She was also sleeping with that other student, too."

I had to think for a second. "You mean Cliff Hogarth?"

"Yes, that one," Dain said. "Another brain trust."

I seriously doubted that Lily had ever slept with Cliff Hogarth, but now wasn't the time to argue about it. "So Lily was sleeping with both Cliff Hogarth and Mr. Jones," I said. "Two men you had little respect for."

"I told you she was a slut," he snarled.

I shrugged. "Maybe you're right. But she refused to be a slut with you, didn't she, Mr. Dain? She wouldn't have anything to do with you, right? I'll bet that burned you up."

His upper lip shook when he tried to sneer. "She was nothing to me."

"And yet you wanted her so badly," I taunted.

"Shut up!"

"So you killed her."

"She was nothing to me."

"She was everything to you," I countered.

"She spurned me!" he shouted, raised the tire iron, and came at me.

Without thinking, I grabbed a paint can and hurled it at him. It hit him squarely in the face and the cap bounced off, spilling a quart of Red Velvet interior satin paint all the way down the front of him.

He was still raging and paint was still dripping off of him like blood when I raced out the front door and almost knocked down Eric, who was dashing toward the house. He crushed me to his chest and I wanted to crawl up inside him and stay safe. But I couldn't—not yet.

"Are you all right?" he demanded.

"Dain," I mumbled. "Inside. He killed Lily."

Days later, the St. Patrick's Day Parade and Spring Festival were a huge success. The high school's production of *The Sound of Music* was lovingly dedicated to the memory of Lily Brogan. Sean actually walked out on stage and said a few words about his sister and how she loved the theater we were all sitting in. His sister, Amy, joined him onstage and also said a few words. Amy had to gulp away tears, and her big brother put his arm around her shoulders to comfort her.

By the time the two of them left the stage and the play began, I was crying like a baby. And judging by all the sniffles I heard, I wasn't the only one.

During the reception after the play, I was thrilled to discover that my plan to get Sean together with drama coach Lara Matthews was a huge success; they had started dating. When I saw him sneak a kiss from her behind one of the stage flats, I had to wipe away more tears. If anyone deserved to be happy, it was Sean Brogan.

Speaking of dating, Emily and Gus finally announced that they were a couple, as if we didn't already know. They revealed everything at Emily's official housewarming party the weekend following the play. She had decided it was time to invite everyone over, even though my crew was still working on several of her rooms. But since the kitchen was almost completed, Emily was more than ready to throw her first of many parties.

I was thrilled that Emily had invited Brad and Denise Jones. They fit right in with my group of friends, and I spent some time laughing and chatting with them before slipping off to wander through Emily's house alone. I couldn't help myself; I wanted to check the work we'd done so far and make a mental list of all the things that were left to do.

I was sipping champagne and studying the plaster corbels on either side of the bay window in the back sitting room when Gus walked in.

"Hey, babe. What're you doing in here all alone?"

"Just checking my guys' handiwork," I said. Then, since I figured I wouldn't have another opportunity to speak to him alone, I rushed ahead. "I'm worried about Emily."

He frowned. "Why?"

"Gus, I've known you my whole life and I love you like a brother. But if you hurt my friend Emily, I'll never forgive you."

"Aw, come on, Shannon." He laughed and gave me a hug. After a moment, he took hold of my hand. "Let's take a walk."

We wound our way through the clusters of guests to the front door and stepped outside. Emily hadn't yet hired a tree trimmer, so the massive eucalyptus and redwood trees surrounding the house still loomed overhead, casting odd shadows as they swayed in the evening breeze. The moon was almost full and I wondered if it really did cause people to act crazy sometimes. My guess was yes.

It took Gus a few minutes of walking and gazing at the sky before he finally got around to telling me what he wanted to say. "Look, I don't want you to worry. I won't hurt Emily. I've been in love with her for more than ten years, ever since she first moved to town."

I shook my head in confusion. "But it's been so long. Why did you wait until . . . I don't understand."

He smiled and shrugged lightly. "She wouldn't have me."

"What do you mean?"

"She refused to get involved with me."

I gaped at him. "Is she crazy?"

He laughed. "Naw. She thought I was too young and wild for her. She was sure I would grow tired of her."

I glared at him. "You wouldn't dare."

"No, I wouldn't." With a scowl, he added, "But she insisted that my reputation had preceded me."

"Your reputation as the world's greatest lover?" I teased. "So, what changed her mind?"

He kicked a small stone across the flagstone pathway. "Would you believe it was Mrs. Rawley?"

I was puzzled for a moment. "You mean the ghost?"

"The ghost," he said, and laughed again. "It happened after she read Mrs. Rawley's diary."

When we'd first started working on Emily's house, my crew had found the old journal inside a wall of the dining room. As a young woman, Mrs. Rawley had hidden it inside a hole in the wall of her bedroom, behind a picture frame. Over the years, the small book had slipped down the inner wall to where we finally found it.

In the journal, the young Mrs. Rawley had revealed her unhappiness and pain. She hadn't had the courage to run away with her one true love, who just happened to be Gus's great-grandfather. Instead, she had done her duty and married the man her parents approved of, and had missed out on any chance of real happiness. If she'd had it to do over again, she would've followed her heart and her life would've been completely different. Apparently, the ghost saw her chance to help another couple follow their hearts when Emily moved in and Gus finally showed up.

"Mrs. Rawley's story opened Emily's eyes to the realization that happiness is fleeting," Gus said. "You've got to grab it while you can."

I wiped away a tear and gave him another hug. "Be happy," I whispered.

He grinned. "You, too, beautiful."

The day after the housewarming party, Callie went home to her mother. There were more tearful hugs and lots of promises to keep in touch. After she left I swore I would never cry again, because I'd shed more tears in the past few weeks than I had in my entire life.

Within a day, Mac and I both admitted that we missed Callie desperately. Mac was already lobbying his sister to send Callie back for the summer. I didn't hold out much hope.

"Girls that age are totally into their friends and boys and the beach," I explained.

"So you think she'll forget all about us old people when she gets back to groovy Bel Air?"

I laughed at the very idea that we would be considered old, but the thought that Callie might forget about me was actually painful. "I hope not."

"Me, too," he said, and wrapped me in a tight hug. "Maybe we'll get lucky and talk her into visiting for a week."

I patted his back sympathetically, knowing how much he missed the girl. "Let's try for two weeks."

*   *   *

Days later, in a police lineup, Dismal Dain was identified by a hospital security guard. The guard swore that the last time he'd seen Dain, the guy was wearing a pair of blue scrubs and walking into the third-floor intensive care unit, where Cliff Hogarth had been a patient. The evidence was piling up, and Dain was finally forced to confess to killing Cliff, as well as Lily Brogan and her unborn child. To hide the crime, he shoved her body into the dumbwaiter. Then he packed her clothes into her backpack and tossed it down the laundry chute.

Dain's excuse for killing Cliff was that he was being blackmailed by him. Apparently Cliff had been hedging his bets, thinking that either Dain or Mr. Jones had to have killed Lily. Cliff had seen both men out at the light-house mansion, when he himself was secretly following Lily.

Cliff Hogarth was a horrible person, but I didn't suppose that was reason enough for him to die such an awful death. I did have to admit secretly, though, that I was perfectly happy to have him gone. He had made my life miserable, too.

The town thrived on all the grisly gossip, of course. And Whitney swore to anyone who would listen that she had never trusted Cliff Hogarth, after all.

One sunny day at the end of March, I drove out to the Gardens to see Denise. I hadn't had a chance to tell her the whole story of my confrontation with Dain at the mansion.

"You must've been scared to death," she said, and gave me a warm hug. "But I love that you showered him in red paint."

"Yeah, that was a nice touch."

We both were able to laugh about it, although Dain's confession was a bittersweet victory.

"I mean, yes, he was a cold-blooded killer," Denise said, "but above and beyond that, Dismal Dain was the worst student counselor who ever lived."

"I know!" I said, shaking my head. "Me, a hairdresser. What an idiot."

"I wish you were," she said, grabbing a clump of her hair. "I could use some help here."

We laughed some more and chatted as I shopped for herbs for my kitchen garden.

"Despite everything that happened, I'm so happy that we've become friends," Denise said.

"I completely agree." I flashed her a smile as I grabbed a pretty little pot of lemon thyme.

She hesitated, then said, "Since we're friends and all, do you mind if I share some good news with you?"

"Please do," I said. I placed the thyme plant in my basket and held up a basil plant to study the leaves. "I'm desperate for some good news."

"Well, then." Her smile was radiant. "Brad and I are going to have a baby. Two, actually. Twins."

The basil plant slipped from my hands and she caught it, laughing. Then I burst into happy tears. Wrapping her in another hug, I whispered, "That might be the best news I've heard in fifteen years."

Read on for an excerpt from Kate Carlisle's
new Bibliophile mystery,

BOOKS OF A FEATHER

Coming in hardcover in June 2016
from Obsidian.

Chapter 1

As soon as I closed and locked my front door, I sagged
in relief. I usually worked at home, so being gone all day
was unusual for me. But after a moment, I perked up,
knowing Derek was already here; I'd seen his car parked
in the space next to mine.

Derek Stone was my fiancé and . . .

Fiancé. It was still odd to say the word out loud, let
alone think it, but it was true. It was real. We were getting
married, and how crazy was that? The two of us had almost nothing in common. I'd been raised in a peace-love-
and-happiness artistic commune in the wine country and

I wore Birkenstocks to work. Derek had been a highly trained operative with England's MI6, and he carried a gun. Think James Bond but more dangerous, more handsome, more everything. I was crazy in love with him. I figured that the old adage that opposites attract had to be true because he loved me right back.

He had proposed two months ago, the night my friend Robin married my brother Austin. Of course I said yes. Duh! Since then, we'd barely had a chance to talk about a wedding or anything else related to getting married. We'd been living temporarily in Sonoma, and Derek had been commuting back and forth to the city while our apartment in town was being remodeled. And that was happening because months ago, Derek had purchased the smaller apartment next door to mine and we'd decided to join the two places together.

We had only been back in town a week. Our place was still in a state of flux, to put it mildly. We'd been rearranging furniture and picking out new stuff and doing all those things you did when you suddenly had two extra bedrooms and a much bigger living room. It was fun and time-consuming and a little bit mind-boggling. I occasionally had to stop and pinch myself.

So no, there hadn't been much time to discuss wedding plans. We'd get around to it one of these days.

With a happy sigh, I slid the case that held my bookbinding tools under my worktable and set my satchel on the counter.

"Derek, I'm home," I called, even though he probably knew it already. He was preternaturally aware of everything that went on around us. Besides, our freight elevator tended to shake the entire building when it rose up from the basement parking garage, thus acting as an early-warning signal. I liked to think it made things more difficult for bad guys to sneak up on us, an excellent selling feature, given the number of times my place had been broken in to by bad guys.

"Hello, darling," he called from somewhere in the house.

"Wait'll you see all the amazing books I got from Genevieve," I shouted as I hung up my peacoat in the small closet by the door. "They're so valuable. I can't believe Joe lost track of them. One of them is probably worth at least forty-five thou—"

"Brooklyn," Derek interrupted loudly, his tone a bit more urgent than usual. "We have company."

I grimaced. In other words, *Shut up, Brooklyn.* I could tell from Derek's voice that our *company* was a person or people I didn't know. Our friends and family were all completely trustworthy. They knew I worked with rare and often priceless books. But even though I trusted our friends, I was still awfully paranoid about showing off the books I worked on. You just never knew.

I'd even taken precautions before leaving Genevieve's shop, tucking the books away in a zippered compartment inside my satchel, which I'd worn strapped across my torso and had clutched all the way to my car. I never took chances with books. And yet here I was, blurting out all my secrets to anyone within earshot.

To be fair though, I was inside my own house. I should've been able to shout out whatever I wanted to, once I'd locked the door behind me. But no.

"Okay," I called out, trying to sound nonchalant. "Be right there." But first, I needed a minute to collect my wits, if I still had any left to collect. I turned in a circle, scanning my workshop for a long moment, looking for a good hiding place. There were lots of them. Besides my worktable in the center of the room, I had three walls of cupboards and counters that held all sorts of equipment and supplies. At the end of one counter was my built-in desk.

I grabbed my satchel and pulled out the eight books—the eight rare, extremely valuable books that I'd just blabbed about loudly—and carefully slipped them into the bottom drawer of my desk and locked it. I would've preferred to stash them inside the steel-lined safe in the hall near our bedroom, but this would have to do for now.

I felt almost silly for taking such precautions. Was I being overly suspicious? As quickly as the thought emerged, I brushed it away. There were plenty of people in the world who were willing to lie, cheat, steal, or kill for a book. *Better safe than sorry,* I thought, and rushed down the hall to the living room to greet Derek and our company.

Derek stood by the bar that separated the kitchen from the living area, pouring red wine into three glasses. Another man, wearing a beautiful navy suit, had his back to me. Though I couldn't see his face, I could see he had straight black hair and was nearly as tall as Derek. He had just said something that caused Derek to laugh. I stopped and listened to that deep, sexy sound.

"And there she is," Derek said, spying me at last. "Darling, come meet Crane, one of my oldest friends."

"I'm not that old," the other man joked as he turned and stared at me. "Ah, how delightful."

If I'd been walking, I might've stumbled. The man was Asian and spoke with a British accent, and he was simply . . . beautiful. Not as dashing or as blatantly masculine and tough as Derek, but then, who was? Still, Crane's smile was brilliant and his dark eyes twinkled with humor. He moved with a natural ease and confidence that made him even more attractive. *No man should be that pretty,* I thought vaguely.

It was a bit overwhelming to have two such gorgeous men smiling at me, but I decided I could endure it. I hurried over to the bar to give Derek a quick hug and kiss, then turned to our guest and extended my hand.

"Hello, Crane. I'm Brooklyn."

His smile grew as he gripped my hand warmly. "I've heard so many wonderful things about you, Brooklyn. It's a pleasure to finally meet you."

I glanced at Derek. He'd never said one word to me about his friend Crane before. And yet the man knew all about me? Hmm.

Derek bit back a grin, clearly reading my mind. "Darling, Crane and I were in school together. I haven't seen him in five long years, which led me to believe he was probably languishing in a federal penitentiary."

Crane laughed. "I always figured you'd be the one to wind up on the wrong side of the law." He shook his head in mock dismay. "Instead, you joined forces with the good guys."

Derek shrugged. "Considering our misspent youth, it's surprising we both turned out this well."

Crane nodded at me. "It was always a competition to see which of us could cause the most havoc in school."

"You won in the end," Derek admitted, handing each of us a wineglass. "But only through a technicality."

I gazed at Crane. "How did you win?"

"He cheated," Derek said dryly. "He came into his inheritance and nothing was the same after that."

"It's true. Money changes everything," Crane admitted with a worldly sigh. "It's not as much fun getting into trouble when you know you can simply bribe your way out of a jam."

Derek chuckled. "I, for one, am grateful for a few of those bribes."

I looked from one man to the other. "I'd love to hear stories of Derek causing havoc."

Crane leaned close. "I'll tell you everything, but first"—straightening, he held up his glass—"a toast, to old friends and new."

We clinked glasses and took our initial sips of the excellent Pinot Noir Derek had poured.

"And as long as we're toasting," Crane added, "I understand congratulations and best wishes are in order."

"Oh." I gazed up at Derek and touched my glass to his. I don't know why, but I was truly moved that he'd told his friend about our engagement. The two of us had barely discussed it since we'd been home from Dharma. I looked back at his friend. "Thank you, Crane."

Crane raised an eyebrow. "You're a lucky man, Stone."

"I know," Derek said, and kissed my cheek.

Happily flustered, I moved into the kitchen and quickly put together a cheese platter along with a bowl of crackers and some olives. Derek ushered Crane over to the living room, where we all sat to talk.

Crane leaned forward with his elbows resting on his knees. "Derek tells me you work with rare books."

I wanted to bite my tongue, knowing Crane must've heard me shouting about the pricey books I'd brought home. Now that we'd officially met and I knew he was one of Derek's oldest friends, I almost felt guilty for hiding them from him. "Yes, I'm a bookbinder. I take books apart and clean them up and put them back together again."

"She's being modest," Derek said. "Brooklyn has a unique gift for repairing the rarest of books. Almost like a skilled surgeon."

"Without all the blood," I murmured.

"But she's also an artist," he continued. "She's designed some fantastic book art."

I felt my cheeks heating up. I knew Derek appreciated my work, but all this lavish praise was going straight to my heart.

He touched my knee. "Darling, Crane has an impressive art collection. I think he would enjoy seeing your work."

"I would indeed," Crane said, helping himself to a cracker. "I collect all sorts of art, including books. I'd like to see your work sometime."

After a glance at Derek, I made a quick decision and turned to his friend. "You're welcome to join us tomorrow night at the Covington Library. They're having a big party to celebrate the opening of a new exhibit featuring Audubon's massive book of bird illustrations. It's a real masterpiece."

He looked taken aback. "Thank you for the invitation. I'd love to join you."

"And while we're there, I'd be happy to show you some of the books I've worked on." I started to take a sip of wine, but stopped. "That is, if you're not otherwise engaged."

Crane flashed me a spectacular smile. "I'm not. I'd be delighted to see everything you can show me."

"Good," Derek said. "It's settled, then."

"I was actually going to invite you both to dinner tomorrow night," Crane said. "Perhaps we can dine together before or after."

"We'd like that very much," Derek said, and relaxed against the back cushions of the couch. "Here's a bit of history for you, Crane. Brooklyn and I met at the Covington Library."

I almost laughed. Derek and I had indeed met at the Covington. It was the night my mentor was killed and Derek accused me of murder. Was it any wonder we fell in love?

"Ah," Crane said. "So the place has a special meaning for you."

"It does," Derek said.

I smiled at him. "And this time we'll make sure there aren't any dead bodies to worry about."

Unfortunately, Derek didn't smile back. If fact, he looked at me as though I were crazy, making me realize I'd just tempted fate in the worst possible way.